Remember Me

IAN C.P. IRVINE

Copyright 2020 © IAN C.P. IRVINE

All rights reserved. Without limiting the rights under copyright observed above, no part of this publication may be reproduced, stored in or introduced into a retrieval system, or transmitted in any form or by any means without the prior written consent of the copyright owner.

This is a work of fiction. Names, characters, businesses, places, events and incidents are either the products of the author's imagination or used in a fictitious manner. Any resemblance to actual persons, living or dead, or actual events is purely coincidental.

This ebook may not be re-sold or given away to other people with the explicit permission of the author. Thank you for respecting the hard work of this author.

The school mentioned in this book was a real school. It no longer exists, having been demolished a few years ago. For many years it was the centre of the community. Many, many thousands of pupils went to Portobello High School. And for most, it was an incredible, enjoyable experience, with special teachers. This book is dedicated to the amazing educators that worked there, and who gave of themselves to help others. All of the names and characters in the book are entirely fictional, and every element of this story is fictional. But the school building was real. And it was blue.

Dedicated to all my teachers at Portobello High School. You were excellent!

With special thanks to:

Mr Marshall

Mr Kirkpatrick

Miss Cook

Mr Wheeldon

Mrs Hamilton

Although I may have forgotten everything you taught me, I will never forget you!

With Special Thanks for help with this book to:
Allan Guthrie
Sue Alexander

I appreciate all your thoughts, suggestions and support!

Books by Ian C.P. Irvine

The Assassin's Gift

Say You're Sorry

I Spy, I Saw Her Die

Haunted From Without

Haunted From Within

Time Ship

The Orlando File.

The Messiah Conspiracy

London 2012: What If?

The Sleeping Truth

Alexis Meets Wiziwam the Wizard

Get Writing! How ANYONE can write a Novel!

Chapter 1

Friday
15.15

The plastic ties forcing David Weir's hands behind his back cut into his flesh, the blood running slowly down his wrists and congealing on his sticky fingertips. The blindfold fastened around his eyes pressed against his eyeballs, threatening to burst them open like two small water balloons.

But that was the least of his worries.

When his captor forced him up the stairs, David had tripped and landed heavily on his right arm. Pain now washed over him in waves, threatening to blot out his senses. He was sure it was broken. Only the threat of the electric cattle prod got him back to his feet.

After the climb up the eight flights of stairs, they had eventually come to the top floor. Although blindfolded, David knew where he was. This was his floor, where he'd taught Geography in the first classroom on the right for over ten years. The one with the best view in Edinburgh looking out to Holyrood Park and Arthur's Seat.

It was the classroom where he'd dedicated his life to the children of Portobello High School - until the council decided to close the school and move them all to a more modern building not so very far away.

Now the school was a shadow of its former self, abandoned, derelict, and awaiting demolition, which David knew only too well, was scheduled for Friday afternoon...

Was that today?

A shove between the shoulder blades sent David staggering down the corridor, colliding with the wall, and releasing another wave of pain from his broken arm.

He fell to his knees and breathed heavily, fighting the urge to vomit. If he did, the cloth his captor had thrust into his mouth would stop the contents of his stomach from going anywhere apart from back into his throat and down into his lungs.

He would choke to death.

David sensed his captor step around him, a waft of wind on his cheek as he passed. The rope which his captor had looped through his arms and the plastic ties connecting his wrists jerked him around and he fell sideways onto the floor.

Another wall of pain.

Behind him, he heard a door being opened, feet clanging up a metal ladder, a few thumps and bangs, and then a breath of fresh air swept over him.

It confused him.

David knew what the sounds were and where the air came from.

He'd expected his captor to lead him into his classroom - why else would he have brought him up here? - but instead, it seemed he'd opened the door to the supply cupboard, pulled down the ladder, and then forced open the hatch leading to the roof.

In all his years of teaching, David had never actually been up there. It was too dangerous.

His captor hauled him back onto his feet, pushed him forwards and into the cupboard.

David banged against the ladder and tripped, falling again.

His captor caught him, steadied him, and then bent down and lifted David's right foot up onto the first rung.

Then his left.

A prod to the back.

"Up! Climb!"

David coughed, and tried for the hundredth time to protest, but ended up once again fighting the urge to vomit.

Instead, he succumbed to his captor's demands and started searching for the rungs with his feet, gingerly testing each one with his weight before committing himself to the next.

"Hurry!"

David almost missed the next step, but a hand forced his foot forwards and down until he found the right position.

As David climbed, he sensed the walls around him disappear and the wind began to buffet his head and shoulders. Somewhere close by he could hear the sound of seagulls crying. The smell of the sea filled his nostrils.

And there was something more... voices. David could hear voices.

"All the way up!" his captor commanded him.

David could feel the edge of the last rung against his ankle as he leant forward, but he was reluctant to step up above it, not knowing what was there.

"Step out on to the roof!" his captor urged.

Fighting the pain, his heart pounding, David complied, every nerve in his body flooding his brain with sensations as he tried to build a picture of where he now was and what was around him.

He felt the crunch of gravel underfoot.

The wind swirled around his legs and blew through his hair and against his cheeks.

Fresh air.

Salty.

He heard footsteps below, coming up the ladder, and for a moment he felt relieved. Relieved that he wasn't going to be left up here all alone.

A hand grabbed his arm, the broken one, and David almost passed out with the pain.

His captor dragged him forward, and yanked the gag out of his mouth. He felt an arm around his throat, grasping his head, and a hand forced his mouth open.

Something was thrust into his mouth...a tablet... a capsule? Then the lip of a bottle, and a liquid was squirted into his throat, forcing him to swallow, washing the tablet down into his stomach.

"Who are you?" David choked and then gasped for air, his body trembling with fear. "What did you just give me? Why are we here, on the roof? Why are you doing this to me?"

He felt the breath of his captor on the side of his face.

The stench of garlic.

Stale aftershave.

Next, his captors voice, loud, straight in his ear.

"It's only fair to let you know, it's nearly four o'clock. In less than fifteen minutes they're going to blow up the school. Good luck!"

Then the sound of footsteps as his captor moved away from him.

"Where are you going?" David screamed, terrified. "Don't leave me here!"

More silence. Then footsteps again, retreating.

"Where am I? How far from the edge?"

There was no reply.

And then David felt very strange. His pulse was racing. He became confused. Dizzy. Weird.

What was happening to him?

Almost magically, the pain was ebbing away now, but it was replaced with a heightened sense of awareness and panic. Random thoughts began to rush through his head. Energy began to course through his veins. He was hot. Very hot. Sweat was running down his face, soaking his blindfold.

He felt an overpowering need to move.

Then in the distance, he heard the bang of the trapdoor being closed.

The sound echoed and reverberated through his head.

His captor had gone.

David was now alone.

Alone on top of the tallest building for miles around. A building due for demolition, in the next few minutes.

"Escape. I have to escape…"

The thought entered his mind, and then started to circulate, round and round. He heard the words being spoken to him, first by one voice, then by another. Soon a choir had taken up the chorus and was shouting the word in his mind, over and over again.

"Escape…escape…escape…"

His eyes had begun to twitch, his arms and legs jerking uncontrollably.

David was growing increasingly frantic and scared, his heartbeat pounding rapidly in his ears.

A rush of warmth down his legs told him he'd just pissed his pants with fear.

David began to weep.

"Help!…" He heard himself cry, his voice weak, pathetic.

"HELP!" he shouted again, several times.

But no one replied.

With each second that passed, David could feel the drug taking even more effect.

Agitated, unable to stand still, and heeding the advice in his head now screaming at him to escape, he started stumbling around the roof, searching for the trapdoor.

At first, he moved cautiously, doing his best to sense the space in front of him before committing to it, petrified he could be near the edge of the building. But as the drug took more of a grip on him, his movements became more erratic.

He was losing control.

He had to hurry…and he had to find that trapdoor…

Chapter 2

Portobello High School
Edinburgh
15.55

Gary Bruce checked his watch. Only five minutes before the demolition when the towering hulk of the old Portobello High School would be reduced to a dusty pile of rubble in a matter of seconds. Another famous Edinburgh landmark smudged off the map.

For once, Gary had mixed feelings about his work. Normally he loved blowing things up: it was every little boy's dream, and to a certain extent, Gary had never grown up. He ran his own demolition firm and enjoyed getting up for work every day. Few people could say the same.

The old Portobello High School was his biggest contract yet. The bulk of the school was spread out over several acres and consisted of numerous buildings averaging two or three floors. At the centre of the campus, however, a massive blue eight-floored building rose straight up into the sky. This part of the school was tall, long and thin, each floor containing two rows of classrooms separated by a long corridor which ran down their middle. At each end of the building was a set of stairs and an elevator, with a third set of stairs and two elevators running up through the middle. In its heyday, Porty High had about two thousand pupils, but the school was now over fifty-five years old, out-of-date, and its structure was tired and dangerous. Bit by bit, parts were falling off the building, and it was a miracle that no pupils had ever been injured or killed by falling chunks of masonry.

It was a large building, covering a large area, and planning its destruction had been a complex and difficult job. But ten minutes from now, when the dust cleared, the first and most dangerous part would be over.

Gary himself was one of tens of thousands of pupils who'd happily attended Porty High. Even though it had been one of the largest comprehensives in the country, the majority of pupils who'd gone there had enjoyed a brilliant education from fantastic, dedicated teachers.

Gary wasn't the only one who'd be sad to see the old girl go. Hundreds of spectators had turned up today, wanting to pay their last respects and see the final few seconds of the school as it was blown to smithereens.

Turning his attention back to the checklist on his tablet, he methodically ran through the last few preparations and radioed around for final oks from his team.

Suddenly he heard a cry go up from the crowd at the end of the cordoned-off street that ran past the school.

His radio buzzed.

"Gary, there's someone on the roof. Abort! Abort!"

Turning the key back to the 'Safe' position and removing it from the demolition console, he stepped outside his cabin and looked across to one of his team who was busy pointing to the top of the building.

From his vantage point, Gary could only see the westward edge of the roof from the side nearest the Holyrood Park. "I can't see anyone."

"A man! Wandering around. His hands are tied behind his back, and he's blindfolded. Staggering around like he's drunk... he's near the edge. Get someone up there!"

Two hundred metres down the road behind safety barriers, a shock wave of fear and excitement ran through the crowd.

Someone was on the roof of the old school.

Some of the mothers began to scream, whilst a few, and thankfully just a small minority of the children, started to shout *'Jump! Jump!'*

They were told to shut up by their parents, who covered their children's eyes, or tried to turn them around.

The policemen handling public safety went into overdrive, shouting excitedly into their radios, and directing the crowds to go further back and clear the road altogether.

One of the more experienced officers called an ambulance and requested a helicopter and assistance from the fire-services.

From that point forward, everything happened very quickly.

The man on the top of the building was moving in and out of view, crossing back and forward from one side of the building to the other.

Stew, the team-member with the binoculars who'd first alerted Gary, was now giving a running commentary to the control room, which was being overheard by several police-officers who'd hurried to the command post.

Outside in the street, a stunned silence descended on the crowd of onlookers, replaced by a rising and descending communal sound of alarm as the man seemed to approach the edge of the building but then turn at the last moment and veer back towards its centre.

A policeman hurrying towards the crowd from his parked car had produced a loudspeaker. Fiddling with the controls, he pushed past the onlookers and ran towards the hulking edifice towering above them. Raising the loudspeaker to his lips, he began shouting instructions at the man above.

"Stand still. Please do not move! You are in danger! Someone is coming to rescue you! I repeat, stand still and DO NOT MOVE!"

For a moment the man seemed to stop and listen, but seconds later he fell forward onto his knees, out of sight.

He was gone only for a few brief moments before he stood up again and then took several unsteady steps towards the edge.

A moan of alarm went up from the crowd below.

The man seemed to hesitate, turning slightly to the side, and then walking a few steps parallel to the side of the building.

Once again, the policeman was heard issuing instructions on the megaphone, but this time the man on the roof didn't respond.

He carried on moving forward, edging to the rim of the building.

Without knowing that the wind at the top of the building was preventing any of his instructions being heard, the policeman made another valiant effort to guide the man away from the side, but to no avail.

Taking another step forward, the man's left foot landed on the edge of the building, and as the weight of his body followed above it, the outside of his foot failed to find sufficient support and the ankle began to turn outwards.

Almost in slow motion, his leg buckled at the knee, and the man leant precariously to his side.

With his hands tied behind his back, the man was unable to compensate for the sudden loss of balance, and he stumbled sideways.

For those looking on from below, in the years to come, the scene that unfolded before their eyes would replay in their minds over and over again. A few of the children would wake up screaming from nightmare-filled dreams, and some adults would find themselves blinking and shaking their heads in an effort to erase the recurring vision and the morbid questions and feelings that accompanied it.

Just a moment before, they had been looking at a man, a human being, alive, breathing, and conscious.

The next, they were watching him fall, accelerating towards the ground, the end of his earthly existence only milliseconds away.

Mercifully, the large blue wooden fence around the side of the demolition site hid the final form which the geography teacher's body adopted: a deformed red mass somewhat akin to shape of the continent of Africa.

Chapter 3

Portobello High School
Edinburgh
17.20

Detective Chief Inspector Campbell McKenzie climbed out his car, brushed down his jacket and wiped away the remnants of his Gregg's sausage roll.

Admittedly, it wasn't the healthiest of foods, but it was warm, filling, and truth be told, rather delicious.

His DI had briefed him in the car on the way over. As McKenzie stood on the road outside the entrance to the demolition site, he looked upwards at the tower block above and couldn't help but imagine what the last few moments of the victim must have been like.

One moment he was on solid ground, the next falling through open air.

How many seconds would it have been before he'd hit the ground?

How far had he fallen?

After he'd stepped off the edge of the building, would the man have had a chance to process any last thoughts before...

McKenzie shuddered.

"DCI McKenzie?" The voice caught him off guard. McKenzie turned to see four men emerging from a door in the fence surrounding the perimeter of the old school.

"That's me. Who would you be?"

"Gary Bruce. Site Manager. I own Bruce Demolition, the company clearing this site. This is Stew, my No 2."

The two men were accompanied by an armed officer and a local policeman, Sergeant Murray Anderson, who McKenzie recognised from previous work together, and who according to his DI was in charge of the local police presence.

The armed officer introduced himself as Sergeant Galbraith. He was a heavy set man with broad shoulders, large biceps and pronounced thighs, someone who obviously spent a lot of time in the gym. He was almost bursting out of his uniform.

"I've got a team of armed officers just started sweeping the campus for any threats. It'll take a while, given the size of the campus." Galbraith explained.

McKenzie thanked him and requested to be informed the moment the site was declared safe. McKenzie then turned his attention to the uniformed officer. Tall, bald with a thick ginger moustache.

"Murray, good to see you again. Doctor been yet to make a formal declaration of death? And any sign of the forensics team?

"Forensics are on the way. And yes, the man who fell has been declared dead at the scene. One of the onlookers came forward and volunteered to help. Doctor from the local practice in Duddingston. For now, I'd rather we kept the footfall around the area down to a bare minimum, so until Forensics arrive, if I may suggest..."

"Don't worry Murray, I saw a picture in the car on the way over. I've got no desire to rush over there until I've properly digested my lunch. Looks like one of the worst falls I've seen in years, and I've handled a fair few. Is it visible from the street?"

"Perimeter fencing's high enough to make sure no one can see."

"Good. Have the press got wind of it yet?"

"Unfortunately. BBC Scotland were filming it. But we've stopped them and they've agreed not to release anything without our permission. We're keeping all other press at bay."

"Excellent." McKenzie smiled at the demolition men. "Is there somewhere we can set up a temporary incident room?"

"It'll have to be one of our portacabins. I'll need time to clear out some papers... How long will you need it for?"

"I don't know. We'll set up properly back in St Leonards later, but there's going to be a lot of activity here in the next few days, so we'll need the space. Can you take us there now?"

The site manager nodded.

"Good, lead the way. And Murray, how many men you do have here at the moment?"

"We had six. Another three just arrived."

"From what I've heard, it's looking like the victim didn't get up there himself. Have you started looking for anyone else? And do we have a name yet for the victim?"

"No. We didn't want to disturb the scene until Forensics got here. So no, we haven't got any ID. His body is badly distorted, so we haven't seen the face yet. Sorry for being so graphic but there's no other way of saying this." Murray paused. "His head, what's left of it, has been pushed inside his chest. Into his rib cage." He hurried on. "And as far as the other question, yes, before the armed response team arrived and took over, Mr Bruce's men had escorted some of my officers on a quick recce of the buildings and we rechecked that all the entrances were locked and reconfirmed that all the exits were cordoned off. I've got some dogs and another ten men on the way over... There's a freshly broken window at the bottom of the far stairwell, and it looks like that's where the victim and whoever was with him may have entered the building."

McKenzie glanced over at the site manager.

"How's that possible? You were just about to blow the place up. The area should have been on tight lockdown."

Gary Bruce turned red, whether from embarrassment or anger, McKenzie couldn't tell.

"It *was*. There's no way onto the campus except through the two main entrances, and they were both closed. All the normal procedures have been followed. We didn't see anyone on the cameras and the dogs on the campus never picked up any intrusions. But to be fair, we withdrew them from the area about forty minutes before the building was due to be brought down. We don't know how anyone could have got inside. All the doors were locked, and the broken window was still intact on the last site inspection thirty minutes before I was due to detonate the explosives. No one entered, and since the man fell off the roof, no one has left."

By this time, Gary had led them into the demolition site, and up a staircase on to the third level of a set of portacabins which had been lifted and stacked on top of each other by a crane, forming a temporary set of offices.

Sweeping a table clear of maps and architectural drawings, and depositing them on another desk by the far window, Gary waved to a few chairs.

McKenzie took his jacket off and placed it on the back of one of them.

"How safe is the site? Once the armed response team have given the all clear, can my officers walk around it without fear of anything falling on their heads or any explosives going off? I'm assuming the area's still wired to blow?"

"It's a demolition site. The explosives have been deactivated, but there's a risk from the buildings. I can't say it's safe, categorically. But given you must access the area, I'd suggest your men be escorted by one of mine at all times. And wear protective hats."

"Agreed. There's a real possibility that whoever did this could still be on site, hiding somewhere. Until the armed response team hand the building over to us, we need men on the ground outside covering everything and everywhere. And if someone is still inside, we need to make sure he doesn't escape. If he has gone, we need to find out where and how. You mentioned cameras?"

Gary nodded. "The CCTV covers most of the campus."

"Good. We'll need full access to whatever you have."

McKenzie crossed to the window of the portacabin, from where he had a partial view of the demolition site and the side of the old school building, the bulk of which towered above them.

He took a deep breath.

The scale of the immediate task was just beginning to dawn on him.

There was a lot to do and time was passing quickly.

If there was anyone still hiding in the demolition site, they had to find them soon.

He turned back to face the room.

"I need maps. We need to know the area we're going to be searching."

Gary nodded. "I can supply those."

"Thanks. And Murray, we'll need those officers and dogs. Get them here soon. Mr Bruce, we'll need those helmets. Can you make sure we have enough?"

Turning to his DI, Elaine Brown, he started verbalising a list of immediate actions that needed done. After a couple of minutes, he finished the list. "... and we need a whiteboard, and some coffees! And find out where on earth Forensics are. The sooner we have an ID the better."

For a moment, no one spoke.

"It's going to be a long night, guys. Let's get going."

McKenzie smiled at everyone and they got the hint. Meeting over, time to go. A moment later McKenzie was left alone with his thoughts, and the growing realisation that as soon as Forensics arrived and the site was declared safe and handed over to them, like it or not, he'd have no choice but to go and take a closer look at the victim.

Or whatever was left of him.

Portacabin No.3
Temporary Incident Room
Operation BlueBuilding
Edinburgh
22.00

McKenzie stood up at the front of the small portacabin and looked around the room at the twenty officers assembled before him. The room was cramped, with a couple of tables pushed against the wall, a window on each side of the room, and a whiteboard and flipchart behind him. Two rows of five chairs were squashed in just in front of him, with everyone else standing around the walls. The room smelt of pine.

"Thanks for coming, especially to those of you who came in at such short notice. For those of you who don't know me, I'm DCI Campbell McKenzie from St Leonards, and this is DI Elaine Brown," McKenzie nodded to his DI who stood at the side of the room. She smiled back. Medium height. Long black hair. A smart dress-suit. Slim build. A small, pronounced mole on her left cheek which blemished otherwise perfect skin.

McKenzie continued. "We've got a mixture of teams here tonight, from both Portobello and St Leonards, and for the near future, it's been agreed that it'll stay that way. I run an informal investigation team. And I one hundred percent believe in the contribution that each and every one of us can make. So, if you have any ideas, any thoughts, please speak up. No prizes for keeping quiet."

McKenzie paused, and looked around the room. He had their full attention. No one had any questions yet. McKenzie knew that would change soon once the team got underway.

"Now, I'd like to welcome our armed colleagues from Fettes Row who're still on the campus going through the process of sweeping the buildings for threats. Until they hand the area over to us, no one else has access to the site. We have to assume that whoever's responsible for forcing the victim to the top of the school building is still within the campus, and could be armed. I don't want any heroes, so no one takes any risks. We do this by the book. Do you understand?"

A round of nods.

"Until the area's declared safe, we get on with whatever we can. So, first things first, the Forensics team have just informed me that there must've been at least two people involved in today's incident. As most of you know, a man fell from the top of the building at 15.59 today. He died instantly upon hitting the ground, and to spare you the details, what's left of his body is a mess."

McKenzie glanced around the room. Everyone looked grim.

"First of all, the man was blindfolded. Forensics have also confirmed that both hands were tied behind his back using plastic ties, so unless he was a contortionist, someone else has to be involved. There are lacerations on his ankles which indicate that at some point he was forcibly restrained. In other words, it seems the man may have been forced to the top of the building against his will. For now, we have to assume this'll shortly be declared a murder, and we'll proceed on that basis."

He paused. Most of the officers were taking notes. Some were slightly white-faced, and McKenzie knew that two of them had seen the body and been sick. Even for experienced officers, this was something horrific.

"The one piece of good news is that we now have a name. Forensics were able to retrieve a wallet from the victim's pocket. Due to the facial trauma we can't make a visual ID, but early indications are that the victim is a David Weir. According to his online records and LinkedIn, he's a teacher. He's got a degree from Murray House, and he's been teaching for most of his career at this school."

A murmur went around the room.

"Until dental records confirm his identity, no one takes that name outside this room. We should have those shortly. At this point I'd like to make you aware of Gary Bruce, who runs Bruce Demolition. For the next few days we'll probably be running the investigation from this portacabin. You also need to remember that this is a demolition site. It's dangerous. The main buildings are in a precarious condition. If you don't pay attention, and you go somewhere you shouldn't, bad things can happen. Not only from the loose fittings and falling plaster, but also from the rubbish and drug paraphernalia which is lying all over the floor. The building has been lying empty awaiting demolition for almost two years, and in the meantime, it's been used by homeless people and drug addicts. When you enter the lower floors, the stench is quite overpowering, I'm told. Make sure you're kitted out safely. Hard hats, thick shoes and gloves at all times please. Masks are discretionary. When the armed response team eventually gives us access, no one will go anywhere without consulting with a Bruce Demolition expert first, got it?"

More nods.

"Any questions, so far?"

"What about the explosives? Have they been removed?" One of the officers at the back of the room asked. McKenzie didn't recognise him.

"Not yet. But I'm assured they're all safe and stable. Just don't go touching any if you see them."

A few people laughed.

"Anybody else?"

There were no takers.

"Okay. Now let's move on to what we've done so far about searching the campus... Before the armed response team arrived to search and secure the area, an initial search of the campus conducted by officers already on site confirmed that all the buildings were still locked up but did discover a broken window at the bottom of the far stairwell...Marked here on this diagram as Staircase C."

McKenzie turned to a map which he'd blue-tacked to the whiteboard and pointed to the far end of the long narrow building. McKenzie then briefly outlined the layout of the tall main building.

"Let's take a moment to make ourselves familiar with the campus. There are eight floors in the main building, with a total of four lifts and three stairwells. I've given each of them a letter. The main building is long and quite narrow. At each end of the building there is a staircase which goes up all the floors, and a lift. Needless to say, none of the lifts are working. The lifts at either end only go up as far as the seventh floor. You would have to walk up one floor to the eighth."

McKenzie now pointed on the diagram to the middle of the tall blue building.

"There are two lifts at the centre of the building which only go up as far as the fourth floor. Likewise, the staircase here also stops at the fourth. I've marked the staircase in the middle as Stairwell B. And the one nearest us at this end of the building closest to the portacabin and the main road is Stairwell A."

McKenzie now pointed to a long spur which came off the main building at right-angles near Stairwell A.

"This part of the building only has two levels, and is serviced by stairs in Stairwell A, and by another set marked Stairwell D, at the far end of this part of the building."

He brushed his hands over the rest of the diagram. "As you can see, there are a lot of other buildings on the campus, all single level buildings. I've no idea what they were all for, but I understand that at one point there were two thousand pupils in the school. My wife being one of them!"

"Me too!"

"And me!"

Several other voices chipped in.

"It was a great school! I loved it. It's weird being back like this," one of the uniforms from Portobello added.

"Good. We might be calling upon your experience at some point. Okay, turning back to the window at the bottom of Stairwell C. I've since been back to visit it again with Sergeant Anderson, and having examined the scatter of broken glass on the ground, most of which is on the outside of the building, we know that whoever broke the window smashed it from the inside, possibly in an attempt to escape. But we can't find anyone on CCTV crossing the playground, and no one was seen leaving the exits of the campus. There are however, a few blind spots on the CCTV, particularly where power to some cameras was turned off in the moments before the demolition was due."

McKenzie took a sip of water.

"I'm going to ask Sergeant Galbraith from the Armed Response Team to say a few words."

McKenzie waved at the Sergeant, who then stepped up to the front beside him.

"Thanks, Guv." Galbraith nodded to McKenzie, then turned to the room. "When we first entered the building, we had to retire to get hard shoes, and in some places, I insisted that officers had to sweep the floor with brooms before progressing forward, just to make sure they weren't stepping on needles. In fact, the stench is so bad at the bottom of each stairwell, and for the first two floors going upwards, that the dogs couldn't pick up any tracks. They were only able to pick up a single distinctive scent once we made it to the eighth floor, whereupon they followed it into a supply cupboard where the trapdoor to the roof is located. We didn't venture out onto the roof, as at this point, we don't have the appropriate safety gear. We've not finished the search yet, but so far, it's all clear. However, our search has been limited to the tower block, and as of yet, we haven't searched any of the two-storey spur," Galbraith pointed at the section of building that ran at right angles from the tower block. "We've also not yet started searching any of the single-level buildings...or the outbuildings dotted around the edges. These sections of the school are therefore not yet secure."

McKenzie patted Galbraith on the shoulder.

"Thank you, Sergeant."

Galbraith promptly returned to his seat.

McKenzie continued after a brief pause. "'*So, what next?*', I can hear you ask. Any suggestions?"

One of the female officers in the second row put up her hand then spoke when McKenzie nodded at her. "The rest of the building areas obviously need to be surveyed as soon as possible. Since it's getting dark now, why not survey the campus with thermal-imaging cameras? Or above from a helicopter?"

Galbraith stood up and turned towards the officer who'd just spoken. "That's exactly what we're going to be doing next, hopefully with the help of a helicopter which should be arriving in about ..." he glanced at his watch "...ten minutes. However, at this stage we aren't going to re-enter the building. The electricity is off, and we only have a limited number of torches and safety equipment. More is coming, but I don't think it'll arrive until tomorrow morning. As soon as this meeting finishes, we're going to split up into teams, and scan the building from the outside using thermal-imaging equipment."

Galbraith looked across at McKenzie.

"Actually, I'm done for now." McKenzie replied. "I think we should get right on to it. Does anyone else want to add anything? If not, please feel free to talk to me at any time. We mustn't wait until meetings to share ideas."

No one else wanted to add anything.

"Good, I'll just say thanks for now. Our next scheduled meeting will be at nine tomorrow morning. I'll see you all then. For now though, if you'll give us a few moments, DI Brown and myself will divide you all into teams and issue instructions, and then we'll divvy up what safety equipment we have. Please remain in the room until you hear your name called."

The next fifteen minutes was spent organising everyone into teams, and handing out instructions and equipment. When everyone was set, they filed out of the temporary incident room, and made their way down to their start positions. If any heat traces were discovered, McKenzie was to be alerted immediately. An armed search party would then enter the building, surround it, and capture any target.

After they'd left the room, McKenzie followed them out, and blue-tacked a piece of paper to the outside of the door. The words '*Operation Blue-Building*' were scrawled on it in big black letters. No doubt their computer system back at St Leonards would allocate them an 'official' Operation's name in the coming days, but for now, this one seemed the most appropriate.

Turning around he looked back up at the tall tower block.

McKenzie was petrified of heights, but he knew that at some point he should go up there and take a look for himself.

Even the thought of it had his pulse racing.

Just then he heard a buzz on his radio and he raced into the room to retrieve it from his jacket.

"Boss, they've just started the thermal imaging, but they've already got two traces. You'll need to get down here quick... you need to see these for yourself!"

Chapter 4

Portobello High School
Edinburgh
23.15

McKenzie stood beside Gary Bruce, DI Brown and a PC Lynch who was operating a thermal imaging monitor. They were staring at the monitor's screen, linked to the hand-held thermal-imaging camera which had been hoisted up on the end of a long pole carried aloft by two PCs.

The six of them were standing just inside the perimeter fence beside the long two-floor extension that jutted out at right angles to the tower block. The camera was facing into the building at the level of the second floor. They were two classrooms along from the tower block.

PC Lynch, a uniformed officer in his thirties, explained what they were looking at. "According to the plans Mr Bruce gave us, this is the RE - sorry, Religious Education - area. We've picked up two images, one stationary and one moving. The first one looks like it could be a person crawling along the floor, keeping low. It's this one here... look..." Lynch pointed to the image. "It's quite large, but to be honest, I don't think it's big enough for an adult."

McKenzie stared at the image, the body temperature showing bright white against the black backdrop of the cold building. Whatever it was seemed to be lying on the floor.

"Can't see much detail. Could be an adult curled up, facing away." McKenzie suggested. "We need to get in there and take a look."

"The lack of detail's because of the thick walls. Unfortunately, we can't reach high enough to see through the windows," Lynch explained.

"The other image?"

"It's in the same classroom. We'll be seeing it side on, against one of the walls at right angles to this front wall. The thermal footprint is much fainter, but we can still make it out."

Lynch called to the PCs carrying the cameras, and they walked a few metres further away.

McKenzie squinted at the image which appeared.

Brown was first to comment. "Looks like a person, upside down. Those look like feet, and that looks like a head..."

"I agree. But the image doesn't make any sense."

"That's why I said you had to see this for yourself, Guv." Lynch agreed.

McKenzie looked up, glancing to his left. "And what about these classrooms? Anything showing up there?"

"We've very quickly scanned along both floors, and nothing else comes up. These are the only heat signatures we found. Another team's scanning the classrooms on the other side of this block, but so far they've found nothing either. They've moved on to the music rooms now."

McKenzie thought for a moment.

He called Galbraith.

"Our team's found two thermal images. I know you haven't given us the all clear yet, but we have to go in now and see what these images are. If you agree, I'd suggest three teams, four men on each team, each team comprising two armed officers, one of my team, and one of Bruce's staff. I'd suggest that at all times Bruce's men are in charge of our safety from a structural perspective. If they say it's too unsafe to proceed, we stop. We also maintain radio silence at all times. Everyone wears a night vision headset, and no torches are allowed. Your armed boys go first, and the rest follow."

There was a pause while Galbraith thought about it.

"Bruce's team are civilians. Normally they wouldn't be allowed in, but this is a weird setup. We're potentially in danger unless they escort us, and they're in danger unless we escort them. Okay. But my men are in charge. What they say goes."

"Agreed." McKenzie smiled.

It was the result he needed.

Portobello High School
Staircase A
Edinburgh
Saturday
00.15

Led by the armed police-officers and the demolition expert, McKenzie followed the two teams up staircase A. There wasn't much moonlight tonight, and there were a lot of clouds. Outside it was dark. Inside it was almost pitch black. In this environment, the night vision goggles they were all wearing were invaluable. With them, they could almost see clearly. Assuming anyone hiding in the classrooms would not be similarly equipped, they would be at a severe disadvantage to the approaching police team. However, thanks to the internet where it was possible to buy almost anything, that assumption could easily prove to be false.

Anderson hadn't been joking when he'd said that the place stunk to high heaven, or that the risk from stepping on used needles was severe. The stench of stale urine and excrement, probably human, caught in the back of McKenzie's throat and almost made him gag. Through his night-vision goggles, the needles on the floor glistened occasionally in the torch beams. It was unlikely that they would penetrate the heavy shoes they were all now wearing, but it wasn't a risk they could take.

The simple broom which McKenzie carried quickly proved to be worth its weight in gold, and where necessary he forcibly widened the existing path through the rubbish and drug debris which had already been made earlier that evening.

When they got to the first floor, Galbraith waved one of the teams along the extension from the tower block, then carried on up to the second floor. Several times Galbraith indicated for everyone to pause, and they stood still, listening to the sound of the building creaking and settling. There were no other sounds, and the team carried on.

They soon came to the junction on the second floor where the corridor ran between the classrooms in the main tower block and the other corridor branched off into the extension.

With a wave of his arm indicating to move on, Galbraith set off down the corridor into the extension. McKenzie and his team followed.

At the first classroom, they paused at the door and discovered it was closed. Not wanting to try the door lest it made a noise and gave away their presence, they moved past it to the RE classroom where the thermal images had been seen from outside the building.

They took up positions on either side of the door, which was half-open, and then paused again. Listening.

Apart from sounds of the building settling, there was silence.

Galbraith gave an 'OK' signal to the other men in the team, and when they all replied in kind, he pointed into the classroom.

The next few moments passed very quickly.

First, Galbraith gently pushed the door fully open.

The armed police-officers rushed into the room, their weapons raised and searching, fingers poised on their triggers. Galbraith took a stance in the middle of the room. The others followed behind, going down into kneeling positions at the sides of the room and poised for a response from the two images they were investigating.

Almost immediately the form lying on the floor sprung up and rushed straight at them.

Seeing it just in time, Galbraith relaxed his finger on the trigger and swept the barrel of his rifle away from his body, aiming to hit the oncoming shape in the head, but missing it by centimetres.

The fox swept past them through their legs and disappeared into the darkness.

The team's attention turned to the far wall.

It was immediately obvious there was no further threat to the team.

Stepping closer to the far wall, the team removed their night vision goggles, switched on their torches and stared at the naked body of the man in front of them.

Upside down.

Gagged and blindfolded.

Wrist and ankles nailed to a wooden cross in the shape of an 'X' attached to the middle of the wall.

As McKenzie took in the sight that befell him, he experienced a strange mixture of emotions.

Shock.
Confusion.
Disgust.
Revulsion.
And curiosity.
How had this been done?
Who had done it?
And how had someone done it without being spotted?

McKenzie walked forward and checked for a pulse on the victim's neck, already knowing the answer.

The man was dead. The body was cold, but still warmer than its surroundings. If they had found him several hours earlier, perhaps he would still be alive.

As it was, however, he had died a gruesome and slow death, either bleeding out as the blood slowly drained out of the violent wounds in his limbs, or asphyxiating on his own vomit and bodily floods.

McKenzie swore loudly.

He pulled out his phone and texted the rest of the search party groups:

'High alert! Just discovered another body. Assume killer may still be in the building!'

For a moment McKenzie stood quietly, deciding what to do next.

His immediate urge was to take the cross off the wall and lay it and the man's body on the floor in an attempt to give the dead man some respect. But the correct thing to do was to leave both alone, cordon off the area and let the forensic team get the body to speak to them in ways that the man himself no longer could.

From experience McKenzie knew that the expression *'Dead men tell no tales'* was completely wrong. On the contrary, in the hands of the right forensics' expert, dead men often gave up their secrets, chapter and verse.

McKenzie was also confident that Police Scotland had some of the best forensic experts in the world.

Backing away from the wall, he put his night vision goggles on and gestured for the others to do the same and follow him.

Whoever did this was probably still at large in the building, and McKenzie was going to find the bastard.

Stepping in front of the armed officers, he headed back into the corridor.

"Sorry, Guv, I still have to go first..." Galbraith insisted.

Galbraith, McKenzie and his officers moved into the corridor, Galbraith indicating that they would move back to the start of the corridor and check each classroom in turn.

McKenzie cleared his mind and tried to think. Whoever was behind both of the murders should not be underestimated. These were unlike the typical killings he normally encountered.

The person - or persons - who had committed them, had done so knowing full well that the site was being watched by the public, guarded and under observation of the police.

In spite of CCTV, the perimeter fencing, guard dogs and regular patrols, someone had managed to get two victims onto the campus - along with a full-size cross - and commit two gruesome murders, without being seen or heard.

McKenzie had two questions:

How?

And why?

He was a long way from knowing the answers but was certain about one thing: he was going to find out.

Chapter 5

Portobello High School
Edinburgh
'Operation Blue-Building'
Incident Room
Saturday
03.00

McKenzie waited patiently for the last of the remaining DS's and uniformed officers to file into the room. The mood was sombre, and everyone was exhausted.

"I'll get straight to the point. The body of a second person was found a few hours ago. A man. The body was found, for want of a better description, crucified to a cross, upside down. Credit cards found on the body and a LinkedIn search indicate that he's Ronald Blake, a Religious Education teacher who, like David Weir, taught at Portobello High School for most of his career. We're still to contact the next of kin, and get a formal identification, but I'm confident he is who we believe him to be. It's worth noting that Mr Blake's body was found in a classroom which used to be given over to the Religious Education Department. When we couple that with another fresh piece of news, namely that we now know that Mr Weir was a geography teacher, and the top floor of the old school was given over to the geography department, I think we can see that these deaths are linked. Two deaths. Two teachers. Both killed in or near to the departments where they taught."

McKenzie wandered across the front of the portacabin, letting the news settle in properly. The assembled team began to talk amongst themselves. McKenzie gave them a few moments then continued.

"Now, since discovering the second victim, the armed response team has completed their inspection of all the rooms in the building. There are a lot, spread out across the campus and up there," McKenzie gestured at the hulk of the building outside the portacabin behind him, "and there's the distinct possibility a cupboard or a toilet has been missed somewhere, but Galbraith has informed me that the building has been searched to the best of their ability, and no threats and no other victims have been found. With their search now complete, the armed response team is handing the site over to us. I'm formally in charge of the investigation from now on. Before continuing, I'd just like to thank Galbraith and his team."

McKenzie nodded at the Sergeant and smiled.

"Anyway, given the late hour, I'm going to dismiss you all and send you home to your beds. I've spoken with DCS Helen Wilkinson and she's allocated extra resources to this investigation. Consequently, reporting to me, Detective Inspector Euan Mather will be arriving in the next twenty minutes with a fresh team to take over during the rest of the evening, and we'll all reconvene later today at eleven. I know some of you will have other plans, but if you can, cancel them. I need you here."

McKenzie turned to Brown, who he caught in the act of yawning with her hand over her mouth, "DI Brown, do you have anything to add?"

"A couple of matters, sir. The first is something I want to establish as soon as possible: when was the second victim actually crucified? How long has he been in the building? And how the hell did someone get a full-grown man and a huge wooden cross into the building without being spotted? I'll brief DI Mather as soon as he arrives and hand over to his team, but one of the questions raised earlier was just how much planning was involved in this. I'm of the opinion that these murders were timed and planned for maximum visibility and attention. Whoever's behind this is not only clever, but also bold. And my fear is that although we've already got two victims, we can't be sure that's where it stops. Lastly, walking around the inside of the building with all the rubbish and used needles I couldn't help wondering how so many people have already had access to the site when we can't find a way in. Does that tell us something?"

McKenzie nodded. "Good questions. And there's going to be a lot more. On the latter, I've already discussed that with Bruce. Apparently, what you see inside the building is mainly there from before. Bruce demolition put up their new fencing only three weeks ago. Before that, the old fencing had several gaps where people broke through and could get in. Which is why the perimeter was redone and reinforced."

Brown nodded, and a few people whispered something to their nearest neighbours. Obviously, Brown wasn't the only person to have had that question.

"Good. Enough for tonight. I want you all to go home, sleep, and come back with your own thoughts later today. In the meantime, I don't want anyone else going back into any of the buildings on the campus, and the replacement shift of officers will be redoubling all efforts to make sure the perimeters are secure and no one can enter or leave the site without permission."

McKenzie scanned the room full of tired faces and finished the first day of Operation Blue-Building by clapping his hands along with the words, "Dismissed."

Thirty minutes later McKenzie and Brown left the portacabin, having fully briefed DI Mather, and given him a long list of actions to get underway.

After Brown had driven off alone in her car, McKenzie waited for a taxi to arrive. Standing on the side of the road, he looked up at the dark building towering above him, and felt a cold shiver run up and down his spine.

He had only just been allowed to return to active duty, but already he was wondering if he should have taken the offer of another month's paid leave instead.

Recalling what he'd seen this evening, he knew this was a case he was never going to forget.

One thing was for certain.

Whoever was behind this was one sick, depraved bastard.

And he needed to be caught.

Before he killed again.

On the side of the street
Further along the road from Portobello High School
03.45

Sitting in the back of the white van parked several hundred metres down the road, the man put down his cup of thermos flask coffee and raised his pair of military night vision binoculars to his eyes.

"Patience is a virtue", one of his fathers, the last one, used to say. Mostly just before another beating was dished out. Looking back now it certainly gave a new meaning to the phrase, 'I'll beat some sense into you'.

Slowly, over the years, yes, he'd learned many a useful idiom, but he'd never really appreciated the why, how, or what for. He just remembered the bruises. And the hate. And the look in his father's eyes.

Nowadays however, some of it was beginning to make sense.

Like now.

His patience had paid off.

The policeman getting into the taxi was DCI Campbell McKenzie. The man in the van had been listening to the police chatter over the hacked police radio he'd bought from a guy in Leith, and he'd picked up that McKenzie would take a taxi as soon as another detective, Mather, arrived.

Focussing his binoculars on McKenzie through the one-way glass windows, the man had watched as McKenzie waited beside the road for his cab. He'd watched him staring up at the hulking edifice of the old school before finally stooping forward and climbing into the back seat of a private hire.

This wasn't the first time he'd seen McKenzie.

The man already knew a lot about him.

McKenzie looked like his old photograph. He hadn't changed much. He had a colourful track record. He'd recently been cleared of any wrong doing in connection with the death of his previous partner, DI Danielle Wessex, and had only just returned to duty after several months off.

But now he was back.

Just in time.

It couldn't have worked out better.

McKenzie's appointment to lead the investigation had been nothing more than a coincidence, but the man in the van still couldn't quite believe his luck. He couldn't have chosen a better or more appropriate person himself!

The man in the van had listened to all McKenzie's Airwave conversations earlier today. Writing down anything of interest. Updating his profile of the man who would now be responsible for tracking him down.

After McKenzie's taxi drove off, heading towards Duddingston, the man in the van tuned back to the police airways and spent the next thirty minutes listening to random conversations, before finally settling on a conversation between DI Mather and Fettes Road.

Now he had Mather's frequency, he would easily be able to follow his conversations too.

Which would be essential in the coming days.

Staying one step ahead of McKenzie and Mather, and anyone else who was to subsequently lead the investigation or direct actions around the school, would be key.

Today had gone brilliantly.

No one had a clue how he'd done it.

Or what he'd actually done.

So far, he was Scot free.

Which was the way he would have to remain if he was going to complete the rest of his plan.

Today had been exciting.

Two deaths.

Two rights wronged.

But there was a lot more work to do.

This was only the beginning.

The Grange
Edinburgh
04.15

"What are you still doing up?" McKenzie reprimanded his wife as he walked into their kitchen and saw her sitting at the island, eating ice-cream from a carton.

"Cravings. Driving me insane. I woke up. Couldn't get back to sleep."

"Fiona, you need to rest. You've only got another two months before Little Bump comes, and once it arrives, you'll never get any rest again!" He laughed, grabbing a spoon from a drawer and sitting down beside her.

"Get your own, this is mine." She laughed back, pushing him playfully away as he went to dip his spoon into her carton.

"Any more in the fridge?"

"Nope. Sorry... that's why I'm being so possessive."

"You're going to eat the whole tub?"

"Don't just blame me. Little Bump is hungry."

McKenzie knelt down and kissed Little Bump through Fiona's pyjama top.

"Naught boy."

"Girl..."

"Boy..." McKenzie insisted, standing up and crossing over to the American-style fridge-freezer.

"There's some cold lasagne in the oven."

"Thanks."

"So, can you talk about it?" she asked, not forcefully, but interested.

"Two deaths. Murders. Very gruesome. Looks like the same person did it. That's all I can say."

A few minutes later McKenzie was standing in front of the microwave waiting for the lasagne to heat up, when he heard his Airwave ringing.

He retrieved it from his jacket in the hallway and called DI Mather back.

"You've seen it then?" Mather asked.

"What?"

"Ah, …so you haven't. Someone posted a video on Facebook of the man falling to his death from the roof of the school. It's gone viral..."

McKenzie swore loudly. "Text me the link. I'll call you back."

McKenzie hung up, waited for the link and then watched the video several times. Now angry, he returned Mather's call.

"I can't believe it! Who'd post something like that? I thought we'd got a news blackout on this?"

"This is Social Media, not the news. And there's more than one. I've seen three. Obviously filmed from different phones in the crowd on the street. It doesn't surprise me in the slightest, Guv, it's what people do nowadays. They'll probably be on YouTube soon as well."

"I want you to get them pulled. Wherever they appear. As soon as possible."

"You mean call Facebook?"

"Whatever it takes, just get them pulled by the time I get back to the school later this morning."

"I'll leave that to the Media team in Fettes Row. I'll chase them. But don't forget it's almost four-thirty in the morning. And it's Saturday."

"Do what you can."

"Guv, do you know about tonight?"

"What about tonight?"

"I just heard from one of the officers here who's going... if it's still on."

"If what's still on?"

"The Portobello High School Reunion Ball."

"The *what*?"

"The School Reunion. Apparently it's the first time all the pupils who left between 1990 and 2000 will be getting back together again."

McKenzie looked up and glanced at his wife.

He ended the call with Mather and then walked over to Fiona.

"Did you know about the reunion ball at your old school?" he asked.

She stared back at him, licking the last remnants of the ice-cream from her spoon.

"Campbell, exactly what planet are you on? I've told you about it a thousand times. Hence the new red dress I just bought. And why your kilt went to the dry cleaners."

It rang a vague bell. McKenzie swore again under his breath, as he returned his gaze to the video on his mobile.

Hitting play again, he watched for the fifth time as the man fell off the edge of the Portobello High School.

McKenzie shook his head.

Things were going from bad to worse.

A school reunion was the last thing they needed just now.

And he could think of at least two people who wouldn't be going.

Chapter 6

Cramond
Edinburgh
Saturday
09.30

Stuart Nisbet parked his Ducati in his garage, hung his helmet on the hook on the wall, and then pressed the button on his key fob to close the garage door.

After watching the large metal door slide back into place, he left the garage by pressing his fingerprint against a sensor on the wall, waiting a few seconds for the door to slide sideways, and then stepping through into the opulent house beyond.

Placing his finger on a panel on the inside wall, he then waited for the door to slide shut behind him, effectively sealing off the garage and its contents - the Ducati and two luxury cars - from the main house.

As he walked through his spacious hallway, he called out to his electronic assistant and told her to run his bath and pour his coffee.

"And Sabrina, tell me the latest stock prices for New Zealand Hydro and GlaxoSmithKlein."

As he picked up his coffee from his expansive kitchen-diner with its floor-to-ceiling, sweeping glass-filled panoramic view of the River Forth, he mulled over the recent stock prices Sabrina recited to him, and made some quick, calculated decisions.

The markets were closed now, but if he sold the stock electronically as soon as the markets opened again on Monday, he'd make another killing.

After instructing Sabrina to call his broker, a human's voice filled the air.

"Mr Nisbet, It's Duncan. How can I help you, sir?"

"As soon as the markets open on Monday, sell forty percent of the stock in GlaxoSmithKlein, and all of the stock in New Zealand Hydro, so long as they don't drop more than ten percent upon opening. Confirm the sales once done."

"Yes, Mr Nisbet. Understood."

As he picked up the paper from the table in the hallway and took the stairs two at a time up the circular staircase to the third floor, Nisbet did the mental maths. Even if they dropped the full ten percent, he'd still make a cool four hundred thousand dollars.

Stripping quickly out of his leathers, he lowered himself into his marble bath in the floor of his penthouse bedroom, took another sip from his coffee, and thought about the day and night ahead.

There was so much to do.

He'd been looking forward to the school Reunion for over twenty years. Twenty years of planning how he'd rub the noses in it of all those who'd treated him like shit while he was at school; all those who hadn't believed he would ever succeed or make anything of his life. Well, he'd have the last laugh. Not them.

Stuart Nisbet was perhaps the richest Scotsman of his age, one of only a handful of billionaires in the country.

He mixed with celebrities, dined with Royals, and raced his horses at Ascot every year.

Not bad for a little boy who grew up in Portobello and left school with only a few elementary qualifications to his name.

After a stint in the Army he'd realised in an incredible moment of epiphany in Afghanistan that it was mostly the uneducated that made up the cannon fodder of warfare. And life. If he wanted to survive, and to make anything of himself, he had to get smarter. Incredibly he'd survived Afghanistan, and as soon as he returned home and left the service, he'd enrolled himself in college, spent years studying, got into University and then graduated with a degree in Economics.

His determination to turn his life around was impressive, and his drive to succeed was inspiring.

He'd easily passed the interviews he'd chased with the financial houses in Edinburgh, and after rapid progression upwards through the ranks, within years he was heading up and managing his own funds.

Several years later he'd left the rat race - being employed by others who pocketed most of his profits was no longer for him. Confident he could do just as well, if not better, by himself, he'd founded his own investment business, establishing and running several incredibly successful funds that invested in high-tech stocks, energy and pharmaceuticals.

He'd taken some gambles - albeit calculated gambles - and made several small fortunes.

Which he'd then turned into bigger fortunes.

And which in turn, had then been transformed into a vast fortune.

His success knew no bounds.

Stuart Nisbet had the Midas touch.

He now lived in one of the most beautiful and richest areas of the UK. His house was amazing, with sweeping views across the River Forth that were unparalleled anywhere. He drove fast cars, dated fast women, did whatever he wanted.

He lacked only two things.
True friends.
And *real* love.
Of which money could buy neither, no matter how much he had.

Nevertheless, Stuart was looking forward to tonight.

Not only would he get the chance to awe those who had dismissed him as trash all those years ago, but we would get a chance to see the few friends he did once have.

And then there was also Maggie Sutherland.

Even thinking of her now made his heart flutter.

He'd had many women since he'd first fallen in love with Maggie. Some famous, some beautiful - and sometimes more than one at the same time - but he knew that one day when he was dying and his life flashed before his eyes, it would be Maggie Sutherland and her blue, blue eyes that he would think of during his last few seconds.

She'd had the softest lips.

The sweetest smile.
And the cutest dimple in the world.

The reality of it all, however, was that at the time Stuart had only been a pathetic little second-year. Not a man like the others in Sixth Form, or even some of the teachers.

He hadn't blamed Maggie - he understood her reactions, he *knew* her only too well, and anyway, the chase had and would make the catch so much more worthwhile - but still it had hurt, a lot, when she had so publicly thrown his Valentine's Card into the bucket in front of all her laughing friends.

Later, he'd heard that one of the teachers had given her a Valentine's card. And two of the Sixth Formers.

Bastards all of them.

The opportunity had been a long time coming, but tonight there would be scores to settle. Not one, but several.

Looking back, Stuart had few regrets. He'd faced life the best way he could: accepting his lot in life, he'd taken charge of his own destiny, and forged a new future for himself.

So yes, Stuart had *few* regrets.

But tonight, he'd make up for the ones he did.

Stuart had a plan.

Duddingston Road
Edinburgh
10.00

Irene Quinn had been dreading this day. For months. Ever since some stupid person had decided to plan the bloody thing and her husband had found out about it. No one had ever considered planning a Reunion before, so why now all of a sudden?

Irene had enjoyed school. She'd done well, had good friends, passed all her exams, and even made it to university.

Now she had two children, and unlike some of her friends, she still even had the same husband.

Barry Quinn and Irene had been married for almost twenty years now. Twenty years ago, Barry had been a catch. He'd played rugby in the First Fifteen in the year above hers, and when they were married, she had been proud.

Over the years, she had got less proud, - as Irene knew Barry had of her - and together they had both descended into a life of mediocrity. They lived in a mediocre house. Did mediocre jobs. Lived mediocre lives.

Yet, in spite of all the mediocrity, their lives were not too bad. In fact, truth be told, they were probably both happy with their lot.

Barry and Irene knew their place in society, and until Barry had come home that day full of the news about the school Reunion, they had been content with what they'd had and the lives they lived.

Lives which were not great. Not bad. But ok.

Since that day however, it had been a very different story.

"Do you think Peter Black will be there?" Barry has asked Irene within an hour of starting to think about the Reunion. "He was a right bastard! Always putting me down and showing off and always going on about all the great things he was going to do when he left school. And what about Andrew Jessop? He was going to be a doctor... or was it a surgeon? And Cammie? He wanted to open up a string of garages and make millions. They all had such big plans. And what have I got? What did I end up doing?"

"You married me. We had two wonderful children. We're happy. Never mind about the others. You can't go about comparing yourself with everyone else..." Irene had started to defend her life, even though Barry had a fair point. What had they done with their lives? Apart from stagnate.

"What about Fiona? I wonder..."

"Fiona who?"

"Lewis. Fiona Lewis. She was beautiful."

"Was she the one that you snogged at the Christmas disco, before you and I got together?"

"Aye, but nothing else happened."

"But you still fancy her..."

"How can I? I don't even know what she looks like now. Anyway, what about you and that guy, Paul Bentford? That English guy, whose mum and dad owned that hotel in Joppa?"

Irene started to blush.

"What about him?"

"I bet you sometimes wish you'd married him instead of me? He was taller than me, his parents were loaded and you got off with him once, didn't you?"

"I went out with him for a whole term, until he dumped me."

"But you still fancy him? You're not going to tell me you've never thought about him?"

Barry was pacing round their front room, playing with his car keys in his hands.

"I'm not going," he finally announced, plonking himself down on the sofa and reaching for the TV remote.

"Good. It'll save a baby-sitter. I'm going." Irene sat down on the chair beside him. "It'll be a laugh, and it'll be good to see everyone else."

Barry glared at her.

"So, if Paul's there, are you going to dance with him?"

Irene blushed again.

"Not if his wife is there with him. And not if you go with me." Irene fiddled with the strings on her apron and then rested her hands on her stomach. "Anyway, why won't you go?"

"Because it'll be embarrassing. I haven't kept up with anyone else. Everyone will have forgotten me. And I know that everyone else will have done so much more with their lives. They'll be living all over the world, doing big jobs, having tons of fun. I was no big shakes at school, and when everyone finds out what I've done since school, it'll just confirm what everyone said at Porty."

"But people didn't really talk about you, Barry."

"Exactly. I was a nobody then, and they'll just laugh at me when they find out I'm still a nobody now."

"Thanks. So, I'm a '*nobody*' too then?"

"You know what I mean..."

"I just hope Paul's there, then. He was never a nobody. And he was sure to God never going to be a nobody either." Irene replied, getting angry now, and deliberately winding her husband up.

"You're not dancing with him!" Barry's face started to turn red.

"I'll dance with whoever I want Barry. Especially if you're not there, you coward!"

"If you dance with Paul, then I'm going to dance with Fiona Lewis."

Irene laughed, stood up and walked out of the room.

When she got to the downstairs bathroom, she closed the door, and stood in front of the mirror.

The reflection staring back at her had changed a lot in the past twenty years.

She'd be lucky if Paul even recognised her, let alone wanted to dance with her. And Fiona Lewis?

She thought of Barry and her, and the disco all those years ago when she'd seen Barry trying to get a hand up her top while they danced slowly to Dire Straits and 'Sultans of Swing.'

For a moment she closed her eyes and fought back the tears, then when she'd recovered enough she escaped to her kitchen, found her phone, and called her hairdresser.

"Sorry, Irene. We're booked that whole week."

"Why?"

"It's the Porty Reunion. Haven't you heard about it?"

Irene lied, hung up and went to get the old yellow pages. She needed to book an appointment with whoever she could get.

There's no way she was going to go the Reunion looking like she did.

After she'd booked something with someone in Leith, she'd searched for and found her old gym membership card.

At the time, she'd had three months until the Reunion.

Three months to get fit, lose weight and tone up.

Whatever it took. Paul was going to notice her. And bloody dance with her.

Maybe it was about time she shook Barry up and made him jealous for once!

Duddingston Road
Edinburgh
10.30

Iain Small stood in front of his mirror, his hand playing with the mound of fat that had slowly and imperceptibly buried his tummy over the past few years.

Underneath there was still a six-pack, Iain was sure of it. There used to be one there, but even though Iain still worked out - although truth be told only very occasionally - years of drinking beer with his rugby pals, had covered the six-pack with a 'one-pack'.

Quite a large one-pack.

Until recently it had been possible to ignore it, but now, with only eight-and-a-half hours until the Reunion started, he couldn't help compare himself to how he used to look then, and how awful he looked now.

Where had his youth gone?

Iain had been popular at High School. He'd had lots of friends, and thanks to the Rugby Club, he was still friends with most of the people he used to hang out with back then.

Iain had got older, life had moved on, but in many ways a lot had remained the same.

The boys he'd be drinking with at the bar tonight, were 'his boys', the same boys he'd been hanging out with since he was eight, or even younger.

Half of them still played rugby together every weekend, and most of them still got together every Saturday night in Town or down in Porty on the Esplanade somewhere.

Even the girls that he talked to most weekends were still the same girls from school. The only difference was that a lot of them were now married to his friends. The fact that most of the boys he still hung out with, had, at one time or another, gone out with or slept with the girls who were now married to *their* friends, was no big deal.

Nowadays, however, life and the choosing of partners had mostly settled down. Most of his friends had kids who were themselves now in the final years of school at the new Portobello High School, and Iain wouldn't be surprised if in twenty years' time, his kids were still hanging out with the same friends they had today.

Outside the rugby crowd, things were admittedly different. A lot of people had flown the nest, escaped their insular ecosystem and ended up in different cities, with flash careers and big mortgages. But Iain had never really seen the point of the rat race. After leaving Edinburgh Uni he'd got a job in a computer company in Leith, and had stayed there ever since.

He was content. Happy. Loved his life. His friends. And his lot.

Iain wasn't a millionaire, and realistically never would be. But he had almost everything he'd ever wanted in life, and was basically happy. Very happy.

He had few regrets. Just one or two. But they were just small ones. Like, for example, never being brave enough to tell one of the girls at school - Marie McDonald - just how much he fancied her, or to ask her out. Marie had been special. Just being in the same room with her had made Iain nervous, and reduced him to a silly, quivering, speechless, spotty wreck!

But that was the past. Iain was now married to Debbie, three kids - two boys and a girl, and a cat.

Debbie had been in the year beneath him, and they'd got together one night after the disco down in the Town Hall in Portobello High Street.

They split up several times, but always got back together and they'd eventually married eighteen years ago. They lived in a bungalow not far from the new school, and he drove to work in Leith every day.

Edinburgh offered him everything he needed in life: employment, rugby, mountains, sea, a great social life and regular time with his friends.

He was looking forward to the Reunion. Although he was in almost daily contact with his main friends from school, there were others who had moved on and found other lives far away from Edinburgh.

He wondered how they were? Why did they leave Edinburgh? What took them away? How were their lives? Were they just as happy as he was?

Perhaps a little part of him did wonder, if the grass was greener for those who had left and gone elsewhere? If they had found better lives, Iain knew that he was unlikely to be jealous. Curious, yes, but no, not jealous.

Standing there, looking at himself in the mirror, the biggest problem that Iain had now was his 'one-pack'.

And if that was the biggest problem he had, then things weren't that bad after all.

Roll on tonight!

Northfield Broadway
Edinburgh
10.45

Marie McDonald stepped out of the shower and towelled herself down in her bathroom. Technically she hadn't lived at her parent's house for over twenty years, but this would always be her home, even though it was her parents' house.

Her parents had left her bedroom as it was the day she'd caught the train down to London, and her new life, the August following her graduation from Edinburgh University. Her old posters were still on her wall, and David Bowie and Duran Duran would be forever staring down at her whenever she woke up in her old bed. *Her* bed. The most comfortable bed in the entire world.

And she should know. She'd slept in most of them.

Since she left Uni, she'd lived the life of a nomad, going to whatever country needed her most.

She'd studied History at Edinburgh, but upon graduating had 'been called' to spend a year doing Voluntary work in Africa. After a year of volunteering and being paid nothing, she'd decided to help an endangered tribe in South America. She moved continents and carried on doing much the same sort of work, but this time for a small salary. Not much. But it was something.

She'd then spent several years in South America before returning to Europe.

Almost accidentally she'd ended up in Poland, where she'd been taken by the plight of Roma children in an orphanage near Warsaw.

When the charity which had run the orphanage had collapsed, Marie had almost single-handedly somehow managed to raise enough money to keep it open.

Without intending to, the lives of over sixty previously abused, neglected and otherwise unloved children, now depended upon her.

She couldn't leave.

Hadn't wanted to leave.

And she now lived there, full time, with no end-game in sight.

In fact, as each year had passed, she'd unwittingly got herself in deeper. The orphanage had grown, expanding from sixty Roma children to a charity with several homes in different parts of Eastern Europe, and a total of over three hundred children.

As the years had passed, Marie had become a recognised expert in many of the issues relating to the problems orphans faced - particularly those from Eastern Europe - and she was often invited to speak to various assemblies at the European Union, or to individual governments, or large corporations - in fact, anyone, anywhere that could help support her or donate much needed funds to her work and her charity.

Increasingly, as her mission had expanded, Marie had done less of the hands-on caring, and more of a managerial and public speaking role, championing the little children's cause, and raising awareness of their plight, and the need to look after and love them.

Marie was a passionate believer in education as being the solution to raise her children out of poverty and their often very hopeless past associations and lives. Through education, her children could empower themselves for good, solid, lives ahead.

Her trip back to Scotland, planned serendipitously so that it coincided with the Portobello High School Reunion, was originally intended to be a long-deserved break, recommended by her doctor who was concerned about the effects of both physical and mental exhaustion.

Although initially reluctant, she'd eventually succumbed to those badgering her to take a relaxing holiday, but no sooner had she booked her ticket to Edinburgh, than she'd started to make plans.

She would visit Loch Ness, climb Ben Nevis, cycle along the Great Glen, and then find out who her parents' local MP was, and try to seek an opportunity to raise some 'Overseas Development' funds from the Scottish Parliament.

And now, having discovered about the Portobello Reunion a week ago, she'd bought a new dress and lipstick.

Marie was sure not many people would remember who she was. Over the years she'd lost contact with everyone, but she was still excited.

She'd been happy at school. Learned a lot. She'd had good friends at the time. In fact, looking back on her youth, all in all she'd had very positive experiences.

Marie knew that she'd been so busy looking after her children that she had neglected her own life, but now, tonight, perhaps there would be a chance to rekindle some friendships and build upon them for the future.

Marie had always believed in fate, and as the hours ticked by and the Reunion got steadily closer, she couldn't help believing that her returning to Edinburgh at the same time as the Reunion was taking place, was more than just coincidence.

There was a reason she was here today.

And tonight, she could feel it in her bones, something big was going to happen. Something very big indeed…

Joppa
Edinburgh
11.00

    Willy Thomson reached from underneath his duvet and hit the top of his clock, stopping the bloody alarm and knocking it off the bedside table.
    His head hurt.
    And as he began to stir, he realised that his right hand hurt too. A lot.
    Pushing back the duvet, he lifted his hand to his face and saw the dried blood and the bruising, and slowly began to remember the cause of it the night before: too much beer, and a cheeky bastard who'd disrespected him on his way back home.
    Willy smiled to himself, thinking about the beating he'd given the man. He'd done a good job, considering how drunk he was.
    Last night had been a good bash, thanks mainly to the wallet he'd got from another stupid tourist in the Grassmarket: drunk, having too much fun, and not paying enough attention to his valuables, which in this case amounted to two hundred pounds, a French driver's license, a credit card and a contactless debit card.
    Willy could sell the driver's license and the credit card, and with a little luck he'd still be able to have some fun with the debit card for a few days, before he passed it on to his mate in Leith.
    As he lay in his bed, Willy contemplated the best course of action for the rest of the day.
    Stupidly, he'd let himself have too much fun last night, and now, even without getting out of bed, he knew he was facing a hangover.
    A hangover was the last thing he needed. There was a lot to do today, and he wanted to be sober tonight, at least at the beginning of the evening, so he was able to think clearly and make plans as events unfolded.
    He'd been looking forward to the School Reunion ever since the rumours started circling that one was on the cards.
    Willy's life was a mess. Since he'd left school, he'd been in prison three times - theft, assault and attempted murder - and he'd struggled to hold down any form of job for long.
    If it wasn't for the Council looking after him each month with dole money, the flat, and the rich pickings he lifted from the tourists who flocked to the eternal honey pot that was Edinburgh, Willy would have long ago wasted away and died from starvation or cold.
    Willy survived from day to day, and when things were going well, from week to week.
    The reason why Willy was a mess was due to a lack of decent parents while growing up (they were drunk most of the time), lack of friends (who would want to hang out with such a loser who stank to high heaven?), and his complete lack of education and absence of any skills or training.
    Probably the most relevant of all that small list, was his lack of education.
    Willy knew he was smart, though, which meant that his ignorance was purely down to his old school teachers.

Willy's life had been one long struggle. He'd had to fight for everything he ever had - which admittedly wasn't much - and Willy couldn't see an end in sight, any time soon.

Things would have been very different if he'd had a decent education. He could have been rich by now. Clever. Living in a big house with his girlfriends. One of them might even have stuck around long enough for Willy to have got married. Maybe he would even have been mad enough to have a few screaming kids. Unlikely, but possible.

At school however, instead of helping him turn his already rubbish life around and teaching him something useful that could have got him into a good job, his teachers had instead belted him at almost every opportunity. Willy had very quickly been identified as a trouble maker, and since that moment his teachers had done their best to make as much trouble for him as possible.

They'd had it in for him since the moment they'd first laid eyes on him.

All of them.

Tonight though, was going to be payback time.

Willy was a big man now. Not small like he was when the teachers took advantage of him and bullied the crap out of him.

Tonight, if Willy could find any of the teachers on his list, he'd make them pay.

Yep. Tonight was going to be dead good, and by the time the evening was over, at least one of them bastard teachers was going to be good and dead.

Chapter 7

Portobello High School
Edinburgh
'Operation Blue-Building'
Incident Room
Saturday
11.05

McKenzie stood at the front of the portacabin waiting for the room to settle down. Recognising the evening shift should have finished several hours ago, he acknowledged with a smile and a nod some of the uniforms who were still present.

McKenzie clapped his hands together to get everyone's attention.

"Okay, good morning everyone," McKenzie began. "Apologies for the late start, but most of you here pulled almost two shifts yesterday, so I wanted you to get some proper rest. For some of you it's also been a long night, I know, and I appreciate you still being here, but I hope we'll get you home and in bed as soon as possible. From tomorrow we'll go back to normal times again, okay?"

There were no objections.

"DI Mather, can you update us on what the night shift covered, and any items for the day team to get going on?"

Mather pushed himself off a desk at the side of the room, nodded at McKenzie and stepped across to the whiteboard assembled against the wall.

"Thanks Guv. It's been a busy night." He lifted up his phone and showed it to the room. "You've all seen the videos. We've had a team in Fettes working on them since three this morning. They've been trying to find out who posted them, and where they were filmed from. Anything that could be useful. And they've been trying to take them down. It doesn't help that it's a Saturday morning, but both Facebook and YouTube have promised to take them both down by lunchtime. That was the good news. Unfortunately, there's very little the videos can tell us. They were posted from burners using fake accounts. Which means they could have come from the public or someone involved in the murder. We'll never know."

"So, what else do you have, Mather?"

"Quite a lot, actually." He paused, turning to a flip chart on which he'd made a number of notes already. "First of all, let's focus on the victims. Early this morning we contacted next of kin from both the deceased, and about twenty minutes ago we had the second of two positive IDs in the morgue. Both of the deceased have now been formally identified. As preliminary reported in yesterday's meeting, they are David Weir, 55 years of age, and Ronald Blake, 57 years of age. Both were teachers at Portobello High School for many years. Mr Weir was a Geography teacher, and Mr Blake, an RE teacher. Mr Blake had left the school and had transferred to Leith Academy, a promotion, but Mr Weir had moved to the new school site on Milton Road and was still a teacher at the new Portobello High school. What's important to note is that Mr Weir was killed after having been taken onto the top of the school via a ladder in the old Geography supply cupboard, and Mr Blake was killed in the same room he'd taught in for many years as a RE teacher, ... sorry, for those of you who have forgotten everything they learned already, that's Religious Education, or was. Nowadays I believe it's called something more PC."

"RS?" someone volunteered.

"Yes, I think that's it. Anyway, back to the victims. Mr Blake was married. His wife had reported him missing after he hadn't returned home on Thursday night. As for Mr Weir, he lived by himself. He separated from his wife several years ago. He has two grown-up sons, both now working down south somewhere."

"Did someone go to their houses?" McKenzie asked, whilst crossing his arms across his chest and leaning backwards against the wall.

"Yes. PCs Daniels and Winston. They visited Mrs Blake. But they visited Mrs Weir in the old family home, not where he's been living recently."

McKenzie scoured the room for PC Daniels and Winston, and upon finding them, asked, "Anything remarkable to report? How was Mrs Blake?"

"Visibly distraught, Guv. She needed to sit down, and it was a while before we left. We ended up calling in a neighbour to sit with her after we'd gone. Mrs Weir was also upset, but when we visited her, there was another man there in his dressing gown. She's obviously moved on since the marriage. Don't get me wrong, she was upset, but you could tell there was a lot of separation between them now."

"Thanks. Sorry, carry on Mather." McKenzie nodded at the DI.

"We sent someone round to Mr Weir's tenement flat in Leith where he's been for the past year and have knocked on the doors in the stair trying to find out when he was seen last. We didn't access the flat yet, as we didn't have a key. We made enquiries in the stair though. A woman on the third floor said she'd seen him on Wednesday morning about seven thirty on the way to the school, but not since. Quite a few of the people who lived in the stair didn't come to their doors, so I've put it down on today's duty roster for another team to go back there this afternoon, and again in the evening or the morning, until we've managed to speak to everyone and gone round the local shops and pubs etc. We also need for Mrs Weir or someone else to accompany us to the flat and to let us look around. That must be a matter of priority. It could turn out that it may be the scene of his abduction, and if so, we'll need to get forensics there asap."

Mather continued, "Moving on, let's talk about the campus here. The school grounds and the buildings are completely locked down. No one's come or gone, and no one can get in without us knowing. We've also got extra CCTV installed in several of the areas I thought were a little blind."

Mather pulled the top of his marker pen off and underlined the word 'Motive' which he'd already written near the top of a list on the whiteboard.

"So, why did someone want to kill two teachers in the classrooms they'd taught in?"

He let the question hang in the air for a while, but continued before anyone volunteered an answer.

"That's one of the questions we need to answer. And quickly. The obvious choice would be that it could be an ex-pupil with a grudge. But we can't be too sure. It could be another teacher. Or maybe someone who knew them both outside the school and thought it might be sick, or funny to kill them where they used to work."

"But why here? In the old school, and not in the new one?" McKenzie asked.

"Good question. That hints at it being an old pupil who attended the old school, but like I said, that could also be just what someone wants us to think." Mather hesitated and pointed to a hand that had just gone up on the left of the room.

"DS McLeish?"

A tall, skinny man dropped his hand and spoke, "If someone has killed two teachers, and we have a bona fide serial killer on our hands, we have to assume that there could be more. This might not be the end of it. Perhaps we should be checking on all the teachers in the school to see if any others have gone missing?"

Mather nodded.

"Good thinking, McLeish, which is why we contacted the school secretary about an hour ago, and said someone was coming round to talk to her about something which was pretty sensitive and needed her immediate help and attention. How do you fancy volunteering?"

McLeish nodded and smiled. "I'll take that one. I'll also get a full list of the teachers from the past twenty years and start enquiries about any other murders or unexplained deaths amongst their number, just in case these are not the first."

McKenzie nodded. "Can you also get a synopsis of their careers, and the contact details and names of the headmasters and other non-teaching staff of the school during that time frame? It would be good to contact them to establish if there's any obvious reason why the victims have been targeted. Mather, is there anything else, before I let you go home to bed?"

"Just one more thing. The pathologist doing the post-mortems is Brian Wallace. He's aiming to start them tonight. He's already made an initial viewing of the bodies, and commented upon one observation common to both victims, namely, that both of them seem to have multiple burn marks on their bodies. He's not sure yet, but he thinks they could be the result of a powerful cattle prod."

"Which might explain how they were coerced to the site of their murders. There's nothing like a million volts being stuck in your side to encourage you to do whatever someone else wants," PC Lynch volunteered from the front row.

"Possibly, PC Lynch. But even if they were forced into the building, we still have to figure out how they got the victims into the school, undetected. And two of them in rapid succession?" Mather replied.

"We need to figure out how long Mr Blake was attached to that cross for, if that's possible. Maybe one victim was brought in before the other? If they were both brought in at the same time, then surely we're looking at more than one murderer, here?" Brown suggested. "What I'd like to know is how and when the murderer brought the cross into the building? If it was in advance, how long before? Was it before they grabbed Mr Blake and brought him to the school? How much preparation has gone into this and how on earth did they manage to do it without being spotted by anyone in the demolition team?"

"And how heavy was it? If it was one murderer, how did he lift and fix it onto the wall alone? We also need to know how long the two men were missing for, when they were last seen alive, and where they may have disappeared from." McKenzie replied. "To help with that we need to find the mobile numbers for the deceased. Then we need to get their phone records and cell site data so we can track down their last movements. Whoever gets their numbers first needs to record it in the Investigation Log, get the appropriate warrants raised, and request the information from the phone operator as soon as possible. Don't bother waiting for my permission. Just do it, and let us all know when it's been done. Understood?"

A round of nods.

"Okay, now I have an interesting one for us all," McKenzie said, standing up and walking to the centre of the room. "It seems that tonight there's going to be a big school reunion of Portobello's illustrious alumni."

"I know, I'm going!" Anderson announced.

"Me too," another voice quickly followed, this time coming from DS Shona Wishart, an attractive woman from Orkney who McKenzie had worked with several times before. When she spoke, it was more like she was singing, her voice rising and falling in cadence and her accent strangely hypnotic and mesmerising. "I did my O'Levels and Higher Exams at Porty High. I wouldn't miss the Reunion for the world. I can't wait."

"Anyone else? I didn't know anything about it until my wife told me this morning." McKenzie admitted. "She's going too... The big question, for me, is, should we cancel it? I'm just not sure it's a good idea to let it carry on as normal."

"Do you think we could actually cancel it? It's a private affair, being organised by a group of alumni, nothing to do with the school." Wishart continued, with everyone listening attentively.

"I think we have to consider it. Shouldn't we be worried that something else might happen? If there's a serial killer killing teachers, isn't a school Reunion like a red flag to a bull?" McKenzie asked, opening his hands outwards and inviting opinions.

"Possibly. But that depends if there are any old teachers going. You could also look at it another way," Mather argued. "What better opportunity is there going to be, to talk to old ex-pupils and find out reasons why someone might want to kill the two teachers?"

"I'll think about it. Wishart, can you find out who's responsible for the event, and sound out their thoughts on cancellation or postponement? If they're not keen on doing that, can I put you in charge of making some plans around beefing up security for the event? Can we also get some more of our team in there somehow? As helpers, or ushers, or waiters? Whatever? If we let the event carry on, we need to have as many eyes and ears in the building as possible. I'll be going too, so that's at least three of us who can mingle and ask a few questions, but more would be good."

A hand went up at the back of the room.

"DC Barnes?" McKenzie nodded and waved to a detective to stand up.

"I was just wondering, what if there's no murderer at large after all? Since it's unlikely that anyone else could've got into the building, is there any chance that David Weir brought Ronald Blake into the building, kept him here for a few days, crucified him, and then took himself to the top of the building and jumped off?"

Both Mather and McKenzie raised their eyebrows and looked at each other. A murmur went around the room.

"Wow... that's a good one. It would certainly answer a few questions if you were right." McKenzie mused.

Mather turned to the whiteboard, popped off the lid to his pen, and made a note of the question.

"Given that could be a possibility, it adds to the argument for just letting the Reunion go ahead as planned," Wishart suggested.

"Possibly. Like I said, I'll think about it. But that's a fair point."

McKenzie clapped his hands together.

"Okay, I think it's time to let the night crew go home. We'll take a few minutes break and then reconvene in ten to make a list of today's actions and assignments. Thanks Mather."

Everyone stood up and one by one they filed out of the room.

As Mather left, a head popped round the door and asked for DCI McKenzie.

It belonged to Gary Bruce.

He looked nervous, and the moment McKenzie saw the expression on his face, he knew another problem was just about to be added to the list.

It turned out McKenzie's instinct, as usual, was right.

Chapter 8

Portobello High School
Edinburgh
'Operation Blue-Building'
Incident Room
Saturday
11.45

Gary Bruce watched nervously as the last of the police officers and detectives left the portacabin and the door behind them was closed, leaving him alone with McKenzie.

"It's a bit delicate..." Gary started, his eyes searching McKenzie's as he spoke.

"I need to know how long this is going to take. How long will it be before I get the site back?"

McKenzie cocked his head to the side, appraising the man before him. From the way the question had been posed, there was obviously a lot riding on his answer.

"The school is now a murder scene. I'm not at liberty to discuss everything with you, because you are a member of the public..."

"Two deaths. A video posted across the media. I know. I get it. I've heard everyone talking and I know what's happening." Gary nodded, wiping some sweat from his forehead. "I just need to know how long these things normally take."

"What do you mean, Mr Bruce..."

"Gary. Call me Gary..."

"Ok, Gary. Thanks. But it's only been a day. Not even that. These things run their own course. At this point, I can't really say..."

"Guess. Give me some idea..." Gary interrupted him.

McKenzie hesitated before replying. The man was nervous. He wasn't the same, cool demolition expert that McKenzie had met yesterday afternoon.

"Gary, obviously there's something worrying you. Can you tell me what the real issue is here, so that I can understand how I can help?"

Gary turned away and walked across the cabin to the window, leaning on the edge of the window frame and staring up at the tall blue building towering above them.

He coughed.

"Explosives." He replied. "The whole bloody building is wired with explosives. And we have a serial killer running around killing people inside, and I don't have the faintest idea how he got in. How do I know that he hasn't found the explosives and done something with them? Or stolen some of them? It took days to rig that building. Almost a week. And if this is going to drag on, I'm going to have to take the explosives out again. Then put them all back later on... I can't let people walk around in the building knowing its set to blow up at a moment's notice..."

"It's safe now though, isn't it? You deactivated everything? That's what you said earlier..."

"Of course it is. But... even so, there're still things that could go wrong. A storm. A lightning strike..."

"And it would all blow up?" McKenzie asked, surprised. Also alarmed.

"No, probably not... but maybe." Bruce shook his head, and turned back to face McKenzie. "But this is crazy. It makes me really nervous. I can't allow it. I need to get my building back..."

"That's not going to happen anytime soon, Gary. I think we both know that. So, if you're telling me now that there's a real risk to everyone with the explosives being in the building, then we're going to have to come up with a plan to remove them pretty sharpish. But something tells me that this isn't the main thing that's worrying you just now. Do you want to tell me what it really is?"

Gary turned towards the DCI and studied his face for a minute. McKenzie could see the man was thinking, and said nothing. He'd long ago learnt the power of silence, and how to let the pressure of it build up until it literally squeezed the truth out of another person.

"Do you know how many people I've got working on this project? Eight. Eight full-time workers. Skilled workers. Expensive. I mean really bloody expensive. And now half of them are doing nothing, but that doesn't mean I'm not paying them. I haven't got any other jobs to send them to just now, and I can't put them on something else until this job is done. In the meantime, I'm also paying for equipment hire. Equipment which I can't use or return because I might not get it back when I need it."

"Don't worry, I'll sign whatever paperwork you want to help get you the insurance..."

"WHAT INSURANCE!? I haven't got proper insurance... I couldn't afford it..."

McKenzie's face went blank, trying to process what he'd just heard.

"No Insurance? Are you serious? Are you sure that's something you want to admit to me?"

"Don't worry... I've got all the important stuff, but with the level of insurance I've got, I'm only covered for five days of delays. I couldn't afford the premiums for longer than that. Beyond five days of delays, all the additional costs come out my own pocket. And my pockets are empty. I've got enough money to keep us going till Friday, but if we're still here next Saturday and that school hasn't come down yet, I'll be ruined. Bankrupt! Finished!"

Gary swore aloud and turned away to look out the window again.

"Yesterday morning I was on top of the world. This is the biggest job I've ever done... I've been building up to this for years. This is the job that was going to *change everything*. For me, after all the years of growing slowly and surely, this is the big time. But I've got everything invested in it. *Everything*. There's nothing left over. So, if I don't get the bulk of the demolition done by Friday, I won't be able to afford to finish the job."

"But you are covered until Friday for all the legal requirements that come along with something like this?"

"Yes. Of course I am. If anyone gets killed here and it's my fault, then the Insurance company will take care of everything..."

Gary sat down hard on one of the chairs beside the window.

"Listen, I'll talk with the others and my superiors about how long it will be before we're done here. Maybe I can expedite things." McKenzie offered.

Gary looked up. "Please. I've only got until Friday next week. Maybe I'm jumping the gun in worrying so much but I've got every moment of the next few weeks planned out, and every minute of delay is literally costing me a fortune."

"Noted. Like I said, I'll make some enquiries and try to get a better indication of when we might be finished here. But can I change the subject for a moment?... Can you give me a list of all your staff who've been working on the site for the past week? We need to establish if any of your staff went to Portobello High School themselves, and if so, when?"

"Absolutely. But why? What are you thinking? Are we suspects all of a sudden? Do you think one of my men did it?"

"I can't rule it out. In fact, I've got to rule it *in*, for now. Somehow two people were smuggled into the building without being seen by anyone else. Either the killer knows a secret way into the building that no one else does, or they have the keys and simply walked into the building when no one when else was looking. Which means it could well be someone in your team."

"Or someone else, who stole a copy of the keys and somehow managed to get past our cameras and my men when we weren't looking!"

"True. But how would they get access to your keys?"

"I don't know. They're under lock and key, but all I'm saying is, that it doesn't have to mean that one of my team is a murderer."

"Gary, it's my job to suspect everyone. Don't take it personally. But can you give me that list in the next hour? And can you please instruct all your staff to keep quiet about anything they've seen or heard here yesterday or today? This is a murder case. We don't want any details getting out. And the public don't yet know that there have been two deaths. We need to keep it that way for now."

Gary nodded, stood up and moved towards the door.

For a moment, he hovered in the doorway, and McKenzie thought he was going to say something. His mouth opened, and words seemed to form on his lips, but then he seemed to think better of it, nodded to himself and left the room in silence.

Just then, McKenzie's phone rang. It was DCS Helen Wilkinson, his boss.

"McKenzie, I've got some bad news for you... and I'm afraid, you're not going to like it."

Portobello High School
Edinburgh
12.18

McKenzie was furious. Facing the portacabin which was now once again full up with his team, he took several deep breaths and tried to control his emotions.

Lifting his right hand up to get everyone's attention, the room quickly fell silent. For a second, McKenzie felt like a school teacher controlling a classroom of pupils, and for the first time ever, realised that he was using the same control mechanisms his teachers used at school.

This one was simple but effective: whenever he lifted his hand, everyone shut up.

"As you know, the Queen is visiting Scotland next week and staying at Holyrood Palace. I've just been informed by DCS Wilkinson that Police Scotland has been passed some intelligence detailing a credible terrorist threat to the Queen. Until further notice, all available hands are now to be made available to join Operation Crown, whose sole mission is to find those behind the threat and protect the Queen. This means that the following people are to report to Fettes Row as soon as possible."

McKenzie read out a list of names, and most of the room stood up, looked around at each other with quizzical looks on their faces, and then exited the portacabin.

By the time they had gone, there was only a handful left: DS Wishart, DS McLeish, DI Brown, Sergeant Anderson and PC Lynch.

McKenzie's face was blank, but the apparent lack of visible emotion did little to hide the frustration beneath.

"I'm sorry guys, but apparently the threat is very serious. There's nothing I could do."

"We understand Guv. The Queen's safety is obviously paramount here, but we need everyone we can get on this, NOW. We've probably got a deranged serial killer running about bumping off his old teachers..." PC Lynch enunciated what everyone was thinking.

McKenzie smiled at him.

"Like I said... there's nothing I could do. I almost lost you two as well, but I managed to persuade DCS Wilkinson that your local knowledge would be invaluable, and she made a few calls for me," McKenzie said, speaking while nodding at both Sergeant Anderson and PC Lynch.

"We'll just have to hope that Operation Crown is successful and wraps ups sooner rather than later. In the meantime, it's just us and Mather on the night shift, so let's make sure that everything we do counts. Okay?"

Everyone nodded.

"Good, so let's put our heads together and do a bit of brainstorming then."

McKenzie grabbed a coloured pen and turned to the whiteboard.

"During the last session we made plans for the rest of the day. Some of them may to be scrapped now we've lost most of the team, but McLeish and Wishart, you two can carry on getting the lists of employees and staff and finding out about the Reunion tonight. Beyond that, let's start from scratch and map out what we know, what we need to know, and how we're going to get it, in order of priority. Then we can divvy up actions from there, okay?"

"Good. So the way I see it, the four big questions we have are, '*How did the murderer get the victims into the school without being spotted*', '*How long were they there for?*', '*Why were they killed?*' and finally '*Is there any connection between the victims themselves?*'"

McKenzie nodded at the team and then made some notes on the whiteboard.

"Comments?" he asked, as he finished scribbling away.

"Thinking about the second question, we need forensics to tell us how long Blake was in the school for, before we discovered him."

McKenzie nodded, and then annotated something on the board.

"Thinking about how they got into the building, is there any possibility that we've missed some gate or door, somewhere? Are we absolutely certain we haven't missed anything?" Brown questioned. "There's no hole in the boarding, a loose panel or something?"

"I've already had the perimeter walked, and all the doors to the building checked, several times." McKenzie responded. "But there has to be something we've missed. Apparently, the perimeter fencing has been up for months. Somehow someone got into the building and then out again, without being spotted, or they're still here. And we're pretty sure they aren't still here. The false panel idea needs checking again, I think. Can I ask you to take that one this afternoon? Go around checking everything to your heart's content. Convince yourself we've not missed anything. And then get hold of Gary Bruce and get him to recheck all the plans for the building to make sure there's no other way in. He's already said there isn't, but get him to do it again."

Brown nodded, and McKenzie put her name against the action on the board.

"Right, now to the question of motive. Why were they killed? Any ideas?" McKenzie asked, leaving the question hanging in the air.

"It's interesting '*how*' they were killed." Lynch commented. "Someone went to a lot of trouble to kill them in or near the departments they worked in. Which means that they must have known that the victims worked there. As mentioned before, the first thought was to consider a grudge from an ex-pupil - someone who was taught by them and took both their classes - but I like the idea that maybe it wasn't a pupil at all. Maybe it was another teacher? Someone who worked with them at some point."

McKenzie smiled.

"McLeish is getting a list of all the staff, past and present. Can you help him, and try to establish what previous teachers thought about the deceased? Is there anything that connects them? Is there is anything obvious we need to know? Does anyone know any reason why they may have been targeted? Grudges or animosities between them, pupils and other staff? I'm also going to leave it to both of you to check the previous list of staff against any reported missing persons. Make as many calls as you can to names on the list and check that they're all accounted for in some way. Just do the best you can."

They both nodded, and McKenzie noted the actions on the board.

"So far so good. Now, because we're so short staffed I'm going to help out as much as I can and start by visiting the relatives and homes of David Weir and Ronald Blake. Anderson, can you come with me?"

McKenzie checked his watch and then added himself and Anderson to the action list.

"It's almost one o'clock. Can I suggest we meet back here about five?"

Everyone nodded.

Nobody smiled.

Chapter 9

David Weir's flat
Leith
Saturday
13.05

It had been several years since McKenzie had last made a house call in the course of investigations. Since being elevated to the grand heights of DCI, he had found himself increasingly office-bound, spending the bulk of his time managing and coordinating the capabilities and efforts of others in the solving of crimes.

Within Police Scotland, Campbell McKenzie was recognised as one of the rising stars. His last few reviews had cited his ability to motivate his teams, who worked together effectively and efficiently, and he had an impressive track record in solving crimes and building cases which more often than not, had led to many successful arrests and convictions.

Were it not for the events which occurred last year during his second last case, he would have had an amazing track record behind him. Thankfully, the recent Review Board had all but exonerated him from any serious wrong doings, and approved a full return to duty, albeit only after several of the officers on the review board had nevertheless expressed concern about his judgement in allowing himself to get so deeply involved with and conducting a short-lived affair with a fellow member of staff, his protégé DI Danielle Wessex. Thankfully, it was recognised that McKenzie may actually have been the victim of a sophisticated attempt to manipulate and discredit him: DI Wessex was the lover of one of Scotland's most notorious criminals, the crime lord Tommy McNunn, who had later murdered DI Wessex and attempted to compromise and frame McKenzie for her death. It was also recognised that it was McKenzie himself who had ultimately brought the real murderer of DI Wessex to justice. Until then, McNunn had been a seemingly untouchable crime lord who for many years had been the subject of many investigations but who had always managed to wangle himself free from prosecution. Following the murder of DI Wessex, McKenzie's fast actions had led to the arrest of McNunn with sufficient evidence to ensure that Tommy McNunn had subsequently been found guilty of the murder of DI Wessex.

Following the case, McKenzie had been suspended temporarily, but had then been allowed to return to duty temporarily pending the final outcome of a review board who were commissioned to investigate the sequence of events and determine if McKenzie had been guilty of any criminality or was in breach of police regulations and procedures.

Upon returning to duty, McKenzie's had found himself the target of a hired assassin, who had been contracted to kill not only himself, but also Tommy McNunn. Threats to his life had resulted in McKenzie then going into hiding. In the weeks that followed Tommy McNunn had been found dead in his cell, and the assassin had tracked down McKenzie and confronted him.

The official record of what had followed, recorded the discovery of a body whose identity had been attributed to the assassin. McKenzie had walked away, alive.

In reality, only two people knew what had happened that day: his wife, and the assassin who was very much still alive.

Immediately after this, McKenzie had taken some time off to assimilate everything that had occurred, and seek some counselling: marriage guidance counselling and also personal counselling to help him deal with the latent psychological effects of the past year.

McKenzie had only just returned to active duty again the week before, and although he was feeling fresh and determined to carry on where he had left off, he now wondered if the lack of staff and resources on this case would now give him an excuse to roll up his shirt sleeves and get out of his office and back out onto the streets. Perhaps it would give him the opportunity to reconnect with some of his early career, and help enliven his skills and freshen up his understanding of current practices. The bottom line was that he was determined to make the most of a bad thing.

It would also give him an opportunity to prove himself to anyone on the review board who may retain any niggling doubts about his ability or right to return to duty.

As the car driven by Anderson pulled up outside the tenement where David Weir had a flat on the third floor, McKenzie closed his eyes for a few moments and took a couple of deep breaths.

Before leaving the portacabin, McKenzie had made a few phone calls, arranging events for the rest of the afternoon, and ensuring in advance that his time would not be wasted. In any homicide, the first twenty-four hours were crucial. McKenzie knew that the clock was ticking. He also knew that news of this double murder was likely to rock the whole country. It was exactly the sort of news that the press and social media would go to town on: an old school about to be demolished, two teachers found murdered in their old class-rooms, a mysterious and clever serial killer on the loose. It had lots of catchy elements to it that would hook the world's attention: crucifixion in an RE classroom, a blindfolded walk off the top of a tall building, and a building that was packed with explosives and set to blow up only minutes after the second murder, whilst being watched by literally hundreds of onlookers. Soon the world's press was going to be focussed on his team. Nothing much had been accomplished in the past few hours, and now with only a tiny team left, they needed to make progress soon or the trail would go cold very quickly.

The worst thing was, McKenzie had a nagging feeling that the two murders were not going to be the last. Whoever was behind this had planned the timing perfectly. Planning was the key to it all. *How* had the killer known what the demolition plans were? *How* had the killer felt so secure and confident in his movements? The building was due for demolition, primed to explode at any moment. If the killer had made any mistakes, suffered any delays, they - and there probably had to be more than one killer — would have been blown sky high along with their victims!

Before they got out of the car, McKenzie motioned to the Sergeant to give him a few moments, and then busied himself in scribbling some notes into his notebook. Most of the DIs, and DSs in Police Scotland had long since succumbed to the temptations of modern technology and made their notes electronically directly into a tablet. McKenzie was often labelled a Luddite for his insistence on using pen and paper, but the others were wrong. McKenzie could easily see the benefits of tablets and using the app the police provided: automatically saving notes to a common fileshare, or the ease by which they were able to share notes with others. But the benefits didn't outweigh the one singular negative: McKenzie hated typing, and preferred to use his God-given hands to scribble away as fast as he could go – he could write down three times as many words on a piece of paper than he could ever manage on a screen before he started swearing at his inability to spell, and the determination of the app to autocorrect his words from something meaningful to gibberish that was completely out of context.

"Okay, done… " McKenzie nodded, closing his notebook and popping the pencil inside his pocket. Anderson looked at him inquisitively, his eyebrows sliding upwards at the sides, as if to say, 'anything interesting?'

"Nope. Just personal thoughts. Good thoughts."

Anderson smiled. "We're going to need as many of those as possible on this case, Guv." He opened the door, climbed out and stretched. "Any thoughts or words of wisdom before we go inside?" Anderson asked.

"You're one of the most experienced sergeants I know. I don't think there's much I can tell you. After the initial introductions though, I'd appreciate it if you'd lead the conversation. I want to look around the flat as much as possible." McKenzie looked up at the tenement above them, appraising it and its local surroundings. "I'd be interested to hear your thoughts, Murray?"

Anderson nodded, almost expecting the question.

"Obviously we need to ascertain if there's any reason Mrs Weir can think of why someone would want to harm Mr Weir. But I'm keen to establish if there's any known association with the other victim outside of school. Is there any connection between them that we should know about or which could help us understand what happened to them yesterday in the school? And are there any signs that Mr Weir had gone to meet someone before he was presumably taken against his will?"

McKenzie stepped up to the door and scanned the list of names that were presented on the intercom alongside the numbers of the flats. He found the one he wanted – 'WEIR' – and pressed it.

"We haven't got a search warrant, and given the commotion that's going on at Fettes Row with the Queen's visit and Operation Crown, it's unlikely we'll get one before Monday or Tuesday. I just hope they're as cooperative as possible. Ideally it would be good to have a look around the flat. See any letters, find a diary. Listen to an answer-phone if there is one," McKenzie said, looking across at Anderson as he waited for someone to respond to the buzzer. "If there's any sign of a struggle, the flat will also become a crime scene."

"Hello?" A soft voice spoke, and McKenzie leaned forward to speak into the intercom.

"DCI McKenzie here. I believe you're expecting us?"

There was a buzzing sound and a loud click as a latch was automatically released on the inside of the door.

"Come on up. Third floor. On your left."

McKenzie pushed the door open and stood aside to let Anderson go first. As they stepped inside the staircase, he felt the hairs on his neck bristle, and he paused in the doorway. Instinctively he looked behind him and up and down the street. There were a few kids on bicycles further down the road, hanging around outside the local shop, but other than that, no one else to be seen. He quickly scanned the cars and vans on the road, then looked up at the other tenements on the other side of the street, but he didn't spot anything or anyone untoward.

"You coming?" Anderson asked, waiting at the bottom of the stairwell for him.

"Yep, sorry, just had that feeling I was being watched."

Anderson laughed. "It's obvious you haven't been out your office for a while. Quite a few of the residents will no doubt be on our books, and thanks to whatever they're taking today, they'll be as paranoid as their neighbours and worried I'm coming after them. They'll be watching me, not you."

"Perhaps…" McKenzie smirked, walking past the uniformed Sergeant, "but I didn't see any curtains twitching."

"Hello, it's up here…" A voice caught them unawares from above, booming down the staircase and echoing loudly of the cavernous, empty, cold blue-painted stairwell, which was typical of almost all the more affordable tenement properties this side of Edinburgh. In some of the others in the more up-and-coming areas, the tenants had pushed up their property prices by making the stairwells warm and attractive, by hanging pictures on the walls, laying out fancy doormats, and filling plant pots with sweet smelling colourful flowers. There was none of that here though. As McKenzie looked up the stairwell and saw the anxious face of Mrs Weir peering down at them from above, he couldn't help but exhale defensively out through his nose as the smell of stale urine accosted him from below, wafting up from the passage underneath the stair that led out to the communal gardens behind the main building.

Anderson pointed to a little empty clear plastic packet lying on one of the stone steps. "I wonder if someone in the stair is dealing?"

"It's worth noting, but it's unlikely there's a connection to what we're here for."

"Definitely worth noting though," Anderson said, bending down and picking it up, sniffing it with his nose. "I'll run it by the boys down at Fettes to see what it is."

Mrs Weir was waiting for them just inside the doorway of the flat.

"I'm DCI McKenzie, and this is Sergeant Anderson," McKenzie introduced himself as they arrived on the third floor. "Thank you coming over to let us look around. I'm sorry for your loss, and I appreciate this will all have come as a shock to you."

McKenzie studied her face as she replied. She nodded, swallowed hard, and for a second her check twitched.

She opened her mouth to say something, then hesitated. Then she coughed to clear her throat.

"I'm sorry, … Sergeant, … DCI McKenzie. It's … just so hard to believe."

"Can we come in?" McKenzie asked.

"Sorry, yes… absolutely. Sorry… " Mrs Weir nodded again, then stepped aside, and waived her hand into the flat behind her. "Please. Please come in."

McKenzie stepped past her. The inside of the flat was dark. Almost as if the woman could read his mind, Mrs Weir stretched out her hand and flicked the light switch on the wall.

They stepped through a short corridor, into a lounge. As Anderson behind him immediately started to engage David Weir's wife, as instructed by McKenzie earlier, McKenzie started to scan the lounge for anything and everything memorable, drinking up the decoration and the contents of the room.

McKenzie noticed that his pulse was slightly raised. This was the first time in years that he'd been out doing this. In recent years he'd relied upon the reports of his team who had themselves gone out and done the legwork.

He'd missed it.

The lounge was clean, contained all the usual contents you would find in any lounge in any home in Scotland. But there was something about it. There were no photographs. Nothing too personal. It lacked soul.

As Anderson invited Mrs Weir to sit down so he could ask her some questions, McKenzie started to peruse the room: a large 55 inch TV, a Hi-Fi, and a wood-burner sitting against one wall. The focus of the room though, was the large window through which the flat commanded an amazing view across the old Leith docks to the sea behind, probably less than a quarter of a mile away.

From here you could see for miles, right across the Firth of Forth into the North Sea beyond.

It was an amazing sight.

"This why David bought the flat. He loved the view." Mrs Weir announced.

"How long has he had it?" McKenzie asked, detecting that perhaps there was a story there. The way she had spoken the words had contained a hint of reminiscence.

"We bought the flat together years ago. We lived here for a while before we got married. But when the kids came along, it was too small, and to tell the truth we were a little worried about the area. We wanted something more for the kids, and luckily we were able to find it. I saw the Sergeant pick up the empty packet of drugs from the stair. That's nothing new. The owner of Flat 11 at the top of the stair is well known to the local police. Always has been, and always will. He's part of the local landscape now and nobody ever bothers to do anything about it. Or can do anything about it."

McKenzie nodded, taking a mental note to learn more about Flat 11 later on.

"May I ask how long you've been separated? I understand you are…"

"Divorced? Well almost. It'll be official in the next month or two once all the paperwork is signed…" she said before pausing and realising the redundancy of what she was saying.

McKenzie glanced around the flat, and back at Mrs Weir.

"I see you have a set of keys. Were you still on talking terms?"

Mrs Weir glanced at the keys in her hand and then back at McKenzie, before realising the significance of what the detective was saying. Most couples approaching divorce were not on talking terms, let alone letting the other person have free access to their home.

"Ah… yes," she hesitated. "Actually, recently things had become a little stressed, and we haven't really seen each other since Christmas… we went out for a meal with the boys on Boxing Day. But technically I still own half the flat, and I still have my own keys."

"When was the last time you were here? Can you see anything odd or out of place?" McKenzie asked, glancing around the room.

"I had a quick wee look around whilst I was waiting, just being nosey really, and everything seems fine. Nothing odd. Would you like to see the other rooms?"

"Yes, please. That would be helpful. After that Sergeant Anderson would like to ask you a few more questions, and if you don't mind, I would like to have a look round the flat by myself, if I may? It's standard procedure in cases like this. We need to learn as much as possible, as soon as possible. The first hours of a murder investigation are the most important."

Mrs Weir glanced across at the Sergeant and then back at the Detective.

For a moment, McKenzie wondered if she was going to ask if he had a search warrant.

Luckily, she didn't.

She spent the next ten minutes guiding McKenzie and Anderson around the two-bedroom flat, and then let herself be guided back to the small kitchen where Anderson was able to make a cup of tea for Mrs Weir, and sit her down at a small kitchen table.

Strangely, there had been no obvious unopened mail lying around, but when McKenzie asked Mrs Weir if she'd seen any, a look of intense guilt clouded over her, and she'd slowly reached for her handbag.

She pulled out a bundle of letters and handed them to the Detective.

"I was just checking… to see if there was anything from anyone else… "

"Did he have a girlfriend?"

"Not that I knew off. My lawyer's always pressing me to find out if there is. Maybe it might help my side of the proceedings."

McKenzie reached out and took the bundle of envelopes from her, several of which had already been opened.

"It would be helpful if you could explain as much as possible to the Sergeant about both your circumstances and your husband's. As much as possible. And if possible, also the details of your current partner and how we can contact your two sons. I think it's likely that we may wish to talk with them at some point in the near future too."

"The boys, John and Sam are coming up later today from London. They'll be here about five, I think. They're both very shaken by all of this."

"Please pass them my condolences. It would be good if they could come into the station in the next two days, if possible, please? Along with your partner? The Sergeant will give you the address."

McKenzie saw the register of alarm on the woman's face, and anticipated the next question, but it never came.

Instead of the usual, "Am I under suspicion?" she looked away, towards the nearest window.

"I saw the videos on the internet of him falling from the building," she whispered.

Then she started to cry.

Outside in the white van, the driver pulled back the sleeve of his blue overalls, and glanced at his watch.

1.35 pm.

It was time to go. He'd done what he needed to.

However, he still had a lot more preparations to make, and time was running out.

Glancing once more back up at the third-floor flat, he saw the outline of the detective looking out from the window and waited a few moments before he retreated back into the room.

Then he switched on the ignition and pulled away.

As he drove away from the tenement, the driver smiled to himself as he counted two other white vans in the street.

Around here, man-in-a-van was the Invisible-Man.

Chapter 10

David Weir's flat
Leith
Saturday
13.35

While Anderson comforted Mrs Weir in the tiny kitchen, and did his best to make his way through all the questions that needed to be asked in a situation like this, McKenzie made his way systematically around the flat looking for anything that could tell him something which might help.

McKenzie trusted the Sergeant to ask the right questions. He'd worked with him before, and although he wasn't a detective, that was out of choice. The Sergeant could easily make the grade if he wanted to, and McKenzie knew that others had suggested it to him before, that were he to apply, he'd be highly recommended. In fact, he would be a very good detective, perhaps better than most of those who preferred not to trudge the beat and wear the uniform.

McKenzie knew that at the top of Anderson's list would be some more questions around the divorce. Although his instinct told him that the woman was genuinely upset, from what she'd just told them, there was a possible motive right there. The divorce was pending, probably due for completion in the coming weeks or months. McKenzie's investigation would now need to determine if there was any financial benefit to Mrs Weir if her husband were to die before the divorce went through. How much did she stand to inherit if he died? And how much better off would she be before the divorce, were they not able to find a will?

Unfortunately, it was a sad truth that many murders were committed by loved ones, and it could be that they'd just established the basis of a motive for Mrs Weir to end her husband's life before the divorce was made final.

A possible motive.

Obviously, it was highly unlikely that Mrs Weir would have committed the murders herself, but she could have paid for others to help her.

After making a note to that effect in his little book, he started to look for a phone. Unfortunately, as was increasingly the case these days, he didn't find one. Mr Weir didn't have a landline. He probably only had a mobile phone, and used that for everything.

Which meant that it would be more difficult for him to check Mr Weir's voicemail or text messages to find out what had been going on in Mr Weir's life in the days leading up to his disappearance.

Not finding a physical phone, McKenzie started to look for any phone bills from which they could get details to contact the phone company. Luckily it didn't take long before he found one on top of a pile of letters and other bills stacked on a shelf in the lounge.

He put it in his pocket and started to look through the other mail.

There were a few bank account letters, already opened.

He scanned the contents.

They revealed positive balances, nothing spectacular, but showing no debts either. One had eight thousand pounds in it, but nowadays that wasn't much at all.

McKenzie pocketed that one too. Later, they'd contact the bank and try to coerce some details from them, checking to see if there were any other accounts that seemed significant.

There was a calendar on the wall in the hallway.

McKenzie scanned the dates of the past week, and the weeks ahead. There was nothing to show any obvious appointments made for the past week that Mr Weir may have attended, but over the next few weeks a few social events seemed to be highlighted, with names he took note of: over the next few days, they would start tracking down friends to see if they knew of anything that could be significant. No doubt, one or two would end up being invited down to the station to help with inquiries.

Rather poignantly McKenzie saw the red ring around today's date, with a note pointing out the upcoming school Reunion.

Entering Mr Weir's bedroom, he quickly made his way around the room.

It had been years since McKenzie had done anything like this, but he quickly remembered the routine.

He checked the bedside table and the pockets of any trousers or clothes lying around.

Then he looked through the drawers, paying special attention to the back of them, where people would often hide things.

Next, he looked for hidden spaces. Over the years he'd developed an uncanny ability to walk into a room, quickly assess the possibilities and then find them.

In circumstances like this one, the job of the detective was to find out as much as possible about the deceased and everything they had done in the last few days.

Who had they met? Where had they been? Why had they gone there?

Was there any motive for a possible murder? Was the deceased hiding something?

Where obvious answers were not forthcoming, then other questions needed to be asked: did the deceased lead another hidden life that others did not know about?

Was there a lover? A mistress? A boyfriend? An ex-boyfriend/girlfriend/ or spurned lover?

Was the deceased in debt?

Who were their enemies?

Why did they have enemies?

In the case of Mr David Weir, he found very little.

Yes, he did find a secret place, just inside the wardrobe, underneath a floorboard.

It contained several porn magazines.

It turned out Mr Weir had a slight fetish, apparently.

He liked high-heeled shoes, and naked, Amazonian women wearing them.

Sometimes McKenzie would feel guilty seeing into the lives of others in this way, especially when they were now dead.

Tonight though, McKenzie did not.

Instead he felt only frustration.

Returning to the lounge he scanned the contents of the book shelves, trying to ascertain more about the deceased's interest or hobbies.

He noticed a number of books on sailing… was he possibly the member of a sailing club? Perhaps a study of his bank accounts would reveal details on subscriptions to clubs or societies he could then contact and visit.

There were a number of thrillers, some books by big names he recognised, and a lot by others which he didn't.

After an hour McKenzie realised that he wasn't learning anything new.
For once, the expression 'dead men tell no tales' was proving right.
A visit to David Weir's flat had revealed almost nothing at all.

Shortly afterwards, they all left the flat together, Mrs Weir requesting that they wait with her while she locked up and made her way down and out of the stair.

Once outside, they escorted her to her car which was parked close to theirs on the main street.

She got in, they thanked her, and she drove off.

"So?" McKenzie asked the moment she was out of earshot.

"She didn't do it. Although you probably also picked up there's possibly a motive for killing her husband before the divorce went through, she'd need someone else to actually do it for her. But why would she then also want to kill Mr Blake? Plus, I just didn't pick up any negative vibes or false answers. She seems totally genuine. Her husband was murdered. She's surprised and genuinely sad about it. I don't think she's going to be able to help us out much more."

McKenzie nodded.

"Thanks. I think you're probably right, but can you brief me on what you asked her and what she replied, en route to Ronald Blake's house?"

Their car was only a few metres away.

"I'll drive," McKenzie volunteered, reaching out to the windscreen to retrieve a flyer which had been left on the windscreen.

McKenzie was about to crush it up when he saw his name scrawled on it in red pen.

Or was it blood?

Climbing into the car beside Anderson he unfolded the sheet of A4 paper and read its contents.

It was two lines: a derivation of a popular children's poem.

> *"One, two, buckle your shoes.*
> *Three, four, watch out for more!"*

As McKenzie digested the words, a chill coursed its way down his spine and he shuddered.

The meaning was obvious. The two deaths at Portobello High School were only the beginning.

But that was only the half of it.

The note was addressed to him personally.

The killer had been here. Had followed them.
Had written this note in advance.
And he'd placed it in full view of McKenzie to find personally.
Whoever had placed this note here, on *his* windscreen, was playing a game.
A game of death.

What worried McKenzie most was that the killer had thought about all of this in advance.

By announcing more deaths to come so publicly, so personally, to *himself*, the man was laying down a challenge.

"Stop me if you can."

Clearly, the killer was convinced that McKenzie couldn't.

Which meant that unless McKenzie could prove him wrong, at least one or two more victims were going to die!

Chapter 11

En route to Ronald Blake's family home
Duddingston
Saturday
14.05

"Will all due respect, if you don't give me some of my team back, I have no chance - none - of finding whoever the killer is before they carry out their threat. I need more people – now - not next week."

There was a pause at the other end of the phone, while DCS Helen Wilkinson took a deep breath and tried to control her response. "Count-to-ten", she was busy reminding herself. "In fact, best count-to-a-hundred."

The conversation was already several minutes old, and McKenzie was not accepting the answers she'd given him so far. She'd made it clear that until the security level was reduced or Operation Crown was cancelled or terminated, every able-bodied officer was working full time on resolving the very real threat that had been made to the Queen.

"And while you think about it," McKenzie went in for the kill, detecting a moment of weakness, and a moment of opportunity, "I want you to realise that if someone else dies in the next few days, then their blood will… "

"One officer. That's all," she replied. "And I'd caution you about what you were just about to say Campbell. That's was unfair and unjustified. You don't go around saying things like that. You know my hands are tied."

"Do I get to choose who?" McKenzie replied, already feeling bad. But it had worked. And one person – one good person – could make a massive difference.

"No."

"Good, then I want DI Fraser Dean. Full of initiative. Works hard. Does the job of two people. Please send him straight over to the school and tell him to call me en route."

McKenzie hesitated for a second, knowing he had been pushing it. Then rather meekly he added.

"Thank you, Guv," and hung up.

For a few minutes they drove in silence, before Anderson broke the spell.

"I'm saying nothing, but, you were a little harsh on her, Guv."

The phone rang before McKenzie could reply.

"DCI McKenzie? Hi, it's DI Dean here. I've just been reassigned to you, and told you need to talk with me urgently?"

As they made their way through the streets of Edinburgh to the house of Ronald Blake, McKenzie briefed Dean on what had just happened.

"There's a number of things I need you to do. Get over to the address I'll text you in a minute, and start chasing down any CCTV cameras in the area, public or official. Check anytime between one-fifteen and two o'clock this afternoon. Whoever placed the note on my windscreen is highly likely to be the killer, or at least know them. If we capture an image of them doing it, we hit the jackpot. It's likely that whoever did it followed us from Portobello High School, so I want you also to look for CCTV cameras in the neighbourhood of the school. We left there just before 1pm. It's going to be a long manual process of identifying traffic that's seen both in the immediate vicinity of the school, and then again near Mr Weir's flat, but once again, if you do it, you might just trace the car straight back to the killer. I don't want to micro-manage you on this. You know what to do. Just do it please. If you get anything, you call me immediately, okay?"

"Yes, boss." Dean replied. He'd worked with DCI McKenzie before so he knew the ropes and what to expect. "I'll get right on to it."

"Just do your best. That's all I'm asking you. It might take weeks to analyse and cross-reference the footage if you get any, but the stakes are high, so it's worth doing."

Dean hung up.

Anderson waited a moment and then commented.

"It's a long shot, but sometimes it's the long shots that pay off."

McKenzie nodded, without speaking. Anderson could see he was thinking.

"Okay," McKenzie finally spoke. "There's a slight change of plan. You're going to drop me off at the Blake household, and then you're going to drive straight down to Fettes Row, get hold of someone in Forensics and give them this note. It's another long shot, but it could possibly have the DNA on it from the killer, or whoever placed the note on the car. Call me when you're done, and either come and pick me up, or meet me back at the school. Also, take this phone bill and get the ball rolling on getting phone records and phone mast data from the phone company."

McKenzie reached into his pocket, pulled out the phone bill he'd picked up in Weir's flat and gave it to the Sergeant. "If I get anything from Blake's house, I'll text you the number to chase that one down too."

Anderson had just turned the car into the road where Ronald Blake lived, and was pulling up in front of a semi-detached three-bedroom house in the middle of a cul-de-sac. It was an expensive area. An expensive house. A big achievement for a family only on a teacher's salary.

McKenzie took a few mental notes, reminding himself to find out from Mrs Blake when they had moved in and what her job was. And how they could afford a place like this.

McKenzie climbed out the car, and nodded at Anderson who then drove off. Before walking up the garden path, McKenzie called McLeish.

"I'm just about to go into the Blake household, and I was wondering where you are with the list of former staff and teachers at Portobello High School?" McKenzie asked, before briefly explaining about the note.

McLeish understood immediately. McKenzie was worried that another teacher may about to be killed, and McLeish and Lynch needed to hurry up the process of calling around and checking that no one else was missing.

"We've got some of the list, and we've just started calling the people on it. We'll have to wait for the rest of the names. We've been promised more later today. Unfortunately, regarding the details we've been given, we've mainly only got home numbers. There are very few mobile numbers. It's Saturday afternoon. Most people are probably out just now anyway."

"It's going to be a long process, but it's one that's got to be done. I also want you to talk to whoever was the headmaster at the time they were both teaching at the school. The fact that they were killed together in the school surely means there's a link between them and the school and something that happened there. Something that was a good enough reason for someone to kill them."

McKenzie thanked McLeish and hung up.

Usually calm and collect, McKenzie was beginning to feel the pressure.

Someone somewhere knew what this was all about. They had to find them soon, before others started to die.

It took several minutes for Mrs Blake to answer the door.

McKenzie held up his badge and was about to introduce himself when the woman interrupted him.

"I'm a neighbour, Detective, not Mrs Blake. She's in bed. She didn't get up today, and she's very upset. I don't know if she will speak with you, but if you come in, I'll have a word with her."

"Thank you, Mrs… ?" McKenzie queried.

"Mrs Duff. From number thirty-six over the road. We're good friends."

Mrs Duff showed McKenzie into Mrs Blake's lounge, smiled at him and then backed out of the room.

McKenzie could hear the sound of the women speaking together, a few tears, and then a few minutes later, Mrs Blake appeared in the doorway, wrapped up warmly in a dressing gown despite the nice day outside.

Her eyes were red, and she looked terrible. McKenzie felt a pang of guilt, almost as if he was intruding. It had been years since he'd done this.

"Mrs Blake. I'm Detective Chief Inspector McKenzie. I'm heading up the investigation into the murder of your husband. I'm sorry for your loss. I just wanted to come around to speak with you personally, and to see how you are?"

McKenzie noticed the spark of recognition in her eyes as she picked up on his rank.

"Chief Inspector?" she half-smiled, nodded to herself, and then took a few steps closer, reaching out to the side of a chair, before easing herself in.

"Yes, we're all very shaken by what has happened to your husband, and we are absolutely determined to find out what happened and who is to blame for his death."

She looked out of the window, and without turning to face him, she asked.

"Helen's going to make us both some tea. Or would you prefer coffee, Detective McKenzie?"

"Tea please, Mrs Blake."

"If you're a DCI, I reckon you'd better be calling me by my first name. Please call me Ruth. I've got the feeling we're going to be speaking quite a lot over the coming days."

She turned to him and looked him straight in his eyes.

Her eyes were a bright blue. But cold. Without warmth.

Which was understandable given the circumstances.

"I knew something was wrong. I felt it. And that's why I reported him missing. As soon as I felt it."

There was something about the way she spoke her words that caught McKenzie's attention.

"You and your husband were very close?"

"Yes. We were."

She began to cry.

"He normally calls me. Wherever he is. Just to check I'm okay. And to say he's okay. Even if he's really drunk. He never wants me to worry."

"Can you remember when was the last time you spoke with him?"

"Thursday afternoon. Just a normal conversation. I asked him what he wanted for dinner. But then he didn't come home. I waited up for him until about 10 p.m. and then went to bed. It wasn't the first time that he ended up in the pub after work in Leith and then didn't come home till very late. I was getting used to it."

"Mrs Blake, may I ask, did he know David Weir? Did Mr Blake go out drinking with Mr Weir?"

"No. Not him. They used to be friends but a few years back they stopped talking. And then Ronald decided he didn't want to work at Portobello High School anymore and he started looking for a new job. That's when he got the job in Leith Academy."

"So, your husband was a friend of David Weir?"

"Yes. Years ago, they used to be very close. Then something happened between them, I don't know what, and he stopped coming round to visit, and they stopped going out for drinks together. They still talked together at the school, I think, but they weren't as close as before."

"Any idea what it was that happened between them?" McKenzie probed, but looked up and nodded at Mrs Duff as she came into the room and offered him a cup of tea.

"No. I think I once asked, but he didn't want to talk about it. And Ronald had lots of other friends, so it wasn't a big thing."

"There's a reason I was asking. I don't know if you know or not, but unfortunately David Weir's body was also found yesterday afternoon. He fell from the roof of the school. We have reason to believe that the fall was not a simple accident."

The expression of sadness and shock that appeared on Mrs Blake's face answered any questions McKenzie may have had about whether she already knew of his death.

"Oh, the poor man..." she half-whispered, then looked down and stared into the cup of tea which Mrs Duff had handed her.

"I'm sorry to be the bearer of the bad news. I've just come from Mr Weir's house, where I met with his widow."

McKenzie said nothing for a few moments. He sipped his tea and smiled weakly at Mrs Duff. She shook her head a little and looked down at the carpet.

"Mrs Blake, can you remember if there were any other teachers or friends that your husband used to spend time with around the same period he was good friends with Mr Weir?"

"No. Sorry. I don't think so," she replied after a moment of thinking. "Why, do you think it might be one of the other teachers that killed Ronnie?" She was looking directly at McKenzie now, her eyes steady, but the pain she was feeling was evident in the warble in her voice as she spoke.

"I can't say. The investigation has just begun. From experience though we can say that sometimes it's just the small things that make the difference to an investigation. Small details that you might not think are relevant, but which suddenly become very important. So, may I request that if you remember anything which you think could be important, would you please let me know?"

McKenzie reached into his jacket pocket, pulled out a card, and passed it over to her.

Mrs Blake nodded.

"Do you know if your husband had any enemies? Anyone who would wish him harm?" McKenzie moved on.

There were a few tears now.

"No. Ronnie didn't have enemies."

The fact that someone had very carefully planned Ronnie Blake's death, clearly indicated the contrary, but McKenzie knew that now was not the right time to point this out.

Instead, he spent the next thirty minutes running through a long list of standard questions, gathering the basic facts, and hoping, just hoping, for a breakthrough.

None was forthcoming.

"Would you mind I were to have a quick look around the house or through his personal things? Does your husband have an office?"

With the help of her neighbour Mrs Duff, she slowly raised herself out of her seat, and made her way through the back of the bungalow and to a room on the left.

"Ronald's private room. I hardly ever go in. It's his domain… was his little den where he could lose himself from everyone else. I don't know what went on in there. But, if you think it might help you, please take your time and have a look around. I don't want to know what you find, but I hope you find something useful."

Then Mrs Duff helped her carry on through to the kitchen, and McKenzie was left alone to sift through the remnants of another man's life.

He turned the handle, pushed the door open and stepped inside.

Chapter 12

Ronald Blake's Den
Duddingston
Saturday
15.10

Only a few days ago, all this had meaning. The notes on the man's desk, the files on the bookshelves, full of records, receipts, letters, and plans. Photographs of distant and past relatives, most of whose identities were known only to Ronald, and would now be lost to future generations. Sadly, Mrs Blake had revealed that her husband and herself had not been able to have children, even though they had desperately wanted them. Ronald had one brother, but he had died a few years ago in a climbing accident in the Cairngorm mountains, and Mrs Blake was an only child.

Standing in the centre of the office, it dawned on McKenzie once again just how meaningless and sad some aspects of life were. All of this, everything that surrounded him had so much meaning to Ronald Blake. Much of it was probably the accumulation of thoughts, feelings and experiences which had taken decades to accumulate, and some of it may even be all that remained from previous generations of Blakes.

Perhaps, somewhere in the Blake's attic, there would be other boxes full of even more photographs, or memorabilia: old plates, books, souvenirs from lives gone by which Ronald Blake had kept and felt too guilty about throwing out or taking to the local dump when older relatives had died, leaving Ronald to inherit the dust of their lives.

Now it was Ronald's turn.

McKenzie could guess that after his funeral, Mrs Blake would perhaps never step foot in her husband's office again, and it would remain like this until the day she died.

Until the day someone was asked to come into the house and clear it out.

Looking around, McKenzie knew that almost everything in the room would end up in boxes, packed into a little white van, and taken to a land-fill.

To be buried without respect, and with no formal recognition of everything which those boxes contained: hopes, tears, laughter, moments of extreme pleasure, and the depths of pain and sorrow.

Everything that makes up a life.

Dreams. Aspirations. Experiences.

Tossed in a box.

Then buried or burned.

"Detective McKenzie? Would you like another cup of tea?" the voice of Mrs Duff caught him off-guard, dragging him back from his spiralling dark thoughts.

"Yes, please. That would nice," McKenzie replied through the door.

Then he took a deep breath, switched on the light in the dimly lit room, and got to work.

Ronald Blake's Den
Duddingston
Saturday
16.30

An hour later, McKenzie left the office, carrying a small box full of a few items he wanted to examine back at the portacabin. He'd just called a taxi, which should arrive soon.

Mrs Blake was back in the front room, sitting on a seat closer to the window, staring out towards the distant view of the sea and the other side of the Firth of Forth.

"Thank you," McKenzie said, interrupting her thoughts, whatever they were.

"Ah, Detective… " she smiled meekly, turning slowly towards him. "I'm sorry, I didn't hear you, and Mrs Duff had to go home to cook dinner for her husband." She paused. "Did you find what you needed? What you came for?"

"Not really," McKenzie replied. "But if it's alright with you, I have a few things here that I would like to take away and look at later. I promise that they will be returned to you as soon as possible."

She nodded.

"One of them is a phone, which I found on his desk. It's password protected. May I take it? And would you perhaps know what the password might be?"

"His phone? Oh, I forgot about that. I'll have to cancel the contract now, won't I?"

She began to cry.

McKenzie fought the urge to step forward, place an arm around her shoulder and cuddle her.

"Yes. I'm afraid you may have to do that, if you don't want to keep the phone for your own use. But if it's okay, I would like to have a look at the contacts he's had recently, which means I need to let one of our specialists look at it once we can get through the password."

"My birthday. 8th August. 0808. Try that."

"I've made a list of everything, could you please just give me your signature on this form?" McKenzie asked, stepping a little closer and offering her a pen.

She nodded, took the pen, and with McKenzie's help, she made her mark on the blue paper covered in legal gibberish which was proffered to her.

"Mrs Blake, I was wondering, this photograph was on one of his shelves amidst his collection of books. Its three men, one of whom is David Weir. Do you know who the other one is?"

McKenzie picked a gold-framed colour photograph out of the box and extended it out towards Mrs Blake so that the light from the window could reveal the figures on it.

Three men. Holding fishing rods and cans of beer in their hands.
Smiling.
Two now dead.
Who was the other?

"Mark. Mark McRae. Sorry, I'd forgotten completely about him, Detective."

"Who is he? Can you tell me anything more about him?" McKenzie asked, studying her eyes as she replied.

"He was another teacher. Yes, that's it. Another teacher from his time at Portobello High School. For a while they were good friends. But then they seemed to stop seeing each other, just like he did with Mr Weir."

"Do you know if Mr McRae is still alive? Or when the last time you or your husband saw him?"

Mrs Blake shook her head.

"I'm sorry. No, I can't. I'm getting old now, my memory isn't what it used to be. And I'm missing Ronnie so much I can't think clearly."

McKenzie nodded. It would be wrong to press her just now.

"Mrs Weir, may I come back and talk with you again? Just in case we have some more questions, and to see if you might perhaps remember anything else?"

"That would be nice. Please do. And I'll let you know when the funeral will be, once all the arrangements are made and the coroner releases Ronnie back to us."

McKenzie felt very sad as he walked down the steps to the waiting taxi. When he glanced backwards, Mrs Blake was standing in the window, watching him.

A little old lady.
Now alone.
In an empty house.

As he got into the taxi, McKenzie remembered just how much he'd hated this part of the job before he'd started climbing through the ranks.

16.45

The first call McKenzie made in the car was to McLeish.

"Mark McRae. A teacher at Portobello High. Find him. Check if he's okay, and then get him into the station for questioning as soon as possible," he instructed.

"He's one of the people we've called already. Actually three times. No answer yet. I've got an address. Shall I prioritise him and go around and visit him? There's only two of us doing this just now, and... " McLeish replied, scanning down the list and the spreadsheet on the computer in front of him.

"I know. Leave it an hour, and if you still have no response, go visit him. He knew both of the deceased. We need to talk with him. And if we start focussing on other teachers in the school as possible suspects, he could be one of them."

Next, he called Anderson and gave him the number of Ronald Blake's phone, instructing him to record it on the incident log, raise a warrant and get the ball rolling on obtaining all the relevant phone records and cell site data.

The next call was to his wife, who'd left two voice messages and a text.

"When will you be back? The Reunion starts at eight, and I don't want to be late. There're drinks and nibbles to start with, then the band starts at nine."

Then there was another discussion about which dress she should wear. The one she'd chosen earlier was too tight, and Little Bump was now not so little anymore. She couldn't make up her mind whether being so obviously pregnant in a dress was tasteful or embarrassing.

"Never be embarrassed. And I don't care what anyone else thinks. I love you, and I love Little Bump!" McKenzie insisted, telling her to go with the green dress, as first chosen.

He promised to be home by seven o'clock, begging his wife to have something ready for him to wolf down the moment he got through the door and before he jumped into the shower.

She jokingly threatened him with a Gregg's in the microwave, but when Fiona detected that he liked the idea, she immediately revealed it was going to be something far more healthy. "Little Bump needs a healthy dad, not one with a coronary bypass!"

He'd laughed, but hadn't found it funny. Fiona was right. His diet had to change. But a few minutes later, as he passed a Gregg's on the main road en route to the school, he only managed to protest to himself for a few seconds, before he pulled over, jumped out and hurried inside.

He was starving.

Getting back into the car a couple of minutes later he was only half way through demolishing the sandwich, when the phone rang.

It was Wishart. She'd got an update on her conversations with those responsible for organising the Reunion.

"They were furious about the idea of possibly cancelling it! They know about the death of someone and the video yesterday afternoon, but they've pointed out that there's almost two hundred people coming tonight, with a lot of them coming from abroad especially for the party."

McKenzie listened carefully, still uncertain about the wisdom of letting the event proceed, but acknowledging the potential opportunity to learn first hand from people who had been at the school when Weir and Blake were teaching there. There's was also the possibility that the killer could show up amongst those at the Reunion. And if they were lucky, *very* lucky, perhaps something would happen that might get them a step closer to identifying or even arresting a suspect.

Unlikely.

But possible.

Although highly unlikely.

"Okay," McKenzie decided. "We go with the flow. The event goes ahead. We probably don't have time to cancel it anyway. Are you still able to make it?"

For the second time in an hour, McKenzie ended up giving advice on a dress.

"Okay, that one sounds wonderful," McKenzie finally agreed. "Go with the blue one. Decision made. I'm only five minutes from the school now. I'll see you back at the portacabin at five, as agreed earlier."

Cramond
16.55

Stuart Nisbet was nervous.
Uncharacteristically nervous.

Apart from the last time he'd been anywhere near Maggie Sutherland, the last time he'd been this nervous was in Afghanistan, the day before his first tour began: arriving at the airport and getting off the transport plane, he'd passed several coffins which were waiting for repatriation to the UK.

Realising that within a few days he could be going home like that, he'd suddenly understood the seriousness of the situation and almost wet himself.

No more schoolboy bravado.

Just plain fear.

Now with only hours to go before he would once again come face-to-face with so many of those whose faces had haunted him for over twenty years, he was having second thoughts.

It wasn't only that he might see Maggie again,… it was far more than that.

Something bizarre. A weird set of thoughts and feelings that he couldn't quite understand.

Even though for twenty years he'd been planning this, looking forward to rubbing everyone else's noses in the dirt of his success, suddenly, weirdly, he'd wondered, *'Was that the right thing to do?'*

At first he couldn't quite understand the thoughts and feelings which were going through his mind. He needed fresh air again, and it was only when he was a mile out in the Firth of Forth on his jet ski, skimming across the water at over sixty miles per hour, that the fog began to clear.

Slowly, a realisation dawned on him.

Yes, Stuart was a success.

He'd been lucky.

Very lucky.

Financially.

But money wasn't everything.

Was it?

And what would it gain him to rub the noses of the others in his fortune, when he was jealous of the one thing most of them probably had, and which money couldn't buy?

Who was the successful one, now then?

And who was the fool?

Perhaps turning up tonight with all guns blazing, splashing the cash and playing the big guy was nothing but the most foolish thing he could do.

Twenty years of driving himself, pushing himself, willing himself on, imagining an evening like tonight…

It was all for nothing.

This wasn't about others.

This was about him.

His inadequacies.

His failings.

No wonder he had no real friends. No one to love.

In spite of owning more than anyone else in his country, he had nothing at all.

A mile out to sea, Stuart Nisbet closed his eyes, twisted the accelerator handle as far as it would go, and shot forward faster, faster, ever faster.

Then he lifted both hands off the steering controls, stood up, closed his eyes, and fell backwards off the jet-ski into the sea.

16.58

Mark McRae shivered, closing his eyes and riding out the muscular spasm that swept up and down his body.

The water dripping from the roof of his prison cell was cold, despite the temperature outside which had to be at least twenty degrees warmer. It was the summer after all. Earlier that week it had been over twenty degrees... but here, inside this damp, dark room, he was almost hypothermic.

The incessant drip, drip, drip of the water drops echoing around the room was driving him mad.

He'd long ago given up trying to scream, and he was even beginning to manage the constant urge to vomit as the gag bit into the back of his mouth.

The others were gone now – where he did not know – but he missed their company – whoever they had been. They too had been gagged, and alone in the dark they had tried for a while to communicate through their grunting, but had quickly realised that their unintelligible sounds were exactly that: unintelligible.

How long they had been gone for Mark didn't know. In almost complete darkness, the hours and days blended into one. The passage of time was imperceptible.

If he'd wanted to, perhaps he could have counted the drops of water as they fell from the ceiling, but something as clever as that was now well beyond his capability.

Mark was starving. He hadn't eaten since he had first woken up in the room and found himself with the others.

Thirst was the other problem.

His mouth was as dry as a bone.

His captor was making no effort to look after him. No water. No food.

Mark was scared. Petrified.

He had defecated and urinated in his trousers several times, both from fear and necessity. At first the smell had been overwhelming, but now he couldn't smell it, his brain compensating for the stench and filtering it out.

His chains were cutting into his wrists and he thought they had been bleeding. But you can't see red blood in the dark, so he wasn't sure either way.

It had been hours since his captor had last come into the cell.

Each time, he'd heard the trapdoor open and then been blinded as the light bulb hanging from the ceiling had burst into life like an exploding sun.

Before he'd had time to adjust, he'd felt the cattle prod in his side again, and he'd fallen back down onto his knees in compliance, at the mercy of whoever his captor was, and awaiting whatever his fate would be.

His captor never stayed long. He just came in, checked the chains, and left.

When the others had been in the room with him, Mark had been blindfolded, but after the second person had been taken out of the prison cell, his captor had come back in and swept the blindfold of his head.

"I need it. I'll give it back to you later." He whispered.

That hadn't happened yet, and Mark had not complained.

With or without it, the blindfold made very little difference.

He sat in almost complete darkness, the only source of light being a slight crack in the edge of the trapdoor through which some light oozed.

It was his only connection to the outside world, and he stared at it constantly, trying to figure out what had happened, how he had ended up here, and how on earth he would get out.

Mark was not a tall man. He was of a slim build, and no match for his captor who was a hulk of a man. His captor wore a mask, which was probably a kid's cheap Halloween mask, but it did the job. All Mark saw of him was a wizened old North American Indian, long fake black hair, and a feather sticking up.

His captor had only ever spoken a few words and even then, his words were muffled by the plastic mask and the small slit for a mouth through which the voice escaped.

He'd detected an accent. Slight, not too pronounced, but the man had obviously lived abroad for some time.

Mark had hoped that might give him a clue as to who his abductor might be, but after hours of thinking about it, he'd still drawn a blank.

Instead he started to worry about what would happen when the man came back for him.

The others who had been here before were now gone.

Where had he taken them?

Was he next?

Were they still alive?

Adrenaline surged through his exhausted and cold body, and once again he began to shake.

In the dark, fear is twice as bad as in the light.

Mark defecated in his trousers one more time.

This time he didn't even notice.

Chapter 13

Operation Blue Building
Incident Room
Portacabin
Saturday
17.00

McKenzie strode into the portacabin, half expecting to find no one there.

There was so much to do, and so few people to do it, he knew that asking everyone to do their job and respect meeting times was a tall order.

But McKenzie was known for his insistence that everyone makes meetings. Not because he believed in meetings for meeting's sake, but because McKenzie believed that the sum of the parts was always greater than the whole. Or that 'one-plus-one' would often make three when people talked together and shared the information they knew.

Breakthroughs came not from lots of people working individually, but from a team - small or large - working together.

Five faces looked up at him as he turned at the front of the room and faced them: PC Lynch, DS Wishart, DS McLeish, DI Elaine Brown, and Sergeant Anderson.

In typical McKenzie style – his own personal quirk – he clapped his hands together and smiled.

Everyone knew the meeting was now in progress.

"I'll kick off, everyone, if that's okay, because I may have the most important news. And it's not good. You might have heard that I was probably contacted directly by the murderer. He followed us and left a note on the car."

McKenzie recounted to the team the details of the note. The looks on their faces said it all: unless they did their jobs, more people would die.

"Murray? Have you got anything?" McKenzie asked the Sergeant. "Any luck with forensics?"

"It'll be at least three days before we get any sort of response. At a minimum. And that obviously depends upon them being able to find any DNA traces. And DI Brown will be handling that from now on, as part of her ongoing liaison with Forensics."

"Thanks Murray. Please keep on it, Elaine. It's a long shot, and I wouldn't bank on the murderer handing us an identify on a plate. My guess is there will be nothing, but you never know."

"Next," McKenzie continued. "We now have two mobile phone numbers for the deceased, and I've handed Murray the task of managing the appropriate warrants and getting all the usual data we can from the telephone companies. Hopefully we'll get that by tomorrow morning?"

Anderson nodded. "If not sooner."

"Good." McKenzie turned to the board and made a note on the action list.

"Right, next." McKenzie continued. "I have a name for a colleague of Ronald Blake who also knew David Weir." He held up the photograph and recounted his visit to Mrs Blake. "McLeish is lead on tracking him down, identifying if he's missing and if not, getting him in for questioning."

McKenzie turned to the whiteboard, and scribbled two words before underlining them: "Suspect List".

Under the heading he quickly scrawled a few bullets: *Other teachers. Ex-Pupils. Mrs Weir (ex-wife to be). Mark McRae (colleague teacher and friend).*

"Has anyone got anyone else to add to the suspect's list?" McKenzie asked, scanning the team, but seeing no response.

"Lastly, I spoke with DCS Wilkinson, and after much begging we've got one more person on the team. DI Fraser Dean. I've got him working on the CCTV cameras trying to find an image of the person putting the note on my car. You'll get to meet later."

"Last from me, is in talking with Wishart it seems we're too late to cancel this evening's Reunion. It's going ahead. I'm putting DS Wishart in charge for this evening's activities."

McKenzie held out an open hand to Wishart and she stood up and came to the front. She gave a quick update on her conversations that afternoon and then started to build a list of names on the board of who was going to the Reunion.

She wrote down her own name, followed by Anderson, and McKenzie. She then spent two minutes negotiating with Lynch if he could come too. He agreed. His wife would have to find someone else to babysit for their children tonight, at short notice. He wouldn't be a popular man.

After giving them instructions on how to get to where it was being held, Wishart gave them duties and tasks to perform during the event, and they all agreed. Including McKenzie. They'd communicate with each other by personal phone and text messages. Airwaves should be left in the car or at home. This was an undercover operation.

McKenzie thanked her.

"McLeish, you're up next." McKenzie nodded at him.

"Thanks," McLeish said, moving forward and swapping places with Wishart at the whiteboard. "I went to visit the school secretary in her office at the new school – which is incidentally very nice. Anyway, she's given me a list of all the staff she has a record of going back forty years. Names, subjects they taught, duration of employment. She's cooperated fully. I also got a list of former headmasters as you requested. In particular we've identified the one who was the headmaster for most of the time that Ronald Blake and David Weir taught at the school. I have his contact details ready for you. I tried calling him but there's no answer. By the way, after serving as Head for about fifteen years, he moved to live on the Island of Coll. It's way out there in the Hebrides. Almost completely off the grid."

"Interesting. I'll have those details immediately after this meeting, please. I need to speak with him as soon as possible."

"No problem. Anyway, I've built a spreadsheet, and I've started going through it, trying to make contact with as many past staff as possible. McRae's top of the list after the old headmaster. As discussed by phone. It's going to be a tough job. At the moment, there's only myself and Lynch. I could do with some help."

"Understood, but until Operation Crown is over, it's just the two of you. Nothing I can do about it. Sorry." McKenzie replied. The answer wasn't ideal, but the decision was above his pay grade. "Thanks, McLeish. Appreciated."

McKenzie nodded at Brown, his partner.

"Elaine, anything interesting to share?"

She stood up.

"My two tasks so far have been to liaise with both forensics and Gary Bruce. Starting with Bruce, this afternoon we went on a long tour of the inside perimeter of the site, searching at great length to find any possible routes of entry onto the campus. As suggested, we looked for false panels. We also walked the outside perimeter looking for low walls, adjoining rooftops, ladders, trampolines, tree branches... anything and everything that could possibly help someone to get over the fence, although realistically speaking we've got to remember that the victims were probably forced against their will and could not be carried over such a large fence. They'd probably put up some sort of resistance, and the people living around the edge of the school would surely see or hear something." She paused, looking for questions, but there were none.

"Okay, so we also then took another look at the schematics and plans for the campus to see if there was any possible tunnel into the school from outside, and there was nothing. To be honest, there's no possible way into the school except through the new entrance that Gary's team has built at the front of the school. Having spent the best part of today chasing this up, I'm completely stumped by it. Short of parachuting onto the roof of the school, I can't see how it was done."

For a moment, just for a moment, Brown could see that some of the team were actively pondering the possibilities of how someone could parachute onto the roof of the school without being seen.

"I was joking." Brown laughed. "But, actually, I suppose we do have to look at all the possibilities, because at this point in time, we're clueless as to how it was done."

"Unless Gary Bruce has got something to do with it?" McLeish volunteered. "Maybe they didn't break in: perhaps they were allowed in or led in?"

McKenzie stared at McLeish. Yet again, he'd come up with an alternative angle that couldn't be discounted. McKenzie stood up, and walked to the board, contemplating adding Bruce's name to the list of suspects.

"Okay, that's a good point." McKenzie admitted. "But for now, we'll leave his name off the suspect list. Mr Bruce is in and out of this room, and right now, I don't want him seeing his name on the list. Everyone just remember that it's there, okay? And it might not be Bruce. It could be one of his employees. They're all suspect."

Nods all round.

McKenzie gave the floor back to Brown.

"Moving on to Forensics, I've got a few interesting things to report. Firstly, Forensics has indicated that both victims had the same traces of brown dirt on their trousers. It appears they were both sitting down in the same place, possibly on the ground, or somewhere which was covered in wet dirt. It confirms that before they were brought to the locations where they were individually killed, they were at some point both in the same place, somewhere. They're now looking at the soil types, and trying to narrow it down further.

"They've also confirmed that both bodies have similar burn marks on them, which are consistent with those that might be experienced as a consequence of being pushed rather forcibly by a cattle prod."

"I've asked if we can narrow the type of cattle prod down, and identify who might have access to one, but it appears they're widely used by many farmers, and aren't controlled. In other words, anyone could get hold of one, if you really want one."

"They've also now said that both bodies had lacerations and markings on their wrists or ankles which could indicate they've been handcuffed or shackled in some way for an extended period of time."

"Also, forensics have informed me that they have found what they believe to be some form of writing on the forehead of Ronald Blake. It looks like it was written in felt pen. Unfortunately, they can't tell *what* was written, because Blake's sweat washed almost all the writing off, but they think they can make out a couple of letters – R, E, M, and that it was written in red. They're going to see if they can find anything on David Weir's forehead too, but because there was not much left of it, that exercise is not straightforward. I didn't ask for any more details on that part."

"The killer wrote something on his forehead?" Lynch asked. "Whatever it was, that could be hugely significant. The killer would have wanted us to read it. It could have been some form of message?"

"Sadly, we were too late. If it was meant to be a message, the killer used the wrong type of ink to leave a permanent note." Brown replied, then continued.

"Lastly, moving on, Forensics have identified a drug being present within the blood of David Weir, which they are trying to identify for us by tomorrow morning. They think that when he fell from the roof of the school, he was high as a kite. He probably didn't know what was happening to him."

"And Ronald Blake? Was he drugged too?" McLeish asked.

"I asked, they weren't able to say yet. Anyway, that's all I have for now."

"No news on how long Ronald Blake was on the cross for?" Wishart enquired.

"Sorry, not yet. That's another thing they can hopefully tell me tomorrow."

McKenzie stood up and moved to the front.

"Okay, boys and girls, if you're not going to the Ball tonight, I want you home for a rest, and some relaxation. If you take a bath, make sure you have a notebook handy to capture any ideas or Eureka moments. We need all the help and ideas we can get on this one. And then we'll all meet back here tomorrow at nine-thirty sharp. I'll give you all a lie in till then." He smiled, jokily, knowing it was no lie-in at all.

"Guv, are you sure there's no way you can talk some sense into Fettes? We need more people on this. If someone else gets murdered… "

McKenzie raised his hand.

"DS Wishart, as long as we try our hardest, there will be no blame and NO guilt felt by anyone on this team if another body turns up. Frankly, this is a ridiculous situation. We can only pray that Operation Crown concludes as quickly as possible. In the meantime, as soon as this meeting finishes, I'll be on the blower to DCS Wilkinson to insist we get an undercover armed team covering us and the party goers at the Reunion tonight. There's a high possibility the killer will show up, and we've been warned to expect more victims."

"What about the school?" McLeish asked.

"Mather is still on the team. He's covering the night shift. Before we came in, Anderson managed to pull a few strings in Portobello and he's going to have a couple of uniforms helping Mather to patrol the perimeter and inside of the school site. And the dogs will be out in the playground. No one is getting in here tonight, that's for sure.

"Anyway, for everyone going to the Reunion tonight, we'll meet in the foyer of the new Portobello High School at about 7.45pm. I'm afraid there'll be no alcohol drunk tonight, no matter how tempting it is. We're all going to need our wits about us. See you there."

McKenzie clapped his hands together. Meeting adjourned.

17.25

"Ma'am, with all due respect to the Queen, I also have a real threat I'm trying to deal with here. Two dead so far, with a real possibility of more to come, and a high likelihood that it could be within the next few hours. What I'm asking is NOT unreasonable, and I think you appreciate that. So, please, can you authorise and pull whatever strings you need, to ensure that my team and the School Reunion event this evening is supported by an appropriate team of armed officers. As you see fit, Ma'am."

McKenzie finished his diatribe and took a deep breath. They'd been at it already for several minutes, with the impatience on both sides growing.

DCS Wilkinson wasn't happy. She'd lost the argument, and she knew it.

McKenzie could almost hear the steam hissing out her ears.

"Four officers, undercover, arriving at 6.45pm. And just let's hope no one assassinates the Queen tonight, or we'll both be going to the Tower."

"Thank you, Ma'am." McKenzie replied, smiling slightly.

There was a moment's pause, and then DCS Wilkinson offered an olive branch.

"So, what are you wearing to the ball, tonight? Are you going fully kilted up?"

"Yes, actually I am." He replied, wondering how his superior knew.

"Campbell, there's something I've always wanted to ask, given that I might be forgiven for being an English woman, working north of the border."

"And what's that, Ma'am?" he asked, noting her use of his first name to still the waters.

"What's actually worn under the kilt?" she asked. "If you excuse me for asking."

McKenzie hesitated, and then replied in one sentence, before summarily hanging up.

"Nothing Ma'am. Nothing's worn beneath the kilt. It's all in perfect working order."

17.35

Mark McRae heard the approaching footsteps and tensed, quickly closing his eyes and attempting to avoid the sudden onslaught of light as the trapdoor was opened.

He knew that if he controlled the amount of light that entered his eyes, by slowly opening his eyelids, he might be able to quickly adjust to the light.

At the very least, it wouldn't hurt so much.

As soon as the trapdoor opened, a draft of fresh air assailed him, the sweetness of it stirring his senses and making him realise, possibly for the first time, how good fresh air actually smelt.

If he ever got out of this hell hole alive, he would never take fresh air for granted again.

Slowly opening his eyes, he could make out his captor coming backwards down the stairs from the trapdoor above, his head covered with the mask as normal.

He was a huge man. Broad across the shoulders, and a slim figure. He obviously kept himself in good shape.

The man turned and came towards him, the cattle prod in his right arm.

For once the man didn't turn the light bulb on, leaving them both relatively in the dark.

As he approached, the man in the Indian mask lifted the cattle prod towards Mark, who immediately fell forward onto the ground in an act of total supplication. By this time, Mark's reactions were automatic.

His captor had trained him well.

"I just wanted to let you know that it's your turn next, *Mr McRae.*"

Mark noticed the inflexion uttered on the last two words, turning the simple sentence into a chilling threat. His captor was mocking his career as a teacher, and the way he'd inflected on his name hinted at all this having something to do with his job.

"For what?" Mark choked, as he tried to speak through the gag in his mouth.

A searing pain immediately swept through his side.

"Talk only when invited to. Otherwise, stay quiet." The Indian commanded, retracting the cattle prod back having made his point.

Mark writhed on the floor, biting hard on his lip.

For a moment the Indian looked down at him, an evil laugh emanating from behind the mask, adding to the terror of the moment.

"I'll be back shortly," the man threatened, and perhaps I'll take you for one last walk. If you're a good boy, that is. If not," he paused. "You'll get eternal detention, and I'll make you stay behind after school, … for ever."

"Water. Some water please… " Mark almost whispered. Begging as silently as he could.

Another searing pain in his side was the only answer he got.

This time, Mark passed out with the pain.

Chapter 14

Duddingston Road
Edinburgh
17.45

"Barry, what on earth is that?" Irene Quinn screamed, pointing at the car sitting in their drive way. "And where the hell did it come from?"

"That," replied Barry proudly through the open window of their lounge, and after coughing a couple of times to clear his throat, "… is a 2019 Porsche Boxster!"

"I KNOW it's a Porsche Boxster… it's got it written all over the tail of the car. I'm not a complete idiot! I meant, what is *THAT*, and what is it doing *HERE*!"

Barry coughed again.

"Think of it like a taxi. Or your carriage for the Ball this evening. '*Yes, Irene, you too can go to the Ball!*' " he answered, mimicking the best version of the Disney voice he could think of.

"BARRY QUINN! You get out here *NOW!* What the hell have you done? And where the hell did you get it from?"

A few minutes later Barry Quinn, survivor of over twenty years of marriage, but probably now heading to the divorce courts, appeared before his wife, tail between his legs, and slightly red in his face.

"You didn't seriously expect me to take you to the School Reunion Ball in our clapped out Ford Escort, did you?"

"What on earth has got into you, Barry Quinn?" she said, stepping towards the red apparition on her drive-way. "Barry, you promised. You PROMISED you wouldn't do anything like this. What are you trying to prove? What does this say to everyone else that knows us? We'll be the laughing stock of… "

"No, we ARE the laughing stock of our year." Barry interrupted, his face turning slightly red. "I'm Barry Bloody No Mates who never achieved anything in his life, and in over two decades didn't manage to make it more than a mile away from the Secondary School. I just want everyone else who doesn't know how pathetic I am to think, just for a moment, that I'm not the complete and utter failure that I am!"

Irene Quinn turned from the car to her husband.

For a moment her heart went out to him, and she felt an overwhelming urge to wrap her arms around him and squeeze him tight.

After taking a few deep breaths, that feeling was replaced with another. An urge to wrap her wrists around his throat and squeeze it until he turned blue.

Instead, she stormed past him, tears running her cheeks.

"I am not nothing, Barry. You've got me. And I AM not *NOTHING*. And our life is fine. Just fine. What on EARTH are you thinking?" She paused in the doorway, before turning and issuing one final torrent of emotion at him. "Send it back Barry. Send the bloody thing BACK!"

Duddingston Road
Edinburgh
17.55

Iain Small sat on his sofa, talking with his friends about the video on WhatsApp which had gone viral. Everyone was watching it. So far it had got over eighty-seven thousand hits. The video had been pulled several times, but someone kept re-posting it.

"Poor bastard!" Iain said, shaking his head. "Do you think it's anyone we knew?"

"Dunno," Kerrin replied, whilst staring at his wife who had just walked into the room topless and looking for her bra.

"Everyone will be talking about it tonight. If someone knows who it is, then we'll soon find out," Iain suggested. "You know, these school Reunions can cause a lot of stress for some people. Some people worry about seeing their old school pals again. They're scared that everyone will judge them for what they've achieved, or slag them off for being a failure."

"Are you thinking that this guy topped himself because he couldn't hack the idea of going to the ball?" Kerrin wondered, whilst blowing his wife a few kisses and smiling at her. They'd just made love, and if Kerrin had his way, they would probably be doing it again, or at least trying, as soon as Iain got off the phone.

"Yeah, something like that."

"It's pretty pathetic really... I mean, dinnae get me wrong, but why get so stressed about it? Just don't go to the bloody Reunion. There's no need to throw yourself off the roof of the school."

"Kerrin, you're a lucky bastard and you know it. You've got your own house, healthy kids and a bloody gorgeous wife. Okay, you've got a crap job, but in comparison with most folk, you're really successful."

Kerrin coughed.

"Okay, straight up, perhaps I do know where this guy was coming from. I mean, I did actually consider renting a really flash car for the weekend, and pretending it was mine. Just, you know... so that people would think... "

"That you were a prat? We all know you, Kerrin. Who were you trying to impress? Who?"

There was a moment's silence.

"Hang on a second, Emma's just leaving the room." Kerrin whispered.

Another pause.

"Can you remember that girl in Brunstane House, you know the one with big tits and the blue eyes that I used to fancy something rotten?"

"What? Yvonne? The one who knocked you back about ten times?"

"Yea. Yvonne McDougall. Well, I was just thinking, maybe if she's there tonight, and I turned up in a flash car, then... "

"Shut the hell up, Kerrin. You're married to Emma. You've been going out since the school Qually dance... what on earth are you still dreaming about Yvonne for?"

"I'm not… I mean, maybe just a little. What about you and that girl Marie? You used to go on about her tons, when you were in fourth year?"

"Marie McDonald? True, but she was *way* out of my league. She'd be about forty-six now. You've got to be realistic about these things, mate. I might have fancied her like crazy when she was sweet sixteen, but we're all getting older. Have you looked in the mirror recently pal? I'm just saying. I've got Debbie, and I'm lucky she doesn't dump me for someone better looking than me. You've got Emma. And you're punching way above your weight with her mate. Way higher."

Kerrin pretended to laugh, but he knew Iain was right.

"I told Emma I wanted to rent a car, and she just laughed. She told me to stop being an idiot. She just said that the car park's probably going to be so full of cars rented by other twats pretending to be something they're not, that I'd just be wasting my money."

"Shit," Iain replied, changing the subject completely. "Have you seen the time? It's gone six o'clock. I've still got to cook the kid's their dinner. What time are you getting there?"

"It's still the same plan. We're meeting in the Forrester's Arms in Porty for a glass of Prosecco first, then getting the taxis from there."

"Seven?"

"Like I said, that's the plan, Stan. Be there or be square."

"Twat!" Iain laughed back, and hung up.

Getting up out of his sofa, Iain walked through to his bedroom and kissed Debbie on the back of her neck, whilst she sat at the dressing table and started to apply her war paint.

"What's that for?" she asked, looking at his reflection in the mirror.

"For persuading me not to hire the Corvette. It was a stupid idea, and you were right."

Debbie shook her head.

What was it with men and school Reunions?

Did it bring out the Twat-factor in all of them, or was it just her husband?

Northfield
Edinburgh
18.05

Marie McDonald was nervous. A little scared. Annoyed. And much fatter than she'd realised.

The dress she'd hoped to wear earlier this evening no longer fitted. Her bust was too large and was barely contained, and the sides of her dress just held her in. If she ate one too many biscuits this evening her dress would probably pop off.

For a moment she did consider wearing it anyway - perhaps getting a little bit of attention due to the bust factor may not be too bad after all - she might need all the help she could get! But after only a few moments serious consideration she admitted to herself that it was not appropriate.

The last thing she needed was someone to snap a photo and pop it on Facebook, only for a colleague of hers in Poland to see her dressed like a decadent Parisian tart.

Although that was probably a little harsh, both for herself, and the Parisians.

Luckily, the TK MAXX near where the old Meadowbank Commonwealth Stadium had come to her rescue.

She managed to find a tasteful, yet rather cheap dress within twenty minutes, and even if she did say so herself, she looked great.

All day long she'd been thinking about tonight.

Would anyone recognise her? Would anyone remember her?

What should she say about herself if anyone asked?

One of the things she did not want to do this evening was to turn it into a fund-raising exercise. But she knew her own weaknesses, and she knew that she often used fund-raising as a method of diverting focus away from herself. And tonight was not about that.

Also, tonight *was* about her.

It was not about her kids. Or the orphanage.

And the last thing she wanted to do was bore everyone else.

Unfortunately, the few phone calls she'd placed to different charities over the past few days had not gone well. Corporations and people in Scotland were tightening their belts. The economy was not doing so well.

Earlier that afternoon she'd found a school diary in a drawer in her old wardrobe. There were a few numbers in there of her old friends. She'd even drummed up the courage to call a few of them, but two of the numbers didn't work anymore, and one had gone through to a family from Lithuania who had inherited the number when they moved into the house.

So, she couldn't arrange to meet anyone before the evening started, and she would just have to go to the Ball by herself.

She looked at her watch.

Only a few hours to go.

Should she get there early, or turn up late?

Deciding to be on time, she planned the timing for the umpteenth time: a small meal, shower, make up, and then an Uber to the Reunion.

The cab was already set for 7.35pm.

She looked in the mirror again.

The person who looked back was no one special.

Suddenly she felt very alone.

Tonight would be dominated by friends hugging each other, air-kisses, real kisses, and people laughing and having fun together.

She'd be lucky if anyone even remembered her.

She closed her eyes and began to sob.

Maybe she wouldn't go after all.

Cramond
18.10

Stuart Nisbet had sunk.

Mentally, and physically.

Whereas he'd probably only gone down about a metre before the buoyancy in his life-jacket had begun to drag him back to the surface, in his mind he'd felt himself falling and falling.

Spiralling down and down.

Deeper and deeper into a place he'd never been before.

And then it had stopped.

He'd found a place where everything was once again in balance, and the world around him had begun to stabilise.

He experienced a strange but pleasantly surprising mental inner calm.

For a moment he floated in the universe, doing nothing, trying nothing, striving for nothing.

Just being.

Existing.

Nothing to prove.

Nothing to do.

Just *being*.

An inner peace like he had never experienced before, engulfed him, and he realised that for the first time in years... perhaps his entire life... he was happy.

Then he had opened his eyes.

The world around him was grey and dark.

Cold.

His chest was hurting.

Not painful.

But full of a desire to breathe, to suck in air, to exist once more.

His feet had taken over, kicking, propelling himself upwards, and almost immediately he was on the surface, surrounded by sea as far as the eye could see.

Stuart gulped air, almost surprising himself with his appetite to live.

He knew immediately that something had changed.

His life would never be the same again.

A few metres away his jet ski bobbed on the water patiently awaiting its master, having dutifully circled in an arc and returned to where Stuart had jumped off.

Smiling, Stuart struck out across the water, climbed aboard and fired up the engine.

A moment later he was speeding back towards the beach, laughing aloud as the salt spray splashed his face and the wind buffeted against his chest.

A man reborn.

Upon arriving at the beach, he'd loaded the jet-ski on the trailer, changed, and headed home.

Entering his garage, he stowed everything away, then found and dusted off his old pedal bike.

His plans for this evening had belonged to his old life.

Now they had changed.

Yes, Stuart Nisbet was still going to the ball, but not in a super-car or a helicopter, but by bike.

God had given him two good feet and a pair of legs, and tonight he would use them both.

Chapter 15

The Grange
Saturday
18.20

McKenzie closed the front door and strode into the kitchen, his arm hiding the flowers behind his back, hoping to catch Mrs McKenzie by surprise.
The kitchen was empty.
The house was silent.
"Fiona?" McKenzie had called out, wondering where she was.
"Up here... in the bath." She'd replied.
Hanging his jacket on the back of a chair, he grabbed a bottle of non-alcoholic beer from the fridge and headed upstairs.
"Are you not cutting it a bit fine?" McKenzie questioned, popping his head around the door, but keeping the surprise safely hidden out of sight.
"Sorry, I was getting ready, but I realised I was a bit stressed, and... Little Bump started to kick!"
"Bump kicked?"
"Yup. It was amazing. So I stopped stressing and decided to relax and chill a little."
"Any room for me?" McKenzie asked.
"No way. Two's fine. Three's a crowd. Sorry."
"Even if I give Mrs McKenzie these?" he asked, proffering the bouquet out from behind his back towards her. "I thought you might want to make yourself a corsage for the ball?"
Mrs McKenzie smiled and blew him a kiss.
"They're beautiful, although I think you're being a little old-fashioned. But the thought was nice, thank you."
"So, why are you stressed?" he asked, dropping the lid on the toilet, sitting down and taking a few sips of the cold beer.
"It's the school Reunion. Of course I'm stressed. School Reunions are the stuff of nightmares."
"Why? You were popular at school. And you've kept in contact with quite a few of your friends, so you'll have plenty of people to chat to."
"I know. But... everyone's going to be there. I'm all grown up now, I know, and I've got Bump on the way, but, suddenly I just feel like a little schoolgirl again, and all the old insecurities and doubts have magically resurfaced. It's bizarre. Last night I even dreamt I was sitting my exams again. And that I failed them all and I have to re-sit them all in October again."
McKenzie laughed.
He knew the dream.
He'd had them too, over the years.
A person's school days never truly go away.

"Okay, I've got a few calls to make before we leave, but we haven't got much time. The cabs coming in forty minutes. What's for dinner? Shall I make something or…"

"I'm not hungry, but I've left you a salad and some cold salmon in the fridge. Make your calls but be ready, Campbell. I promised to meet the girls at the bar at eight sharp!"

Downstairs in the kitchen he wolfed down the salmon and salad, and then walked back upstairs to his study. Or what used to be his study. In a few weeks' time the transformation to a baby's nursery would be complete, and his book shelves and desk would have been replaced by a cot and a baby mobile hanging from the ceiling.

He'd begun the redecoration a few weeks ago, but hadn't made much progress yet. He'd miss his man cave, and he knew it.

He was incredibly excited about Little Bump.

Somehow, though, it still all seemed a little unreal.

Fiona was getting pretty huge, but was there really, *really* a little person in there?

And was it a boy or a girl?

In a few years' time, would the walls of his office be covered in Hibs posters, or pictures of ballerinas and sparkly handbags?

Laughing to himself, he sat down at his desk, and pulled out his phone.

Trying to get hold of Daniel Gray was proving more difficult than anticipated.

According to the list McLeish had given him, Mr Gray was headmaster at the old Portobello High School for over ten years, covering much of the period during which both Ronald Blake and David Weir had been teachers at the same time.

He'd been the headmaster there until 2001, then moved elsewhere, before retiring in 2010.

After Portobello he moved to a school in Oban, and from there had retired to the small Hebridean Isle of Coll.

According to the map McKenzie had looked at, you couldn't get much more off the Grid, than there.

The Google Maps view of Gray's cottage was beautiful, located on the top of its very own beach, but miles from the nearest house.

Based upon his retiring date, and assuming that he'd retired when he was sixty-five, that would make him seventy-four now.

McKenzie couldn't help but wonder if the reason Gray wasn't picking up the phone was because he was dead, having passed away without anyone noticing.

It was rather a morbid thought, but given McKenzie's recent luck, he couldn't put it past the realm of possibility.

Fortunately, the next few seconds proved him wrong.

"Hello?" a gruff but strong voice bellowed down the phone at him, picking up after only a few rings.

"Good evening. This is DCI Campbell McKenzie of Police Scotland, based in Edinburgh. I'm calling you just now in connection with two murders that took place very recently within the premises of the old Portobello High School. I understand that you were the headmaster at the school for a number of years, and I believe you may know the victims, both of whom were serving teachers during your stint at the school."

There was a moment's silence.

"*TWO* murders? At Portobello High School?"

"Yes sir. Unfortunately."

"Oh dear… " the voice quivered at the other end of the line. "Hang on, please,… I think I'd better sit down."

The voice seemed less strong than before and McKenzie felt guilty for being so brusque and matter of fact without any social preamble. For all he knew, Gray, Wier and Blake could have been very close, and this news might be quite shocking.

"May I ask who was killed?" the old headmaster enquired, his voice shaking.

"Yes. Normally we wouldn't do this over the phone like this, but given your current location, and the situation we have here in Edinburgh, I can't really afford to send anyone over to speak with you from my team at this current time. Time is also of the essence, so if you would promise me not to repeat anything I am about to tell you, I would like to share two names with you, if I may, Mr Gray."

"Yes, I promise. Who were they?" the headmaster pressed, with McKenzie detecting a sense of urgency in his voice.

"Okay, but I repeat, you must not reveal the following two names to anyone without discussing it with me first." McKenzie reiterated. He was taking a risk. He didn't know this man on the phone from Adam.

"I've promised you once already. Please, get on with it man! Who were they?"

"David Weir, a geography teacher, and Ronald Blake, an RE teacher."

"Oh shit… " the old man, immediately swore, then went silent.

"Mr Gray? Are you still there? Are you okay? Again, I apologise for just breaking the news to you so… "

"I'm sorry, I can't help you officer. And I'm very busy. My apologies, but I have to go now… "

"Wait!" McKenzie interrupted him, fearing that at any second he was going to hang up. "I just wanted to ask you a few questions about them. To establish if you could think of any reasons why someone may wish to kill them both? Did you know of anyone who had a grudge against both of them? Or either of them individually?"

"No, sorry, I'm really busy. And I can't help you. Please don't disturb me again. I'm an old man, and … *Goodbye!*"

The line went dead.

McKenzie nodded to himself and smiled.

'Bingo.'

Mr Gray's actions, contrary to his insistence that he knew nothing, had just spoken volumes.

Gray knew something.

There was a reason why Blake and Weir had been killed, and McKenzie's instinct had immediately began shouting at him that headmaster Gray almost certainly knew what that reason might be.

McKenzie glanced at the map again and googled how far away it was.

He swore to himself as the answer came up.

Coll was over one hundred and seventy miles away through the mountains and across the sea via a ferry from Oban.

Unless Gray could be persuaded to be a little more cooperative over the phone, McKenzie was probably going to have to do a road trip.

McKenzie picked up the phone and dialled the number again.

This time it was not answered.

Joppa
Edinburgh
18.35

Willy Thomson's right hand was hurting. *Really* hurting. It turned out that the eejit he'd wacked in the face on the way home last night had been harder than he'd first thought. The chances were that Willy's hand was broken.

It hurt like shit.

Willy was used to pain, but tonight he could have done without it.

Tonight was going to be a special night. His night. The night he'd get payback.

It also didn't help that to take the edge off the pain, he'd now drunk most of a small bottle of whisky.

Admittedly, it hadn't been all at once, and he had managed to drag it out over the past two hours, but he still did feel the buzz and the adrenaline that shot into his veins whenever he thought of those who were guilty for his lack of success in life.

Whisky was a good friend of his.

In his line of work, and with his lifestyle, it was the fuel he needed to complete and succeed in a lot of the things he did.

Whisky.

And a knife.

Like the two he'd been sharpening for the past hour. Just checking that he'd be sufficiently tooled up for this evening.

Willy was no fool. He knew that he might get searched on the way in to the Reunion Ball, so he was taking his special DMs with him: the ones with the hollowed soles and the slit underneath where he could slip in the knives and simply walk through the detectors with the knives hidden underneath.

Sometimes the alarm went off when he marched into a night club, but then he lifted his feet and showed them all the metal segs he arranged in a horseshoe around the heel. The bouncers always took one look, shrugged or laughed and waved him in.

The knives weren't that big but Willy didn't need anything large. It was what you did with a knife, not its size, that really mattered.

As he'd proved so many times before.

Willy was excited. Really looking forward to the Ball.

He'd spent the majority of his time that day thinking about all his victims over the years. He'd been proud to admit to himself that it had taken quite a while to think them through, because there had been so many. In particular, he'd thought about how close he'd come to actually killing someone.

So far, none of the bastards he'd knifed had actually kicked the bucket.

He'd always thought that was actually quite a good thing. In a way, it sort of made him a virgin.

He'd never really done it before.

Tonight that was going to change though.

This evening was going to be the one when he finally popped his cherry: he'd bloody really do it tonight.

He'd kill someone.

Bloody *really* do it.

Who he was going to kill he wasn't quite sure.

Which of them bastard teachers was about to die, Will didn't actually know yet.

He'd not made up his mind.

But one of them would.

Whoever he saw that pissed him off the most.

Or whoever was the easiest.

Tonight Willy was going to do it.

For real.

Chapter 16

The New Portobello High School
Milton Road
Saturday
19.45

One by one the flashy cars turned into the car park from Milton Road, and ex-pupils from Portobello High School got out, smoothed down their clothes and then loitered with the sole intent of being seen by as many others as possible, standing beside their expensive cars, before wandering almost reluctantly over to the entrance to the new school.

Without doubt, the car rental firms were doing a roaring trade tonight, and never before had the Portobello High School produced such an amazing crop of actors.

As Willy Thomson sauntered into the car park after getting off the Lothian bus, he whistled as he saw all the cars lined up. Before he went home that night, he was going to have a fair old time with his house key!

Just inside the school entrance, the foyer was chock-a-bloc with air-kisses, hugs and high-fives. People who had never ever really liked each other where hugging and kissing, and almost immediately begun to jostle and reposition themselves in a new 'Post-Reunion' hierarchy of students.

Sadly, for many, the past twenty-five years seemed to vanish in the blinking of an eye, and old-feelings, insecurities and emotions resurfaced as if from nowhere. All their successes, all the therapy and all the education so many had gone through to better themselves in life, were quickly superseded or swept aside by the comments of their peers. Within minutes, the old school order was being reimposed, and everyone was once again a pupil back at school: a geek, a swat, a bully, a tart, a clart, a hack, teacher's pet, a perfect Prefect, Head Boy, Head Girl.

Friends who were actually once friends quickly gathered at the bar, and were friends once more. Those who had few friends, began to circulate in the main hall, looking for others like them, who were lost and desperately seeking some form of post-school validation.

Stuart Nisbet watched it all, standing just inside the main hall, but having crossed the demarcation line from the foyer into the main event.

He was one of the very few who had cycled to get here, and for now, probably also one of the very few who was genuinely unphased by all the social complexities and shenanigans which were going on around him.

He wasn't judging anyone. Just observing.

Until his 'epiphany' – for want of a better word to describe the weird self-realisation that had overcome him just a few hours earlier, he'd been planning the same as most of the others: how to impress everyone else, and how to best make others regret any negative comments they'd made about him when he was at school.

Stuart was fascinated by what was now happening.

True, in the first moments, the veneer of the last quarter century was swiftly blown away, and old social values resurfaced and were reestablished, but what was happening next was truly brilliant.

People HAD changed. After school, everyone had gone in different directions. Their values had evolved. Their likes, their dislikes. The words they used, their mannerism. Who they were.

They were all different.

So, it came as no surprise to Stuart that as the evening progressed, he saw some people who were initially immediately thrown back into their prior selves, actually emerge from their old ways, and walk away from their pasts.

After initially standing by some of their school heroes, or bullies, or friends, some pupils realised that they were no longer 'pupils' or their former selves. And they saw that the old school bully who had always scared them was now still tiny, or smelled terrible, or even that previous school heroes were actually cowards, or boring, or that friends who once were, were now no longer friends, simply because they no longer had anything in common. As a result, as the boredom set in, or the initial attractions slowly vapourised, and previous heroes became today's fools, some people just began to walk away from others.

A new group of people formed in the big hall, who joined the lost souls of earlier, and they too began to circulate, and mingle, and attract and detract others.

New relationships were formed: numbers, email addresses, Facebook, Instagram, WhatsApp numbers were swapped.

The old world order was turned upside down, and a brave new world was formed.

The beautiful thing about it all was that, without saying much about his past successes, without having arrived in one of the most expensive cars in Scotland, and without anyone realising what he was or who he had become, some of the other pupils he recognised saw him, greeted him, and stopped to talk with him.

Casual conversations were had.

Stories were exchanged.

Memories were shared.

After an hour of just experiencing the Reunion for what it was, Stuart decided to do something positive.

There was someone he wanted to meet.

The New Portobello High School
At the Bar
20.46

Barry Quinn stood at the bar, waiting for his turn to get a fresh round of drinks for himself and two of his friends.

Stupidly though, he couldn't drink, because he'd decided to drive the Boxster after all.

Irene had sworn there would be no sex for a month, and she was busy getting drunk with her usual friends, and several people Barry couldn't remember at all, but whom Irene had recognised at once and for whom she'd immediately abandoned Barry.

Not only did Irene now think that Barry was a prat of the largest magnitude but Barry also knew that she was right. He'd spent almost a grand hiring the Boxster for one day, thinking it would really set him apart from the others and get everyone saying, '*Wow… is that Barry driving the Porsche? He must have done well!*'. As it had transpired though, there were another two Boxsters in the car park, seven sports cars, and ten top-end elite cars.

Everyone had had the same idea as him, and far from bragging about it at the bar, those who'd been stupid enough to rent a flash car, were now disowning them as fast as possible.

What a bloody waste of money!

On top of that, both of his friends were giving him a really hard time over the Boxster. The number of flash cars in the car park was the second biggest topic of conversation so far this evening, second only to the video of the man falling of the old school building's roof. When Barry had admitted that one of the Boxsters was his, they'd almost wet themselves laughing. He'd only offered them a drink each to shut them up and give him a chance to escape.

They were both good mates. They'd stayed friends since school, but Barry didn't want to just hang out with them tonight. He wanted to 'mingle'. To see who else was here.

And to find Fiona Lewis.

He also wanted to catch Paul Bentford before his wife did, and then keep an eye on him for the rest of the evening.

While he waited for the drinks to come, Barry thought about the slow dance with Fiona all those years ago. He'd touched many breasts since then, but for some reason, he would never forget that fleeting second when he managed to touch Fiona's nipple, before she'd pushed his hand away.

From that moment forward, Dire Straits, Fiona Lewis and her right breast had been connected in time, and branded indelibly on his mind.

Barry was just beginning to ponder, for the hundredth time that day, just what the possibility of another dance with her might be, and were it to happen, could there possibly, *perhaps*, be a chance of recreating that wonderful moment from all those years ago?

"Barry Quinn?" A voice suddenly caught him unawares from behind, dragging him back from his daydream. "Is that you?"

Barry turned, recognising the voice immediately, and feeling a surge of panic traverse its way up and down his spine. It was the voice of Peter Black. One of the people Barry least wanted to see this evening.

As he spun around, there was a microsecond of confusion when Barry found no one behind him, but immediately realised that by looking down, - quite far – Peter Black was there, after all.

He had hardly grown at all.

The man was bloody tiny.

"Peter?" Barry questioned himself aloud.

"Aye, that's me. Barry, I recognised you immediately! You haven't changed at all!" Peter said, his eyes lighting up and seeming genuinely pleased to see Barry.

"Neither have you. You've not changed either!" Barry replied. Meaning every word.

Peter moved forward to give Barry a man hug, but Barry was quick enough to thrust out his hand and avert the impending disaster.

"How's life? What have you been up to?" Barry asked, dreading what he was about to hear. Peter had always made Barry feel like a piece of shit. Not by bullying him, really, but just by being so positive about his plans, and all the things he'd wanted to do with his life. Barry didn't have any plans. And hadn't done anything.

"Not much, actually." Peter replied. "Just surviving really, I suppose. And you?"

Barry shrugged his shoulders back.

"Me? Nothing, really. I still just live around the corner from the old secondary school. I've done the same job for the past twenty years. And I'm married with two kids." Barry glanced across at the barman. Where were his drinks?

"Two kids? Wow, that's great." Peter smiled. "I'm jealous. What're their names?"

"Gregor, and Derek. Two boys. Grown up now, one's in third year at Edinburgh Uni, and the other is on a gap year, but going to St. Andrew's next year."

"Both at Uni? That's brilliant! You've done really well."

"Not just me," Barry replied, smiling. "Me and Irene. She's a great mum."

"What, Irene Gillespie?"

"Yes. You remember her?"

"Too right. She was one of the best catches in the year. Bloody hell, Barry. You've done brilliant. I'm really jealous."

"Why? How's things gone for you?"

Just then the drinks arrived.

"Listen, can you hang on a second, I'll just take these two drinks over to my friends, and I'll be straight back."

A moment later, Barry Quinn returned to speak with Peter Black. Voluntarily.

Ten minutes later, Barry began to realise, perhaps for the first time in his life, just how lucky he actually was.

Unlike Peter, he'd never had testicular cancer.

Unlike Peter, his wife had not run off with another man.

Unlike Peter, who'd desperately wanted kids and couldn't have any, Barry'd had two.

And unlike Peter who'd got a high-pressure job in London, just as he'd always planned to, but who'd then hated almost every day of having to commute three hours a day in and out of London, and who was bored to tears with his work, Barry quite liked his job.

Barry's life, it was beginning to seem, was not so bad after all!

The New Portobello High School
At the Bar
21.05

Fiona Lewis was surrounded by a quorum of giggling 'girls' in the large hall of the new modern secondary school. They were standing in front of a row of tables stretching down one length of the hall, all covered in memorabilia from their days at school, behind which were large boards covered in things stuck to them with pins. There was a lot to see, covering school concerts, sports events and achievements, school musicals put on over the years, news articles about the school, details on school trips abroad: photographs, posters, school prizes, news articles, programmes from the school musicals, large collective pictures of all the pupils in the different years of the school standing in rows, some standing on long wooden banks in the back row, others sitting down in the front row, cross-legged.

There was a board covered with articles on ex-pupils and their achievements in the outside world since graduating: scientists, businessmen, teachers, professors, senior positions in Scottish government, one Member of Parliament.

There was also one board covered with Obituaries of former pupils from their years. Fiona had found this a little morbid, but also very sad. It was constantly surrounded by groups of people chatting and pointing at the pictures.

There were also tears from some who were surprised and shocked to find that an old friend was no longer with them and wouldn't be coming this evening.

Outside the school in the carpark, McKenzie had summoned a quick meeting of his team and the three members of the armed support team. As requested, apart from one, the rest were in civvies. Wishart had thought long and hard about whether there should be any detectable police presence there that evening, but had in the end decided – after talking with the organisers – that they didn't want to alarm anyone unduly. They had agreed a compromise: one visible armed police officer, sitting outside the school in a police car belonging to the armed response team. He was still there, looking ominous, and not welcome at that point in this impromptu meeting.

His presence there was mentioned at the start of the evening in the opening address from the stage in the hall, and had been excused as a necessary precaution for all public meetings taking place in Edinburgh at that time, due to the heightened state of security alert as a result of the Queen's state visit.

Everyone had bought it and seemed unconcerned. However, if the serial killer was amongst them, it was hoped that the armed presence would be a strong deterrent.

"So, has anyone got anything? Any leads? Any thoughts?" he asked the team.

To any passer-by, McKenzie knew they would appear just like a bunch of friends having a drink and smoke outside in the fresh air. They wouldn't warrant a second glance.

No one had anything. Yet.

"Everyone's talking about the video, but as you would expect, no one is aware of who it is or that there was a second death as well. So far, it's an unfortunate suicide. Possibly a school pupil who chose the day to make a statement to everyone attending here tonight. Or possibly just a coincidence." Wishart said.

"Okay, but keep digging. Try to find out casually if anyone had any thoughts about the best or worst teachers in 1993. Or before. Or even after. Any thoughts about Blake or Weir. Or even McRae would be good. Positives or negatives. Grudges, misdemeanours, anything that makes them stand out. And if so, any other names that could be connected with them."

McKenzie knew he was preaching to the converted, and eggs and sucking came to mind, so with no new thoughts coming forward, he was about to dismiss them, when Lynch spoke.

"I was speaking with McLeish just before I left home tonight. We're both still really bothered about something. Not only how did the killer get the body into the school, but how did the killer get them *to* the school. And the cross. You can't just turn up outside the school in a car, offload two people, and a cross, and not raise any suspicions from passers-by. And even before you get the victims to the school, how do you stop others seeing them in the car?"

"A blacked-out car, or a van?" Anderson suggested.

"Yep, something like that. And when did the killer bring them? At the same time, or one at a time?"

McKenzie nodded. He'd been thinking about this already.

"Great thoughts. I've already got Dean looking at CCTV feeds. I'll ask him to expand his search to vans or large cars acting suspiciously or caught repetitively in the neighbourhood of the school. The question is when should he look at? What time frame? Until we can narrow down a timeframe it's probably too much to ask for. At the moment it's only Dean, and he's focussing on the area around Weir's flat in Leith. This is madness. We need more people on this."

Everyone nodded.

"Okay, point noted. Something we need to progress further. For now, everyone get back in there. Mingle. Listen. Discover. Got it?"

He was just about to clap his hands together, but thought better of it. Instead he smiled at them all.

Everyone headed back inside.

"Fiona? Fiona Lewis? Is that you?"

A man's voice. Strangely familiar. It immediately tickled the memory banks, but it didn't trigger anything fast enough before she turned around and found herself face-to-face with Barry Quinn.

She smiled, and laughed out loud, a little nervously. Another blast from the past. This one perhaps not the most welcome of all.

"Fiona McKenzie, now." She smiled. "Barry, how are you?"

She saw his eyes scan down, taking in Little Bump, and for a brief moment she registered what she could only think was a disappointment in his eyes.

Which was true. Barry couldn't believe how attractive Fiona still looked, but in the smallest instant of time possible, as soon as he saw how large Fiona was at the front, he knew that his outrageous fantasy of possibly snogging Fiona on the dance floor and having a quick 'feel-up' as they used to call it as teenagers, had gone from being not only extremely, *incredibly* unlikely to just plain impossible.

He couldn't climb over *that* to get near her, even if he tried.

"Congratulations!" Barry exclaimed, the disappointment in his voice ruining all his attempts to sound enthusiastically surprised.

"Thank you." Fiona smiled, acknowledging his acknowledgment.

"So… how have you been? How's life treated you since school?" Barry asked, moving on, and surprising himself with the sincerity with which he transitioned into the normal mode of questioning for that evening. 'Okay, so Plan A's not happening,' he said to himself, 'but I do actually want to know about her life.'

"Good. University. At Durham. Then some years in London working as an editor in a publishing house in London. Then I moved back up to Edinburgh and started working in a publishing house here. I still do it, sort of freelance."

"Wow. You always loved to read. You were the local book worm!" Barry remembered.

"A few years back I got married, and now we're just about to have Little Bump."

"Boy or girl?"

"It'll be a surprise. We prefer it that way. And you?"

Barry hesitated. This was the bit he was dreading. He had nothing impressive to say.

"I always loved Edinburgh, and could never really face moving away, so I just stayed. I married Irene Gillespie. Do you remember her?"

"Wow. Yes. Congratulations! She was a real catch."

She seemed genuinely happy for him.

Barry felt a warmth inside himself. He'd had this conversation several times this evening so far and everyone always lit up when he talked of Irene, several quite honestly saying that she was a real catch and joking that he'd obviously been punching above his weight.

"Kids?" she asked, her hand stroking the surface of her own huge bump.

"Two… " Barry replied, before launching into an explanation of who his children were. He spoke with genuine pride for them, and even showed Fiona some photos on his phone.

Barry talked of his life since school. Irene. His job. His house. This time all a little more positively than he'd ever described them before.

A sudden feeling of guilt descended upon him. It dawned on him then just stupid he was, and also what a dishonest bastard he was, for fantasising like he had about trying to snog Fiona tonight. Irene had been brilliant to him. And this was how he'd treated her.

"And where is Irene?" Fiona asked.

"Good question," Barry replied, scanning the room urgently.

"Oh, there she is… I think that's her. Over there, talking to Paul Bentford." Fiona pointed across the room.

A sudden quiver of panic shot through Barry as he turned and saw Irene and Paul together. It looked like he was just about to lead her to the dance floor, in response to the band just starting up.

"Fiona, sorry, I'd better go… " Barry started to excuse himself.

What happened next both surprised and pleased Barry.

Fiona reached out and touched him on his arm. At the same time, she leant forward and kissed him gently on the side of the cheek.

"It was a pleasure to see you again, Barry. Good luck! You're a very lucky man. You've been one of the successful ones, obviously. Say 'Hi' to Irene for me."

Barry paused.

Smiled.

And grew up.

He'd been an ungrateful hypocritical, disrespectful prat.

Seconds later he was heading over to Irene to save his marriage, a curious mix of fear and anger surging within him.

Irene Quinn was his, and there's was no way that Paul Bentford was going to cop a quick feel with his wife on the dance floor!

Chapter 17

The New Portobello High School
Saturday
21.15

Willy Thomson hovered on the edge of the dance floor, scanning the faces of everyone to see if there was anyone who he might call a friend. Or for Scott Davies.

He'd recognised quite a few people, but no one that he had anything in common with. He'd also noticed that most people chose not to see him. He'd seen the recognition in their eyes that he existed, but as soon as they clocked him, their eyes diverted in the other direction, or looked through him to an imaginary point beyond.

The only positive to be taken from it all was that people remembered him. Obviously, he'd made an impression on them all those years before, and that impression still remained today.

Surely that was a good thing?

He'd taught them to respect him then, and obviously they still did.

At school, Will had not been the school bully.

There had been a strict pecking order, where a lesser bully looked up to the one above. Typically, the older bullies in the years above were highest in the ranking, but Willy had been different.

Even in his second year of secondary school, with still another two years to go before he could legally leave, and with four years of pupils above him, Willy had been considered the third bully in the school.

People were scared of him.

He was a rough fighter.

And unlike the animal kingdom where most animals didn't fight battles which they might lose in case they got injured and could die from an infection of their wounds, Willy was different. Willy simply 'didn't give a fuck'.

He often fought even when he knew he would lose. Just for the kudos of trying.

For a perverted sense of entertainment.

And to gain respect.

Willy had been fighting all his life.

Life was a battle, after all.

Survival of the fittest.

Before coming this evening, Willy had wondered if he might see Grant Patterson tonight. Or Scott Davies.

Grant had been the No. 1 school bully. Scott had been the second.

Standing on the edge, watching everyone else dance and have fun, Willy was excited.

He was looking for Scott Davies for a reason.

According to the pictures on one of the boards on the edge of the hall – it was a list of former pupils who had kicked the bucket since leaving school – Grant Patterson was now dead. He'd died several years back. There was a newspaper article pinned up, saying he was found dead full of bullet holes. Shot dead in connection with some drug stuff.

Willy had smiled when he'd read that. It meant that he'd just gone up the pecking order. He was now the No 2 Bully.

And if Scott Davies was not around - maybe if he'd been killed too - then that would make him No 1!

Willy couldn't see him even though he'd been looking.

As he stood scanning the crowd, Willy started to feel really edgy. It was the anticipation. He didn't like it.

He needed something to take the edge of it.

His fingers nervously felt the packet in his pocket, which was calling his name.

He'd wanted to keep it till later, to take just before he did what he'd really come here to do this evening.

Maybe he should take it now though. A quick visit to the toilets.

A quick snort.

Then he'd feel brilliant.

And if he did meet Scott Davies, perhaps, he'd take care of him tonight too.

Yeah, that was a good plan.

Willy nodded to himself, smiled, and turned to go and find the bogs.

Almost immediately he bumped into a tall, well-built man in a casual suit standing behind him. Willy was forced to look up into his face to see who it was. A set of perfect white teeth and a tanned face greeted him back.

"Good grief! It's Wee Willy!" the man said.

Willy's fists clenched. No bastard ever called him Wee Willy and got away with it. Willy's willy wasn't wee. It was massive… At school people had stopped daring to call him that, thanks to the lessons he'd dealt out to anyone who had.

Looking up at this guy in front of him though, Willy wondered if he'd be able to give this guy a kicking or not. He wasn't only tall, but he was obviously very fit.

"You don't recognise me, do you, wee Willy?"

"Dinnae call me that, pal."

"Or what?" the man smiled back.

"I'll *do* you."

The man laughed.

"You and whose army?"

Willy's mind froze. The expression the man had used immediately recalled memories.

"I wondered if you'd remember that, *Wee* Willy."

"Dinna CALL me that, ya bampot!" Willy threatened again, squaring his shoulders and trying to be as tall as possible. "And no, I canna remember who the hell you are. Should I?"

"Scott Davies."

Willy froze.

"What? Scott Davies? Ye canna be. He wis small and fat!"

"Yes, about twenty-five years ago. People grow up. Well, not everyone. You didn't, did you, *Wee* Willy?"

"Scott? What happened to you? You're massive!" Willy asked, now genuinely in awe of how one person could change so much. He looked nothing like the Scott Davies he'd remembered.

"Fancy a drink, Wee Willy? Do you want to go to the bar?" Scott asked, surprising Willy altogether.

"Aye... actually, aye, that wid be braw."

They left the noisy hall and the dance music playing over the speakers and made their way to the bar in one of the rooms at the back.

"Vodka, whisky or beer? Or all three?" Scott asked.

"All three, if you're serious!" Willy laughed.

"In one glass, or three?"

Willy thought about it for a second.

"One. It's a party, isn't it?"

"Ah... so it's Mad Wee Willy, then. Not just 'Wee'."

Willy hesitated.

"I was just joking. Gees a beer."

"*Please*?"

"Aye, please."

Scott got two beers and then moved across the bar area to a table and sat down.

"Did you hear about Grant?" Willy asked, lifting up the beer and 'cheersing' Scott's bottle by banging it on the bottom.

"Yep. What a waste. Stupid bastard. So, how are you Willy, what are you up to?"

"You know, surviving. Apart from that, nothing special. And you? Are you still up to no good? I haven't heard about you in years. I thought you might have gone inside, or something."

"You thought I'd been sent down. To jail?"

"Aye."

"Far from it. I thought you knew... "

"Knew what?"

"I left school, gave up pissing around, and decided to make a go of my life. No more messing around, or hanging around with neds like you."

"I'm no a ned."

"Course you are. But's it's still possible to change. If I managed to, so can you!"

"What do you mean?"

"I mean, I gave up being a loser, and became a winner."

"How?" Willy laughed. "Life ain't that simple, mate."

"I never said it was simple, Willy. I just said I did it."

"So, what was this big thing you did then? How did you '*change*' your life?" Willy asked, mimicking two big inverted commas in the air when he said the word change.

"My dad convinced me that I needed to get a trade. You and me obviously weren't the brains of the school back then, but that didn't mean we were stupid, did it? It just meant we weren't good at school stuff. So I left, got an apprenticeship and became a plumber. Then after working for other plumbers for years, I realised that instead of working for others, it would be better if I could get others working for me. So I quit, set up 'Portobello Plumbers' and I've never looked back!"

"What?" Willy's jaw dropped. He couldn't believe what he was hearing. "You OWN PORTOBELLO PLUMBING?"

"Yes."

"But that's massive. You're bloody everywhere... I was in Glasgow last year, and I saw the adverts everywhere... !"

"Yep. We've got forty shops and plumbing centres across Scotland and the North of England. And we're expanding south."

"You must be bloody minted!" Willy couldn't believe his ears.

"I am." Scott replied, without blinking, or smiling.

Just a simple acknowledgement of the truth.

"Shit... that's amazing."

"Why, Willy? Why's it amazing?"

"Because... "

"Because you and I were no-hopers? Stupid-wee-bastards that everyone else had given up on? Listen to me, Willy,... " Scott said, leaning forward and resting his hand upon Willy's. "In this life, you can have anything you want. Anything. If you work hard, are willing to learn, and you're no afraid to take some gambles along the way. As long as you don't stop believing in yourself, you can do anything you want."

Willy was silent. Something amazing had happened to Scott Davies. The guy oozed power and charisma and wealth. And with his hand resting lightly on his, Willy felt a strange, intense intimacy that was really unsettling him to his core. Scott was speaking not to Willy, but right into him. Messing with his mind. Stirring up the emotions deep inside him.

Challenging him.

"Willy, I know what you're thinking. But don't think like that. No man is a loser. He loses ONLY if he wants to. One man, any man, no matter what background he comes from, can change the world. Think of all the world's greatest leaders. They were just simple men, from simple backgrounds. Then they rose, became better versions of themselves, and became leaders of men. They changed, and became great. And so can you, Willy. So can *you*!"

Willy shivered. He pulled his hand away from under Scott's, and stood up.

He suddenly felt really uncomfortable.

"What are you doing? Are you gay or something?"

Scott laughed.

"See that woman over there at the bar, surrounded by those men? That's my wife. She was Miss Scotland five years ago. Now she's the mother of my two children."

"Wow... " Willy uttered, glancing across at the most lovely woman he'd ever seen.

"Okay, Willy, it was nice to see you." Scott said, pushing back in his chair, standing up and taking another drink of the beer. He put it back down on the table. The bottle was only half-empty.

"You going?" Willy replied, suddenly feeling that he didn't want Scot to leave.

"Got to. Sorry. I need to do the rounds and talk with a few others. Listen, I wanted to see you tonight, Willy. I remember you. And I wanted to say something to you. Everyone deserves a second chance. Everyone. And no one is ever too old to learn. I believe that. I'm recruiting for my apprenticeship scheme. It's a special scheme to give back to the community. I'm offering a second chance to people who have the balls to take their life and turn it around. Who believe in themselves."

"What are you saying? I don't understand!" Willy shook his head, suddenly feeling under pressure.

"You still think you're a loser Willy. Always have, and still do. But I think there's something more in you than that. You just need a good break and some support and encouragement. I've got a team of people who can help you become more than you are. If you want."

"Become what?"

"A plumber. Get a trade, Willy. Learn to work with your hands and your brain. And then take charge of your own future!"

Scott was holding out his hand. He was offering him a business card.

"Think about it, Willy. And if you're willing to make a fresh start, willing to learn and willing to work HARD, then call this number. Someone will take care of you, and you won't regret it."

Willy took the card and stared at it.

His hands were shaking.

"Okay, well, I've said my piece, Willy. The rest is up to you. I wish you well!"

And with that, Scott smiled, turned and walked away towards Miss Scotland, who'd broken off from those lusting around her, and was now waiting attentively for her husband to join her.

Willy just stood there, gawping after them, his jaw wide open.

A moment later, the crowds of ex-pupils closed around Scott and his wife and and they were gone.

When Willy sat back down in his chair, he was shaking.

He tried to swallow but found he couldn't.

Ten minutes later, he was still just sitting here.

Emotionally a wreck. Feeling vulnerable. Overpowered. And challenged.

The past ten minutes had been the most intense in his life.

Wee Willy had just been offered a chance to become Big Willy.

To shake off his past life, and reach for a new life in the future.

For the first time in his life, Willy was really scared.

Chapter 18

The New Portobello High School
Saturday
21.45

"Hi Everybody!" the voice boomed from the stage at the end of the hall. "Can I ask one of the stewards at the back to round up everyone from the bar and the foyer and bring them in here? It's time for a few wee speeches. And then, afterwards, we'll introduce the surprise band for this evening, and we'll start rocking the rest of the night away!"

The hall immediately started to fill up with the people from the bar, and soon all eyes were on the speaker on the stage.

"My name is Sofia Waterson. I'm head of the organising committee for this evening. It's been years in planning, but it's paid off. I can't believe we've got so many ex-pupils back here from 1991-1993 all at the same time. I hope you're all meeting up with old friends, and having a great time!"

"Okay, so before I invite the organising committee up on stage for a quick round of applause, I do want to acknowledge the incredible sponsorship we received for this evening which actually all came from the generosity of one man. He's an ex-pupil of the school who's become a great success. You can see on the posters and the advertising that it's all come from Ben Venue Capital Assets, and originally the owner had agreed to come up here and make a speech to you all and announce the surprise band for this evening, but earlier this evening he changed his mind. He said, and I quote, *'This event is not about any one person, it's about everyone here. About the school and the pupils.'* So, he's chosen to remain anonymous and not take any credit for this evening. Frankly, I've been blown away by his generosity. Not only has he agreed to cover ALL costs for this evening, but he's also agreed to pay for another event next year, for all the pupils from 1994 to 1996! Now, one last thing about the generosity of this man which I know *is* going to blow you away and make you cheer wildly and give him a huge round of applause – whoever he really is - is that once the band starts playing, it's going to be an open bar. In other words, drinks will be on the house!"

There was suddenly a huge cheer and as predicted, a wild round of applause.

At the back of the hall, Stuart Nisbet joined in with everyone else.

"Okay, but before you rush back to the bar, I also want to say thanks to the organising committee, now assembled in front of you. You might recognise a few friends and familiar faces."

Sofia gestured to a line of people who'd made their way quietly up on to the stage. She then ran through a few names, noting their responsibilities and asking for a token show of appreciation. Several rounds of applause ensued.

"Okay, now I would like to invite one of our old teachers up on to the stage to say a few words and introduce the band. We did ask the headmaster from 1991-1993 to come and say something this evening but he couldn't make it. He sends his regards. Instead, I'd like to hand you over to Jason McIntosh, who you know taught maths to most of us."

She gestured to a man in front of the stage and he walked up a few wooden steps and took to the microphone.

"Wow. I can't believe tonight. What a fantastic event. Personally, I'm finding it all a bit emotional. So many faces that I've recognised. But they're not just faces. They're success stories. I am so proud to have taught at Portobello High School. In my opinion, probably the best Secondary School in the whole of Scotland!"

There was a spontaneous outburst of cheers and massive applause.

When it died down, Jason went on to give an emotional speech about the opportunities that the old school had given everyone, how it had helped change and form lives, turning children into valuable members of society. Creating happiness. Creating opportunities. Creating successful people with the right attitudes in today's society.

The speech touched all those who listened, and many of those in the audience found themselves with wet eyes, and tears rolling down their cheeks.

Everyone who listened to Jason speak, agreed with everything he said.

Everyone apart from one person.

Willy Thomson stood at the back of the hall, nursing a whisky, and seething with anger and hate.

The bastard on the stage in front was top of Willy's list for a doing. Before Willy had come, he'd made a mental list of three names as candidates for the main activity Willy had enthusiastically planned for later this evening.

Although there were a lot of former teachers milling around, two of the teachers he'd marked for personal revenge didn't seem to have turned up.

Only one had.

And he was now standing on the stage in front of him.

Spouting drivel and talking a right pile of shite.

But as he listened to him drone, Willy's anger was conflicted.

He was confused.

He was glad to see Jason McIntosh, and relished the opportunity which he now had to definitely take revenge and to kill the bastard later that evening.

However, since talking to Scott, his mind had been all over the place.

Scott had offered him help.

A new future.

An opportunity which Willy instinctively knew would never come again.

Willy had a shit life.

But Scott's words and offer had really inspired him.

As Willy watched and listened to Jason McIntosh continue to talk, his mind went round and round.

"Do I kill the bastard and get the ultimate street cred I deserve, or do I let the bastard live and accept the help Scott offered?"

The whisky didn't help make his thinking much clearer, either. For a moment he considered stopping with the drink. But the words 'free' resounded in his mind.

For Willy this was turning into a truly amazing night of opportunity.

An opportunity of a new life, as much drink as he could swallow, and the chance to kill one of the teachers who Willy blamed more than all the others for being personally responsible for Willy's especially fucked up life!

"Okay, that's enough from me. Now I know it's the moment a lot of you've been waiting for… " Jason began to round his speech of. "I was going to do it myself, but then I just saw Loudon Galloway standing down there… who was Head Boy in 1993! Let me invite him up here to introduce the band… "

There was a small moment of confusion as the running order of the speeches was changed, and the 'big announcement' was delayed once again, but then within a few seconds, the old Head Boy of Portobello High School in 1993 was up on stage and everyone was cheering.

Sadly, the years had not been good to Loudon Galloway. Once a fit, handsome man popular with everyone in the year, and voted for as much for his looks as his personality, the man on stage was now fat, bald, and so drunk he could hardly speak.

He managed to say a few almost unintelligible words, before mentioning the name of a band which everyone immediately recognised.

"Runrig!"

Everyone went wild.

How on earth the school Reunion committee had managed to book what was one of the biggest bands in Scotland in 1993 and was still popular today, was incredible.

A moment later, the band burst out onto the stage, picked up their waiting instruments, and everyone went crazy.

An already good evening had just got ten times better!

Stuart Nisbet smiled to himself. He'd done the right thing. Three times.

From the way everyone had reacted, calling on a few personal favours and pulling a few strings in order to book Runrig had obviously been the right thing to do.

That was the first thing.

The second decision had been a long time coming, actually.

He'd called up his two girlfriends and suggested they shouldn't see each other anymore.

Stuart knew they weren't real girlfriends. He had been interested in just one thing from them, and in return, they had wanted just one thing from him.

Originally, he had imagined turning up here tonight with both of them on his arms, each of them looking stunning, and wearing clothes which showed of all the assets they had.

Stuart was after all, an expert asset manager.

Somehow however, that plan now just seemed totally superficial. And wrong. So Stuart had axed it. And them.

The third decision was even better.

When he'd originally approached the organising committee and offered to sponsor the Reunion Ball, it was because he'd wanted to get as much publicity as possible for himself. For a long time, he'd dreamt about standing on the stage and bragging about how his company had been the only sponsor for the evening, and how his personal success had enabled him to splash the cash in order to make everyone else happy. The whole thing had been about him, and his plan to show off. To tell the world how great he was.

Earlier that afternoon though, everything had changed.

Everything.

Now, he knew that his original plan had been wrong.

None of this was about him.

And making it about him would be pointless. Wrong. Stupid.

Something *had* changed in Stuart earlier that afternoon. Something fundamental.

Exactly what, he didn't know.

Who he had changed to, he didn't recognise.

Who he would become, was exciting, but unknown.

Stuart knew that he'd been lucky in life. But instead of rubbing other people's noses in his personal success, how much better would it be if he used his success to help others?

Earlier that day, Stuart had realised that the pursuit of *wealth* did not make anyone happy. It was the hard work en route which did. It was the journey, not the destination.

Stuart also realised that although he had so much, he also had so little.

If he offered to share what he had, perhaps he could persuade others to share with him, some of what they had?

His thoughts were not yet perfectly formed, he admitted to himself, but they were ... *interesting*.

The others around him, most of whom were very poor, seemed to be a lot happier than he was. Almost everything that he wanted and still lacked, they had. So how could he boast that *he* had so much, when in comparison, he felt he had so little?

He had nothing to show off to them.

They on the other hand had a lot to show off to him.

"Penny for your thoughts?"

A woman's voice. Soft and gentle.

Stuart turned to his right, and was met by two beautiful green eyes, level with his own.

"You probably don't remember me, Stuart, but I remember you. You owe me 50p."

Stuart laughed, and screwed his face up in an obvious effort to try and remember the name of his creditor.

"And that's not to mention the interest, which I think probably comes to about £3000, at the extortionate rate of interest which you agreed to." Her eyes twinkled when she laughed.

"Sonya?"

"No!" the woman hit him playfully on his arm. "Marie McDonald. I sat in front of you in the German class in second year, and you were always flicking rubber bands into my hair. And you borrowed 50p one day to catch the No 5 bus into town, but never paid it back."

Slowly recognition dawned on Stuart. A faint memory of a rather spotty, gangly girl about thirteen years old, with the same infectious laugh.

"Marie?" Stuart turned around to face her full on, his body language now transformed.

For a second he considered reaching for his wallet and pulling out the pretentious wad of notes he always carried, and offering to make a settlement on the money he owed her. But he stopped short of doing it, remembering that such ostentatious behaviour was now consigned to his former self.

"Wow. You've changed. A lot." Stuart stumbled. "And I mean for the better."

"For the better? So, you mean I was a horrible toad before, small and ugly… ?"

"No, I mean, that… " Stuart started to dig a hole for himself, then decided to go for it. "Actually, yes, I do mean that. The last I can remember of you in German class, you were small and toad-like… " he said, smiling, "but now… wow… you've turned into a beautiful princess. Presumably because some handsome prince, now your husband, has kissed you?"

Marie blushed slightly, and Stuart found her reaction strangely endearing.

"I don't believe in fairy tales. At least, not ones like that."

"So, there's no husband or kids?" Stuart asked, rather forwardly.

"No. Not yet. But I do have about ninety children."

Marie watched the reaction on his face, and laughed again.

"It's a long story." She added.

"I'd like to hear it. Can I get you a drink from the bar? And perhaps we could sit down in the Chill-Out Zone next door away from the band. I used to love this music, but for some reason, just now I'd rather listen to Marie McDonald than them."

It was a little bit forward, Stuart knew, but it came out before he could stop himself.

Marie's eye twinkled again in the disco lights which were now sweeping the dance-floor, and for a moment Stuart saw a rush of thoughts pass through her mind. A moment's hesitation.

Followed by a nod.

And a smile.

"But you're paying. After all, you owe me £3000."

Chapter 19

The Dungeon
Saturday
22.45

Mark McRae staggered to his feet and held out his hands in obedience to the commands just issued to him. The Indian stood in front of him, threatening Mark with the cattle prod.

"I'm going to put this blindfold back on you. The other guy doesn't need it anymore and you can have it again. Then I'll unshackle you from the pipes, and we're going to go for a walk. If you try anything, I'll use this and then bring you back here, and leave you alone for a week. Do you understand me?"

The Indian's voice was deep, and as he listened to every word he said, Mark desperately tried to place it. Surely he knew the man? Why on earth would a stranger be treating him like this?

Try as he might though, Mark couldn't place it.

Mark took a few steps forward and then stumbled. He felt so weak.

"Water… " he tried to utter, hoping that his captor would take some form of pity on him, and let him drink something.

"What did you say? Did you just try to speak with me?" the Indian bellowed.

Mark was desperate for water, but the imminent threat of the cattle prod being used again drove him to shake his head instead. Silently. With no further effort to speak.

"Just in case, I'm going to put a gag in your mouth." The Indian said, then pulled a cloth out a pocket, and forced it roughly into Mark's mouth.

Then, a moment later, the blindfold was once again thrust onto his head and the world went black. He felt a tug on his hands as the chain around his wrists was yanked several times, and Mark realised that he was free from the pipe, although the handcuffs still held his wrists tightly together.

He felt a push from behind, and he stumbled forward, a powerful hand catching him by the elbow just as he worried he would fall forward onto his face.

"Watch out for the steps. You'll go up them slowly, and I'll guide you forward. It's about a ten-minute walk, and then we'll have some more stairs. You won't make a sound. If you try to talk, cough, or even fart, I'll stick this cattle prod so far up your backside, I'll fry your kidneys from the inside out. Do you get me?"

Mark nodded.

Then he started to inch his way forward towards the ladder.

Fear once again started to course its way through his veins.

A cold, silent fear that engulfed him and amplified itself with every step he took.

A few days before he'd watched the other two leave, just like this.

Neither had come back.

McKenzie watched his wife with admiration as he saw her mingle with the other old pupils of the school.

She seemed to have many friends, and those she spoke with seemed genuinely pleased to see her again.

McKenzie also couldn't keep his eyes of Little Bump. It was growing every day, and standing on the side of the dance floor, watching Fiona stroking her stomach, McKenzie felt incredibly proud and happy.

The past few months with Fiona had been brilliant.

A man could not have a better wife than her, and he knew it.

He was a very lucky man.

Unfortunately however, their investigations this evening were not being so 'lucky'. They were all drawing a blank.

Conversations about old teachers, and the antics that everyone used to get up to in school were all over the place. His team were finding it easy to drop Weir's or Blake's names into a conversation and fish for results, but so far, no one had volunteered any information or reason which could for one second, suggest a motive for an ex-pupil - or another teacher - to want to kill them.

Both teachers had been popular. Well liked. And seemingly very good at their jobs.

So far, the main reason for the team being here was drawing a huge blank.

McKenzie was beginning to feel like nothing was going to happen this evening. He was even tempted to let everyone relax and have a drink.

That thought was crushed, however, the moment he set eyes on Willy Thomson who'd just walked into the back of the main hall.

Slimy and as gormless looking as usual, McKenzie recognised him immediately. Willy and McKenzie had form together. He'd been one of McKenzie's first arrests, and they'd hated each other ever since.

Too late, Willy saw McKenzie approaching.

"So, William Thomson. What brings you to the ball tonight?"

"Went to Porty, didn't I? Got a right to be here."

"I can't believe what I'm hearing. William Thomson defending his right to be in a school? Without stealing anything?"

Almost as an afterthought McKenzie raised his eyebrows to question Willy.

"No. Ain't stolen nowt. I just wanted to be back at the school. See my mates an stuff."

"William, I'm sorry to have to break the news to you, but as far I can recall, you *'ain't got no mates!'*"

"Listen, Detective Superindependent McKenzie, or whatever you call yourself nowadays, I ain't done nothing, so back off. Leave me alone to enjoy the night, okay?"

McKenzie studied him for a second.

"Who were your favourite teachers at school, Willy?" McKenzie asked.

"Didn't have any. I weren't anyone's teacher's pet."

"Okay, so which teachers did you like the least. Even hate, maybe?"

"All of them."

"Any of them in particular?"

"Why?"

"Nope. They were all the same. Bastards all of them. They were all so full of themselves, and none o'them could teach for shit."

"In *your* opinion."

"Exactly."

"It's nothing personal, William Thomson, but you must admit that wherever you go, trouble is not far behind. So, I just want to say this to you, and I want you to listen hard. If there's any trouble tonight, if there's any fighting, if anyone's hurt, and particularly if any of the *teachers* are *hurt*, I'll be looking for you. You understand?"

Willy Thomson stared at DCI McKenzie.

It was almost as if he *knew*.

But how?

How did he know what Willy had been wanting to do tonight?

"See you, you've got me all wrong, DCI Bloody Pie-in-the-sky McKenzie! I've gone straight, I have. I'm getting myself a trade. And I'm gonna get rich. So bloody leave me alone and go find some real criminals!"

Willy had said the words without realising it, but once they were out, they excited him.

It seemed that tonight, the bloody universe was conspiring against him, trying to steer him onto a new track, forcing him down the path of the straight and narrow.

Obviously, any plans he'd had for sticking an old teacher later tonight would have to be put on ice for now. McKenzie would be after him in a second if anything bad happened. Plus, since he'd bumped into Scott Davies, he'd been unable to think of anything else except what they'd talked about.

It was quite exciting really. Tonight was the night that Willy Thomson's life was going to change.

Maybe in a few years he'd be able to come back to the next school Reunion and turn up in a fast car… a big red one… just like those that everyone else had brought with them tonight.

Willy Thomson smiled at the thought.

Yep, the future was looking so bright, he needed sun glasses!

Saturday
22.55

McKenzie's phone buzzed in his pocket, and after checking the caller display, he apologised to Fiona and the couple she'd just introduced him to, and hurried outside into the foyer.

"Guv, hi, it's DI Dean. You told me to call you on your mobile if I got anything."

"Fraser, it's almost eleven? Are you still at it?"

"Yes, Guv."

"It's appreciated. Thanks. So, what have you got then?" McKenzie was impressed, and grateful. The man had been watching CCTV images for hours, and should have knocked off ages ago.

"A white van. Seen twice at the school today on the road outside, and also passing through a traffic light at a junction in Leith about five minutes before you said you left the flat. I can't get it any closer to you in Leith at the moment, but I thought it might be worth mentioning, because the same van was reported stolen about two weeks ago."

"Interesting." McKenzie pondered the news for a second. "And yesterday or Thursday?"

"Nothing, Guv. As soon as I got the match for today, I double-checked for the past few days. I couldn't find any reports of that van in the vicinity of the school in the past few days. I've picked it up a couple of times in Portobello,... "

"But since that's the main road in and out of Edinburgh, that doesn't mean too much."

"Yes, I was just about to say that."

"And what do we know about the owner who reported it missing?"

"Definitely not a suspect. An older man, about sixty-three years old. He's been freaking out about the loss of his van, and the impact it's had on his small business. He called to report the van missing within hours of it being stolen, as soon he noticed it had gone."

"Okay, good. Keep trying to tie that van closer to the flat in Leith, any closer sightings if possible... and also keep looking for any other vehicles, just in case the van has nothing to do with it. And last thing, put an alert out on that van, and if anyone spots it, or any automatic alerts come through from the ANPR system, let me know."

"Will do, Guv."

"Good work, DI Dean. Thanks!"

Saturday
23.05

Barry Quinn sat at the bar, getting drunk.

He hadn't seen Irene in over an hour. The last he'd seen of her was when she'd disappeared onto the dance floor with Paul Bentford. His first instinct had been to go over to them, warn Paul off and then grab his wife.

His wife.

But as he'd stepped onto the dance floor, he'd hesitated. Something held him back.

What would he gain by forcibly preventing anything between Irene and Paul? If she wanted to be with *him*, rather than himself, then he should let her.

Surely it was better to find out now, than continue to live a lie.

So, instead, perhaps rather stupidly, he'd let Paul put his arm around his wife and guide her into the mass of frolicking party goers.

Standing on the side, he'd watched them dance together.

Not once had Irene looked around to see where her husband was.

Then, when the dance had finished, she'd stayed for another.

Barry had felt a mixture of emotions as he'd seen Paul wrap his arm around Irene and pull her a little closer.

Forlornly Barry had hoped that Irene would push him away and establish a safer distance between them.

Instead she'd thrown her head backwards and laughed, loving the moment.

Faster and faster they had danced.

And then it had happened.

Paul had leant forward and kissed Irene on her cheek.

It was only a small kiss, but after he had withdrawn, Irene had looked up at Paul, adoringly, then after a moment, she'd had moved towards him and kissed him on the cheek back.

It was as if someone had stuck a spear in Barry's heart.

He couldn't quite believe it.

He'd stared, at first in disbelief, then in acceptance.

Then the realisation dawned on him that he deserved it.

After all, he'd been fantasising about doing the same with Fiona Lewis.

He couldn't watch any more.

He'd turned around and left the hall.

At first, he'd left the building and gone for a walk to cool down, calm down and think about what he'd seen.

Then he'd returned to the school, headed to the bar, and lined up a series of drinks.

Sometimes it is only when you've lost something, or someone, that you realise what you truly had.

Too late, Barry Quinn had found out exactly how much Irene had meant to him, and just how good their life together had been - until then.

It was funny how things worked out.

All the time he'd been a success, he'd thought himself a failure.

Then, just as he realised how much of a success he actually was, his life had collapsed around him, and he'd become the failure he'd always been scared of being.

Saturday
23.10

Marie and Stuart edged their way slowly along the side of the dance hall, looking at the tables of memorabilia and the displays of posters and pictures stuck to the vertical boards which lined its perimeter.

The lighting was subdued now, so Stuart used the torch function on his mobile to cast some light on the information they read together.

They'd been chatting and dancing together for over an hour, and in truth, they were getting on really well.

Surprisingly well.

Neither wanted to say it, but both felt it.

There was the spark of a connection between them.

They were enjoying each other's company.

"It's really strange, looking at all these photographs, and so-called memorabilia. How can they be 'memorabilia' when to me it's all just like yesterday? Where have all the years gone? How can this have happened to us?" Stuart mused, as he stood side by side with Marie and they edged along the displays.

"Sometimes I think that too. My memories of school are so vivid, but then I think of the years in between and all the things I've done since then, and I realise that time *has* passed. And the years have just flown by."

"True. So, I would love to hear all about what you've done since..." Stuart's voice trailed off, and his facial expression changed dramatically.

An intense show of sadness had just swept away the smile which Marie was quickly falling in love with.

"Stuart, what's the matter?" she asked, then followed his gaze to the board and what he was looking at. It was the section that talked about former pupils who had died and were not coming tonight.

"Maggie Sutherland. She's dead." Stuart said, pointing to the photograph of a lovely young woman on the board.

"I remember her... she was in Crighton House, I think. She's dead...? How?" Marie bent forward studying the photograph. "What a shame..."

Stuart stood up straight, his eyes narrowing.

"Marie, do you mind if I have a moment to myself? I think I'd just like to step outside and get a breath of fresh air."

"Certainly. No problem." She replied, looking at him, concerned. "Are you okay?"

"It's a bit of a shock. That's all." He turned to Marie and smiled at her. A beautiful smile. Reaching out, he touched her gently on the shoulder. "I just need a few moments. But please don't go away. How about we meet in the bar in ten minutes?"

Marie nodded and gave a quick fleeting smile in return.

When Stuart turned and left, Marie glanced back at the board, wondering if there was any more information about why she'd died.

There was none.

Just then, two voices called her name from behind her. She turned round to find two girls on her right, and a man on her left all vying for her attention.

"Marie McDonald? Where on earth have you been all these years?"

Saturday
23.15

As the group of people in front of them moved away from the boards on the side of the hall, McKenzie and Wishart moved into the gap to take their place.

"I'm sorry that we've messed up your school Reunion, Shona. I know you were coming anyway. Same for Sergeant Anderson. I hope that you are at least managing to have some decent conversations with friends?"

"Yes, it's a bit of a pain not being able to drink all the free champagne which is being handed out at the bar, but hey, I guess that's the way the cookie crumbles."

"One of the great perks of the job." McKenzie nodded, sarcastically.

"Anyway, Guv, this is what I wanted to show you. This is the Remembrance Board, which shows the pupils and teachers who have passed away and couldn't make it today. I've taken some snaps, so we car share them with the team later, but I thought it might help the work that McLeish is doing in identifying any previous deaths amongst the past pupils etc." Wishart gestured at the board.

"Absolutely, I saw this already, and I noted that it doesn't really give much information on the 'why' some of them died. A couple died of cancer in relatively quick succession, and one in a car accident, but the rest are a bit vague."

"Do you want me to do some digging? Get some more details if possible?"

McKenzie nodded.

"Did you know any of them? Were you close to anyone of them?" he asked Wishart.

She pointed to a picture of one of the boys.

"I fancied him, I have to admit. We were close for a few weeks. It was a very fleeting thing. We were only fourteen. But you never forget…"

"Your first kiss?"

Wishart nodded, now silent, and biting her tongue.

"I'm sorry."

"He had cancer. And a wife and two teenagers."

McKenzie never said anything. He just nodded silently.

They turned their backs to the board and faced the revellers.

"So, Shona, did you come here alone tonight? Or were you meant to meet up with friends?" McKenzie asked DS Wishart.

"My partner hates Reunions. He refused to come. So I arranged to come with two of the girls. They're over there, Karen and Sally." Wishart pointed to two girls dancing with two men near the stage.

"Oops, just got a message… " McKenzie pulled out his mobile. "Two messages from Dean."

The first message was good news.

"I've got more CCTV of the van actually in Weir's street in Leith."

The second was even better.

"Call me. We've found the van!"

Chapter 20

The Dungeon
Saturday
23.25

Mark had fallen twice, each time heavily.

He'd almost definitely broken a couple of fingers on his left hand, and the pain swept over him in waves.

"Move!" the voice commanded from behind, a hand on his shoulder urging him forward.

Twice he'd felt the cattle prod in his back, but thankfully each time it had just been to urge him on, and he'd not been subject to the electricity shooting through his body.

Mark was trying his best to comply with the instructions issued.

"Bend down a little... move forward, turn to your left, turn to your right. Slowly, lift up your feet... there's a pipe there, step over it carefully... straighten up."

Mark was exhausted, ravished with thirst beyond belief. Before now, Mark had never been truly thirsty in his life. Not like this.

His tongue was swollen, his eyelids half-closed, his throat so dry that it felt like it was made of wood.

They'd been walking for about ten minutes now, slowly, negotiating a range of unseen hurdles.

Even though Mark wore a blindfold, he could tell that they were still in pitch black. There was no extraneous light trying to fight its way through an edge, or no faint glow beyond the darkness of the cloth.

With his eyes-blindfolded, and sitting in the dark for what must have been days, his other senses had become acute. He'd never realised how sensitive human skin was... he could feel the slightest variations in heat and cold across his body, and whenever a drop of water fell from above onto his skin, he'd feel it crashing against his body.

His hearing was now amazing. Like a bat, he could sense when objects where near or far, and all around him he could hear water dripping from the ceiling, or the occasional scurrying of an animal somewhere around them.

Mark knew he had to be in some sort of tunnel, or narrow corridor. He could hear the echoes of their movements reverberating off the walls on either side of them, and occasionally directly in front, just before he guessed they would have to turn a corner.

"Stop!" the voice had commanded.

Immediate obedience, Barry paused, awaiting his next instruction, and forming a shape in mid-air like the game of statues which they'd played as children growing up.

For a few minutes they did not move, listening or waiting for something to happen, Mark didn't know what.

"Okay. Carry on. *Quietly.*" His captor commanded. The voice was once more accompanied by the tip of the cattle-prod, but again without any charge being applied.

Mark's brain was racing. Why the brutality before, but not now?

Then it dawned on him.

His captor was worried that someone might hear them!

Perhaps, if Mark somehow made enough noise, someone would hear it.

Maybe, if he kicked the next pipe, as loud as possible?

This was his chance!

It was a risk. If he was wrong, if it didn't work, then with absolute certainty the cattle prod would be applied at its maximum setting.

Mark knew it.

"But without the risk of pain, there could be no gain!"

The thought rushed through his brain, appearing from out of nowhere, either mocking himself or encouraging him, Mark was not sure either way.

It took a few seconds to make the decision, to risk everything for the slightest possibility of being heard, and rescued, but once he'd made it, Mark felt a wave of adrenaline course through his body.

He primed himself, ready to kick the next pipe they passed.

It would be all or nothing.

Perhaps the last chance he might have.

Slowly he let the tension and energy build up within him.

Any.

Second.

Now…

Saturday
23.35

Outside the school Stuart had taken some time remembering Maggie Sutherland. The announcement on the board hadn't said why or how she'd died, but Stuart would find out, and send some flowers to her grave, wherever it was.

Stuart couldn't believe she was gone.

Over the years he'd thought a lot about her. In Afghanistan his thoughts about her had bordered on obsession, but in Afghanistan an obsession like that had been healthy. It had kept many a man sane: pick an emotional moment with a woman - or a man – and replay that moment in your mind over and over again. Perhaps each time, twisting the reality of the memory slightly, morphing it from one truth to another, evolving the reality from a kiss, to a full-blown phantasy sex session that last not seconds, but hours.

In Afghanistan, where details had been missing, they'd had months to imagine every single new pixel, fitting each of them together, perfectly.

More than one wet dream had ensued. Sleep and dreams had become a man's best friend.

For Stuart, Maggie Sutherland had been his mental pin-up, the girl-at-home whom one day he would track down and marry.

In reality, it never happened.

He'd survived Afghanistan.

He'd returned to the UK.

Met first one girl. Then another.

And the insecurities which had surrounded him around Maggie at school, had once again kept him from finding or calling her.

Tonight though, he had promised himself that he'd tell her the truth.

How he'd felt about her.

He knew that the reality would be that she'd be married, with children, but he was still going to find a moment, and tell her just how he'd felt.

And to thank her personally for helping him survive Afghanistan.

Without the memory of her, he would not have made it, of that he was sure.

Discovering as he had just done, that she was dead… several years ago, without him knowing, rocked him to the core.

Whatever had killed her, she had died without knowing just how important she'd been to him.

He cursed himself for not having done anything about it sooner.

And now… it was too late.

Maggie Sutherland was gone.

Saturday
23.45

Fiona McKenzie rested a hand upon her husband's shoulder, and as he turned she planted a huge kiss on his lips.

For most of the evening, their conversations had only been short and sweet as their two ships had passed on the dance floor, or in the bar.

McKenzie had done his best to keep her hydrated and her glass topped up with water, but she understood that he was on duty tonight and although she missed him, she was not mad.

She was a policeman's wife and she had long ago learned to accept it.

Along with all the inconveniences that came with the job.

The past few years had been difficult, but they had come through them together, and now they were stronger than ever.

Of that she was sure.

In less than six weeks, they would be having a baby together, and Fiona McKenzie could not be happier.

She was enjoying every single second of her pregnancy.

A couple of times this evening she had cast a glance over to her husband as he'd been talking to others, and she loved the feeling of pride that surged within her.

He was a good-looking man, commanded respected from all those around him, and was doing an important job.

"Did you see the year photos?" Fiona whispered in his ear so he could hear her above the last few songs from Runrig.

"Nope… you want me to guess which one is you?" McKenzie laughed, nodding at Anderson and breaking away from him, their conversation now over.

Fiona took his hand, and guided him towards the last of the boards nearest the stage, right under one of the stacks of speakers which was blasting away at full volume.

"That one, top right, in the middle. That's our year photograph from 1996. We were in 6th year then. The final prom. That was the last time we all saw each other before we left school. It was taken a few days after the school had officially finished. Guess which one I am!"

McKenzie edged along a little more and peered closely at the photograph.

There were three rows of pupils, almost all about 18 years old, dressed to the nines, and looking the most glamorous they ever had, at that age.

McKenzie whistled a few times, playfully, and Fiona punched his arm.

"What? What's the matter? I'm whistling at you… "

"Which one is me?"

"That one?" McKenzie asserted, only the tone in his voice giving away the uncertainty. The other girl in the photograph he'd been looking at was quite similar.

"No… " he corrected himself quickly. "THAT ONE!"

Fiona smiled.

"Correct."

"Wow… you're so much thinner. You look just like a school-girl… "

"I *WAS* a school-girl, idiot. Although technically, when that photo was taken, I'd finished with school, and I was eighteen!"

"Legal jail-bait, then."

"Is that appropriate? DCI McKenzie?"

"Legal is the key word there, darling."

Fiona was standing in the front row, on the right, wearing a bright red ball gown. Perhaps a little over-the-top for today's standards, but nevertheless very nice.

"How come I've never seen this photo before? You look lovely in it!" McKenzie asked, genuinely surprised.

"I think I've got it somewhere, probably buried in one of my many tins in the attic."

"Shame you haven't got it on the wall somewhere… "

McKenzie's phone buzzed.

"Sorry… " he apologised, looking at the screen and seeing it was Dean returning his call They were playing phone ping-pong.

He kissed Fiona, stroked Little Bump, and excused himself out into the foyer where he could hear what DI might want to tell him.

"We found the van."

"Brilliant! Well done… "

"Not so well done, Guv. It's a burning wreck down in Seafield. An anonymous phone call. By the time we got there it was already too far gone. I reckon it's been burning for an hour or two. Only the bottom rear back-end and part of the rear tyre seems to have survived in any way, but even that's pretty much melted. We're just waiting for it to cool down now, so we can load it onto the back of a van and take it away for forensics."

"Blast!" McKenzie swore and absorbed what he'd just learnt.

His mind was racing.

"Are you there now?" McKenzie asked.

"Yes, Guv."

"Make sure you pay due diligence to checking out for possible footprints or anything else that forensics might find at the scene. Don't let the pick-up people trample over the scene until forensics have had their moment."

"I'm all over it, Guv." Dean replied. "I mean, I'm not all over it, and I'll stop anyone else too. I get what you mean."

McKenzie smiled.

"So, what does this tell us then?" he asked Dean.

"I'm trying to get a trace on the caller, but my guess is that it won't tell us anything. The question is, was it a passer-by or the killer, rubbing our nose in it?"

"Exactly. Is that part of the game he's playing with us? And did he know we'd identified the van, or is he just clever and not taking any chances?"

"I'm guessing he probably cleaned the van before he burnt it. I wouldn't hold out much hope that it'll tell us much."

"Okay. You're probably right, but just go through the process properly, okay? And then as soon as you've got it sorted and handed over, go home and get some sleep."

Sunday
00.05

Iain Small was drunk. He'd had an amazing evening, spent mostly at the bar. His wife had been on the dance-floor, but both were content, chatting with their friends, and occasionally bumping into and catching up with some they'd not seen since the last school prom.

Iain had been looking forward to the evening, and he was loving it. It made him feel even more warm and fuzzy about his old school days than before, if that were at all possible.

Thanks to the amazing wisdom of his wife Debbie, he'd not turned up in a Corvette, and had just come to the renunion as he was: plain old Iain Small.

He was happy with who he was. Loved life.

What was there not to love?

Iain didn't need the world. He just needed his mates, Debbie, and a good social life, and he had them all.

He was sorted.

However, when just past the stroke of midnight, a space cleared at the bar and from afar he saw Marie McDonald, he drunkenly almost fell off his chair.

Wow!

Marie had been one of the girls he'd always fancied at school, and seeing her now… she was even more gorgeous than he'd remembered.

She seemed to be alone, at least for the moment, and remembering that the last time opportunity had knocked like this was almost a life-time ago at the last school prom, he stood up, excused himself from his mates, and wandered over towards her.

She saw him coming, and incredibly, she smiled.

"Iain Small!"

"Marie!"

They stood in front of each other for a few moments, not saying anything, then Iain went first.

"Are you happy?" he asked.

She laughed.

It was a very direct, honest, and probably alcohol-inspired question, but it deserved an answer.

"Yes, I am. And you?"

"Actually, yes I am Marie. Very!"

Just then a tall handsome man appeared by Marie's side.

"Blast... !" Iain said under his breath.

He shook his drunken head, and then stood tall, his mind made up. He was going to go for it.

"Listen mate, sorry to disturb you, but would you mind giving me ten seconds alone with Marie. There's something I need to tell her, privately. Then I've got to go back to my rugby team, over there... " he said pointing, "and get on with the rest of my life. My *happy* life."

Stuart Nisbet looked at Marie, who smiled back, and passed him both the drinks she'd just ordered for them.

"I'll be a few minutes, and I'll come find you." She reassured him.

"Handsome man," Iain said, watching Stuart wander away. "Anyway, Marie, the thing is... you see. I'm drunk. And there's something I want to tell you now that I wanted to tell you twenty years ago, but didn't. Because I was a spotty coward, with no self-confidence."

Marie said nothing but continued smiling, in spite of the smell of alcohol drifting over from Iain.

"The thing is Marie, I think you're gorgeous. I always did. And at school I always wanted to ask you out. And I dreamt of one day kissing you."

Iain Small blinked and smiled to himself.

He looked deeply into her eyes, and for a moment lost track of what he was going to say next.

"Anyway," he continued. "Now I've done it. I've told you. So there."

Marie hadn't looked away yet. She was still smiling.

"Anyway, that's it. I'm going now. I'm happily married to my wife Debbie, and I only told you that just now, because I wanted you to know that at school, we all thought you were lovely. And sometimes, in life, people should just be a bit more honest and tell people what they think. I'm sorry for disturbing you, Marie. And now I'll let you get back to your husband."

Iain nodded, and was just about to turn and go back to his mates and his drink, mission accomplished, when Marie put out a hand, touched him gently on the cheek, lent forward and kissed him softly on the lips. Quite quickly. And only once.

"Thank you Iain Small. I really appreciate that."

It took a few seconds for Iain to recover, but when he did, he just smiled and said, "This has been a BRILLIANT night! The best ever!"

Then he turned and went back to his drinks and his friends.

The happiest man in the world!

Chapter 21

Somewhere
Sunday
00.07

Mark had resigned himself to his fate. Previously primed, ready to act, and anticipating the moment he would be able to finally act and do something that could act towards his own salvation, his spirit had finally been smashed when his captor had informed him, "Good, we're almost there."

Mark could hear the slight easing of tension in the Indian's voice. Whatever risk his captor had been worried about, was now gone.

Once more his captor was back on a solid footing, and was in total control.

"Wait here. Do not move."

His captor stepped past him.

Mark could hear him fumbling with something just ahead of him, followed by a slight scraping sound, and a draft of fresh air being sucked down the passageway they'd just negotiated.

Mark felt the captor reach out and pull on both of his hands. Urging him on.

"Forward. Step up and over. Don't fall."

For a second Mark hesitated.

Where were they?

Why had his captor gone to all this trouble to get him here, wherever here was?

If they were close to the final destination, how *final* was it?

Was the Indian going to set him free? At long last?

Or was it more final than that?

"Hurry up!" The Indian commanded. Not in a raised voice. But more quietly than normal.

Mark sensed that perhaps all opportunity had not passed altogether.

If the Indian was speaking quietly, perhaps if Mark could just scream for one final time, just loud enough to be heard by whoever the Indian might be worried about.

Surprised by his own resilience, Mark struggled to summon up the courage and the strength to scream for just one more time, hoping that enough sound may escape past the rag gagging his mouth.

Perhaps the last opportunity he may have to save his life.

"*MOVE!*" the Indian commanded, this time louder.

Mark hesitated.

And then screamed.

As loud as he could.

Only to discover that his swollen, dry throat no longer had the power to make any form of sound.

Instead, he felt a muscle tear in his throat, and he started to gag.

"MOVE!" the Indian commanded again, this time pushing the cattle prod into his side, with the power turned on.

Pain surged through Mark's torso, and he dropped to his knees, a white searing light exploding at the front of his skull, blinding him momentarily, in spite of the blindfold.

"That was the lowest setting. Stand up and move, or the next one will be half power, in your testicles."

Mark began to cry, but no tears emerged.

Slowly, he struggled to his feet, and one by one he moved them forwards towards his final destination.

Sunday
00.08

Sofia Waterson, head of the organising committee for the Reunion once again took to the stage, now quite merry but thankfully still understandable.

"Wow! Please, join me in a final massive, MASSIVE, round of applause for Runrig. I still can't quite believe that we managed to book them for this evening. Perhaps you would also like to thank the evening's sponsor, Ben Venue Capital Assets - and its generous if not slightly mysterious owner - for everything: the entertainment, the FREE alcohol and drinks, and the surprise gift each and every attendee will receive before they leave this evening!"

There was a loud and drunken roar of approval and applause, that needed quelling by Sofia before she could carry on.

"Okay, so, that's it with the live music, but we still have another hour to go before '*Carriages*' at 1 a.m., so I'm going to hand over to the DJ now, who I believe is going to play a fantastic selection of music from our schooldays. Including, I am assured, a few slow dances. So find your partners, cuddle up, go wild... but most importantly, have fun!"

The lights then dimmed, the DJ started playing hits from the nineties, and the energy in the hall went up another level.

Everyone was having the time of their life.

Except for Willy Thomson.

He stood at the back of the hall, looking on, watching everyone else, surprisingly sober, but very edgy.

Willy Thomson was confused.

He knew that this evening his life stood at a cross-roads, and that he had been given an opportunity that he could ill afford to turn down.

No one had ever given him an opportunity before.

Ever.

And there was a certain irony in that the opportunity had been given to him in the school.

Not to take the opportunity would be madness.

But taking it would set him on a new path that he'd never ventured down before.

It would also mean abandoning his plans for killing one of the teachers.

Willy knew that if he wanted to, he was ready to commit that ultimate act.

He'd selected Jason McIntosh to die, and he was worried that if he didn't go through with it, he'd leave the school this evening feeling even more of a failure than he did now.

Willy didn't like this feeling.

The packet of cocaine in his pocket was burning holes in his trousers, and he kept fingering it to assure himself that if he needed it, instant relief would be there.

So far, he'd managed to prevent himself disappearing into a toilet cubicle and sniffing the lot, and he was actually quite surprised by his ability to resist the temptation.

Willy knew though, that if he did take the coke too soon before killing the maths teacher, then it might wear off. If he was going to kill the bastard, and take the coke, he had to time it right.

On the other hand, if he was going to 'renounce' his bad ways, and embark on a new path, taking the coke would not help.

As soon as he took it, he'd lose his self-resolve, and next thing he knew he'd be doing something he might regret later on.

Faced with what was probably the first really important choice that Willy had to make in his life, he discovered that making choices was proving far more difficult than he would have expected.

Willy tried to weigh it up…

Getting a trade, a real education, would be difficult. It would be a struggle. The rewards would be there…but only after a long time.

Killing someone and carrying on his life of violence would be easy.

There was no challenge, and the self-gratification would be immediate.

But… perhaps easy wasn't right?

Willy was really struggling.

Knowing what to do, and summing up the resolve and the courage to decide, was difficult.

Then he remembered his conversation with DCI McKenzie and the warning, and he made his choice.

Perhaps, for the first time in his life, he was grateful for the helping hand of the law.

Decision made.

Willy Thomson was going straight.

Sunday
00.15

Barry Quinn stood outside in the car park, staring at the Boxster.

How the hell was he going to get it home now?

He was drunk, and he couldn't drive.

If he left it here, it would be stolen.

Or at least keyed by some ned.

He wanted to go home now, and escape.

Where Irene was, he had no idea. He hadn't seen her in ages, and no doubt she'd gone off somewhere with Paul Bentford.

He really missed her.

And thinking of her with another man made him realise how much he actually loved her.

If only he hadn't been such a prat.

If only…

"Barry? Where have you been? I was getting really worried about you!"

Barry turned around to face his wife, tears hovering on the edge of his eyelids. He said nothing.

"What's the matter? Are you drunk?" she asked, reaching out with her hand, and stroking his cheek lovingly.

"I saw you. With Paul." He said.

"Who?"

"Paul Bentford. On the dance floor. I saw it all."

"What are you talking about? You saw us on the dance floor… dancing? So what?"

"I saw him kiss you… "

Irene was shaking her head slightly and frowning.

"What… "

"On the cheek. And then you kissed him back. And then you disappeared off together somewhere."

Irene's face went blank. She looked confused. Blinked.

Then laughed.

"Barry, are you jealous? Do you think that I got off with Paul Bentford?"

She laughed again, and then stepped forward, kissing him solidly on the lips.

"You're such a prat, Barry! Sometimes I can't understand why I love you so much, but I do!"

"But I saw you kissing!"

"Idiot. He kissed me. Said how lucky I was to be with you. Said I looked lovely, and congratulated me on my life and how much we'd achieved together, and thanked me for the advice I gave him a long time ago to ask Sandra Roper out. He did. They went out. And got married. Thanks to me, *apparently*."

"What? You never told me that?"

"Why should I have? It was never important."

"So why did you *kiss* him then?"

"His wife is pregnant again. A big surprise. It's going to be a girl, and he wanted to call it Irene. As a token of gratitude. So I kissed him… ON THE CHEEK. And then he took me over to meet Sandra and we had a drink together, me and Sandra and dished the dirt on our husbands and had a good old chin-wag!"

Barry stood silently, staring at his wife.

The tears began to roll down the side of his cheeks.

"I thought you'd gone off with Paul… "

"Why? You idiot. I love you. Always have. Always will."

She stepped forward and hugged him and then kissed him passionately.

Barry wrapped his arms around her, tightly, and pulled her close.

"I'm such a complete and utter prat," he said, and then began to sob into her shoulder.

"I never argue with my husband, Barry. If you say you're an idiot, then I must agree!"

Sunday
00.30

Marie McDonald and Stuart Nisbet stood on the edge of the dance-floor, talking.
About life.
About everything.
For two people who'd just met, they were getting on surprisingly well.

Stuart seemed very interested in learning as much about Marie as possible. He asked questions, and listened attentively to her answers. Then asked more questions.
Marie was an attractive woman. In her experience, when men started to express an interest in her, they generally spoke a lot about themselves.
In contrast, Stuart was in no hurry to talk about himself.
It was refreshing to meet a man, obviously capable, and strikingly good looking, who did not seem to want to impress himself upon her at all.
Stuart also had the knack of getting her to talk about things that she didn't want to discuss.
He was able to dig, without her feeling uncomfortable.
Soon, against all her intentions for this evening, she was talking about her children and her fundraising activities.
At one point, she got so passionate and worked up about the challenges she faced in caring for her little ones, that she began to cry.
Stuart had offered her a fresh handkerchief to wipe away her tears.
Who did that anymore?
Seriously, who was this guy?
With about thirty minutes to go before the evening was due to draw to a close, the DJ started to play slow dances.
It happened very naturally, and without any awkwardness.
Stuart smiled at her, gestured to the dance floor with his left hand, and stepped slightly to the side, as if to let her go past, should she accept.
Without thinking about it, she smiled back, and walked onto the dance floor, gently scooping up his hand in hers as she went.
He held her close.
Not just for one dance, but two.
Neither one of them seemed in a hurry to go anywhere.

Chapter 22

Somewhere
Sunday
00.35

Mark McRae fell to the floor, landing heavily on his chest, and banging his head badly. He immediately knew that his scalp had split and was bleeding, but Mark had other problems.

The Indian had just turned up the power on the cattle prod and hit him with it on its maximum setting.

A fire was burning down his right side, leaving him in excruciating agony. For a moment Mark passed out, all his senses seeming to stop.

When they returned, it was with a vengeance.

He was lying on his back, looking up at the ceiling.

It was dark, but his blindfold had been removed.

He tried to move his hands, but found them bound tightly to some heavy objects on either side of his body. Likewise, his feet were also similarly immobilised, with the ropes around his ankles cutting sharply into his skin.

It took him a moment to realise it, but the gag from his mouth had been removed.

He tried to move his jaw, but found it difficult to do.

Neither was he able to speak, even though he tried.

His mouth was so dry, no sound came out.

As the clouds of unconsciousness lifted, the darkness around him became more manageable and he was slowly able to make out his surroundings.

"Recognise the place?" the Indian asked, stepping forward from somewhere behind him, and now towering directly above Mark's head.

Mark's eye started to dart around the room, a feeling of dread welling up within him.

The room was empty now, with all the tables and chairs removed, except for a few solid structures which were rooted to the floor, and to which he was now pinioned and spread-eagled on the ground.

The strenuous climb which he'd been subjected to, struggling up four flights of stairs, blindfolded, exhausted, and in pain, now also made perfect sense.

Mark closed his eyes and remembered one of the last times he'd been here before. Standing in front of a class-room full of students, congratulating them on their exam marks and wishing them well at university.

For the first time in days, Mark knew exactly where he was.

Sunday
00.45

McKenzie had gathered everyone together at the back of the hall.

The School Reunion Ball was just about to finish, but before it did, he wanted to have a status check with everyone on duty.

No one had anything much to say or report, except that everyone in the hall and the bar seemed to be having a wonderful time.

"Keep an eye out for Willy Thomson. Most of you know him, and he's here this evening. He's the only concern I've had so far." McKenzie offered, before instructing them all to keep extra vigilant until everyone was off the premises.

Nothing had happened yet, but that wasn't to say something bad would happen in the next hour.

"One last thing, before you go. I've sent you all a photo of one of the boards in the hall, which shows photos of some of the pupils and staff who've died and didn't make it tonight. If you didn't see the message yet, please look now, and then check the board, and if you can, in the remaining time or with your friends or contacts later, try to find out what you can about the causes of death for those where it's not listed on the board? Just in case there's anything significant there."

Sunday
01.00

Sofia Waterson climbed slowly back onto the stage, this time being helped by her husband.

The music had stopped and the lights had gone up.

The fun was coming to an end.

"I'm drunk!" Sofia announced to the hall, which was now full of everyone who had come this evening.

"I'm drunk. I've had a wonderful time. I hope you have too!" she laughed aloud, and everyone replied immediately with a raucous roar of *'Yes!'*

"Let's do this again, shall we? In ten years?" she asked.

"YESSSSS!" was the answer.

"Okay, I'm not going to make a big speech. But seriously, it's been great seeing everyone here tonight. Portobello High is a brilliant school. I think we all miss it. I'm very proud I came here, and I always will be! So, on behalf of all of us, I want to say thanks to all the teachers we ever had, and to everyone who helped get us through the school, who cared for us, and helped us start our lives."

There were now tears in her eyes, and she was obviously struggling with her words.

"Okay, enough. There's going to be one more song, and then we're going to ring the school bell for the last time. After that, and we're getting kicked out. Get home safe and sound. AND STAY IN TOUCH!"

She waived to everyone, then almost tripped coming down the stairs from the stage.

The lights dimmed a little, and incredibly Runrig came back on stage.

They picked up their instruments and slowly began to play 'For Auld Lang Syne'.

A chill went through the hall. An emotional moment that touched everyone that was there.

The ex-pupils of Portobello High School joined hands, began to dance and to sing, and to a man and woman, by the time the song came to an end, there was not a single dry eye in the hall.

The hugs, the kisses, the tears, and the '*I love you*'s' lasted another thirty minutes, but slowly the hall emptied out and the Reunion came to an end.

Standing outside in the car park, small groups of ex-pupils lingered and clung on, not wanting to go home.

Some not remembering where home was.

Saturday
01.00 a.m.

Mark's eyes opened again. He must have fainted with the pain, or the dehydration. Or both. Just for a second, a fleeting second, he wondered if the Indian had left, but as soon as he moved his head to look for him, the voice spoke.

"I'm still here. And we're almost ready." It said.

"First, I'm going to give you a little drink of water. I think you need it."

Mark couldn't believe his ears. If the Indian cared enough to give him a drink, perhaps there was still hope.

He felt a hand at the back of his head, lifting it up, raising it towards a plastic cup which had appeared in front of his face.

"Drink. Very slowly. You need to lubricate your throat. It might hurt."

Mark tried to take a sip, but most of the first mouthful just ran out down his chin.

It had nowhere to go.

"Slowly." The Indian said. "Let the first few mouthfuls sit in your mouth and be absorbed."

Mark obeyed.

It took a few moments, but then Mark felt the muscles in his neck slowly beginning to respond, and with incredible relief he felt the cold water beginning to trickle down the back of his mouth and down his throat.

The Indian urged him to drink some more, and then warned, "Do not attempt to talk or scream. If you do, I will cover your mouth and put the cattle prod on your testicles. I'll make sure no one hears you scream. Do you understand?"

Mark nodded.

Then drank some more.

Slowly.

He coughed a few times involuntarily, but the amazing, wonderful thing was, he could!

The Indian seemed pleased.

"Good. Now I need to fix your tooth. Open wide."

Mark was confused. He felt a momentary surge of panic.

"What tooth?"

The Indian raised the cattle prod in front of his face, and Mark immediately froze.

"Open your mouth. I'm going to put in a frame to keep your cheeks away from the tooth."

For a moment Mark hesitated. What was going on?

Then he saw the cattle prod in front of him again, and felt it prod against his nether regions.

He immediately opened his jaw as wide as it would go.

"Good boy." The Indian said, and quickly pushed a cold metal frame inside his mouth.

It felt massive.

Nothing like any dentist had ever used before.

Mark tried to shake his head.

"Ah, good point. I need to keep your head still, so you don't hurt yourself." The Indian laughed. "I forgot. How stupid of me."

Mark felt something being placed across his forehead.

A leather or plastic belt?

The Indian was reaching behind his head, fiddling with something.

Slowly the belt began to tighten, and Mark felt his head pulled backwards, forcing him back on to the floor, and a frame of some sort that cut into the back of his neck. Mark tried to move his head, but found he couldn't.

He tried to speak, forgetting about the cattle prod, but found that now he could only make childish sounds.

"Last warning, Mr McRae. Next time you make a sound, I'll blow your balls off!"

Mark wanted to scream. The panic was becoming like a blinding white light which clouded his vision, and threatened to drive him insane.

His hands and arms were beginning to shake. If he'd had enough fluids in him he'd no doubt have wet himself, but there was nothing left within him to come out.

"We're almost there, now." The Indian whispered, close to his ear.

"First, I'll just adjust this so I can get better access… "

Mark felt the Indian's cold fingers on the side of his cheeks - it felt like he was wearing rubber gloves - then he felt a weird vibration as the contraption in his mouth seemed to expand, forcing his jaw open wider.

"Aahhhh… ," Mark uttered, involuntarily. It hurt like hell.

Somewhere behind his head, Mark heard the Indian fiddling with something, then a sigh, an exhaling of air.

"Done. Now we're ready." The Indian informed him through the pain.

"Ah… sorry, apart from one thing."

The Indian picked something up from the floor and then came around to the front of Mark from behind. He knelt on the floor above Mark's prostrate body, leant across toward him, and then started to write something on Mark's forehead with a soft pen.

Rocking backwards on to his heels, the man in the Indian mask surveyed his handy work and nodded.

"Good. I think that's clear enough."

The Indian laughed.

"Now, it's time," he nodded. "Oh, but, first, perhaps you want to know what I wrote on your head?"

Mark blinked.

The Indian leant forward and whispered into Mark's left ear.
"It says, '*Remember me?*'"

Having uttered the words, the Indian sat back and studied Mark's eyes for recognition of what he'd just said.

Sure enough, it only took a few seconds.

As the man who was pinned on the floor in front of him and at his mercy, realised the meaning of the words, the blood drained from his face, and in spite of the metal contraption in his mouth, he managed to scream for the very first, and last, time.

The look of terror on Mark McRae's face instantly made all the preparation for this worthwhile.

The Indian smiled.

Then he removed the tops from the two glass bottles on the floor beside him and picked them up.

Laughing aloud, the Indian leant forward and began to simultaneously pour the contents of both bottles down the back of Mark McRae's throat.

Chapter 23

The Portobello School Reunion
Milton Road
Sunday
01.45

"I'd offer you a lift," Stuart said to Marie, "but I cycled here and I don't have a seat on the back."

"Thanks. So not a knight in shining armour that will whisk me off into the night then?" she quipped.

"Is that what you'd like?"

"It has a certain appeal." She laughed. "But there is one problem. I don't know anything about you at all. I told you everything about me, and bored you to tears with my stories about my children and my ideas how to raise money for them, but you told me nothing. My parents taught me not to go off with strange men."

"So now you think I'm strange?" Stuart raised his eyebrows, quizzing her.

She laughed.

"Very."

"That, Marie McDonald, is a great shame, because to tell you the truth, I think you are quite amazing."

Stuart looked straight into her eyes as he said it, and for a moment their gazes were both locked together.

Marie started to blush, but without breaking away, she answered.

"Thank you. And I think that you, Stuart Nisbet, are also very interesting."

"Very *interesting*? That doesn't sound particularly good. And there was I wondering if I should ask you if you'd like to have lunch, and possibly also dinner with me, today? But, if I'm only very interesting… "

"I'd love to." She replied.

Just then her phone buzzed, and she pulled it out of her handbag.

"My Uber. It'll only be a few minutes away."

"Can I pick you up somewhere tomorrow?" Stuart asked.

"Outside the Lady Nairn hotel in Duddingston? One o'clock? There'll still be time for lunch somewhere."

A car turned into the car park and pulled up alongside them.

She nodded at the driver, then turned to Stuart and kissed him lightly on the cheek.

"I'll see you this at lunch time, Mr Nisbet. But come with answers. I'm bringing lots of questions with me."

Sunday
01.55

Willy Thomson watched as the couple outside the foyer gazed deeply into each other's eyes.

The woman eventually got into a taxi, and the man retrieved a cycle from around the corner of the building and then cycled off.

Almost everyone had gone now.

Luckily, he'd managed to avoid being seen by DCI McKenzie as he'd said his goodbyes to a crowd of people, which included two other detectives and policemen that he recognised. Obviously also former pupils of Porty that he hadn't clocked before.

Willy had been standing outside of the school for some time now.

Looking at the sports cars lined up in the car park.

Fighting with the urge to go down the line and key them all.

Normally he'd never ever miss the chance to do something like that. It was such a simple act to do, but one which was so effective in making a statement.

One by one however, the owners have come outside, got into their cars and driven off.

Only one car was left, and Willy couldn't keep his eyes off it.

This has his chance. No one else was around.

In a way, Willy knew that he was testing himself. Testing his resolve to actually go straight.

If he didn't do this, now, if he could just walk away, without touching it, then he knew he would have the strength to go straight.

He'd keyed thousands of cars in his life.

It was so easy to do. With no risks.

But it was oh-so-bad!

"Don't even think about it, Willy Thomson. Remember what I said?" DCI McKenzie's voice caught him by surprise.

Willy spun around.

"I thought you'd gone?"

"I just walked my wife to her car. I'm not done here yet. But you are."

"Aye, you're right about that. I was just leaving." Willy smiled.

Actually smiled.

McKenzie had never ever seen him smile before.

He was always the ultimate sad bastard that carried the biggest chip on his shoulder, blaming the world for everything.

Willy took a step forward onto the car park towards the exit, but then turned and came back, reaching out his hand to the detective.

"Here, this is for you. I found it on the ground, and I don't want it falling into the wrong hands. Can you get rid of it for me?"

Then he turned and walked away.

McKenzie looked down at the little plastic packet that Willy Thomson had just handed him.

Cocaine.

McKenzie looked up and watched Willy disappear.

McKenzie was a good detective, but why Willy Thomson had just voluntarily handed him a packet of cocaine, he just didn't know.

It made no sense.

None at all.

Sunday
02.00

Barry and Irene were the last people to leave the school building. Outside, the continued ominous presence of the police car put paid to their secret, clever plan: to wait until the police car left, then for Irene to drive home.

She'd only had two drinks, then stopped. By now she'd probably be almost completely sober.

Safe enough to drive home, but probably not yet under the zero-tolerance alcohol limit in Scotland.

"Plan B, then?" Barry laughed, and together they walked across to the car, opened the doors and climbed into the back seat.

A voice caught them off guard, almost immediately.

"Hello? I hope you're not planning to drive that home now?" DCI McKenzie said, looking through the open window at Barry and Irene.

"No, but who are you anyway? What's it got to do with you?" Barry asked, very defensively. Irene immediately put her hand on his arm, indicating restraint, even though it probably wasn't necessary. Barry wasn't a violent man at all. If anything, he was worried and stressed about the stupid car.

"DCI McKenzie. Police Scotland."

"Okay, we're in the back seat. We're going to wait here and sleep until about 6 a.m. Then my wife will drive us home. I stupidly got upset and drank too much and I can't drive, but equally, I can't leave this car here unattended. It's not mine."

"Where do you live?"

"About five minutes from here in Duddingston."

"It's not your car?"

"I hired it. To show off."

"My husband's an idiot, officer. But I love him anyway." Irene added, trying to diffuse any possible situation before it developed.

"Okay, how about this? You give me the keys. I drive you both home, and the police car will follow, then pick me up at your house?"

Barry stared at the man, then glanced across at Irene and back again.

"You'd do that?"

"If I don't, and you fall asleep, you'll probably wake up and find that you've got no tyres left. Give me five minutes, and I'll be back."

"Result!" Barry laughed aloud.

A private police escort home!

That would certainly get the neighbours talking, if any were still awake to see.

Wishart was waiting for McKenzie just inside the foyer. She'd confirmed with the caretaker that everyone else had gone, and McKenzie agreed that it was okay for the remaining police presence to leave, most of which McKenzie had already dismissed.

After saying goodnight to Wishart, McKenzie walked over to the police car, where three armed officers sat waiting for the final all clear, and then explained what was going to happen.

All teachers and all pupils had left the school.

Everything had gone smoothly.

It had been a good night.

Three minutes later, the Boxster and the police car left the car park.

Just for a joke, one of the officers put on the blue flashing lights.

Barry and Irene laughed.

What an incredible end to an incredible evening!

And what a wonderful way to start the rest of their lives afresh, now that after all these years, Barry had finally left school and grown up.

Chapter 24

Portobello Beach
Sunday
02.30

Willy Thomson was high.
Not on drugs. Not on alcohol.
Just on life.
Probably for the first time ever, or maybe for the first time since he'd lost his virginity when he was fourteen.
Tonight, above all the odds, the person he'd least expected to ever do so, had extended the hand of friendship to him, and offered him an opportunity.
No one, NO ONE, had ever offered Wee Willy Thomson an opportunity before.
And now he'd made up his mind to take it, the rush he was experiencing was quite incredible.
He was excited.
Nervous.
Afraid.
And happy.
All at once.
The incredible thing was, the rush was free.
A natural thing.
Which was amazing.
Aside from shagging women, Willy hadn't thought that natural highs like this existed.

He walked back from the ball, down to Porty Beach, and along to his favourite spot on the sand, down in front of the Bath Street Baths.
In recent years, it had become quite the tradition for people to come down in the evening at the weekend and build a wee bonfire, then sit around and drink and chat.
Or just sit staring out across the sea and think.
Tonight, Willy had gathered up some wood and paper from one of the skips in Bath Street, and had got his own wee fire going in no time.
He now sat beside his wee fire, thinking.
Planning.
How his life was going to be from now on.
He was going to work hard.
Train hard.
Become a plumber.
And then get the hell out of Edinburgh to somewhere new, where no one knew him, and start a new plumbing business.
Turn it into an empire.
Rule the world.

"The future's so bright, I need sunglasses." He laughed, repeating a line to himself that one of his few mates had said to him, once.

Willy had learnt the line, but never used it, because until now, there had never even been the faintest glow on the horizon, let alone an enticing light as bright as it was now.

"What the fuck are you doing?" A rough voice shouted at him from behind.

Will spun around, expecting to see a policeman, or someone telling him to put the fire out. Everyone made fires, but maybe they were illegal?

Instead Willy found himself surrounded by a gang of about seven kids, all wearing hoodies, hands either stuffed inside and most likely holding onto something, or balled into fists and ready for action.

It didn't look good.

Willy was about to be mugged.

"I recognise you. Willy Thomson. *Wee* Willy Thomson. You're the bastard, that gave me this last night!" the man, obviously the leader of the gang, shouted at him whilst pointing at a massive black eye.

Willy recognised him then. It was the guy Willy had mugged on his way home the evening before. The one who'd practically broken his hand when he hit him.

Willy didn't respond. He slowly stood up, and was busy appraising his chances, and his escape route. Which was basically to run down to the sea, and swim.

"Big mistake. We're the new boys down here, and you dissed me big time. You're dead, pal!"

The man nodded, and the gang crowded in closer around Willy.

Willy saw the first flash of a blade before he was able to reach down and retrieve his from his shoes.

Six more appeared almost simultaneously.

The gang circled Willy before he could run, and within seconds it was all over.

From the promenade, the beach was too dark for anyone to make out what was happening.

Afterwards, the gang ran down to the shoreline, dispersed, and disappeared off in both directions, black figures running against a black sea, their black deed done and unseen.

Within seconds they were gone.

Willy lay beside his fire, his unseeing eyes gazing up at the stars, little hot embers rising like fireflies into the night sky above.

Far, far above, a shooting star shot across the wide expanse of sky.

Normally an omen of good luck, this time Willy was unable to make a wish.

Operation BlueBuilding
Incident Room
10.00

McKenzie stood up in front of the assembled, bleary-eyed team and clapped his hands.

"Mather gave me a quick update this morning before he left, and basically reported that nothing happened here last night. Gary Bruce slept all night in his office downstairs, and did a regular patrol with the other police officers, but they observed nothing and reported nothing. So far so good."

"As I think you all know, the Reunion Ball last night went well and passed without incident. The pupils who attended it enjoyed it, that much was obvious, and we used the event to learn as much as we could about the deceased teachers. Suffice it to say, they were well liked, and there seems no obvious reason, at least none that anyone told us about, which may provide a motive for their deaths. Again, so far so good."

From the downbeat tone of his voice, the team could guess that some bad news was coming.

"There is a little positive news, in some ways, bad in others. Due to some brilliant and very patient investigating, Dean was able to identify a white van that was seen here outside the school, and also very close to the flat of David Weir during the time we were visiting there. Unfortunately, within an hour of identifying it on CCTV, the van was discovered smouldering on wasteland in Seafield. It's been recovered and examined. A footprint was recovered from the ground near the van, but forensics aren't hopeful that it relates to the van. Apparently it's a popular dogging site." McKenzie paused.

"Now for the bad news. Anderson has something to report."

The Sergeant stepped up to the front, and McKenzie made way for him.

"Early this morning a dog walker on Portobello Beach reported a body on the stretch of sand in front of the Portobello Baths. He'd been stabbed forty times. He was quickly identified as local thug William Thomson, who I know is well known to several of you. Time of death was estimated at about 3 a.m."

"From the varied positions of the knife wounds, it's already obvious that he was stabbed from numerous angles and positions, indicating multiple attackers. Thomson was found with two knives hidden in his shoes, but he hadn't had time to extract them, so the attack seems to have happened quickly. When examined, his right hand was closed, and after opening it up, he was found clutching on to a card in his hand. It was the personal business card from Scott Davies, the Managing Director and owner of Portobello Plumbing."

"Scott Davies?" Wishart exclaimed. "He was the No.1 bully in the school for years. Thomson was No.2. I'd say that Scott Davies would have to be the top suspect for this murder."

"I actually saw them talking together in the bar last night. Davies was at the Reunion too." Anderson added.

"Okay, we need to get Davies in for questioning. Wishart, can I ask you to take that one. Bring him in, question him. Get his story. This afternoon if possible."

McKenzie walked across to the board and added the action to Wishart's list.

He also noted down that Dean was liaising on the burnt out van.

"Thank you Anderson." McKenzie nodded at the Sergeant, and took the floor again. "After this meeting, I'll be heading down to the beach to look at the crime scene, and if Thomson's body is still there, to check out the situation for myself. I know what you're all thinking. At this stage I think we'll have to assume that there could possibly be a connection to the Reunion last night, and possibly to the deaths here in this building. We'll continue on that assumption. Which means that the killer's note '*One, two, buckle your shoes, Three, four look out for more*' could have been warning us about yesterday. In which case, as I said yesterday, no one here should blame themselves for this happening. I think we all did a sterling job last night. And there's no way we could have known this would happen. For the record, I have to add that I personally spoke with Thomson last night, on two occasions, and I warned him to behave, just in case he had anything to do with anything." McKenzie stopped and swallowed. "And I just want to say, that although we are proceeding on the grounds that Thomson's death is connected, *I am* noting that the Sergeant is suggesting that initial investigations suggest he was pounced upon by a gang of at least several people. Which is probably not the same modus operandi as our two deaths here. My suspicion is that we are looking at one or two suspects behind the death here in the school, not a whole gang. Although I could be wrong. At this stage we simply don't know. But I just don't think we could have a gang running about this building without being spotted by Gary Bruce's team."

There were a few nodding heads.

"By the way, on Monday I'm hoping to get a proper office manager assigned from St Leonards so we can start managing all the assignment properly. This is all getting a bit ridiculous and old fashioned, so I apologise, but as I've explained, I'm doing my best to get more people. In the meantime, since we don't have someone taking notes at these meetings, I have, just in case you didn't notice, set up the audio recording system over there... I may be asking one of you to listen to the tapes and make notes later on."

This time, there were a few moans.

"Don't worry, once we have an office manager in place, they can assign all the action numbers to your actions, and then it'll be down to you to keep the incident log updated as normal. Okay? Now... is there anything else? Anyone got anything to say?"

Anderson stood up.

"I've got the phone records and the phone mast data back from the phone companies for Weir and Blake's phones."

Everyone sat up. A ripple of anticipation ran round the room.

"Anything?"

"I took the data to the analysts in the office in St Leonards and they'll do the usual analysis to see what info we can learn from usage patterns. I'm going to spend some time this morning going through the phone records and making a few calls to people in their recent contact lists. The bad news is that both phones are no longer active, presumably dumped in the sea or a river somewhere. We know when the last contact was that Weir's phone made to a phone mast in Leith. It's close to the river. I think that's probably where his phone ended up. Likewise, we know when Blake's phone also last established contact with a phone mast. The phone mast is on the edge of the Holyrood Park. I'm guessing the phone probably ended up tossed into St Margaret's Loch. Maybe when the analysts have done their magic, we'll be able to get a better picture of the last movements of Weir and Blake."

"For now though, the time's you just gave us did tell us the times the murderer finally had full control of each victim. We can probably assume the victims were snatched or captured, somehow, just before those times. That's a big step forward.

Excellent work. Thank you! And please let us know as soon as you have anything else back from the analysts that you think's relevant."

The Sergeant nodded.

"Fine, now... anyone else?"

There were no takers.

"Okay, we'll be finishing up just now. If you've got actions you can pursue this afternoon, please do. Otherwise go home and rest. I think next week's going to be full on once we start getting more information back from various people, and forensics. And just to let you know, the meetings will be here every morning at nine, then again at five. I may be away later today, or tomorrow. As soon as I can, I'm heading up to the Island of Coll to interview Daniel Gray, the old headmaster from a while ago. If I'm not here, DI Brown will be in charge in my absence. I'll be going to Coll by myself, since we're so short staffed. And as soon as this meeting is finished, I'll be sharing words with DCS Wilkinson. We have another death. And this team is understaffed. We warned her. Dismissed."

McKenzie clapped his hands together, and everyone dispersed.

Sunday
Portobello Beach
11.00

McKenzie stood inside the tent which forensics had erected around Willy Thomson's body.

It was a hot day already, and the heat within the canvas was building up.

McKenzie had got there just in time. They were about to remove the body, but McKenzie had requested a little time alone to review the crime scene and gather his own personal thoughts. Brown stood beside him. Silently.

McKenzie walked around the body, then bent down and looked into Willy's face. Just last night he'd talked to him, warning him from doing anything silly. Then the incident as they left the Reunion venue, with the packet of cocaine.

What did Thomson mean when he handed it over to him? Was there a message there that McKenzie was missing?

Or was Thomson making a statement.

Had he given up drugs? Had he been selling drugs at the event, and that was the last packet left?

Had something happened at the Reunion that McKenzie and his team had missed?

And why the card from Scott Davies?

Was Willy trying to pass on a message about who murdered him?

Was Davies the gang leader behind Willy's murder, and had Willy in actual fact been the victim of a gang attack?

Was there a connection to the deaths of Weir and Blake?

And thinking of the poem from the killer, was Thomson No.3 in the sequence, "One, Two, Buckle your shoe... ?"

"Thoughts, Guv?" Brown eventually broke the silence.

"Many. His death throws up a whole pile of questions, which we're going to have to work through."

"Are his parents alive?"

"I don't think so. But can you please look into who the next of kin is? We'll need to inform them. I'm heading off to Coll as soon as I can, so I might have to leave that one down to you."

McKenzie adjusted the tightness of the plastic gloves on his hand, then lent forward and gently brushed away the hair from Willy's forehead.

"Checking for any writing?" Brown asked.

"There's none."

"It'll be interesting to find out if there is anything showing on David Weir's head, if they're able to determine that."

"Agreed."

McKenzie stood up.

"I think we're done here. I just wanted to see him for myself."

Pulling off the gloves from his hand, McKenzie looked down at Thomson for one last time.

"The guy was an absolute pain in the neck. To be honest, Portobello will probably be better off without him. But you can't help but feel that he was still some mother's child. And perhaps maybe somewhere along the line, the system let him down."

"Guv, we all make our own choices. He made bad choices. Others suffered as a result. I certainly won't miss him."

"The sad thing is, few will."

McKenzie pulled aside the curtain to the tent and stepped outside into the sunshine.

He blinked, held the curtain open for Brown and checked his watch.

"Time for lunch. I'm buying. How about the Espie in Bath Street?"

Wandering back to their car, they left the forensics team and local uniforms to get on with removing Willy to the morgue.

"Can you call me when you get the autopsy report, if I'm up north? I know the cause of death is obvious, but I'd be interested to see if there's anything else to know…"

"Sure thing, Guv."

As they approached the car, McKenzie glanced at the windscreen.

There was a piece of paper pinned behind the windscreen wipers.

"Oh dear, I've got a bad feeling about this," he said as he reached across and retrieved it.

It was a single sheet of paper.

Two lines of printed text.

"First three, then four.
It's now the time to look for more."

Chapter 25

Sunday
Operation BlueBuilding
Incident Room
Portacabin
11.55

McKenzie's face was expressionless, but for those who knew him, they recognised that it was a mask which covered a host of emotions.

He clapped his hands together harder than normal as soon as the last of them entered the incident room and sat down, and immediately started the session.

"First of all, I'd like to welcome DI Dean, who is joining us for the first time. I asked him to drop everything and come straight over." He nodded to DI Dean, but didn't smile.

"There's no pleasant way to say this, but I think we have a problem. DI Brown and myself were visiting the crime scene in Portobello, and when we came back to the car, I found another note on the windscreen."

He held it aloft, although it was now in a protective plastic sheet.

"It continues on from the first note we received, and says, '*First three, then four.*

It's now the time to look for more.'"

He let the words and their significance sink in.

"Does that mean that Willy Thomson's death is now more likely to be from the same killer? Given that the note was placed on your windscreen immediately following your visit to the body."

"For now, I think we have to treat it like that. However, I think you can read it two ways. My gut feeling is that Willy Thomson's death is not by the same killer, although there may be a link. The timing and the placing of the note could be totally coincidental. The person who placed the note on the screen just followed me and took the opportunity to put it on the car. In which case we have a problem. The note seems to be telling us that there is another body. Even if Thomson's is number three, there could be a number four. And if Thomson's *isn't* number three, then I think we have to start looking for another body now, with a very real threat that another one is already out there , or will be on the way, soon."

Two of those sitting down stood up and started pacing the room. The others started talking to each other. The tension in the room went through the roof.

"Okay, simmer down. We've got to get on top of this immediately. We have to start looking for another body with the expectation that we're going to find one. And we have to be very, *very* careful that one of us doesn't become the fourth person in the poem."

"Do you think it could be a hoax?" Wishart asked.

"I hope so. I fear it is not." McKenzie replied monotonically.

"How about this? Is the killer trying to refocus our attention onto him? What if Willy Thomson's death has nothing to do with the killings in the school, and the killer is trying to refocus our attention back onto himself?" Lynch suggested. "I mean, the killer took a huge risk in approaching your car and putting a note on it in broad daylight with so many other people and police around."

"Interesting idea, but we haven't even found another body yet, so let's not go down that route just now. But if we find one, might we need to bring in the help of a criminal psychologist so we can begin to understand how they are thinking."

"So where are we going to look for a body?" Anderson asked.

"Good question. We were really worried that something might happen at the Reunion. We thought we'd got away with it, but maybe we didn't. No one has reported anyone missing, but it's early days for people who live alone and attended by themselves. No one might miss them for days. So, I think we have to consider that something could have happened last night at the Reunion after all. We'll need to have the school searched. All the classrooms and the grounds, just like we did here." McKenzie said sternly.

"However," he carried on, pausing, and then moving over to the window and looking out and up at the towering blue building above them, "my suspicion is that we're most likely going to find something here. A continuation of the same series of deaths from before."

The team all stood up and moved towards McKenzie and joined him looking out of the window at the old school tower.

"Have you contacted Gary Bruce? Can we go in alone, or do we need the armed response team to sweep the building first again?"

"I would say we should go in now - we can't really wait for the armed squad - but the rules are clear. Theoretically they need to sweep the building and ensure it's safe first. Then hand it over to us. I've called them and they're due here in the next ten minutes. But I'm going to insist we go in together just like last time."

"It's going to take us hours again." McLeish said, the frustration evident in his voice.

"Actually," Lynch started to say something, then turned away from the window and went to the map of the school which had been pinned to the cabin wall. He raised a finger and put it against the fourth floor. "... actually, I think this may be quicker than we think. Has anyone been able to talk with Mark McRae yet?"

A round of 'nos'.

McKenzie came across and stood beside Lynch.

"Why?"

"He's on our list for both a possible victim and a suspect. If he's a victim, then my money is on the fourth floor. It's where the Chemistry Department used to be. McRae is a Chemistry teacher. It would fit the pattern established so far for murder locations."

"I hope you're wrong, but unfortunately, I think you may have just hit the nail on the head."

There was a knock on the door of the portacabin, and Brown hurried over to open it.

"It's the armed squad," she said, turning in the doorway.

"Okay," McKenzie instructed the team, "Wishart, I want you to carry on with tracking down Scott Davies and bringing him in. As soon as possible. The rest of you, everyone follow me. Let's go!"

Outside the portacabin, the team waited while McKenzie explained the situation and the plan and the seven-man armed squad prepared their weapons and adjusted their clothing: they would head straight to the fourth floor, the armed team sweeping ahead, with one of their team backing them up.

Regardless of what they found up there, the rest of the school would then have to be swept, but McKenzie's team would leave the armed squad to do that.

"*Three, then four*," the note had warned.

If they found a body in the chemistry department, there could be a fourth elsewhere.

Once again, the detectives found helmets and then put on hard-shoes to protect themselves from the needles.

Ten minutes later they assembled at the base of the middle stairwell, Stair B.

They moved up in silence until they got to the fourth floor, the Chemistry Department. The stairs ended here, with no further access upwards to the building above.

Here the leader of the armed team gave strict instructions for the detectives and uniforms to wait whilst his team swept the floor, handing McKenzie a radio and telling him to listen for instructions.

The armed squad then split into two, three men in each team, leaving one man behind to protect the detectives. Each group then disappeared into the corridor and the classrooms on either side of the stairwell. Within a few seconds McKenzie's phone buzzed.

"One body. A male. Very cold. There's no hurry. Stay put, we're continuing the sweep."

Sunday
The Chemistry Department
Portobello High School
12.45

McKenzie stood above the body of Mark McRae, fighting the urge to vomit. Two of his team, both extremely experienced officers, had lost that same fight.

"Bastards." McKenzie said quietly and coldly.

He'd seen many, many things in his career, but the deaths here in the Portobello High School had been amongst the worst.

"I can't believe that someone would do this. It's incredibly premeditated, carefully planned and diligently executed. This is one sick serial killer. I didn't think anyone like this existed in Scotland." Brown said.

McKenzie's team had just been let into the room by the leader of the armed team who had then immediately deployed to search the rest of the school.

The risk that there was another body in the school was now real. Only a few days ago they had found two at the same time, and perhaps they would again now.

McKenzie was already wearing plastic gloves, as were his team.

He knelt down beside the body and searched for a wallet in the dead man's pockets. He'd already recognised his face from the photograph he'd taken from Mrs Blake's house, but he wanted to see if there was any ID to confirm it.

Bingo.

The man's wallet.

Credit cards, money, and a driving licence, which McKenzie quickly showed to the rest of the team.

The man was Mark McRae.

And there were two words very clearly written on his forehead.

"Okay, no more touching. Everyone step back. Elaine, please call forensics and tell them to get down here smartish. McLeish. Tell me what you see?"

McLeish stepped forward, still wiping his mouth. He'd been one of those who'd lost his lunch.

"The victim has been spread-eagled and tied to the floor. His head has been restrained, and a metal vice of some sort has been inserted into his mouth. There are two glass bottles. One positioned in each hand, as if the victim had been holding them. The bottles are almost empty but each contains some substance still in liquid form. The victim appears to have suffocated. The victim's throat is full of a solid material which has blocked his airways and prevented him from breathing. There are traces of liquid on the lips, neck and on the floor under the neck. I would surmise that the liquids have simultaneously been poured into the throat."

McLeish stopped, took a step back and gagged again, but this time managed to prevent himself from vomiting.

He apologised and stepped back towards the body, looking around the room.

"Oh dear, I've just realised what this is! This is the chemistry department and the killer has poured two chemicals down into the throat of the victim and there has been some sort of weird chemical reaction, resulting in the formation of a solid foam-like substance which has blocked the throat and airways. Shit, sorry... "

McLeish stepped away again, and this time he vomited.

"What a horrible way to die." Brown said, returning from her phone call.

"I think it was intended that way. It's all part of the show." McLeish said.

"You're not finished, McLeish. You've missed the most important part."

"Sorry, Guv, I was just imagining what it would have been like to die like that."

"You're forgiven."

"Okay... " Mcleish steadied himself to continue his report. "And the most important part is the two words scrawled on his head." McLeish continued. "Two words. They say, 'REMEMBER ME?' "

Chapter 26

Sunday
Operation BlueBuilding
Incident Room
Portacabin
13.30

McKenzie's team had returned to the portacabin to review what they'd just seen and to wait for the armed response unit to finish their search of the rest of the campus.

So far they'd found nothing new.

Wishart was not in the room. She'd gone to bring Scott Davies in for questioning with a policeman from the Portobello police station.

McKenzie had filmed the murder scene on his phone, and the team were now watching it cast up onto the electronic whiteboard.

He'd not yet called DCS Wilkinson to report. McKenzie wanted to wait for the results from the building search and to carefully plan what he was going to say.

He also needed some more time to gain better control of his emotions.

He was furious. Mad. Angry. And sad.

McRae had been on their lists. If they'd had more people on the team, they might have been able to find him before he'd become the next victim.

"Okay, thoughts?" McKenzie said, taking a deep breath.

"We've got to get this bastard!" McLeish said loudly.

"Or bastards." McKenzie corrected him. "This would have been a lot of work for one killer."

"How the hell did the killer manage to get the victim into the building whilst it's under maximum security?" Lynch voiced the thoughts of them all.

"Or was it?" McKenzie replied. "Maybe we let our guard down. Most of the team was at the new school attending the Reunion ball."

"To be fair, Mather had several PCs from Portobello helping him cover the building from the outside. Throughout the night they did regular patrols of the campus and the perimeter. And nothing was seen on the CCTV. And there were two dogs running around the campus. There were no reports of anything." Anderson replied. "And on top of that, Gary Bruce stayed the night downstairs in the other cabin. I don't know how much he slept, but Mather said he spoke to him quite regularly. He was also keeping an eye on things."

"So HOW did the killer or killers get the victim inside? HOW?" McKenzie said, his voice raised.

It was a rhetorical question, and one which had everyone stumped.

McKenzie walked over to the map of the campus.

He stood in front of it, studying it for the hundredth time.

"There has to be another way in. There has to."

He raised a finger and pointed to the revision number of the map, which was marked on the diagram in the bottom right along with the map's scale and other details.

"This is not the original. It's a copy of a later version that's had changes made to it. Brown, I want you to make it a priority to track down one of the original versions of this architect's plan. Get the original if possible, but if not that, one of the very first revisions. We're missing something here, and we need to find out what it was. Also, try to get plans of what was here before they built the school. What existed here prior? Did any part of any previously existing structure survive?"

"Yes, Guv."

"And I mean, *today*. I don't care if you have to break into the Scottish Land Registry, or the architect's office, just get us the original plan. And one that's not so dirty. Look, there's smudges all over this. It's not easy to read some of the writing or the numbers or symbols."

"Understood, Guv. I'm on it."

"Okay. Now onto the message on the forehead. 'Remember me?' What does that tell us?" McKenzie asked, starting to pace the room.

"It links two of the victims together. Blake and McRae. Both had writing on their forehead. Possibly also David Weir but we don't know that yet. They still have to find his forehead." Lynch said, then paused for a second. "I think the message on Blake's forehead may have been the same." He stood up and stepped up to the whiteboard and picked up a pen, then continued. "Forensics have said they found writing, with the following letters: R, E, M. These letters are some of the main letters in the words 'Remember Me?' It could be the same message." Lynch said, writing the words 'Remember me?' on the board, and underlining the Rs, Es and the M. "We need to get a photograph of the writing and compare the positions of the letters which were still visible."

" , please. I suspect you're going to be right." McKenzie said, and added the action to the list on the board.

Anderson next had a thought. "Willy Thomson didn't have any writing on his forehead."

"Noted. Which suggests what?"

"That he isn't part of this."

"It certainly looks like the killer wants to brand his victims. Three teachers, all killed in their place of work, two with red writing on their head. I agree, it's increasingly looking like Willy Thomson doesn't fit the modus operandum of the killer or killers."

"Can I ask, has anyone interviewed or looked into Gary Bruce? He was already on the list of suspects, and given that he was camping out downstairs last night, and he has all the keys and knows the campus better than anyone, is he now even more of a suspect than before?" McLeish asked.

"I think it's a valid point. Since you raised it, can you sit down with him, semi-formally and interview him? But be gentle. Now there's another body, it could mean continued difficulties for his business, and if he's innocent, he's got enough on his plate already. Plus, we need to keep him on side." McKenzie directed.

"That would tend to make us consider him a victim as opposed to a suspect, but that could be what he wants us to think?" Dean spoke. "I haven't met the guy yet, I'm just saying. By the way, I also have something to say."

"Yes?" McKenzie asked, giving him the floor.

"I just heard something from the forensics team. No formal identification yet, but they've been looking at the burnt-out van, and as I mentioned to you previously, one corner of the van at the back got off comparatively lightly in comparison with the rest. The rear driver-side tyre had only partially melted, and the forensics team have recovered some dirt residue trapped within the treads of the tyres. They're running some analysis on it now. I think they're making a thing of it, because it's about all there is left of any significance. The van's not going to tell us anything else." Dean finished.

"Okay, Brown, you're managing the relationship with forensics. Add that to your list and keep us up to date. McLeish, we've had three deaths now. It sounds like we're being warned about a fourth. That means the work you're doing to try and identify any missing staff is even more important now. We found one person who was missing, and now he's dead. Who's next?"

"It's a lot of work for one person to get through in a hurry."

"I understand. Just do your best."

"It would be good to know if a cattle prod was used on Mr McRae, as it was on the others?" Anderson asked.

"True. And also, were there any similar dirt residues found on his clothes, similar to the dirt found on Blake and Weir's clothes?" McKenzie added.

"Okay, I know some of you were given actions last night at the Reunion ball, and you won't have had a chance to do anything about them yet. Just keep us informed when you get any information." McKenzie added.

"Are you still going to Coll?" Brown asked. "It's getting a bit late for you to make it to Oban and catch the ferry."

"I don't know. I'm going to speak with DCS Wilkinson first, and also wait to see what happens with the rest of the search of the building. If I do go, DI Brown's in charge, and it's down to you to liaise with Mather and his team for this evening. Also, for now, no one mention to Gary Bruce anything about the third body. He doesn't need to know just yet."

"Anyone for anything else?" McKenzie asked. There were no takers.

McKenzie did his best to manage a smile, instructed everyone to make sure they got some lunch, if they could stomach it, and then clapped his hands.

Everyone was dismissed.

When they filed out of the portacabin, no one felt hungry.

Sunday
The Chemistry Department
Portobello High School
14.35

DCS Helen Wilkinson stood beside McKenzie in their white forensics suits, looking down at the body of Mark McRae.

McKenzie had called her, and insisted she come out and see the scene of the crime for herself.

He hadn't warned her just how brutal the experience would be.

To his boss's credit, she had taken it in her stride.

No uncontrollable vomiting had occurred.

"We're looking at Scotland's worst serial killer in years. When this eventually gets out, we're talking international media camping out on your doorstep, Ma'am. You're going to be a media star."

"Don't put this on me, McKenzie. This is your case. You'll be the media star, not me."

"I want more people."

"You can't have them. Not for another few days at least."

"There's at least one more death on the way. You saw the note. *'Three, then four.'*"

"The Queen leaves in a few day's time. Given the state of the Union at the moment, everything that can be done to maintain and build relationships between England and Scotland is of paramount importance. He visit's been arranged to build bridges, swing the popular sentiment away from the nationalists and back to seeing sense and saying 'No' to independence in the next referendum. If anything happens to her, it could cost us the Union."

"I get all that. I do. But you tell that to Number Four."

They were still both looking down at the body. The look of horror frozen on Mark McRae's face was something that McKenzie would never ever forget for the rest of his life.

"Ma'am. This is just a thought, but go with me on this, for a moment at least."

"Go for it, Campbell."

Again, the use of his first name. Not uncommon, but he knew she was trying her best to empathise with the ridiculous situation he was in.

"Okay, so just how real is the terror threat? The person or persons behind these series of murders are very clever. Quite frankly, at the moment, they're running circles round us. I just wonder, could your terror threat actually be of their making? Could it be part of their plan to get people taken off the case and give them maximum flexibility to do what they have to do without detection? With as few people chasing after them as possible?"

The DCS took her eyes of the body for the first time and turned to look at her DCI.

McKenzie was a bright man. One of the best.

His idea sounded a bit desperate, but on second thoughts, she couldn't discount it.

"Campbell, it's highly unlikely. I know, for a fact, that the threat is being taken very seriously by everyone. A valid code word was issued. I don't want to say any more than that. So… "

"How current was the code word? And how many people might know the code words?" he interrupted his boss. "What's the chances that someone managed to get privy knowledge of an acceptable code word, used it to generate a threat, and get everyone taken off this case?"

"I'd say slim."

"But not impossible."

"I'll get back to you on that, Campbell."

"So, you'll consider it?"

"The Queen's going back in a few days. You can get as many officers as you need when that happens."

"Ma'am, I appreciate that, and I'll take you up on the offer when it happens. However, and this is the thing, Ma'am... I get the feeling that the killer is one step ahead of us and he or she or they *know* that. I'm worried that by the time the Queen goes back down south, this thing will all be over. None of this is coincidental. It's all been planned in advance. And very cleverly."

"So, what are you saying, exactly?"

"I'm saying that in the next few days, there's going to be one, and possibly even more deaths to reckon with. Who they are, I have no idea. And this school doesn't help. It's like a flame to the moths. The sooner they blow it up, the better!"

Chapter 27

Sunday
Operation BlueBuilding
Incident Room
Portacabin
15.30

McKenzie sat in the incident room, eating a Gregg's sausage roll and some hot Tomato soup.

His revulsion at the latest death hadn't left, but hunger was beginning to affect his ability to think clearly.

Brown sat opposite him, eating a sandwich.

One was all she could face.

McKenzie was quiet, chewing away and mulling something over in his mind.

"I'm going to Coll." He finally announced. "I need to speak to the headmaster as soon as possible. If anyone knows why three of his staff have been slaughtered in his school, he will."

"The ferry from Oban to Coll is at seven fifteen in the morning. You'd have to drive to Oban tonight. If you spend time on Coll interviewing the headmaster, you're talking several days back and forward, mostly travelling."

McKenzie nodded.

"But I've got to go. This guy knows something. I'm sure of it."

McKenzie also knew that if the theory he'd expressed to DCS Wilkinson was correct, by the time he'd gone back and forward to Coll to conduct the interview, the serial killer might have struck again several times.

McKenzie pulled out his phone.

It was time to play hardball with DCS Wilkinson one more time.

McKenzie had just thought of a solution, and he wasn't going to take no for an answer.

Sunday
The Grange
Edinburgh
16.25

Fiona McKenzie hurriedly packed a few things into an overnight bag, just in case, along with some Tupperware containers full of food from the fridge.

"I know you say you'll be back tonight, but the weather on the islands is notoriously changeable. So… this is just in case you get stuck there this evening," she warned, handing him the bag and giving him a kiss on the cheek.

"I won't. I can't afford to. I need to be back here tonight, and on the job tomorrow."

Just then McKenzie's phone rang.

It was his boss, DCS Wilkinson.

"Okay, I've done it. I've pulled a few strings, and blown a hole in our budget for the rest of the year, but you've got what you wanted. Be at the airport at six o'clock. Ask for Sergeant Danny Alexander at information. They'll direct you."

McKenzie smiled.

"Thanks, Ma'am. I appreciate it."

"Take a sick bag with you. Apparently, it's a rough crossing and I don't want to have to fork out extra to clean the helicopter as well. When will you be back?"

"Tomorrow morning. I'm planning to visit McRae's house. We can't track down his brother yet, so the next of kin haven't been informed. I've left that with McLeish."

"Good. I hope you make progress with the headmaster and get what you need."

"So do I. I'm sure he knows what it's all about. But if he doesn't tell us, there's going to be more deaths. And soon."

McKenzie hung up, hugged his wife and stroked Little Bump, then left the house.

Brown was waiting outside in his car to escort him to the airport.

As they made their way through the Edinburgh traffic, McKenzie admitted that he was a little nervous.

He hated flying.

And he'd never been in a helicopter before.

He'd managed to hold his stomach down earlier that afternoon, but unfortunately, McKenzie's instincts told him that this evening he might not be so lucky.

Sunday
Cramond
16.30

Marie McDonald relaxed back into the arms of Stuart Nisbet, and laughed aloud as the water spray splashed her face at over 40 miles per hour.

During a wonderful meal, Stuart had persuaded Marie to 'live a little' and step outside of her comfort zone.

"It's a surprise!" he'd said, and next thing she knew, she was standing on a beach in Cramond, wearing one of Stuart's spare wetsuits and just about to climb on board a jet ski.

"Don't worry, I think I know what I'm doing." Stuart reassured her.

"'*Think*'? What sort of reassurance is that?" she asked, raising her eyebrows nervously.

"I'm teasing you. Actually, it's just a ploy to trick you into letting me put my arms around you. If you sit on the jet ski first, I'll put my arms around you and help you with the controls. Or if that makes you feel uncomfortable, you can sit on the back, and put your hands here and here, and just hold on as tightly as you can. Or you can hold on to me, if you prefer. Whatever is best for you." Stuart explained, showing her what to do, and then explaining how the jet ski controls worked.

"I want to try it myself please, at least for a while. Just hold on to me and make sure I don't fall off, though."

"Okay, let's do it." He laughed. He reached out a hand and helped her aboard. A moment later, she was flying across the Firth of Forth, bouncing off the waves and screaming her head off with the exhilaration.

At first, Stuart took the controls, and she enjoyed his arms around her, and the feeling of closeness and security it brought.

Then when they came to a temporary stop about a mile off the beach, she asked if she could try driving it by herself.

"Absolutely." Stuart encouraged her, and then once more explained how the controls functioned.

It turned out she was a natural.

Stuart was impressed.

"How far can we go?" she asked.

"Let's go along the coast underneath the bridges. You're in charge!"

And so they did. Under Marie's control, they roared off towards the three awe-inspiring bridges that spanned the Firth of Forth river estuary just outside of Edinburgh.

Hurtling underneath the massive bridges that towered overhead, Marie couldn't believe just how much she was enjoying herself.

As they passed underneath the last bridge, the new road bridge that connected South Queensferry to North Queensferry, she slowed down and then turned towards Stuart.

Before he could ask what the matter was, she kissed him.

Twice.

The first was just a practice.

By the second time, she'd mastered it.

It turned out that Stuart was a fast learner too.

Sunday
Edinburgh Airport
18.00

The helicopter from the Police Scotland Air Support Unit sat on the runway waiting for McKenzie to join them. It had already flown over from its base in the Clyde Heliport in Glasgow.

During his career, McKenzie had often summoned the help of the helicopters in the pursuit of criminals on the run, using their thermal imaging cameras to hover over the ground and spot where a criminal was hiding, but so far he'd never actually been in one.

He'd avoided it.

Tonight however there was no alternative.

In the car over to the airport, McKenzie had made a few calls and established contact with the local police force responsible for Coll.

It turned out the tiny island of Coll, which had only 221 inhabitants, did not have a local police officer on the island. Instead, McKenzie had to contact the police officer on the neighbouring island of Tiree. After explaining to her why he was flying to Coll, who he was visiting and where he had to go, the PC was just able to make the last local ferry and make her way to the island.

McKenzie arranged with the officer that she would track down the headmaster's whereabouts - most likely the local pub or at his home – and ensure he was available to answer questions in a sober state by the time McKenzie arrived. The last thing McKenzie wanted was to land on Coll and find the man was too drunk to question. A few drinks might help the process, but too many would not be good.

As the helicopter took off and began the flight to Coll, McKenzie mused over the crime rate on Coll in comparison to what he was facing: the last big reported crime wave on Coll was in 2011 when someone went mad in the only public toilet on the island and destroyed a hand towel dispenser, pulled a pipe off the wall and smashed a sink.

Although it was serious stuff for the outraged locals, it couldn't help but make McKenzie smile.

An hour later, smiling was the last thing on his mind. Having forgotten to request a proper vomit bag, he was making do with the large plastic bag Fiona had put some food in for the evening.

Knowing that the pilot and crew would be laughing their heads off upfront, McKenzie kept himself to himself, and the plastic bag.

Thankfully, it all came to an end thirty minutes later when they landed at the island's small airport, where they were the only visitors.

As the doors opened and McKenzie jumped down onto the tarmac, he was tempted to bend down and kiss the ground, so grateful was he to be back on terra firma. Thankfully, he decided against the amateur dramatics, and found himself almost immediately greeted by PC Eileen Grant, the policewoman from Tiree.

"DCI McKenzie? Welcome to Coll. I hope you had a pleasant flight?" she said warmly, then upon seeing the colour of McKenzie's face and the sick bag he was still carrying, she pointed to the bucket by the small airport building.

"Don't worry, I was listening to the weather forecast, and the winds are dying down tonight. You'll have a much smoother trip back."

"I think I'd rather swim." McKenzie replied.

"Probably not a good idea. Anyway, Mr Gray is waiting for us at his cottage."

"How is he?" McKenzie asked, wondering what to expect.

"He was in the bar, but I caught him in time before he'd drunk too much. I don't think he was very pleased to hear about your visit. He seemed very nervous, and a little distraught. Mr Gray and I are already acquainted. We've met several times before."

"Good. I'm glad you were able to make it. He might find your presence and mannerism reassuring." McKenzie thanked her. McKenzie turned to the pilot's who'd now left the helicopter and he made some quick arrangements about the return trip. "Okay, let's go. I can't wait to meet Mr Gray. I've got a lot of questions to ask him."

Sunday
Island of Coll
Port na Luing Cottage
21.05

Now the world had stopped spinning McKenzie was able to appreciate the scenery of the island, and the attraction of it for people who just wanted to get away from it all.

The island was small and very beautiful.

Now the heavy clouds from earlier had been blown over to the mainland, an incredible sunset was developing, the sea was a beautiful turquoise against the shallow pristine white sandy coves and inlets, and he was sure that not too far from the beach, McKenzie had just seen a pod of dolphins jumping and playing in the evening light.

The narrow roads were empty, and although the island was dotted with small cottages and bothies here and there, the land was mostly open and wild.

Having left the airport, they'd passed through what passed as the only town on the island. Grant had pointed out the only hotel on the island, aptly named 'The Coll Hotel'.

"That's where you and the crew will be staying tonight, if we leave it too late. I've already checked into my room. The next ferry isn't until the morning."

The PC didn't seem at all perturbed that her plans for the evening had been ruined. The pace of life here was markedly slower than on the mainland. It was simpler and more relaxed.

Except McKenzie suspected that for those who lived on the island all year round, things could probably get pretty harsh during the winter months.

"Here we are," Grant announced, pulling off the main road and down a dirt track to a white cottage overlooking an idyllic private beach in a secluded bay.

McKenzie immediately fell in love with the place.

He could see the attraction of retiring here, and sensed the calm and peacefulness the moment he stepped out of the car. The smell of the salt in the air was invigorating, and within a few seconds McKenzie was fully revived, the experience of the helicopter trip now forgotten.

The door to the cottage opened.

Daniel Gray emerged through the front door, an old man, a little overweight, white hair, and a beard.

"Good evening, Detective."

"Good evening to you, Mr Gray. Thank you for agreeing to meet me."

"I wasn't given much choice in the matter. Anyway, come in and have a seat. I've already made the tea."

Grant and McKenzie walked into the back of the cottage, and were immediately impressed by the panoramic view of the beach and the sea directly below the cottage. It was truly amazing. McKenzie could imagine sitting there hour after hour, just staring out at the waves. The word relaxing was possibly an understatement.

Looking round the room, McKenzie took in as much as he could of the ex-headmaster's living space.

He was struck by the fact that there was no television.

A large pair of binoculars on a tripod stood by the window, beside a table with a laptop on it.

Floor to ceiling bookshelves, full of books, dominated one wall.

An old fashioned 1920's gramophone with a large brass flaring horn rising out of it was the main feature of the room, beside which sat a stack of old 78-inch shellac records.

The room was spacious, with enough room for two sofas around a fire place which formed most of the other main wall.

McKenzie suspected that two rooms had been knocked through to one. It was unlikely that rooms in these old cottages were originally that large considering the cold winters and howling gales that would sweep across the island and batter the coastline.

Although he could be wrong. Perhaps he was just prejudiced by watching too many old films. Having never really visited the Scottish islands before, how could he know what the houses really looked like inside?

Grant wandered through to the kitchen enquiring if she could help carry the tea. She was met by a sharp rebuttal which McKenzie could hear from several rooms away.

"Eileen, I'm old, but not dead yet! I can manage fine by myself, thank you."

While Grant hovered around the kitchen just to make sure he could manage after all, McKenzie ambled around the room, checking out the bookcase and its contents. From his experience, the choice of books could reveal a lot about a person.

There were a number of photos on the wall which caught McKenzie's attention, notably one of Portobello High School itself.

Beside it there was a series of horizontal photos showing the pupils from subsequent final years of school, spanning at least ten years.

"I knew them all." The headmaster's voice declared, as he walked slowly into the room carrying a large tray. Grant followed up the rear.

"Would you take a seat please, Detective, and I'll serve you some tea. Do you take milk or sugar?"

"Just milk please." McKenzie replied, sitting down on one of the sofas.

"Well leave it a moment to brew, then I'll serve you." Mr Gray announced, putting the tray down on a table between the sofas. He sat himself down and exhaled loudly. "It's been a long day, and I'll be needing my bed soon, so I think we'll best be getting on with this. Although to be honest, I think you've had a wasted journey coming up here to see me in person. I told you yesterday, quite clearly I think, that I can't help you."

"I appreciate that. But I really do think you can help us. You were the headmaster at the school for a long time, and if you knew all the pupils as you just said you did, you must certainly have known your teachers even better. If you can't help us, no one can."

"So, what do you want to know?" He asked, leaning forward and lifting the lid of the tea pot, inserting a spoon and stirring the tea-leaves.

Settling back into the sofa opposite, McKenzie had the sense that Gray was holding something back, and that he was very nervous about the discussion, maybe even scared.

"When I spoke to you yesterday, it was in connection with two deaths. Those of David Weir, a geography teacher, and also of Ronald Blake, the religious education teacher. Can you remember them?"

"Yes, of course. I remember them both very well."

"Good. Unfortunately, earlier this afternoon we also discovered the body of Mark McRae, one of the Chemistry teachers. Like the others, his body was found in the classroom where he taught at the old Portobello High School."

When McKenzie spoke, Mr Gray was lifting the teapot to pour the tea, but as soon as McKenzie mentioned the death of Mark McRae, the ex-headmaster lowered the pot, almost dropping it, and spilling a little of the tea through the spout onto the table beside one of the cups.

Resting his hand on the table beside the teapot, the old man lowered his head and closed his eyes and took a deep breath.

"How did he die?" he asked, without looking at McKenzie.

"He was found pinioned to the floor of his classroom, with a mixture of chemicals poured down his throat that seemed to react with each other upon contact and form a blockage in his throat that blocked his airways and asphyxiated him. It was without doubt a terrifying and horrible death." The detective didn't hold anything back, studying the reaction of the teacher as he explained it all.

The old man's hand had become to shake, quite visibly.

"Are you okay Daniel?" Grant asked.

The man said nothing for a moment, then opened his eyes and picked up the teapot. He tried to pour the tea out, but missed the cup completely. Grant moved closer to him, placed a hand gently on his and said, "Why don't you let me do that for us, Daniel?"

The man nodded.

McKenzie spoke next.

"Mr Gray, that's three teachers, now all dead, and each killed in a most horrific way near where they taught, within the building of a school at which you were the headmaster for quite a number of years. From talking to the wife of Ronald Blake, I believe these three men were good friends. Then something happened, and their friendship seemed to dissolve. I can't quite help but ask myself, if there is a connection between the reason their friendship dissolved, and the reason they were all killed? I also wonder if you know what that reason is?"

The old man said nothing. He was visibly shocked, but still silent.

"Mr Gray, may I make myself clear. Subsequent to the discovery of the deaths of Mr Weir and Mr Blake, we had a series of communications from the killer warning there would be a third and possibly fourth death to follow. We've now had a third death. Please, if you know what this is all about, or can tell us anything that could connect these three deaths, please tell me now. It could help us avoid a fourth death." McKenzie stressed the last sentence.

Still no reaction from the old man.

"Mr Gray, I sense that you are actually scared to tell me what you know. Being scared is possibly understandable, especially if you know what this is all about. But not telling me what you know could be problematic. If it another death occurs, and it transpires that you had information which could have helped us in our investigations and prevented that death, you could be guilty of withholding valuable information and you may be found liable to sharing responsibility for their death. In addition, if another person is murdered, how would you feel if you knew you could have prevented it?"

McKenzie let the last few words hang in the air for maximum impact.

Grant put another gentle hand upon the old man's.

"Daniel. If you know something, and have done all these years, perhaps now's the time to share it? Let it go. Tell us. *Please*? For your sake, if not for anyone else's?"

The old man shook his head, took a deep breath and pushed himself up out of the sofa.

He walked across to the window and stared out at the sea. The sun was setting now, and the sky was turning a beautiful orange.

"Okay," he whispered quietly. "I'll tell you."

Chapter 28

Sunday
Island of Coll
Port na Luing Cottage
21.35

"What I will tell you now happened many years ago. It's part of a past I try to forget, but which I think will haunt me for the rest of my life." The headmaster began. "As a headmaster you have to make many tough decisions, and sometimes you get them wrong. Perhaps this is one of those. Or perhaps not. But it doesn't stop me feeling guilty."

"About what" McKenzie nudged, when the man seemed to drift off into his memories and stop speaking.

"David Weir, Ronald Blake and Mark McRae were three of the best teachers I had. They were young, enthusiastic and great motivators. They were great friends of each other, both inside school and socially. They knew their stuff and were part of the new generation. The students loved them. Literally."

"One girl in particular. She came from a troubled background. An only child with parents who mostly ignored her. She lacked self-confidence. She was an intelligent girl, and very, very pretty. A lot of the boys at the school had crushes on her, but quite early on during the second year, she developed a crush on Ronald Blake, the Religious Education teacher. She also never really accepted just how attractive she actually was. I think mainly because the one man she did like, did not reciprocate. Ronald Blake didn't see her that way, and she took it very personally. Ronald was a very handsome man, and took a keen interest in his pupils. He'd travelled widely as a student and young man, and was very spiritual. While his main focus in teaching at the school was Christianity, I knew that he'd begun to combine the philosophies he learnt from his different studies in religion, and he used them to help students who increasingly came to him with their problems, and who sought help or counselling. He was a good man. And like I said, a wonderful teacher. His grades were brilliant, sorry, by that I mean that the pupils in his class all scored excellent grades. At the time, I wished I had more teachers like him."

McKenzie sat silently, letting the old teacher reminisce, and mentally storing everything that was said.

"As the years went by, I think it's fair to say that the girl became slightly obsessed with Ronald Blake. She didn't bring him an apple every day, but she tried almost everything else. Although Ronald Blake himself never discussed it with me, until it was too late, she talked about it with her school counsellor, who later told me everything when I conducted an internal review, after the incident."

He paused then and looked at McKenzie. It was the first time he'd referred to the fact that something of significance had occurred. McKenzie didn't probe on what that incident had been, trusting that Mr Gray was just about to elaborate on it.

When McKenzie gave him the freedom to continue, Gray did exactly that.

He came over to his sofa, sat down, took a sip of the tea that Grant offered him, and then pushed back into his chair and closed his eyes.

"I was told later that she became increasingly jealous of another girl in the school, who she nicknamed 'GasBag'. I wasn't sure who Gasbag was, but apparently, as far as the girl who'd fallen for Ronald Blake was concerned, Gasbag was the reason why Blake didn't like her. Instead, Blake liked Gasbag. Not her. So, increasingly, she tried to be just like Gasbag. She dressed like her, copied her. Took the same classes as her. None of which worked. As far as I know Blake never did anything with the other girl, 'GasBag', but I think that Blake's admirer believed that he had. Anyway, like I said, I was oblivious to all of this until things got way out of hand."

The headmaster opened his eyes, and tears formed on the edge of his eyelids and began to run down his cheek.

"It was the final year of school for the girl... " the headmaster began again, but McKenzie interrupted him gently for the first time.

"May I ask, what was the girl called? Her name?"

The headmaster hesitated, seemingly reluctant to say anything.

"Can we just call her... Amelia, for now... that wasn't her name. But it's the first name I thought of... ."

McKenzie nodded. He sensed that if the name was important, it would come out later.

"Okay, so Amelia stayed until the 6th year, did some SYS... Sixth Year Studies, and added to the very good Highers she'd already got in the fifth year. The end of the school year came. School was finished. Technically, she'd now left the school and she had nothing more to do with me, or the school."

"But... " McKenzie couldn't help but asking when the conversation seemed to dry up and Mr Gray reached for some tea. The cup hovered in front of his lips but he didn't drink from it. Slowly he began to speak again, and the tears which had now dried up, started to flow again. The cup began to shake, and some tea spilled out over the sides and dripped onto the table below. Grant reached out with two hands and steadied the cup, and then guided Mr Gray's hand back to the table top.

He looked across at her, a bewildered look on his face. She smiled back.

"But... ,"McKenzie prompted again. "What happened after the school had finished?"

"It was the end of the school ball... people like to call it the School Prom nowadays... you know, another one of those things that's infected us from the States. It was just getting popular than, and because the school hadn't officially organised one, the Sixth Year pupils got together and organised it themselves instead. We agreed to give them the use of the school, or rather, the Council agreed, and they planned the rest. The teachers and staff were invited too. Not all went, but some did."

"Did Ronald Blake, David Weir and Mark McRae all go?"

"Yes." The headmaster answered. "They did. And so did Amelia. Apparently, she turned up at the ball looking exactly like Gasbag. Same dress. Same hair. She was going all out to get Ronald Blake that night. Her last chance. And why not? She was over eighteen by now. School was finished. Technically she was an independent adult, and he was no longer her teacher."

"How long after the school had officially finished was this?" McKenzie asked.

"About two weeks. During the holidays… I mean, what would have been the holidays, but since… "

"Since, they had now left school, it was no longer part of the holidays anymore?" McKenzie agreed, using the point to strike some empathy with him. McKenzie could sense that they were getting to the crux of the matter, and that the closer they got, the harder it was for Mr Gray to continue.

"Exactly."

"Did you go?"

"Yes. But I didn't know what happened until much later. I was completely unaware of it. I was so busy in the main hall enjoying the ball. At the time, I thought it was truly wonderful. My wife was there too. We both enjoyed it. Everyone did… Except Amelia." He sobbed.

"Why?"

Mr Gray took a very deep breath and then committed himself. McKenzie could tell this was going to be it. This was the moment of truth…

"Amelia started to get drunk. I'm told she was flirting heavily with Blake. He was dancing with her, too. I don't think flirting, but he was relaxed. School was finished. His pupils were all adults now. It was a moment when they could all relate to each other as adults for the first time. Blake was drinking too. Quite a lot. I also think he'd been smoking some weed with some of the other teachers. It was quite common then, and this was not a school event, really. After a while, everyone got very, very relaxed. Barriers began to fall. Perhaps too far. At one point, Amelia was drinking with some friends, and she saw Blake dancing with Gasbag. Same dress. A bright red dress. And the same hair. It really upset her. She didn't say anything then, but she told me later that was the point when she decided to get Blake for herself. To prove she was better than Gasbag. To make sure she got him, and not her. Apparently, she'd hovered around until Blake and Gasbag had stopped dancing, and then she'd slowly moved in and taken her place. They started talking. She was really flirting. He'd said he wanted to go for another smoke, with his friends. She'd asked him what they were smoking. He'd told her. She'd smiled. He'd asked her if she'd wanted to join him. Bingo. Oh, yes please! So, they'd left the hall, he'd gone to get his friends together. They all gone upstairs. They found a classroom in the RE department, two floors up. They got perfect peace and quiet there. Nobody would disturb them. They'd all started smoking marijuana together, getting really high. And then… "

Gray coughed. Took a quick sip of tea, and then continued. McKenzie sensed that Gray was keen to get it out. To reveal the truth about what had happened. To get it off his chest, finally, once and for all.

"I don't know exactly what happened then, just what I was told, but I had four versions of the truth, and from hours of conversations, perhaps even days of talking about it, I believe I know roughly what happened. Incredible and no matter how bad it may seem." A final deep breath. And then it all came out.

"At some point Amelia had taken Blake's hand and led him out of that classroom to the one next door. Blake's classroom. The one he taught in during his time at school. They sat on a desk together, smoking some more marijuana. On top of the alcohol which Amelia had drunk, it all became a bit too much. Amelia came on to Blake in a big way. She was a very attractive girl. I don't know exactly what Blake had ever thought about her before, but here was an incredibly attractive girl, now an adult, no longer a pupil, basically throwing herself at him. She kissed him. He kissed her. He'd been drinking and smoking too. They were both very relaxed. Both drunk. Both adults. He'd started kissing her. She took her top off. Then something changed. Amelia later insisted that at some point then, she lost control. He began to take the initiative. It was no longer her pursuing him, but him lusting after her. For the first time ever. He got on top of her. Removed her bra. Then took off her panties."

Gray sighed, wiped some sweat from his forehead, and then continued, committing himself to the events of that night, so long ago.

"He was kissing her neck, was just about to enter her for the first time, - and Amelia had later insisted that at this point she was still a virgin – when Blake had called her by the wrong name. He had called her Gasbag's name. Amelia went nuts. She started to cry. Apparently, she claimed later, she'd cried 'Stop!', repeatedly, and tried to get him off her. But Blake didn't stop. He claimed that she hadn't said stop. Or at least that he hadn't heard her. That she was really keen for it. That she'd been coming on to him for years. And so he made love to her."

Grant had coughed and was about to say something but McKenzie shot her a glance and warned her not to interrupt the flow. He knew that Gray was not finished yet. There was more to come.

"Just when he'd finished, you know… making love to Amelia, they'd heard voices at the door. It was Blake's friends. They'd been watching from the doorway. They came into the classroom then. They closed the door."

Mr Gray coughed several times, closed his eyes, shook his head and finished what he'd begun.

"She later claimed that after closing the door, they'd come into the room and had both raped her at the same time while Blake had watched. But when questioned later, Weir and McRae had insisted that she had invited them in and initiated it. She had wanted everything that had happened, that she willingly incited them on, and that everything that had taken place had been mutual, between consenting adults. Admittedly, it was unusual. But they had insisted that she had been a willing party if not the instigator of everything that happened."

"In spite of her insisting that she had been gang-raped?" Grant suddenly burst out, no longer able to contain herself.

"Yes." Mr Gray, the ex-headmaster of the school had admitted. "But I wasn't there, and I don't know what really happened that night. In spite of everything that happened since."

"Can you tell us who Amelia and Mr Blake's friends were?" McKenzie asked. "I think we need to know that now."

"Mr Blake's friends that evening were David Weir and Mark McRae."

"And Amelia?" Grant pushed.

"I'll tell you, but I wonder if it's all best left in the past now. Amelia can't have had anything to do with the recent murders in Portobello, … with any of this," the headmaster insisted.

"Why not? Blake, Weir and McRae are all dead now, and it could be highly likely that their deaths and that evening, no matter how long ago, are all connected together somehow."

"No, Amelia can't be responsible."

Mr Blake looked quickly from McKenzie to Grant, as if seeking some form of understanding.

"Her name was Maggie Sutherland. She's dead now. She committed suicide three years ago."

Chapter 29
Sunday
Forth Rail Bridge
South Queensferry
22.05

Stuart Nisbet and Marie McDonald left the Hawes Inn restaurant and crossed the road hand-in-hand to sit on the sea wall. They sat directly beneath the Rail Bridge which stretched above them for over a mile from one side of the River Forth to the other.

They had just enjoyed a wonderful meal, with candlelight, and Marie was still on a natural high from the jet skiing adventure earlier that day. She couldn't stop laughing.

"I can't believe you made me do that! I've never done anything like that before… it was amazing." She gushed, recalling the experience excitedly.

"Would you do it again?" Stuart asked.

"Absolutely. If I lived here, I'd buy one of those things and commute to work on it!"

"Actually, you probably wouldn't when it was cold and miserable, and the rain was pouring down. Today was a good day. The conditions were just right."

"Thank you," she said, and kissed him one more time.

"Have you been here before?" Stuart asked, moving his head to indicate the bridge above them and the spot beside the river where they were now sitting.

"Yes. Many times. I love it. It's one of the places I sometimes come to think when I'm back home. Either here or the top of Arthur's Seat."

Stuart smiled.

"Me too."

"Thank you for today, Stuart. It's been wonderful and a big surprise. I never expected to meet someone last night that I'd get on so well with, let alone end up here, sitting with him like this, having spent such a lovely day together."

He squeezed her hand and smiled back. "Actually, genuinely, the pleasure has been all mine. I was pretty nervous about last night, and how it would be to meet everyone again, but thanks to you, it was actually very bearable. I'm sorry if I was a little distracted for a while when I found out that Maggie Sutherland had died. It was a bit of a shock. I want to be honest with you… I had actually hoped to see her again last night. When I was at school, I had a massive crush on her - which went nowhere by the way - and last night I was hoping to show her that I'd not turned out so bad after all. Meeting you and then finding out about her death conflicted my emotions for a while, but I don't want you to feel that I was ignoring you at all. Does that make any sense?"

Marie smiled gently and squeezed his hand back.

"It's funny how our past lives influence our futures so much. The memories of those who we knew when we were so young have such a powerful effect on us all our lives, even if we grow up and become people who are completely different from those who we were when we were younger. That includes our past crushes.

You never forget them. Ever." Marie said, turning her head and looking out over across the water.

"And for the record," Marie continued. "You didn't make me feel bad. So far, I have enjoyed your company immensely."

He smiled back, then adjusted his sitting position slightly and sat with her side-by-side on the wall, their feet dangling over the sea which lapped against the sea wall beneath them.

They sat like that for quite a while.

Neither feeling the need to speak to fill up the lull in their conversation. Each just enjoying the moment, and comfortable to think their own thoughts, whatever they were. In silence.

Stuart's mind filled momentarily with a vision of Maggie Sutherland the last time he had seen her.

Then he blinked a couple of times and consigned her to the past.

Where she belonged, and where, in truth, she had always been.

Maggie Sutherland was gone now.

He would never think of her again.

Sunday
Island of Coll
Port na Luing Cottage
22.10

"I need to get a breath of fresh air." Daniel Gray announced, and slowly pushed himself up out of his sofa. Grant went to help him, but he shrugged her hands away. "Just give me a few moments, please."

McKenzie and Grant watched him make his way out the back door and over to some rocks at the bottom of his garden, where he sat down and gazed over the beach below and at the sky beyond.

"There's still a lot more to tell," McKenzie cautioned Grant. "I appreciate that this may be very uncomfortable for you to listen to, but for now we need to give him the space to say what he feels able to tell us. If he clams up now, there's going to be a lot of unanswered questions."

Grant nodded.

"A *lot* of questions," she replied. "It's very likely that the poor girl was raped, repeatedly, and those three men got away with it!"

"We don't know that, Grant. But it's one of the possibilities we will need to consider. I'm afraid we will also now need to bring her death into the case and view it with suspicion until we can establish the exact cause of death from the records. Could she, for example, have been killed by one of the three men? Or even Mr Grant? He could maybe even be a suspect. Unlikely. But possible. There's going to be a lot of questions. Which is why we need to get as much as possible out of him while he's still willing to talk. Agreed?"

"Yes," she replied. But McKenzie could tell that she was upset.

"Could you please make another cup of tea?" McKenzie asked. "I'll go out and talk with him. If we don't come back in, please join us. Since we're not recording this, I need you as a witness to all that is said."

Grant nodded, and McKenzie wandered outside.

It was almost dark now, as dark as it was going to get anyway, but the sky on the horizon still held on to some light. Enough to see by, or walk around in.

"May I?" McKenzie asked, as he came to sit beside Mr Gray.

"Yes. Please."

McKenzie lowered himself on to the rock beside the old man, and for a while sat silently, admiring the curve of the bay and the white sands, and listening to the hypnotic lapping of the waves as they ran along the beach and broke gently on the shore.

It was truly a wonderful place.

It reminded him of the film 'Local Hero', the classic film from his childhood where an oil magnate from the States fell in love with the Scottish scenery and a beach just like this, and refused to build an oil refinery that might threaten it all.

"You have a wonderful home, Mr Gray. I love your front room and the sweeping vista of the sea and the beach. It's incredible."

"Aye, that it is. It's the source of all my inspiration. And it's where I get all my work done."

"Work? What do you do? I'm sorry, I thought you were retired."

"Retired? Only from the rat race of life in the city. No, I write. I'm a writer. At least, I have been for the past twenty years."

"Aha... yes, I saw your laptop on the table in the room. Is that where you write?"

"Every day. Three thousand words. Without fail."

"Wow. What do you write? Is it possible I've read any of your work?"

"Thrillers mainly. Psychological thrillers. But you won't have heard of me. I write under a pen-name."

"That's a big achievement. I hear it's almost impossible to get a publisher these days."

"Aye, it is. I gave up on that malarkey a long time ago. I self-publish. I do it all myself. I'm not so successful. I don't sell many. But that's not the point. I write because I want to, because I have to... that's what a writer is, someone who has to write, must write, even if no one else is reading what they do. Although that's always a bonus."

"So, who reads your work?"

"My friends. The people I want to read my work... sometimes I send them my books for free. Writing is a good way of expressing ideas and sharing them with others. Anyway, enough about that. I'm sure that's not why you came all this way out to see me."

"No, but it's interesting."

McKenzie took the hint and didn't pursue it any further.

Instead, they sat together for a little longer, watching the distant colours in the sky, and listening to the sea.

"Okay, I'm ready." Mr Gray announced sometime later, and slowly raised himself to his feet. "Shall we?"

Back inside, the tea was already poured and waiting. They sat down and took a few sips.

"So, I know you've probably been asking the big question, 'was she raped'?" The old man looked at them, and they could see the stress in his eyes. "I've asked myself the same questions for the past twenty-five years. And honestly, I don't know. But the older I get, the more I think that perhaps she was. But it was all very different then."

"How?" Grant interrupted. "Rape is rape."

McKenzie shot her a look. She immediately shut up.

"Did she go to the police?" McKenzie asked.

"No. She didn't. And that's the thing."

"A lot of rape victims stay silent. Especially in those days." Grant added, gently. This time McKenzie let it pass.

"So how did you come to hear of it, Mr Gray? You mentioned earlier that you didn't know about Maggie's issues until the school's councillor brought it up with you later."

"That's true. The whole time this was happening, I was down in the school hall with the rest of the pupils… sorry, graduates. And I never heard anything about it for about six months. Maggie went to university and started studying Psychology and Philosophy at St. Andrews. About a month before Christmas, later that same year, she came to my office one day. She was in a terrible state. She told me she'd been raped by three of my teachers on the evening of the Ball. I listened to everything she had to say. Very carefully. I took it very seriously. I spoke to all the teachers at the school who'd known her, including her old councillor, and I got a lot of mixed reports from everyone. The girl was obviously very intelligent, but confused and emotionally damaged. I talked with the teachers concerned, Blake, Weir and McRae, and their side of the story was very different to hers, as I alluded to earlier."

"And what happened then? Did you get the police involved?" Grant prompted. This time McKenzie did glare at her, and a lot more menacingly than before.

"No. Maggie was adamant she didn't want them to get involved. But she wanted me to fire the three teachers, and to make an example of Blake. She particularly wanted me to punish Blake. Even then I got the impression that she felt very strongly for him, and that matters weren't as simple as she claimed. There were a lot of complex emotions at play, that was evident."

"Rape affects victims very deeply, Daniel, and many victims are raped by people they love or are deeply acquainted with. Familiarity, however, does not equate to permission."

"Thank you, Grant. I think we all appreciate that." McKenzie declared, "However, for now, please let Mr Gray elaborate on the situation as he experienced it at the time."

McKenzie sipped his tea, then offered some more from the pot to Mr Gray. He shook his head.

"I don't think that we should forget that this was 1993. Attitudes were very different back then."

"Rape is rape, regardless of where or when it takes place." Grant responded immediately.

"Grant, could you please take a moment to make a fresh pot of tea, and if possible, call the hotel and reserve a room for me for this evening along with the crew of the helicopter?"

Grant glared at McKenzie for a moment, then stood, uttered "Yes, Guv," and left the room.

"Grant is correct," McKenzie continued. "What happened in the end? Did you discuss this with anyone else? How was it left?"

"I could think about nothing else for months. My work at school began to deteriorate. I need you to know that I took this very seriously indeed. But, at the end of the day, she was accusing three of my best teachers of something that in all honesty I couldn't see them guilty of doing. They were *good* people. And she was now a consenting adult. A *consenting* adult. After all my considerations on the matter, I eventually decided that she *was* consenting. I knew that she was a very mixed up young lady... sorry... woman, now. *Then...* I came to believe that she had taken the initiative, and she had seduced them. They were young men, she was beautiful. They'd only done what many other men would have done too. Maybe even you, Mr McKenzie? Have you never ever done anything that you regretted?"

A shudder passed down McKenzie's spine. Did Mr Gray know that McKenzie had slept with his colleague at work, who'd then ended up dead because of it? Had Mr Gray done his research? Or had he just hit the nail on the head, by accident?

"I understand the point you're making, but did you discuss it with anyone else, or did the final action rest with you?" McKenzie probed further, deflecting the need to answer. Refusing to answer.

"I decided not to do anything more." He replied. Then waited for a response from McKenzie. He offered none.

When the silence became uncomfortable, Daniel Gray continued.

"The girl seemed reluctant... no she refused to let me get the police involved. I did suggest we should, but *she* said no. Just 'no'. I thought that if she had been raped, as she claimed, then she should, *would* be happy to get them involved. But she didn't. She was worried about her family, her career prospects, her university place... She seemed determined to ruin *their* careers, but refused to put her own in jeopardy."

"To be fair, that is probably understandable, I think, if she had been raped." McKenzie added. "If she was raped, then she was already a victim, and she may not have wanted to make it even worse by setting herself up to be the victim once again."

"Anyway, the point is, she made me the judge and the jury, and left it all down to me to decide. Which I did, but at the end of the day I placed the careers and statements of the teachers above hers. I told her I would take no action against them. She was furious. She made threats against me. And then I never heard from her again. Or about her, until I later read of her death in the obituaries, a hobby which a lot of us fall prone to when we start getting older."

McKenzie nodded.

He drank some more of his tea.

More silence.

But this time, Mr Gray did not continue.

It seemed that he had said all he was prepared to.

For now.

McKenzie looked up and saw that Grant had been standing in the doorway. Silently. For once not speaking. How long she had been standing there McKenzie did not know.

After several minutes, Mr Gray announced that he was tired. Very tired. He wanted to go to bed.

McKenzie went through the formalities of handing him a card and requesting Mr Gray to contact him if he could think of anything else that might aid them in their investigations.

"I don't know who killed the men. Or why? All I can tell you is about the incident which I know connected them together. Which I've done. It's probably got nothing to do with their deaths. But I told you what I know, because you asked me to."

McKenzie nodded and shook the man's hand.

They walked towards the door.

"How did you find me here, by the way?" Mr Gray asked.

"We got your name and details from the school office. That gave us enough information to track you down from official databases."

"Good. I'm ex-directory now. I've become a bit of a hermit in recent years, and that's the way I prefer it. I keep myself to myself."

Three minutes later McKenzie and Grant climbed into their car and left Daniel Gray standing in the doorway of his cottage.

After they had gone, Mr Gray wandered down the side of his cottage, carrying a bottle of whisky and a glass.

He sat back down on his favourite rock overlooking the beach, poured himself a drink, took a mouthful, and closed his eyes.

From deep within, waves of emotion rolled up and washed over him.

He made no attempt to stop the tears, and for the first time since his wife's death, he sobbed his heart out, howling like a child.

Finally, at long last, it was out.

Now, hopefully, it would all end.

Chapter 30

Sunday
Island of Coll
Airport
23.00

McKenzie stood on the tarmac at the airport waiting for the last moment before he had to board the helicopter for the return trip back to Edinburgh.

Although he'd thought the lateness of the hour would necessitate an over-night stay on the island, the pilot was keen to fly back that evening.

The good news was that a break in the weather would last for the rest of the evening so the flight back should be much smoother than it was on the way up. The bad news was that McKenzie would not be able to visit the old headmaster in the morning before returning to Edinburgh.

"Would you please check on him before you go?" McKenzie asked Grant.

"No problem. It might mean another night on the island, if I miss the ferry again, but I think it's a good idea just to stop by and make sure he's okay."

"I might have some more questions to pop to him. Or you might think of some yourself. But go easy on the questions about rape and if he should have done more about it then. All those who were involved are now dead, so rightly or wrongly, that case is dead too. The big question is, was what happened then related to their recent deaths? And also, did the poor girl really commit suicide, or was there another reason for her death? I'm not saying there was, but we have to just ask the question."

"I agree." Grant said simply, not venturing into any other conversation either way about what had happened so many years before.

McKenzie shook her hand, thanked her, and she agreed to keep him updated and to act as a future liaison with Mr Gray, should it be needed.

Not much later, they were airborne, and McKenzie settled back, closed his eyes, and started to think.

Thankfully, this time around, everything was a lot smoother. In spite of his mind being awash with questions, the movement of the helicopter and the rhythmic drone of the engines soon lulled him to the edge of sleep.

McKenzie didn't resist.

The next thing he knew, he felt a jolt, opened his eyes and found they had landed at Edinburgh Airport.

An hour later he was home, tucked up in bed beside his wife and Little Bump.

Monday
Outside Marie McDonald's House
01.20

"Please, wait for me here for a few minutes." Stuart instructed the taxi driver, before climbing out and rushing round to the other side to open Marie's door and help her out.

She smiled.

"Are you real?" she laughed. "Not only are you handsome, a pleasure to be with, but you're a gentleman into the bargain."

"Not true. I'm just helping you out of the taxi as quick as possible, to save money on the meter."

She laughed, then Stuart followed her as she walked towards the front door of her house and searched for her key in her handbag.

"When are you going back?" Stuart asked.

"I'm meant to be heading back down to London on Wednesday. I could perhaps put it off a few more days, but not much longer. I promised my children I'd be back by Saturday."

They stood in silence for a few moments, each looking into the other's eyes.

For the first time that day there was a moment of awkwardness. Marie's eyes were searching his, anticipating a moment that did not seem to be forthcoming.

"I've had an amazing, and totally unexpected day, Mr Stuart Nisbet. I mean, an *amazing* day."

Stuart smiled.

Standing in the doorway to her childhood home, she reached out and took his hand in hers. "But I still don't know anything about you. We never talked. We were just too busy laughing and enjoying ourselves."

"I'm glad you enjoyed yourself so much. That it wasn't just one sided. Not just me." He coughed lightly. "Can I be honest with you for a second?"

"Stuart, please." She reached up and stroked the side of his cheek with one finger. "Always be honest with me. Tell me no lies."

"Marie, I really like you. I would love it if we could see each other again tomorrow? But I have a problem. I have to work in the morning. If you were free, maybe I could take the afternoon off? Or... "

"I'm sorry, I'm busy tomorrow." She replied.

"Okay, sorry, I know that was a bit forward of me... never mind... "

"But I'm free in the evening, if you are? I'm sorry I can't make it during the day, but I've arranged some meetings to try and arrange some funding with various charities I know of... "

Stuart's eyes lit up. "What time at?"

"Can I meet you at the bottom of the Walter Scott Monument in Princes Street at 6 p.m.?"

"How about 5.59 p.m. So that I can get a little more time with you? Plus, there's a restaurant I'd like to take you to, if you would like to go with me?"

She smiled, leaned forward, and kissed him.

"If you promise to greet me with a kiss, I'll meet you at 5.58 pm!"

"It's a deal."

For a moment, Stuart hesitated. As if he wanted to say something else. Then, the moment passed, and he lifted a hand and stroked the back of Marie's head, gently pulling it towards him.

Leaning forward he kissed her on the forehead, then stepped back.

"I'll see you tomorrow, Marie McDonald. 5.58 p.m. on the dot."

Then he turned, walked down the steps, climbed into the taxi and drove off.

As Marie watched him go, for the first time in a long time, she suddenly felt a very weird sensation.

She felt alone.
In the nicest possible way.

Monday
Mark McRae's house
11.20

The morning meeting in the Incident Room at the portacabin had gone quickly.

Everyone had a lot to do, and not much had changed since the last meeting except for McKenzie's news and an update from Wishart on the questioning of Scott Davies.

When McKenzie told everyone what had happened and what he'd learned, everyone was shocked. McKenzie could sense the added emotion that the news brought to the case.

The action to check on the coroner's report for Maggie Sutherland was given to Wishart, along with the task of learning about her family. Who were the next of kin? Did she have any surviving relatives they could talk to?

Next, Wishart's report on Scott Davies's questioning was short but sweet.

He'd been happy to come into the station for questioning and was genuinely shocked to hear of Willy Thomson's death. Scott Davies had explained the offer he'd made to Thomson at the Reunion Ball, and had an alibi for the rest of the evening which had been checked and confirmed.

For now, he'd been released.

Given the latest death of another teacher, McKenzie had asked Dean and Anderson to help McLeish and Lynch make faster progress on calling round all the ex-members of staff and checking on them. Anyone they couldn't locate after a day was to be flagged up for special attention.

The meeting had then closed, and McKenzie had successfully managed to escape the campus and avoid being collared by Gary Bruce who would no doubt soon be asking about why there was a new team of forensics people working on the fourth floor.

McKenzie knew he'd have to face that problem later, but for now he and Brown were on the way over to the house of Mark McRae.

The house was an attractive two-bedroom semi-detached bungalow in Musselburgh, with a front door that opened onto a quiet road, and a view of the river not far away.

It was a bit tucked away from the city and its night life, but an easy Uber ride which wouldn't break the bank. It was an upcoming area, and although quiet, McKenzie could see its attractions.

The locksmith and a local PC were waiting outside the front door as McKenzie and Brown climbed the small flight of steps from the main street up to the front of the house.

The local PC had already made a few door-to-door enquiries to see if anyone had been given a key to the house to look after, as good neighbours sometimes do, but had found none.

Armed with a digital copy of the warrant that had already been issued that morning, McKenzie nodded at the locksmith, and he went to work.

It only took a few seconds, and the door was opened without any damage to the lock.

McKenzie thanked the locksmith who promptly disappeared, and the detectives and the PC stepped inside, wearing protective gloves and covers over their shoes.

The house smelt fresh, was clean, and showed no sign of any disturbance. From first impressions, it seemed unlikely that McRae would have been picked up from the house. The questions concerning how the victims were physically abducted, where from, and at what time, would all need to be given greater focus. If they could find some answers, then perhaps Dean could work his magic on local CCTV cameras to identify the killer in action. McKenzie made the mental note for the next Operation's Meeting.

Brown took the upstairs rooms, and McKenzie walked the lower floor, checking for mail, bills, and an answering machine. Finding a mobile phone bill with McRae's number in it in the kitchen, McKenzie called Anderson and passed him the number. The Sergeant knew what to do with it.

The kitchen was bright and airy, with a view onto to a small garden with some beautiful flowers and a vegetable patch.

Just from looking around the walls, the décor and the photographs on the window ledge, it was obvious that the house lacked a female touch. The kitchen was practical, but lacked the interior design that made 'a house a home'. McKenzie guessed that McRae probably spent the majority of his time outside, and only used the house as a base from which he conducted the rest of his life. *Had* conducted.

Moving through to the lounge at the front of the house, McKenzie's eyes immediately found a landline phone on a side table.

There was a light flashing on it.

Waiting messages.

Bingo!

Moving swiftly across to it, he picked the phone up and dialled 1571.

Two messages.

He played the first.

It was a message from a dentist's surgery reminding McRae of an appointment last Friday.

The second message caught McKenzie completely by surprise, and upon hearing it, the recording sent shivers down McKenzie's spine.

It was the sound of a man laughing.

An evil laugh.

Mad, but not hysterical.

Then a voice.

A man's voice. Deep. Cold. Twisted. Evil.

A simple sentence. Six words that McKenzie would never forget.

"You've found three, now expect four!"

Monday
Mark McRae's house
11.46

Brown, the local PC and McKenzie stood around the phone, listening to the message again several times.

Every time he heard it, the voice had the same effect on him. It chilled McKenzie to the bone.

It was the sound of the killer. Taunting them. Playing with them.

By pressing 1471 they found the call was made at 11.00 that morning, but the number of the calling party had been withheld.

"The killer called McRae's phone while we were on the way over to the house. It's almost as if he knew we were coming." Brown said.

"I think he did know we were coming. That's the whole point. He's making a statement. He's always one step ahead of us." McKenzie replied, moving to the window and looking down at their car on the road below. There were no notes on the window, but McKenzie couldn't help but feel that the killer was out there somewhere. Watching them.

"How does he know what we're doing?"

"I don't know. He might not. But he might. The big question is does he actually know what our movements are?"

"How could he do that?" Brown asked.

McKenzie thought for a second, then spoke.

"It's just a thought, but can you find out what Gary Bruce was doing this morning? Where was he? And can you pay a visit to his office when we get back and see if you can hear us talking in the room above? If someone downstairs can hear what we're saying or planning, it might explain a few things."

Brown nodded.

McKenzie dialled Anderson and told him what they had.

"Contact the telephone operator, get a copy of this message and get them to do everything they can to track down where the caller made the call from, and from what number. Even though the number was held from the phone at this end, the network still has all the details about the source and destination of every call. And Sergeant, also call Fettes and contact the Electronic Surveillance experts… I can't remember what they're called, but speak to the front desk, explain what the problem is, and they'll direct you. I want you to expedite the analysis of this voice message and get us everything you can on it. I'm guessing he's speaking through a voice digitiser of some sort to disguise his voice. And that's probably not his real laugh."

Anderson took the actions and agreed to get right on it.

"Okay, we listen to this one more time, then we get back to work. We don't let this detract us from our work. It sound's scary. That's the point. But the person behind that message is deliberately trying to play with our minds and we mustn't let him."

Brown and the PC both nodded.

They then listened to the message another three times.

Each time, the message generated the same result.

It sent a chill down every spine in the room.

"Enough." McKenzie finally said. "Back to work."

Brown disappeared upstairs and McKenzie returned to examining the rest of the front room.

He started with the bookcases built into the walls on either side of the chimney piece opposite the large sofa in the room.

Scanning along the books he quite quickly picked up that McRae had been an avid hill walker and rambler.

There were numerous books on the Munroes in Scotland, and travel books of Switzerland, the Alps and mountains in Spain, France and South America.

Around the house McKenzie had also spotted numerous photographs taken during walking trips. All stunning photographs.

McRae had obviously been a very active person.

It was notable that there were few photographs of any women. McKenzie knew that McRae wasn't married, but they would have to establish if there was a partner somewhere. Female or male.

There were also several travel books for Petra, Egypt and Syria, which correlated with a couple of photographs that he'd seen on the wall in the kitchen.

Stepping around the fireplace wall, which now proudly boasted a wood-burner inset into the chimney, with a large flat screen TV on the wall above it, McKenzie began to scan the books on the shelves nearest the window. From the lowest to the highest.

Looking up to the top shelf he scanned the books there but was unable to read all the titles.

He was just about to move away from the book shelves altogether when something began to niggle him at the back of his brain.

A thought. A feeling. A nascent question...

Walking through to the kitchen he retrieved a chair from the table and carried it back through to the front room and placed it before the shelves nearest the window.

Stepping up onto the chair, he steadied himself by reaching out and holding onto the top shelf, then began to scan along the shelf again.

Something was bugging him.

He went along each book one by one, touching the edge of each book in turn.

He closed his eyes.

"What?" he asked himself.

And then it was there.

An image.

Another book.

On the book shelf in Ronald Blake's house.

A blue book with a blue spine.

McKenzie opened his eyes.

Almost immediately McKenzie's eyes landed on the same book.

Ten books from the left of the shelf. A blue book. A blue spine.

Reaching out, he slowly edged it out from the other books on the top shelf and brought it down.

Turning it on his side, he read the title on the front cover.

Two words.

"Remember Me?"

Chapter 31

Monday
Ronald Blake's House
13.00

McKenzie and Brown stood on the doorstep, waiting for Mrs Blake to come to the door.
They hadn't called ahead, and there was a possibility that she wouldn't be at home, but from the state she was in a few days ago, McKenzie thought it would probably be a few days before she started leaving the house again.
He was right.
The door opened slowly in front of them, revealing Mrs Blake, looking tired, still dressed in her pyjamas and with a red face. She'd been crying.
"Oh," she exclaimed upon seeing McKenzie. "Detective Chief Inspector? You're back. Is everything okay?"
"Actually no. May we come in?"
Mrs Blake looked down at herself and for a moment she hesitated to reply.
"You like fine, Mrs Blake." Brown consoled her. "Shall I make us all a cup of tea?"
Mrs Blake smiled back and ushered them in.
"Would it be okay if I visit your husband's office again? There's something I need to check."
"Help yourself." Mrs Blake agreed.

Stepping into Ronald Blake's office, McKenzie crossed the room and went straight to the shelves. The second shelf. Somewhere in the middle... Bingo.
Another blue book, exactly as he'd remembered it in his mind's eye.
He pulled it off the shelf and checked the title.
"Remember Me."
Turning the book over, just like the others, there was no blurb on the cover.
And no author name.
It seemed that the book had been written anonymously.

Impatiently, McKenzie returned to the lounge where Brown had only just had the time to sit down.
"I'm sorry, Mrs Blake, but we won't be able to stay for that cup of tea after all. I need to visit David Weir's flat as soon as possible. We'll have to go immediately."
He held up the blue coloured book to Mrs Blake.
"This was in your husband's office. Have you seen it before? Do you know if it meant anything of significance to your husband?"
Mrs Blake stared at the book.
"I haven't seen that book for a while, but I recognise it. Ronnie used to read it quite a lot, over and over again, a number of years ago. I think it quite upset him.

Then he put it away, and I never saw it again, until now." She coughed. "Why? Is it important?"

"It could be. Do you happen to know where he got it from?" McKenzie asked.

"Sorry, no. Ronnie used to read a lot. He had lots of books. I think he must have bought it somewhere?"

Listening to what she had just said, McKenzie turned the book over and scanned the back for the name of the publisher and the RRP. There wasn't any.

Opening up the front cover, the first page was blank, but turning to the next it said, "Remember Me?" The next few lines were blank, then the words, 'Published by Createspace 2015'. There was no author name.

Flicking through the pages, and feeling the quality of the print, McKenzie immediately realised that this was not a normal book that you would buy in the shops. Probably more likely a self-published book. He didn't recognise the publisher's name.

"Unfortunately, I have some bad news for you Mrs Blake. I'd appreciate it if you would not tell anyone else for a while, but after you told us about your husband's friend Mark McRae, we discovered his body yesterday afternoon. It looks like he was also murdered, but we're awaiting the Procurator Fiscal's report to confirm the cause of death."

"Oh... " Mrs Blake gripped the sides of her chair with both hands. "How terrible." She began to cry. "Poor man. Ronald would be... " then her voice trailed off.

"I feel guilty leaving you, but we have to go. Would you like us to call anyone for you?" McKenzie offered.

She declined, explaining that her neighbour would be popping round for a cup of tea later that afternoon. She'd be fine till then.

On the drive down to Leith to visit David Weir's flat, McKenzie flicked through the pages of the book, scanning the text. Without his reading classes he couldn't read anything, but his instinct was screaming at him that the book held the clues to what was going on.

The title of the book was the same two words which were scrawled over the bodies of both Blake and McRae. And two of the three victims had copies of the books on their shelves.

The big question was, did David Weir also have a copy?

Arriving in Leith, they had to wait another thirty minutes before the appropriate warrant was issued and another locksmith turned up and let them into David Weir's flat. Whilst he was waiting McKenzie called DCS Wilkinson and updated her as to the message left on the answering machine at McRae's house.

McKenzie didn't tell her about the book yet. That could wait till later, until he knew a little more about its significance and what it contained.

Instead, he laid into his boss, demanding to know where his assistant was. She promised him an office manager yesterday afternoon whilst standing over the body of Mark McRae, but so far none had turned up.

"We're all drowning in actions here. We're detectives, not secretaries. If we don't get a proper process in place, we'll drop the ball somewhere, forget to chase an action, and possibly miss out on something that could mean success or failure in finding the bloody sick killer behind all of this."

"I've already assigned you PC Dania Jordon. She should be there now. I'll chase her up for you." His boss promised.

"Thanks Ma'am. But can you do it soon please? And please ask the Queen to go home now. I need my team back, *now*, not later this week."

"No problem. I'll just call her on her mobile as soon as you hang up. Now, is there anything else DCI McKenzie?"

McKenzie noted the fact that she wasn't using his first name any more.

But he didn't care.

He was just about to call Anderson and get him to chase PC Dania Jordon up, when the locksmith arrived.

Three minutes later they were inside Weir's flat.

McKenzie went straight to the shelves in the lounge whilst Brown searched the other rooms.

Unlike in McRae and Blake's houses, the book was not to be found on display.

Tramping through to the bedroom, McKenzie started to look inside all the drawers. Finding nothing, the cupboard was next.

It took twenty minutes, but he eventually found it in a shoe box underneath some porn magazines at the back of the top shelf in the wardrobe.

It was the exact same book.

"Remember Me?"

McKenzie popped the book into a see-through plastic bag they had found in the kitchen, had another quick look around the flat, then left, McKenzie kicking himself for having not noticed the book during his initial search of the flat a few days before.

They had just climbed back into McKenzie's car when his phone went.

It was Wishart.

"Guv, I've found something. Can you drop everything and get back to the Incident Room now? It's really important."

"Why? What have you found?"

"I've got an original architect's map of the school. I'm not sure... but I think I've found the way the killer got into the school without being seen! It's been under our noses the whole time!"

Monday
Operation BlueBuilding
Incident Room
Portacabin
14.45

McKenzie and Brown took the stairs up to the Incident Room in the portacabin two at a time.

They were just passing the cabin on the first level when Gary Bruce stepped out.

He was fuming.

"DCI McKenzie? What the bloody hell is going on? When were you going to tell me you had another body in the school? And why was I dragged into your Incident Room – MY OFFICE – for questioning? Since when did I become a bloody suspect?"

"Not now, Mr Bruce. Not now." McKenzie stepped passed him and started to continue up the stairs but then turned to face him again. "Please, can you wait inside your office? We may need to speak to you urgently in the next few minutes… . Don't go anywhere!"

It was more of a command, than a request.

McKenzie didn't stop to see if he'd heard or not. He turned and bolted up the remaining stairs.

Bursting into the office, he found the rest of the team all huddled around a big table against the wall. There were several large maps spread out before them.

They all looked up and stepped aside to let their Boss into see the contents of the table.

"What do you have?" McKenzie asked, inviting a full report.

"You tasked me with trying to track down the original architect plans of the school, or of any other structure that may have existed here beforehand. The original architects don't exist anymore. They closed about ten years ago. But I found someone who used to work there and who told me that the practice had been sold to another firm, EdinStudios. I approached them, and they spent the past few hours digging these out. They're the originals. I promised to get them back to them unscathed." Wishart explained, almost breathlessly.

"Guv, this is the one we were looking at before which showed us the schematics of the ground level workings… I mean, the pipes and underground structures." She pointed at the plan attached to the wall just above the table

"And this is the new one. What do you notice?"

McKenzie bent forward, screwing his eyes up. Without his reading glasses he really had to strain his eyes to make out the detail.

"The last time I looked at these I was wearing glasses, but I remember I was looking at the size of all the pipes and voids in the ground. We were looking for any form of tunnel or underground access into the school." McKenzie replied. "Right now, I can practically see nothing. My reading glasses are at home. What should I be seeing?"

"We've all been over this first plan a thousand times, looking for a tunnel, something, anything…but there was nothing of significance. At least, that's what we thought. There is this pipe or duct… " she pointed to the map on the wall, "that goes right across the campus under the ground, but according to the scale here, and the figures here, it would only be 8 inches wide at its biggest point. Look… " Wishart pointed to several numbers on the diagram, and then to a section at the bottom which indicated scale.

"Look, see this figure here… it has two single slashes top right above the number… it's a bit blurred, but we all took that to mean the old imperial sign for inches. Obviously 8 inches is nothing. A rat can't even practically squeeze through down there… " Wishart paused, took a breath, and then continued at pace.

"But… here, look at the new diagram we got. You can see here from the revision marking it's one of the original versions. Version 1.3. The other one we were looking at was Version 4.5. Anyway, here is the same duct going right across the centre of the campus and disappearing across to the back, but coming forward here, and then appearing to run under the lift shaft in Stair B into the main building.... Look... " DI Wishart pointed to the course of the duct as it ran across the campus.

"Now... Look here. Look at the scale. On this original it's not blurred at all. It's very sharp. You can read it clearly. And there are not *two* little marks above the number. Just one!"

"Bloody hell!" Anderson exclaimed, probably the oldest amongst them, and quite used to the old Imperial nomenclature. "It's not 8 inches. It's 8 FEET! That's almost two and half metres wide!"

McKenzie bent forward and stared at the numbers on the new chart. Then turning to the copy they had been working from until now, he ran his forefinger across the chart where the number had two little marks appearing above to its right, which seemed to indicate inches not feet.

Still incredulous, he leaned even closer and inspected the two tiny markings. Sure enough, the mark closest to the number was definitely a printed mark, but the second, slightly to its side, was not so pronounced, not so clear. In fact, with the benefit of hindsight, it could possibly now be seen as a spurious mark on the paper, or a shadow or blurring of the first mark somehow caused during the photocopying process.

He whistled aloud then laughed.

"I can't believe it. All this time we've been misreading the bloody map. There's a bloody great tunnel running right under the school from one side to the other, right into the main building and we didn't see it!"

DI Wishart stood up and stretched.

"Exactly. Well, there is according to the plan. Perhaps it's not there, but if it is... it explains everything." She said.

McKenzie turned to face the rest of his team, his back now to the charts which had confused and bamboozled them all up until now.

"DI McLeish, get Gary Bruce here now. Elaine, call the armed squad and tell them to get over here within the next twenty minutes."

Dropping the three copies of "Remember Me?" onto to the table top, McKenzie stood back from the table, stretched and exclaimed loudly.

"Okay, ladies and gentlemen. Suit up. We're going on a bear hunt!"

Chapter 32

Monday
Operation BlueBuilding
Incident Room
Portacabin
15.00

Gary Bruce stared at the chart and shook his head.

Everyone else had left the room apart from him, McKenzie and Brown.

"I didn't know about this. I've been over these charts a thousand times, and just like you and the other detectives, I've always read that mark as an indication of inches, and not feet. This is incredible."

"Mr Bruce, I can see why you would make this mistake. But, and this is a big but, as the prime contractor for this building's demolition, I can't help but wonder if you should have made more effort to understand what was under the ground as well as above it?"

"What are you getting at? Are you blaming me for you not being able to read the charts properly?"

"You also complained to me just a few moments ago that you were being questioned as if you were a suspect? I have to say, unfortunately, that that is actually the case. Whereas my gut feel has been that you are not responsible for these killings, there is slowly a body of circumstantial evidence building around you to the contrary that I am no longer able to ignore. Consider this: you have full access to the building. You may have known that there might be a tunnel stretching across the campus - we will soon determine if there is a tunnel or not as soon as the armed squad arrive - and you have been camping out for the past few days, maybe even before - we don't know - at the school. You were also a pupil at the school so you may have known the deceased and had a reason to dislike them or hold a grudge..."

"AND KILL THEM? Are you MAD?" Bruce interrupted forcibly. "This is crazy. I'm just as much as victim here as any of those you've found murdered in the school. If I don't get to pull this building down in the next few days, I'm going to be bankrupt! I'll lose everything! My life will be over... And I'll tell you what, if that DOES happen, I'll find the fucking bastard who's responsible for this and I will kill him. I *will*... mark my words!"

McKenzie said nothing. Neither did Brown.

Gary Bruce looked at them, from one to the other, searching their eyes desperately.

"But that doesn't mean I killed the teachers in the building... they've got nothing to do with me."

Brown replied. "How do you know they are teachers?"

Gary Bruce laughed.

"You're kidding, right?" He started to pace the room. "I think DCI McKenzie mentioned it, or someone. It's not been a secret from me. Everyone's been talking about it openly as I've walked or guided your team around the building. Don't start trying to pin this on me."

"Okay, okay, let's all calm down." McKenzie interjected. "I understand your worries and your concerns, and your anger… but I would advise that when we do find the murderer or murderers that you take no independent action. In the meantime, it would help the investigation and yourself if you do put yourself in our position when we ask you questions, and you try to answer them as clearly and honestly as possible. If you assist us, if and when we require your assistance, as helpfully as possible, then I promise to help move this investigation forward as fast as possible and work with my superiors and other authorities in obtaining permission to complete the demolition as soon as we can. The likelihood of that happening will all depend upon whether we now find a tunnel and what it leads us to."

There was a knock at the door. The now familiar face of Galbraith, the officer in charge of the armed response team, stuck his head around the door.

"Me again. Ready for business, *again…* "

Monday
The bottom of Stair B
15.30

Four armed officers, fully equipped to support advancing into a possibly dark and confined space, entered through the glass doors at the bottom of Stair B.

Immediately behind them McKenzie, Brown and the rest of his team followed in single file.

A few moments before, they had stood outside in the foyer entrance to the old school and received a briefing from McKenzie.

"According to the map, the duct or tunnel comes into the building below or just to the side of the lift shafts in Stair B. We don't have any schematics or diagrams of how… I think that's all detailed in another plan which we don't have. So, we're going into the building and checking the floors and walls around the lift shaft and underneath the stairs to see if we can find any indication of an entrance or exit from the tunnel or duct or whatever it is, leading out into the building itself. We've suspected from day one that there has to be a way to get into the building that we didn't know about, so this has to be it! Now, if there is a duct, it's a possibility that the air might be stale, contaminated or even poisonous. We've agreed that if anything is found, Sergeant Galbraith will be first into the tunnel and will assess the air quality. If it's poor, only he and his team will be allowed in, aided by their breathing equipment. We'll take their lead. For now, no talking, and silence at all times. Don't bang anything, and be careful where you put your feet. We don't know who's at the other end of the tunnel. Any questions?"

There were none.

Everyone just wanted to get on with it.

Once inside, using brooms, plastic bags, thick rubber gloves, dustpans and even shovels, they cleared away the debris and trash that covered the entrance area in front of the lifts, often just tossing it outside into what used to be the playground of the school.

Gary Bruce stood outside with another member of his team, watching on and champing at the bit.

He'd been forbidden to go inside and follow them in spite of his vehement protestations.

In the old days, pupils would enter Stair B through a double set of glass doors which led directly to two lifts standing side-by-side, both of which serviced the first four floors of the building. Pupils who didn't wish to ride the lifts could walk around the lift shaft to its right, and then around another corner to the back of the lift shaft where a flight of metal stairs led upwards, twisted around on itself and then led upwards to the next four floors, one after another.

Between the metal staircase and the edge of the concrete encased lift shafts was a small gap. Large enough for a person to slip between.

On the other side of the gap there was effectively a hidden space on the right occupying the underneath of the first flight of stairs. On the left was the wall of the lift shafts.

Rubbish was piled up high on either side, both against the back of the lift shaft and the other wall on the right of the staircase.

The space stunk to high heaven. Needles and dried human excrement were everywhere. The place was a midden.

Everyone held their noses, except for the armed response team, all of whom now wore respirators.

On the left-hand wall at the back of the lift shafts, there was a large piece of plasterboard, covered with tiles, and a selection of rubbish, which on closer inspection, seemed to have been stuck to it by hand.

To inspect the walls for any opening, Galbraith reached out to pull the top edge of it away from the wall and let it fall towards the floor, but the moment he did so, he realised that something was holding it to the wall, and resisting his pull.

Cautiously he leant towards it, and inspected it from the top and its sides.

The top of the board seemed to be attached to the wall. Switching on his torch and directing its light behind the large piece of plasterboard, he saw what looked like a rectangular line or edge marked in the wall.

Possibly a panel in the wall to which the plasterboard was attached.

To disguise its existence.

Which it did brilliantly.

"Okay, this could be it." Galbraith announced, and waved at a colleague to take the other edge of the plasterboard panel. "On the count of three, we pull the top of the panel away from the wall."

There was no real resistance.

With a little more strength, the plasterboard and a panel moved horizontally away from the wall.

Immediately behind, there was a large opening, wide enough for a bended man to climb through.

As McKenzie and Brown huddled closer around the entrance, Galbraith flashed his torch into the opening.

A small flight of metal stairs led away from the entrance downwards to a concrete floor beneath.

"There's your tunnel!" shouted Galbraith. "I think we've just solved how your murderer squirrelled the victims into the school without being seen."

McKenzie took one look and turned to Anderson.

"Just to be sure, can you go and escort Gary Bruce and all his coworkers into the portacabin. Take one of the armed officers with you. Keep them there and don't let them leave."

"Are they under arrest?"

"No. But if it is one of them, once they find out we've found a tunnel, I don't want any of them running away."

The Sergeant nodded, peered one last time into the tunnel, then turned and left.

A moment later, McKenzie could hear a stream of protest coming from an even more irate Gary Bruce.

Ignoring it, McKenzie pointed to the tunnel and gave the signal to proceed.

Galbraith bent down and stepped through the entrance.

Once inside he lifted his hand and indicated for the others to move away from the entrance. As they stepped back, wondering what Galbraith was up to, Galbraith lifted a rope that was dangling from the wall and started to pull it towards him inside the tunnel. As soon as he did, the panel and the plasterboard which now stood outside of the tunnel entrance started to slide back towards the tunnel mouth. A moment later it had covered the entrance, once again making it almost invisible and hiding it away from anyone on the outside. Located as it was at the back of the lift shaft and in the shadow of the stair, no one would ever accidently see it or discover it. The mess would easily deter anyone from going anywhere near it, especially the needles which had lay dotted around the floor. Which, McKenzie now realised, was deliberate. The mess was part of the disguise.

As they waited, the panel and plasterboard slid back out towards them, away from the wall.

Galbraith peered out, lifted his respirator and spoke quietly.

"It's very easy to control from the inside. Easy to open, and easy to close once inside. Someone's gone to a lot of trouble to hide this tunnel. There's a lot of dust in here on the floor, but I can clearly see footprints around the bottom of the ladder. People have definitely been going back and forward through here in the recent past."

Galbraith indicated for the rest of his team to follow him into the shaft and waved at McKenzie to hang back.

"I'll send for you as soon as we've cleared the tunnel and its safe. I've already deployed two of my men in the street around the back of the school, just in case someone pops up into a garden somewhere as we approach the end of the tunnel, wherever it goes. There has to be an entrance at the other end, somewhere."

McKenzie turned back to his team and issued some more instructions.

"Dean and McLeish. Get outside as fast as possible and drive round to the back of the school. Drive around and look to see if there's any obvious exit points on the other side."

McKenzie closed his eyes again and recalled his mental picture of the map which they'd left upstairs in the Incident Room. Before they'd come down, they'd taken another look, in particular looking where the duct led underneath the school, and where it went.

The problem they then realised, was that the scale of the campus area shown on the map was larger than the campus area which now existed.

At first it hadn't computed. It didn't make sense.

Then McLeish had spotted an obvious answer.

The original plans they were now looking at were for a first phase of building for a new school, the then new Portobello High School. At the edge of the grounds on the map there were several buildings marked which clearly didn't exist now and according to Gary Bruce had not been demolished by him.

Clearly, since the first round of building of the school in the sixties, changes had been made.

These included selling some of the ground of the school at the very back, and the building of a new hall which Gary pointed out as existing now, but which didn't appear on the plans, and which contained a swimming pool.

The ground which had been sold, was now occupied by several rows of houses.

More problematically, on the original plan, the school campus extended all the way out to the park – the local Figgate Park.

It wasn't obvious to the team in the Incident Room where the end of the tunnel or duct would be in relation to the new houses which had been built and the new edge of the Figgate Park.

For a few moments they had discussed whether to get new plans and figure out where the tunnel ended before looking for it.

"And if it doesn't exist? We waste hours, maybe a day, getting plans of the new houses, and taking measurements and figuring out what's what. No, we haven't got time for that!" McKenzie answered them, remembering the voice on the answering machine. "The threat to life is real. Every second we stand here discussing this, could delay us preventing another death."

Decision made, he'd authorised the search for the tunnel to go ahead, and everyone had assembled below outside the entrance to Stair B.

In hindsight now, McKenzie wondered if he'd been a little rash. If someone had heard them opening the entrance to the tunnel up, or if it had been alarmed in some way, anyone at the other end may have scarpered and escaped before Dean or the armed response team figured out where the other entrance was.

Worried that he might have just made his first mistake of the investigation, McKenzie tried to focus on the positive: now they'd found the tunnel, there was no way they'd let anyone else be murdered in the school!

Chapter 33

Monday
Underneath the Portobello High School
16.00

Galbraith edged along the tunnel. His night-sight vision headset lit up the darkness in front of him, revealing a large metal pipe suspended from the roof and supported up off the floor, effectively running down the right-hand side of the duct. Every ten metres, another pipe joined it from the left, also suspended from the ceiling, but easy to duck under. Occasionally a pipe a few centimetres off the ground forced them to step carefully over it.

The tunnel sloped gently away from them, curving slowly, but with one or two sharper bends.

There was a lot of dust on the ground, but with an obvious trail of recent activity with footsteps pointing both back and forward going through it.

Every twenty metres Galbraith stopped and glanced at the meter hanging from his jacket, which indicated the quality of the air and its level of toxicity.

Strangely, for a tunnel that had supposedly been shut off for many years, the level of oxygen was high, and toxic gases were mostly absent.

Another sign that the tunnel had been in use recently, and that fresh air had successfully blown out any stale air that may have gathered previously.

A sudden sound ahead alarmed Galbraith and he threw up his balled fist in the classic command for everyone to a halt.

No lights showed anywhere ahead.

Suddenly a large rat ran along the top of the pipe beside him. As it drew close, it stopped and hesitated, looking across the gap between the pipe and the man, and staring straight at Galbraith's face.

Its little whiskers bristled, and the rat rose up on its hind legs as it sniffed the air.

Galbraith gave the sign to move forward, and in response to the sudden movement of his arm, the rat turned and scuttled rapidly away back into the darkness further along the tunnel.

Galbraith and his team followed, their guns raised in front of them, searching the tunnel ahead for any threats, but being careful to manoeuvre around any of the obstacles that presented themselves.

It took them five minutes to walk the distance of the piping-duct, longer than Galbraith had expected.

As they neared its end, Galbraith could see a wall ahead of them, and at first thought that it was going to be a dead-end.

However, with only a metre to go, he realised that the tunnel and the pipe turned quickly to the right, through an archway. Once through the archway, the tunnel disappeared down into the ground, but the walkway on which Sergeant Galbraith was progressing came to a metal ladder which went down a few steps into a larger chamber.

Galbraith waited at the top of the ladder until the other two in his team were beside him, then he indicated for them to provide cover, and he stepped very slowly and cautiously down the ladder, being extremely careful not to make any accidental sound.

At the bottom of the ladder, he turned and surveyed the chamber they were in, gun extended and continuously sweeping the space in front whilst the others came down behind him.

The chamber was quite large. The ladder had brought them down into the middle of it. On the left, about two metres away, another ladder went upwards to the top of the chamber where a trapdoor could be seen. On the right, a trapdoor lay open, revealing a gaping dark hole underneath it.

Galbraith indicated for two men to go left to the base of the ladder, whilst he and another man stepped slowly to the right and took up positions on either side of the hole in the ground. At first kneeling, then lowering themselves down flat, upon another signal from Galbraith, they both extended their arms down into the hole with their weapons in front and followed quickly by lowering their heads through the hole and searching for a target.

Once again, their night-sights lit up the darkness below, enabling them to see that no threats were present.

Another ladder extended downwards beneath them into another chamber.

Several large pipes entwined each other with large stop valves at the far end of the chamber.

Descending the stairs into the empty room, Sergeant Galbraith crossed the room to the far wall.

Human excrement was everywhere, as well as puddles of urine, the ammonia from which now set off a flashing alarm on the air-meter hanging from his jacket.

In the corner there were a few items of clothing, and a ripped sheet.

Galbraith bent down and picked up one of the pieces of clothing, a jacket.

It was filthy and covered in faeces, and the Sergeant was just about to drop it when he saw some writing scrawled on the label at the back of its neck.

Pulling it closer he read one word: 'Weir'.

His colleague, now on his left, tapped him on his shoulder and pointed at one of the pipes. A chain was dangling from it, an open set of handcuffs at its end.

Confirming that the rest of the room was empty, Galbraith led his colleague back up the stairs to the room above, and moved across the chamber to the other ladder.

Indicating his intentions, and holding onto the ladder rungs with one hand, he started to climb the ladder, slowly but steadily.

Until now they had made none or very little noise. Now was not a time to start.

The ladder was about two metres tall, and as soon as Galbraith reached the top, another man got ready to climb behind him, his weapon raised above his head, pointing upwards.

Galbraith put his hand on the trapdoor above him and started to push it upwards, expecting to meet resistance.

There was none.

The lid started to lift upwards.

Galbraith immediately stopped, and signalled to a man below him, who immediately reached into a backpack and pulled out a long thin bendy cable with a camera embedded in one end, and a small LCD Screen on the other. The man handed the camera up to Galbraith.

Slowly, very slowly, Galbraith inserted the tube with the camera in it through the gap in the trapdoor, and then rotated it in a wide circle.

The man below scrutinised the screen and what was revealed.

Nothing.

Another empty room.

A door at its far end.

Handing the camera back down, Galbraith moved upwards through the trapdoor, noting as he went a discarded heavy duty padlock on the floor, which had perhaps previously been used to keep the trapdoor secured, but which now lay abandoned on the floor.

One by one they came up the ladder into the room.

Another concrete room.

This time no pipes.

Just a wooden table and four chairs.

And nothing else.

Galbraith and the others gathered around the door at the far end of the room. The seal around the door was good, with no obvious gaps. No light came from the outside.

Whenever everyone was ready, he gave the sign, and one of his men placed a hand on the door and pulled it inwards.

The door moved slightly but did not open.

Next, he tried gently to push it open.

Again, the door moved forward a little, barely, but did not open.

Kneeling down on the floor, Galbraith looked for a pattern of scratching on the ground which might present itself, but saw none. To his experienced eye, he realised that this told him that the door opened outwards, not inwards.

Pointing to two men, he indicated for them to force the door on the silent count of three.

One finger.

Two fingers.

Three…

Two powerful feet lifted, and kicked, and the door burst open and outwards from them.

Almost as one, the men inside the room stepped back and swore aloud, the sudden light from outside temporarily blinding them with its brightness against their night vision headsets.

Ripping them off and stepping through the door, guns still searching, they were greeted with the screams of children who, only a few metres below them, were cycling along a footpath along the edge of a small loch.

They were standing in the middle of the Figgate Park.

Monday
Figgate Park Entrance
16.30

McKenzie stood at the entrance to the tunnel in the Figgate Park.

Immediately Galbraith had emerged into the afternoon light outside the tunnel, he'd phoned back to McKenzie and told them not to enter the tunnel. It was clear, but it was perhaps best not to disturb it until Forensics had been over it with a fine-tooth comb.

Instead he suggested that McKenzie came around to the Park, climbed into some protective overalls, and took a quick look at the set of underground chambers the tunnels had led into. Upon arrival, Sergeant Galbraith had given them a quick report on what they had seen and experienced within the tunnel. He'd then handed the scene over to McKenzie and declared it safe from any immediate threats.

Now suited and booted in their white forensic overcoats, Brown and McKenzie were just about to enter the small concrete building on the edge of the Figgate Park.

He'd instructed the others to start setting up a cordon around the building and do their best to chase away the gang of children who were now gathering on bikes and skateboards around the building, wondering what on earth all the excitement was about.

McKenzie stood and studied the area around him, sizing it all up.

They were standing outside a small, rather nondescript concrete building on the edge of the Park, only metres away from a road behind them. The road itself was small and quiet, and ran along the back gardens of one of the two rows of houses that had been built on the grounds of the school since the original plans of the school had been drawn up. Most of the small road was shaded by trees, and the bottom of the gardens ended in high-walls, providing both privacy and security to the inhabitants of the houses.

A few metres from the side of the building there was a small parking area on the quiet road. A fence ran along the side of the park, but there was an entrance to the park through a space in the fence, where long ago a metal gate probably had hung, but had long since disappeared.

Trees lined the edge of the park, which ran around a small Loch, and a river, known locally as the Figgie Burn. It was obviously a popular area. The concrete building however was set about five metres back from the path on a steep grassy incline, and McKenzie could immediately see that foot traffic close to the building would be minimal. In fact, most people would not even notice the building from the park, with their being no real reason to climb the hill to see it.

The building was just part of the scenery.

It had probably always been there, looking quite official, with no one ever challenging its purpose.

It also had easy access to it from a nondescript road which hardly anyone ever used, and no one saw or paid attention to.

A few metres away from the building to the right, a little further down the steep incline that led down to the path and the pond, a clump of weeds, shrubs and trees hid a large pipe that partially emerged from the ground, and from which a steady trickle of water emanated and ran down a tiny stream into the pond below.

Brown had spotted it, and pointed out that this was most likely the end of the pipe that Galbraith had reported as running through the duct then disappearing into the ground.

"I would take a guess that this whole area was probably very marshy before they built the school, and even once they cleared it and then started building, keeping it dry was probably a problem. From what Galbraith said, and from studying that map, the whole campus seems to be criss-crossed with drainage pipes. When it rains it must get very wet, with a lot of surface runoff to deal with. It's only a trickle now, but there's probably a lot of water coming out that pipe when it rains. My guess is that they built the system to drain the ground, then elaborated on it to keep the ground dry and stable when they built the school." Brown mused. "Sorry, my dad's an engineer." She said, turning to McKenzie and smiling.

"No, they're all good thoughts. Can I ask you to talk to the council and find out more about this whole set up? And who had access to this building when the school was in operation? Who would know about this? That's the key question here."

"I'll get right on it after we've been inside."

"Okay, let's go in."

Stopping at the entrance, they studied the door for a moment.

The armed response team had managed to kick the door open from the inside, bursting out and breaking the rotten wood around what looked like a new metal padlock and fixing. The padlock was still locked and now hung from a metal support which was no longer attached to the broken door.

"A new padlock, but an old door. Effective in stopping people getting in, but not out!" McKenzie had pointed out. "Make sure that Forensics check that for fingerprints and DNA." He said to McLeish who stood close by, but who remained unsuited and not able to enter the building.

"Okay, let's go."

Switching on their torches, they stepped inside the room.

The first thing that hit them was the stench.

Stale, damp air accosted their nostrils immediately.

Unprotected by the respirators which Galbraith's team had worn, McKenzie and Brown were exposed to all the delights the tunnel and concrete building had to offer them.

Shining the torch around the building, they found nothing but the table and chairs.

A light fitting hung from the ceiling.

There was a switch on the inside wall, but apart from that no other fittings of any sort.

The ground was concrete, as were the walls. There were no posters, markings or anything of significance.

The trapdoor was the only remarkable object in the room.

A round metal half-circle protruded from the concrete on one side of the hole in the ground, and a heavy padlock was attached to it, closed, but with no key.

Interestingly, when Galbraith had come up from the tunnel, the trapdoor had not been locked shut.

Carefully McKenzie and Brown descended the ladder and disappeared into the gloom beneath.

Here the smell changed. It was no longer just damp, but disgusting.

The smell of rotting human habitation.

Faeces. Urine. Sweat.

Flashing their torches around the room, they found the entrance to the tunnel which carried the pipes, the ladder up into it, and they saw where the pipes disappeared into the ground. The same pipe which presumably emerged on the other side of the wall out into the Figgate Park a few metres away.

To the left, they saw another trapdoor, another padlock which could secure it shut similar to the trapdoor through which they had just come, and another metal ladder which led further down into another chamber.

Following the steps down into the chamber below, they realised that the air they had left behind smelt almost pure in comparison.

The latest chamber was putrid, and they both had to fight the urge to retch.

Finding nothing of significance on the floor or walls, they crossed to the far side of the chamber.

As Galbraith had observed, there was a collection of pipes coming out of the walls, and disappearing into the ground, some chains and padlocks, a few rags or piecing of clothing, and a significant amount of faeces, some now dried, but others looking still slightly moist.

And there were puddles of urine.

There were no signs of any forms of food or drink being consumed by whoever was here. In hostage situations like these it was common to find discarded paper plates, or plastic bottles, or wrappings from junk food. There was no such thing here.

"The victims were kept here, in the dark, probably without food or water, before they were taken along the tunnels to their deaths." McKenzie voiced what Brown was thinking.

"If they screamed, no one would hear them."

For a few moments they both stood in silence, absorbing the horror of the scene before them. Memorising as many details as possible.

"Okay, let's go. I can't stand this smell any longer. Please, when you speak to Forensics, can you get them to confirm from the faeces and any urine samples how many different people we had here? Was it three, or are we talking more?"

Brown nodded, then turned to go.

"Actually, please, just give me a moment here by myself, Elaine. Just a few moments and I'll be up."

"Are we going through the tunnel to the school?"

"Not for now. Galbraith says there's nothing special along there, and there are quite a few footprints in the dust. Best not disturb anything more unnecessarily. We can have a look later once Forensics have been and done their thing."

"Okay Guv, I'll meet you outside."

McKenzie watched her disappear up the ladder, then turned round again to face the pipes and where the victims had been shackled and kept prisoner for the last days of their lives.

McKenzie needed a few moments alone to process an uncomfortable train of thought. He switched off the torch and stood there in the pitch dark.

When McKenzie and his team had been preparing for the visit to the Reunion Ball, the likelihood was that Mark McRae had been down here, alone, waiting for his death.

If he and his team had discovered the tunnel earlier, McRae may well have been alive now.

He didn't blame his team for not reading the scale on the plan of the building properly… he had seen it too, and he hadn't noticed it.

Was there a case for blaming Gary Bruce? Should he have known more about what lay under the ground and not just above it?

Or was DCS Wilkinson to blame for taking back most of his team, and not giving them the resources to do a proper job. Maybe none of this would have happened if he'd had someone focussing on this earlier, not later.

Or was it his own fault? Was he not ultimately to blame?

They'd had the maps, they'd known there was a mystery about the access to the campus, so should he not have insisted on getting hold of the original maps a day earlier? Or immediately?

McKenzie closed his eyes.

A myriad of thoughts ran through his brain. His heart was beating faster, and he was starting to breathe more rapidly.

This was all his fault. Ultimately. He hadn't done enough. And people had died because of it…

"Guv! Quick! You need to come!" Brown's voice dragged him back to the present, her tone urgent and pressing.

McKenzie turned to find her hurrying down the metal ladder towards him.

"Anderson's been trying to call us, but there's no reception down here. As soon as I got outside he got through to me… " Brown explained.

"What's up? What's happened?" McKenzie questioned.

"It's Mark McRae's mobile number. You asked Anderson to contact the phone company… "

"Yes, and?"

"It's still active. It's still on. And the phone's been moving. It's not stationary."

"Where is it now?"

"The phone company is going to give us the last location in about five minutes time. Anderson is in the Incident Room. He's asked if you can join him? It looks like we might've just had our first break. It could be the killer has forgotten to dump the phone or take out the battery. As soon as we get a fix on the location, the Sergeant is going to dispatch a helicopter for surveillance and get some uniforms to the location. With luck, if we play our cards right, we'll get the bastard who did all this!"

Chapter 34

Monday
The Figgate Park
17.15

McKenzie emerged from the underground chambers into the daylight of the Figgate Park and sucked in lungfuls of clean fresh air. Never before had air smelt so wonderful.

His phone buzzed.

"Guv, we've got the latest location. I've passed it to the squad cars and the helicopters. They're on the way... They're tracking the mobile signal in real time now. At the moment it's stationary... "

"I'm coming. Be there in a sec." McKenzie replied and hung up.

Just then McKenzie could hear the sound of a helicopter. It was getting louder.

Looking round, scanning the sky he couldn't see it, but he could definitely hear it.

Scrambling as quickly as possible out of their forensics suits, they headed towards McKenzie's car which he'd parked a few hundred metres down the road before he'd found the entrance to the park and the concrete building Galbraith had described to him.

They were just nearing the car when the helicopter flew over ahead. Jumping in, he fumbled with the key in the ignition then sped off down the road to the junction and turned left towards the main road on which the old school sat.

As he headed up the road and neared the lights, he slowed down and started to turn left onto the main road.

The helicopter was very loud, almost directly overhead now. Brown opened the window and strained to look out and up.

"Bizarre... it's very close." She commented.

McKenzie's phone buzzed again. It was Anderson.

"The phones on the move. It's quite fast. It must be in a car. But, it's really strange... it seems to be very close to... "

Flashing blue lights suddenly lit up the inside of McKenzie's car.

Brown and McKenzie both spun round in their seats to see a police car rapidly approaching them from behind, and almost at the same moment, another car shot up the road past the old school and swerved across the front of McKenzie's car, blocking his way forward.

Two policemen immediately jumped out of the car and ran across to them. Behind them the other squad car drove up fast and stopped threateningly close to their tail end, blocking any rear escape. Another two police officers jumped out, one of who was now brandishing a gun.

Above them, the helicopter swooped down lower, and hovered directly overhead.

"What the hell's happening?" McKenzie shouted, smashing his fist on the steering wheel.

"Stay in your car. Keep your hands where I can see them!" one of the approaching police officers on the road was shouting at them.

McKenzie wound his window down and thrust his hands out as instructed.

The police officers were now surrounding his car, with one of them, gun levelled straight at McKenzie's face, only a metre away.

"Sir, slowly, please step out of your car and put your hands on the roof."

"Officer, I am Detective Inspector McKenzie. It's my team that called you out!"

Unable to hear McKenzie yell because of the helicopter, the officer waved his weapon again and reissued the command.

McKenzie swore aloud and then stepped out of the car, as instructed.

"Slowly..."

"I'm Detective Inspector..."

"Remain silent..."

McKenzie felt powerful hands grab his, wrap them behind his back, and handcuff him. Across the top of the car, he could see Brown going through the same experience.

"We have the suspects!" McKenzie heard the policeman shout into his radio, before beginning to spin him around so that his back was against his car.

For a second, there was a look of momentary confusion on the young uniformed police officer's face.

"I know you. I've seen you..."

"Before? Yes, I'd hope so. I'm Detective Chief Inspector Campbell McKenzie. And the other person you've just handcuffed is Detective Inspector Elaine Brown. Good job, officer. Well done!"

Monday
The corner of Duddingston Road and Mountcastle Drive South
17.30

The look of confusion on the young policeman's face was priceless.

It compared only with the same look on McKenzie's and Brown's faces.

"Just exactly what is going on?" McKenzie demanded. "And call that helicopter off. It's too close."

"Sorry, sir, but we've been ordered to chase down the person in a car who's carrying a mobile. It's a moving target. You're the only car on the road just now. We just assumed... I mean..."

Anderson rounded the corner, running from the school, and appeared by the young PC's side, his Airwave phone in his hand.

"It's okay, officer. You've done fine. There's something funny going on here though." He held up his airwave and brandished it in the air. "The latest message from the people tracking the phone is that it's here. Exactly here."

"How's that possible?"

"It was stationary, and from the map reference they just sent me, that was just round the corner beside the Figgate Park. Then it started to move... and now it's here." Anderson explained. "Basically, Guv, either you're carrying it, or it's in the car."

They all turned to look at the car.

"Are you going to unlock us or are you actually arresting me?" McKenzie asked the young officer, but with a smile on his face to diffuse the tension.

The officer jumped to it, and within seconds McKenzie and Brown were both free.

"I'll check the inside of the car. Elaine, you check the back. And Murray, could you please give me ten?", McKenzie joked, pointing at the ground, and making it obvious that he wanted the Sergeant to drop to the floor and check the underside of the vehicle.

It only took a few minutes to find the answer to the mystery.

"Got it!" shouted Anderson from just underneath the front of the car. Standing back up, he held out a small plastic box. It was attached to the underside of the engine, stuck on with a powerful magnet. "Looks military."

Anderson opened the box and held it out for everyone to see: it was a mobile phone.

McKenzie swore, turned and hit the roof of his car.

Monday
The base of the Sir Walter Scott Monument
Edinburgh City Centre
17.45

Stuart Nisbet stood at the bottom of the Sir Walter Scott Monument, scanning the crowds of tourists who passed him by.

He was looking for one person.

Someone, who in an incredibly short period of time, had turned his world upside down.

Marie McDonald.

Stuart was a powerful man. If he wished to flex his financial muscle, he would be one of the most powerful men in the United Kingdom. He was a complex man. Capable of manipulating others, controlling them, persuading them. He knew how people worked. What made them tick.

Yet, in the past forty-eight hours, something amazing yet incredibly dangerous had happened.

He'd fallen in love.

It made him feel weak.

But at the same time it was totally exhilarating.

Standing there, waiting for Marie, was more exciting than anything he'd done in years. Just waiting. Doing nothing, but straining every nerve in his body.

Would she come? Or not?

Once, several years ago, he'd had to wait in a room in Dubai with a telephone, sitting by the phone, staring at it, waiting for it to ring.

At the time, if it rang, it would have been because a deal worth almost £100m was going to go through. If it didn't he was going to lose tens of millions.

Sitting in the room back then, he didn't know which way the deal was going to go.

He'd thrived on that feeling back then, both hating it and loving it at the same time.

But the feeling now was far worse. He couldn't believe how nervous he was. Would she show? *Or not?*

In Dubai, although the call had come in late, the phone *had* rung. He'd become even richer.

Now, standing in Edinburgh all those years later, he looked at his watch. The big hand was almost at six, the little hand...

"I have two seconds left. It's five... fifty-eight!"

Stuart looked up and laughed. He was smiling.

Maggie kissed him then, slowly and passionately, even better than she had promised.

When they stopped, Stuart knew that in those few seconds he had become richer than ever before.

"So,... Mr Stuart Nisbet. Where are you taking me for dinner? I'm starving." Marie declared.

"The Witchery, just beside the Castle. I can't think of any place more suitable, given that you have totally bewitched me and seemingly cast a spell over me." Stuart replied.

"Seemingly? Only *seemingly*?" she cocked her head to one side and raised an eyebrow.

"Definitely. Not seemingly. You Marie McDonald have *definitely* done something to me that I can't yet figure out. Most definitely. And in return, I would like to do something to you... "

And before she could object, Stuart had wrapped his arm around her, dipped her theatrically and kissed her passionately.

"I've been wanting to do that all day. I've thought of very little else. Apologies. Normal service will now be resumed." He joked, mocking an apology.

"Oh, that's a shame. I quite liked that! But perhaps if I can get you to drink a little too much over dinner, maybe you'll do it again."

"Is that a command, or an invitation?"

"A command."

Stuart laughed.

"I am but your humble servant."

Sticking his arm out, he offered her his elbow. "We'd better go. Our table is for 6.15 a.m., and we shouldn't really be late."

They started walking.

"How on earth did you manage to book a table at the Witchery at such small notice? I've never been there before, but I know it's one of the best restaurants in Scotland."

Stuart smiled, resisting the temptation to admit, quite simply, that he'd recently bought it.

Instead he tapped his nose with his forefinger and raised an eyebrow.

"That, my dear, is for me to know, and you to be impressed by. *Please*."

She laughed. "I am impressed. But, I should warn you that tonight I have brought a list of questions with me, and we're not leaving the restaurant until you've started giving me some answers. I must admit I do quite like this 'international man of mystery' persona you're exuding, but I've only got a few days left in Edinburgh, and I would like to learn more about you."

"Why spoil the little time we have left then? There's nothing special about me at all. I'd rather talk about Marie McDonald."

Marie stopped, took a pace forward and turned to face Stuart.

"I'm actually serious, Stuart. I don't know anything about you. I'll be honest. I'm interested in you. And I want to know who you are."

As if to prove her sincerity, she kissed him.

Stuart responded, then when she pulled back, he nodded.

"You win. If we have time, you ask. I'll answer."

They started walking again, and then he added, quietly. "But only ten questions. I have about a hundred questions I have to want to ask you too. And there's something very important I want to tell you. Something very exciting indeed, Miss Marie McDonald. Just don't forget to ask me what it is, after you've asked me your first question."

"Why the first question?"

"Because after I tell you what it is, you'll forget completely to ask me the other nine."

Just then, Stuart's phone rang.

He pulled it out of his pocket, and looked at the display.

It was an important call.

Potentially worth millions of pounds.

"Anything important?" Mare asked, seeing the look on his face.

Stuart smiled, hit the button on the side that switched it off, and replaced the phone in his pocket.

"No," he replied. "It might have been important before, but now it's not important at all."

Monday
Operation Blue Building
Incident Room
18.30

The full team had assembled in the portacabin, including the night shift led by Mather, who had been called in early.

McKenzie stood in front of them, his face looking haggard and drawn. Everyone could see the strain the case was beginning to put on him, and everyone else too. They were all tired, and most of them had missed lunch. Again.

There was also a new face present.

"Before we start, I'd like to welcome PC Dania Jordon. She is our new Office Manager. Over the next few days she's going to become the most important person here. From now on, we do everything by the book. The leads and actions are piling up and we can't afford to miss one thing. I'm instructing her to be on all our backs, including mine. Report to her twice a day, or more. As soon as you complete an outstanding action. When you completed one action, go to her and she'll assign you another. If it's the middle of the night and you can't get hold of her, update the incident log yourself but make sure she knows about it first thing the next day."

"I've ordered in pizza. It'll be arriving in thirty minutes. This is going to a long session, so apologies in advance, but we've got a lot to cover. A *lot* has happened, and I don't want to leave here until everyone has updated us on their actions, and everyone has contributed to the team with new ideas, no matter how stupid they may seem."

"I'll give you a full report on all my activities in a moment, but before we start, I just want to frame the seriousness of this. We've had another threat. A phone message directly targeted at us, picked up on Mark McRae's answering machine when we visited his home: - *"You've found three, now expect four!"* In other words, unless we can find the killer or killers soon, we're going to be dealing with another death in the imminent future. The killer used the word 'expect' so I don't think it's happened yet. But this is just another example of the killer being one step ahead of us. Whoever it is, is *playing* with us. It has to stop. I've spoken to DCI Wilkinson and given her a full update. Tomorrow she will finally be assigning us a Criminal Psychologist to start profiling the killer and their motives and hopefully help predict their moves and actions, and to help catch him. A bit late, but it's better late than never. Oh, and last thing for now on the phone message – I've asked Murray to work with the phone companies and our forensics department to try and do as much analysis on the message and the voice as possible. Can we get a voice print from the message? Was that real laughter that we heard on the call, or something tagged on, or recorded from something else? Is there anything in the message that can tell us about the killer?"

"Okay, now, I'm going to go first because there're a few things I need to tell you about, then we'll go through the existing action register and get updates from you all. Agreed?"

Everyone agreed.

McKenzie then spent the next thirty minutes explaining what he'd been involved in and what had happened recently. Not everyone had heard all the details yet, and there were a few gasps and choice swear words openly exchanged in the room as some of the details were revealed.

In quick succession he covered off everything, including his visit to Mark McRae's house, the threatening phone message, the mobile phone number he'd retrieved, the discovery of the book called 'Remember Me?' which he'd subsequently retrieved from both Blake and Weir's house, his conversation with Gary Bruce, the discovery of the tunnel and their investigation of it, and the incident with McRae's phone being found attached to the underside of his own car.

Actions were given out left right and centre, and for the first time they were all recorded professionally by PC Jordon.

The team all engaged, throwing their suggestions into the mix and expressing opinions and ideas, many of which were recorded on a new ideas board that had been brought into the room.

When the pizza arrived, they took a small break, but it was consumed so quickly they carried on only ten minutes later.

Several big questions arose.

'How did the killer seem to know where McKenzie was all the time, and how did he manage to stay one step ahead of the team?'

'With *'Remember Me?'* being the message scrawled on at least two of the victim's foreheads, and also the title of the book found at their houses, what was the connection?'

'*Who* were the victims meant to be remembering? Did they know the killer?'

McLeish had a good question: 'Who was the message meant for, the victim or those investigating their deaths?'

'Who might be next?'

And the biggest of all: 'who knew about the tunnel and would have access to it?'

McKenzie parked some of the questions for later, making sure that they first had reports in from everyone. He wanted everyone to have the same common solid foundations based on everything they knew, before building fresh ideas and planning what came next.

First up from the team was Anderson. He'd got back the analysis on the call records from the three phones belonging to the deceased. The last call records for Weir and Blake were from the area of their homes. They'd discussed this at the last meeting, but there were no new conclusions to be drawn. The actions on those two phones were now closed. The discussion on McRae's phone was more interesting. It had gone dead last Wednesday evening, but then suddenly become active again while McKenzie was in McRae's house, just outside his house. The presumption was that the phone had been dismantled when McRae was kidnapped, the phone and SIM having been taken out, and the phone being kept in a metal Faraday cage somewhere. Then it was suddenly resurrected just outside of McRae's house at the time McKenzie had visited. As later discovered, it had been attached to McKenzie's car. The whole affair showed expertise on behalf of the murderer – he obviously had knowledge that phones could be tracked even when they were switched off, and the battery possibly removed - and had taken precautions. It also showed, as Anderson declared quite angrily, that the murderer was quite blatantly '*taking the piss out*' out of them all.

The comment made everyone angry. Because they all knew it was true.

The phone had since been handed to Forensics for analysis, but quite frankly, they did not expect it to reveal anything.

"We can't ever make those assumptions!" McKenzie had rebuked him. "The killer or killers are working at breakneck speed here. They're achieving a lot and striving to stay ahead of our whole team. At some point it is very likely that they may make a mistake. And when they do, that may be the only chance we get, or the break we need. We have to be all over it. Don't assume anything!"

Next up was McLeish. He and Lynch had been calling the list of all teachers, current and previous, who'd been working at Portobello, trying to check on their safety. The work was ongoing, but so far no further alarm bells were ringing.

Lynch, next, was able to share a photograph of the writing on Blake's forehead, and had confirmed that the shape and position of the letters which were still discernible were consistent with their belonging to the words 'Remember Me?'

Wishart had brought in Scott Davies. He'd been interviewed and discounted. It had been agreed that the death of Willy Thomson needed pursuing but was not part of Operation Blue Building. It would be handed over to some other team to investigate. PC Jordon both entered and closed those actions on the system with the appropriate responses and notes. Next, Wishart had managed to get hold of the coroner's report on the death of Maggie Sutherland. She had fallen in front of a train in Edinburgh Train Station one night. The inquest had decided it was suicide.

"Although someone could have pushed her!" Lynch remarked.

"For now, the Procurator Fiscal considers it was suicide. We'll accept that in the short term. We can't boil the ocean. We've got enough on our plates for now."

"But what if someone killed her because of the fuss she raised? Could McRae or Weir or Blake have done it, then someone killed them in retaliation?"

"Too much speculation for now. But we'll keep an open mind on all of this. For now though, like I said, we accept that Maggie Sutherland ended her own life. Why she did, we may never know." McKenzie ruled.

"Anyway, I've printed off a photograph of her. I'll pass it round."

She handed it first to McKenzie. She was a striking young woman. Undoubtedly beautiful, with sparkling blue eyes. McKenzie looked at the picture, and memorised it, then passed it on.

On the other point relating to Maggie that Wishart had been asked to check, she'd discovered that Maggie was only an only child. Both parents were dead. There were no cousins or immediate relatives to consider. And she was unmarried, and did not seem to have any record of a partner, or at least, nothing had been recorded in the file saying that there was a next of kin at the time of her death.

Brown was up next. Since a hidden entrance to the campus had now been discovered, her action on that was now resolved. She didn't yet have an update from forensics on the possible sources of dirt found in the tyre from the burning van but they were working on it.

Brown had also been in contact with the Procurator Fiscal with respect to the autopsies on Weir, Blake, and McRae. They had now been completed, having been fast-tracked by DCS Helen Wilkinson in response to demands from McKenzie. The Procurator Fiscal's autopsy reports confirmed dehydration in the bodies of all three. They had not been given water in the days leading to their deaths, although McRae had seemingly had water poured into his body via his mouth just prior to his death. McRae had burn marks on his body similar to those found on Weir and Blake, which were also suspected to be from the application of a cattle prod to the victim. The autopsy on McRae confirmed death by asphyxiation caused by a chemical blockage in the throat, but the report was leaving it to forensics to provide more detail on the chemical makeup of the blockage. The report confirmed that the blockage formed after two chemicals were poured into the throat of the victim, which subsequently mixed, expanded due to a chemical reaction, and formed a solid, preventing McRae from breathing. The coroner's report also noted low level traces of a drug in his system and noted a puncture wound to the neck which could indicate that McRae had been injected with a substance several days before. The drug was of the type that would induce temporary unconsciousness. The coroner's report on the autopsies on Weir and Blake also noted the presence of the same drug within their blood, and upon re-examining the bodies, had found a puncture wound in the neck of Ronald Blake. Given the state of Weir's body, it wasn't possible to look for and find a similar puncture wound. Brown went on to give details relating to a few more minor points but finished by stating that the analysis of the faeces found within the chamber at the end of the tunnel should be complete by the following evening. This was intended to confirm who it belonged to, and how many people were held there that may have left a sample. Similarly, forensics would be examining the cloth material found, taking fingerprints, swabbing for DNA and examining the urine samples. The hope was to identify no more than three individuals having been held captive in that room, otherwise they may be looking for another victim. Lastly, there was an outside hope they may find some DNA belonging to the killer.

"I wouldn't bank on it," Lynch had commented.

To which McKenzie had immediately interjected.

"I know that a lot has happened, but I don't want us to start becoming negative. We mustn't. On the contrary, we've just made a major discovery, which could lead us to the killer. It definitely opens open new avenues of investigation. The killer may appear clever, at the moment, but I promise you, if you guys believe we will catch him, we will. Do not, and I repeat, do NOT start thinking anything to the contrary. He just needs to make one mistake and we'll have him. Or her. Remember, the killer is warning us that some other person out there is just about to die. It's up to us to save them. Every second counts. So, no negative thoughts allowed. Agreed?"

A round of nodding heads.

Nobody, however, was entirely convinced.

The clock was ticking, someone else was about to die, and for now, they were powerless to stop it.

Chapter 35

Monday
Operation Blue Building
Incident Room
19.15

McKenzie had given everyone a five-minute break. His wife had called him but he'd missed the call. She'd sent a text, saying only 'Call Me!' but she now wasn't answering her phone.

He'd try again as soon as the meeting was over.

During the break he'd stepped down to the other portacabin room immediately beneath the incident room and had a quick word with Gary Bruce and the others who were still in the room waiting for permission to leave it.

McKenzie had effectively set them free, saying they should go home for the evening, but all return in the morning. One of his officers would take a statement from each of them the next day.

McKenzie had discussed the matter briefly with Anderson beforehand. According to the information Gary Bruce had provided the Sergeant with, no one else in his team had gone to Portobello High School. Only Gary Bruce.

Unfortunately, although Gary Bruce would make the perfect suspect, the more McKenzie thought about him and talked with him, the less McKenzie felt that he was the man they were looking for.

Standing in the 'dungeon' they'd discovered at the other end of the tunnel, McKenzie had begun to sense for the first time the type of man they were looking for.

Cool under pressure. Clever. Sophisticated. A cold-blooded killer.

On the contrary, Bruce was not cool under pressure. He was agitated, getting angrier as each day passed, and McKenzie didn't think it was an act.

McKenzie also trusted Anderson's judgement, and after spending an hour questioning him earlier that day whilst everyone else was standing at the end of the tunnel, Anderson also admitted that he didn't think Gary Bruce was their man.

So tomorrow, they'd take statements, then cross them off the suspect list.

As soon as everyone was assembled, they continued the meeting.

McKenzie stood in front of the whiteboard.

"Okay, the good news is that the actions are progressing. We're making some progress. Which is positive. I want to reiterate we must not allow ourselves to get negative about this. The tide is about to turn, in our favour. I believe it, and I want you to believe it too. Okay?"

Some smiles. But not from everyone.

"Good, now we're going to decide the key actions for the next few days, and discuss the big questions that need to be answered."

"First up, is the tunnel. Who knew about it? Who had access to it? Who *used* it?"

McKenzie turned to the board, and wrote that down, put a big No. 1. beside it and ringed it in red marker pen.

"Wishart. I'd asked you to look into any unexplained deaths amongst Portobello pupils or teachers. I know you haven't had time to do that yet, but for now I want you to park that one. We're short staffed, and we can't do everything. We've got to prioritise, so I'm giving you the action to find out all you can about the tunnel. Find out who would know about it? And who would have access to it or have a key to the concrete building on the other side of the tunnel in the Figgate Park. And find out why the original plan we have is different from the plan now... I mean, when were those houses built? And... And find out why the tunnels are needed, and why they were built?"

McKenzie cast a glance over to PC Jordon.

"Are you getting this, or is it too fast?"

She smiled and nodded.

"It's perfect. All good so far. The pace is fine."

"Excellent. McLeish, you're helping Wishart. You're not dropping the action to chase up on ex-teachers, you're just parking it. She'll supervise you."

A nod from McLeish.

"Lynch? Dean? I want you two doing your best to use the phone records to pinpoint where and how Weir, Blake or McRae may have been picked up. We know they might have been injected and sedated or knocked out. They were probably bundled into the white van we found before it became a burned-out wreck. I know the phone records didn't tell us much, but do what you can to see if there's anything we can get from local CCTV cameras. Was the van we found in the neighbourhood? Can you see any suspicious activities in the streets? There's just the slightest possibility we might get the murderer on film kidnapping his victims. A long shot. But possible. Okay?"

This time two smiles and nods.

"Brown?"

"Yes, Guv?"

"I want you to talk with Forensics and agree a time-schedule for getting them out of this building. As far as I'm concerned, we only have two murder scenes. The room where Ronald Blake was crucified, and the room Mark McRae was killed in. The rest of the building is no longer of interest. Obviously, the tunnel *is* of interest, but I suspect they will not find much there. The dungeon – for want of a better word – and the rooms at the other end of the tunnel are sufficiently far away from this building that I think that although they may need more time there, we should still be able to consider blowing the main building up as soon as possible. I don't want anyone else dying here. Let's ensure that Mark McRae was the last. When this gets out to the press, which it will soon, we're going to have a media circus outside. The best plan is to bring the building down as soon as possible. I'd suggest you give forensics two days. We've also to consider that the building is still wired with explosives. Every second we delay the demolition, the more we put everyone at risk who is anywhere near it. Two days?"

Brown made a face, but nodded.

McKenzie knew that getting permission to blow the building up so quickly may be a challenge, but there were more reasons to destroy it now, than to keep it.

Plus, now McKenzie was becoming more convinced that Gary Bruce was not a suspect, he was inclined to do everything he could to help ensure Bruce wasn't driven into bankruptcy and became another victim of the killer.

There was also a growing feeling at the back of his mind that the building had served its purpose for the killer. When they entered the tunnels and investigated them, they were empty. There were no traces of anything that might lead them to the killer. It was almost as if the killer was satisfied that they had served their purpose and had moved on. Yet again, McKenzie's team were behind the curve, but he didn't want to admit that to his team, even if other's may have thought it too.

Which all led to another big question: if the next murder wasn't going to take place in the school, where was it going to be?

"Okay, does anyone else have any suggestions? Thoughts? Comments?" McKenzie asked, stepping back from the whiteboard after writing the rest of the questions and ideas down.

"I have a question," McLeish volunteered.

"Go for it." McKenzie nodded at him.

"That's three times now the killer has known where you were, and then placed something on your car. Are we chasing the killer? Or is the killer chasing you? And if he is, how does he or she know where you are all the time? Are we confident that it's not one of the demolition squad on site here who's listening to our conversations and then following us to where we say we will go during our meetings?"

A few people in the room looked back and forward at each other.

"A good question. I don't know the answer to that."

"Or is your car bugged?" McLeish asked, quite pointedly.

The question stunned McKenzie. Both in the way McLeish uttered the question, and also in terms of the point it raised. McKenzie immediately began to consider the question more: 'Could his car be bugged?' If it was, it would explain a lot.

"I'd like to say that we're getting a little paranoid by asking that, but actually, in reality, it's not a stupid question. I'm afraid it's actually a real possibility. Since you came up with the question, I'm giving you the action to call Fettes tonight or tomorrow morning, first thing, and find out if there's any way we can scan the car to see if it could be bugged. Do we have that capability?"

McKenzie added the action to the list on the whiteboard.

"Okay, right, you're probably all wondering what my action is? Well, I'm taking this home with me tonight and going to try and read it." He held up the blue book, 'Remember Me?'. "I need to find out what it's about and if it reveals why each of the deceased had a copy. I also then need to contact the publisher and see if we can find out who wrote it, who published it, how many copies were printed, and how they were distributed. How many other people apart from Blake, Weir and McRae got them?"

"Good," he started to conclude, but as he started to speak, his phone rang.

It was his wife Fiona.

Knowing that Fiona would never call him at work unless it was urgent, - messaging was fine but a call might interrupt something, like this important operation's briefing – McKenzie took the call.

"Are you okay," he asked, signalling an apology to the room, and turning his back on them.

"No, I'm in an ambulance. On the way to the hospital. Campbell... I've just gone into labour!"

Monday
McKenzie's Car
19.30

McKenzie's mind was all over the place.

He had instantly clapped his hands to end the meeting, explained that his wife was unexpectedly in labour, and excused himself.

Brown had offered to drive, but McKenzie politely declined. He needed the car, and he didn't know when he'd back.

"You're in charge now. You know what to do." He told Brown.

And he left.

From where he was, it was about a ten-minute drive to the Royal Infirmary of Edinburgh Hospital, down through Duddingston, round past Craigmillar and over the hill past the incredible Craigmillar Castle, not that McKenzie had time for sight-seeing now.

He was scared.

Fiona was only thirty-two weeks into the pregnancy. Little Bump was not expected to arrive for another eight weeks.

He and Fiona had been to all the NCT classes together to learn everything they could about pregnancy. Fiona had also devoured every book she could on childbirth and what to expect.

This was definitely not part of the plan.

It was against the law, and McKenzie knew it, but he popped the blue light on top of his car, and sped across several junctions without waiting for the lights.

Blue lights were for emergency use only.

And this was an emergency.

Pulling into the car park, he abandoned the car without a ticket in one of the parking bays nearest the maternity department, and ran full speed into the maternity ward.

A calm woman at the reception desk smiled at him as he burst in.

"My wife just called me. She arrived in an ambulance just a few minutes ago. She'd gone into labour prematurely. Her name's Fiona McKenzie."

The woman seemed to recognise her name, and the smile slipped slightly from her mouth. She picked up a phone and dialled a number, and asked to speak with someone.

Her face became very serious.

McKenzie began to feel a heavy sick sensation in the pit of his stomach.

His heart was racing, and he could feel the sweat beading on his forehead.

At that moment, all the stress and horror of the past few days seemed to coalesce in those few small seconds.

"Little Bump.

Please God.

Please let Little Bump be okay!"

Monday
Royal Infirmary of Edinburgh
20.00

McKenzie sat on the edge of the bed, stroking his wife's hand.

She had been crying.

The obstetrician had just left them, having explained the situation.

The news had been... good.

An incredible relief.

The words 'Braxton Hicks' had just been indelibly added to their vocabulary, at least McKenzie's. Fiona had known about them already, but they were both relieved to hear that the sensations she'd been having were not true contractions, at least not the type of contractions that heralded the arrival of a baby.

They were common, apparently, and not signs of immediate problems.

Fiona had been advised to go home and rest, and was shortly to be discharged.

"I want you to go to your sister's in Stirling." McKenzie had suggested, quietly, just after kissing her on the forehead and wiping away some more of her tears. I don't like the idea of you being alone in the house. You needed me today, and I wasn't there. And things are not going to get any easier in the next week or two. We've got a serial killer on the loose threatening to kill another victim, and we have to do everything we can to find him in the next few days, before it's too late. I want to be with you, and Little Bump, but three people have already died... and we have to stop the next death."

Fiona smiled.

"Don't worry. I understand. The doctor said I'm fine. There's no problem. The important thing is you came tonight as soon as I called you. You dropped everything."

He smiled.

"But I have to go back... "

"Now?"

"Okay, not now. I'll take you home, get you to bed and give you some food. But then I've got some work to do at home. I'll call your sister and get her to come and pick you up tomorrow morning."

"I can drive myself. There's nothing wrong with me. Actually, it's quite good, because I've just been given a full once over, and they've said everything is brilliant. Apart from the Braxton Hicks Contractions, everything is great."

"I was so scared." McKenzie admitted.

"We both were. But get used to it. Once Little Bump is born, we're going to be scared for 'It' for the rest of our lives. Parenthood never ends."

McKenzie smiled.

"I know. And I love the sound of that. I can't wait."

He stood up, took a deep breath, and clapped his hands together.

"Okay, let's get you home!"

Fiona laughed. "I'm not one of your team. Less of the clapping, please."

They gathered their things together, signed a form at the reception and then walked slowly out to the car.

As they approached the car, McKenzie spotted something lying on his windscreen.

Adrenalin instantly surged through his system, and he stopped in his tracks, looking around him, watching for anyone who might be watching them.

"What's the matter?" Fiona asked, stopping beside him and scanning his face.

"Nothing." McKenzie lied, then approached the car and retrieved the item from the screen.

As he took a closer look at it, the surge of relief was immense.

He was probably the only person to ever react in that way upon receiving such a notice, but he couldn't help smiling.

It was just a parking ticket.

Chapter 36
Monday
The Grange
The McKenzie Household
22.00

McKenzie sat on the leather chair in their bedroom at the end of the bed. Fiona had finally managed to stop fussing about one thing or the other, and settle underneath the blankets, and McKenzie had at last managed to pour himself a glass of wine and open the first pages of 'Remember Me?'

He started the first few pages.

Then his phone rang.

It was Brown.

"Can you talk?" she asked.

"Hang on..." he replied, dropping the book on the chair and sneaking out the room. Fiona had already nodded off.

"What's up?" he asked, as he got downstairs to the kitchen.

"How's Fiona?"

"Ah... she's fine. She just fell asleep. She wasn't in labour after all, and everything's fine."

"Excellent. We were all worried about her. Anyway, I have some news for you. After you left, I managed to catch the school secretary at Portobello High School. She's given me her home number. She has all the records going back years for the school. I asked her who the janitors and caretakers were during the period 1990-1996, and she'd already dug that information out as part of the task we gave her to find out about all the ex-teachers at the school. She was able to go to her laptop and tell me straight away."

"Brilliant. And who was it?"

"The old school had one caretaker stroke janitor for over twenty years. Completely dedicated to the school. It was his life. Apparently, a brilliant man. Totally capable. He retired in 2009. Sally knew him. She's been the school secretary for about fifteen years now."

"Can you call him? Can we talk to him?"

"Nope. Sorry. He died a few years ago."

McKenzie was silent for a few seconds.

"Obviously that rules him out. He would have known all about the tunnel. The question was, who else did? Did the secretary... Sally?"

"Nope, I asked her. She had no idea that there was a network of small and large tunnels under the school, but she wasn't surprised. It's a big campus. Apparently, drainage was often a problem. There're several big ponds in the main area, which often flooded and overflowed during storms. There's a lot of concrete covered area and little natural run-off. The pipes and the tunnels were very much needed."

"So, who else might have known?"

"I'm on that one. I asked. But she couldn't think of anyone else in the school who would be interested or have any responsibility for them. However, the janitor lived in a house within the premises. He looked after the school all year round. It wasn't a seasonal thing. It was a full-on job."

"So, who lived in the house with him?"

"His wife. Cathy."

"Can we talk with her?"

"Nope. I asked that too. Unfortunately, she died of cancer in 2006. He only survived her by a few years. He took it very hard."

"Ouch."

A moment's silence.

"Before you ask, Guv, I also asked about children. The campus must have been a brilliant playground for children, especially during holidays when it was empty. And things like tunnels would be brilliant for children to explore. Cathy might not have known about the tunnels, but I've got nephews and I know for a fact that if their Dad was responsible for looking after them, any kids would have known all about them."

"Good thinking. So, did he have children?"

"Sadly, no."

"Blast."

"But… "

"But what?"

"But… according to Sally, they did *foster* some children. At least two that she knew of. A girl, for a few months, but the parents took her back. Then there was a boy, Michael. A good boy. Apparently. They had him for about six years."

"Excellent. How old would be now? Do we know where he is?"

"He's dead."

"*What?*"

"Died in the Gulf War in Iraq, a couple of months before it ended. He was in the army. Apparently, Mr Banner, the Janitor, was in the army too, and the boy followed in his footsteps."

"So, where does that leave us."

"I don't know. I want to check tomorrow with the council if the Banners fostered any more kids, but for now, it looks like we've come to a dead-end."

McKenzie swore.

"This can't be. Someone knew all about that tunnel. And that person is probably the killer. We find the person, we find the killer."

"Like I said, Guv, I'll be on this first thing in the morning. I'll be camping out on the Council's doorstep before they open."

"Stay as long as you have to at the Council. There's got to be somebody else who knew. Enquire about any work done at the school. Did they ever do any construction that might have led others to discover the tunnels?"

"I asked already. Apparently nothing that Sally knew of. They built an annexe on the other side of the campus, where the tennis courts used to be, but that was a temporary structure, and didn't have any foundations."

"Okay."

"Guv, I'll also be chasing down with the council the history of the campus, and when the ground at the back was sold-off and some houses were built on what used to be part of the campus."

"Good. Thanks. Maybe you should get on home now though. It's late."

"I will. But there's a few of us here, and we might end up at the Forrester's Arms in Portobello afterwards. We're just waiting for the others to finish up."

"Say thanks to everyone else for all the hard work. I'll see you tomorrow… and good luck at the council."

McKenzie walked over to the kettle and started to make himself a fresh cup of tea. Whilst he waited for the kettle to boil, he thought of what he'd just learned.

The janitor was dead, and so was the boy who might have known about the tunnel. But someone else had to have known. McKenzie was positive that they were on to the right track. If it wasn't Mr Banner or his son, it had to be someone else.

McKenzie finished making the tea, put some good relaxing music on in the lounge, then snuck upstairs to say goodnight to Fiona.

Popping his head around the door, he saw that Fiona was still fast asleep. Creeping inside, he picked up the copy of Remember Me?, then returned downstairs, settled down and started reading.

Within minutes, one thing had become very clear.

It was a terrible book.

Monday
Café Royal
Edinburgh
22.25

Marie and Stuart sat in one of the small booths at the Café Royal, nursing their drinks and neither in a hurry to go anywhere.

They'd had a wonderful meal. Actually more of an experience than just a meal.

The Witchery had certainly lived up to its reputation.

Marie had also been true to her word.

Halfway through the meal she'd pulled out a list of questions she'd written down, and started to go through them one at a time.

"Where were you born?"

"Do you have brothers or sisters?"

"Are your parents still alive?"

"What music do you like?"

"What hobbies do you have?"

"What do you actually do, Stuart? Where do you work?"

All the questions were easy to answer up to that point. Now faced with the question he'd been dreading, he didn't want to lie to Marie, but neither did he want to tell her the truth.

Evasion was the answer.

Or the truth, but not exactly the whole truth.

That way he wouldn't be lying.

"I used to be in the army. Then I came out, got a degree as a mature student and then got a job. Now I work in finance."

"Who for?" the interrogation continued. Although, to be truthful, it was the nicest 'interrogation' he'd ever had. Marie was genuinely interested in his answers, and he knew she was asking not because she was nosey, or making any judgements about him, but because she wanted to get to know him. For who he was. As a person.

It was really strange.

Marie made no bones about hiding the truth that she had nothing.

She was very poor. Owned no property. Had no real assets.

Yet she seemed to be incredibly happy, and driven, and her life had real meaning.

In some ways they were polar opposites, yet in other ways they were so similar.

The word 'soul-mate' had popped into his mind earlier on, but he had immediately silenced it. Did soul-mates really exist? Was such a thing possible?

Probably for the first time in his life, Stuart was nervous about admitting anything about his wealth. He was worried that Marie would find it obscene. She certainly would not be impressed by it.

She had no need for money for herself.

She needed money, yes, but only to help the others that she cared for.

Any money she received, she would give away.

Marie fascinated Stuart.

She was, ... amazing.

Stuart could also not quite believe his luck in meeting her.

Only last Saturday afternoon he'd experienced some form of epiphany. He'd realised how little he'd had. He'd changed. Then he'd met Marie that same evening.

Was it all coincidence?

Or was his guardian angel somewhere smiling down on him and pointing him gently in a new direction?

An opportunity to become truly wealthy, in a way that had nothing to do with money.

It was ironic.

He had everything,

She had nothing.

And he wanted what she had.

The last thing he wanted was to lose her.

"So," she probed, tenaciously. "*Who* do you work for? Do you actually have a job?"

"Would it matter if I didn't?"

"Probably, because I think you said something earlier about having to work. And I would hate to think you were then or are now, not telling me the truth."

There was an edge to her voice when she said that, which had scared him slightly.

He'd been warned.

Don't mess her around.

"I work for Ben Venue Capital Assets."

"Hang on, were they not the company that sponsored the ball on Saturday?"

"One and the same. More money than sense."

"Interesting."

"Actually, you given me quite a good entry into what I wanted to say to you... my surprise for the evening... ."

"Ah... you're trying to change the subject... I have more questions... "

"One more... just one more... then I have to tell you something. It's important."

"Okay... " she made a show of scanning down the list of questions. Then dramatically picked one. Her last for the evening.

"How about this. Where do you live? With your parents? You seem to be rather shy about it, actually."

Stuart thought about it. This was the second big question he'd been dreading.

"It's not the most impressive of places. I don't think it would impress you at all. And it's very messy. I have to admit to being a typical bachelor. I sleep there, but ... the truth is, I'd be embarrassed to show it to you. So I don't want to. *Yet.*"

Marie laughed.

"I'm still curious. I'm a woman."

"I'd noticed... "

"And that's the sort of thing we wonder about, when we meet eligible bachelors that sweep you off your feet."

"And that's what you think I've done to you?"

She stopped laughing.

Her eyes twinkled.

"Actually, yes, you have."

He couldn't help but feel a surge of emotion within himself. He reached out and gently took hold of her hand.

He swallowed hard.

"That's not possible. I couldn't sweep you off your feet, because you'd already knocked me off mine. I'm worried I'm falling in way over my head here."

She smiled. They were both nervous.

"I have another question for you Stuart. And please, tell me the truth."

He nodded. He knew it was serious, and would probably be the third important question of the evening.

"Are you married?"

"No."

"Are you involved with someone else? Do you have a girlfriend?"

"No."

She shook her head.

"Are you gay?"

His turn to shake his head.

"Then what's the matter with you, Stuart Nisbet?"

"Ask me if I *have been* married. You missed that one out."

"Have you? Been married?"

"No."

"Then why not? How come... , *seriously*, how come someone like you is not already taken? Is there something I should be scared off? Are you a serial killer?"

Stuart didn't reply.

Should he tell her the truth?

"What? You *are* a serial killer?" she pressed.

"And if I were?" he asked.

It was a strange answer, and for the first time since meeting Stuart, Marie McDonald felt a little uncomfortable.

Chapter 37

Monday
Café Royal
Edinburgh
23.05

Stuart saw the reaction to his question in her eyes, and immediately squeezed her hand.

"I'm teasing. Sorry. I didn't want to make you feel uncomfortable. There's nothing wrong with me, I don't think, but you might need to formulate your own opinion on that. I haven't been married, I'm not gay, and I'm not a serial killer. But, and this is what I was hesitating to answer, I have had a lot of relationships. I know it's not the best answer, but I also don't want to lie to you. So, I'm just saying it the way it is."

"A lot?"

"Yes. Quite a few. I love women, but I've never found the one. You know, *the one*. I did think I'd found someone very special once. I was really in love. But then she committed suicide. Without discussing it with me. Completely out of the blue… "

His voice trailed off, and he looked away, lifting his head and obviously fighting his emotions.

"I'm so sorry. I didn't know… I wouldn't have asked… " she began to apologise, reaching out and resting both her hands on his.

"It's okay. You weren't to know… " He coughed and shook his head lightly. "Anyway, the truth is, in the past, when I've got close to someone, I end up feeling really insecure and not sure what it is that the woman really wants from me."

He stopped short of admitting that he often found out that the answer to this question was typically quite simple: 'millions of pounds'.

Apart from that one special person, who'd let him down and left him wondering for the rest of his life, if he had failed her, and if he hadn't been there for her enough. After that Stuart had tried but failed to find love again. Instead, he'd had sex. Trophy partners. And a broken heart from the one woman that he'd trusted, and then been very hurt by. Devastated by.

So far, his experience of women had left him unable to trust again.

"Talking about me is not something I'm very good at. I avoid it. There's very little about me that I think you would find impressive. And I there's very little I probably have that I can offer you. Apart from what you see here. In front of you now."

Marie listened to his answers, and processed every word he said.

Stuart was different from other men she'd met.

Unlike most men, he had not yet tried to get her into bed. He'd made no real sexual approaches on her, not even alluded to it, in spite of the fact that they were obviously really attracted to each other and there was some very real chemistry between them.

Stuart wasn't pushing her at all.

She felt, had an instinct, that he wasn't lying to her.

He seemed genuine.

And she also sensed, in spite of his obvious strength, both physically and mentally, that inside he nurtured and hid an area of emptiness.

She felt a desire to reach out and comfort him.

Not only that, she also felt a strong desire to reach out and rip his clothes off.

It had been a while since she'd last felt like this.

She squeezed his hand.

"Thank you for the answers. I like what I see, Stuart. And for now you don't have to offer me anything else. Just you. I must admit to enjoying what I see quite a lot." She blushed. "I'm sorry for all the questions. Don't worry. The Inquistion is over. You passed. Do you want to tell me your news now?"

Stuart nodded, and he turned his hand in hers and squeezed it.

"Yes. It's good for you. I hope *really* good for you. I hope you won't be angry with me, but I had a word with some people I know in the company where I work, and I told them about your selfless and pioneering work in Poland and Eastern Europe with your orphans. My company, *our* company, is always looking for good causes. Cynically, you could say they sometimes take advantage of opportunities to give money away so that they can manipulate their tax position, or maximise a public relations or advertising opportunity, but the way I see it is that if you get the money you need, do you really care?"

Marie shook her head. "All companies are the same. That's the way it works. I'm not worried about that. But in the case of children there are specific things we have to watch out for. Publicity has to be limited to make sure there's no photos of the children, and no exploitation."

"Exactly! Absolutely. And you'd have to be all over that with anyone you talk to... but the thing is, I've set you up a meeting with a couple of people where I work, and they would be keen to talk to you about funding, if you would like?"

Marie's face lit up.

"Are you serious? That would be amazing! Today has been a horrible day. Everyone I spoke to said 'no'. No one seems to be interested in the plight of my orphans. They just say I should go to the EU for help and it's not their problem - although they don't use those exact words."

"I'm sorry to hear that. I hope this is different. If you can, please call this person tomorrow and let them know if you can make an appointment in their offices at 5pm?" He handed her a card from his wallet.

"Will you be there?" she asked.

Stuart shook his head.

"They know I helped set up the meeting, but I won't be needed. I've told them what they need to know."

She smiled, and her eyes moistened a little.

"Regardless of what happens, I want you to know that I appreciate this. A lot."

"Just don't be late."

"I won't." she paused. "I'm in no rush to go home this evening. And I'm free tomorrow evening, if you are?"

"I was hoping you would say that. I want to hear all about your meeting and how it goes. But now, if you want, we could go for a walk up Carlton Hill and see the city lights. It's a lovely evening."

Marie squeezed his hand back, and Stuart smiled.
He felt excited for Marie.
She was in for a BIG surprise!

Tuesday
The Grange
The McKenzie Household
08.00

McKenzie woke with a jolt. For a moment he wondered where he was, and then he realised he was in his armchair in his lounge.

He'd been reading 'Remember Me?', which he'd at some point let slip from his hands and let fall onto the carpet.

He'd struggled to stay awake through most of it. The book was terrible. It was obviously written by an amateur, someone who'd made the effort to write a book, but had no idea how it should be done.

The book was dominated by terrible grammar, spelling mistakes, and the most boring storyline in the world.

The only thing that kept McKenzie going was that he knew it was probably based on truth, and that aside from the discovery of the tunnel, it was probably their most important lead so far.

Right from page one, McKenzie knew he was reading the story of Maggie Sutherland.

The book told the story of a female pupil who fell in love with a teacher at Portobello High School, and who was then raped by that teacher and two others.

It named the teachers.

It described what happened.

And then went on to describe how the girl plotted revenge and then carried it out.

The book described in great detail what happened to each of the teachers who raped her.

In fact, the fates which Weir, Blake and McRae had recently met in real life matched those as described in the book almost *exactly*.

Whoever had killed Weir, Blake and McRae had obviously used the book as a template for their deaths.

The crime scenes they were now investigating were all recorded, there, in the book, almost exactly as they had found them.

McKenzie knew that the book was dynamite. He'd done his best to read as much as he could, but even though the material was very revealing, he'd really struggled. It was hard reading.

Picking up the book from the floor, he walked through to the kitchen to make some strong coffee.

Flicking through the pages, he guessed that he'd probably read three-quarters of it. He'd need to freshen up and read the rest as soon as possible.

McKenzie was excited. Perhaps the rest of the book would reveal who else was going to die, and help McKenzie's team to save them?

The book did differ in certain ways from reality. In the book, the teachers were murdered during a school ball, a year later, on the anniversary of when Maggie was first raped. The old school was still open with no plans for its demolition.

In the book, it was Maggie Sutherland herself who'd lured each of them individually to their deaths in the rooms of the school, or to the top of the roof where she'd let David Weir wander around until he fell to his death stoned on drugs.

In the book there was no tunnel used to enter the building.

Just the staircases and the lifts, which were fully operational.

Also, in the book, the revenge was all hers.

She was the victim who turned hero and then meted out justice to her assailants on behalf of all womankind.

The book was undoubtedly written from a very biased perspective. In the writing, the men were one hundred percent to blame for everything that occurred. Maggie was the victim.

McKenzie felt very uncomfortable reading it from that perspective. Although the writing itself was poor, the anguish she'd suffered really came across, and for that reason McKenzie began to question whether the headmaster had got it wrong in finding fault on both sides, or erring toward the fault lying solely with Maggie.

Ever since he'd spoken with the headmaster and learned what had happened, he'd struggled with trying not to take the side of one or the other.

McKenzie had dealt with many rape cases, and he always sided on letting the facts speak for themselves. In this case, neither Maggie, nor the men, could defend themselves further.

So who had told the truth?

Who was the victim?

Sadly, it seemed that now they were all victims.

The big question was; 'Who wrote the book?' Was it Maggie? That would be the obvious assumption.

But when was it printed? How many copies were printed? And did all the pupils in the year receive a copy? Was that Maggie's way of telling everyone the truth and outing those who were guilty? At least, 'guilty' as she perceived it.

However, the most important question that the book raised was about who'd read the book and then killed McRae, Blake and Weir - just as was described *in* the book.

Maggie Sutherland couldn't have done it. She was already dead.

So who did?

It was now 8.10 a.m. Fiona was normally an early riser, but peaking into their bedroom McKenzie could see she was still fast asleep.

Slipping downstairs again, he showered in the utility room.

Towelling himself down and getting dressed, the same question kept running through his mind.

'Who wrote the book?'

He knew that the only way he could get that answer was by contacting the publisher. With any luck, they'd be open very soon, hopefully at 8.30 a.m, but if not, then most likely 9 a.m.

So, making another coffee he walked through to his office, fired up his laptop, and Googled 'Createpace', the name of the publisher on the first page of 'Remember Me?'

Curious, McKenzie spent the next ten minutes devouring any information he could about who Createspace were. It turned out the company was part of the 'self-publishing' revolution which enabled anyone who had written a book to publish the book themselves. Typically, the service was used by people who didn't have a normal publishing contract with one of the usual publishing houses, but who wanted to see their own books in print, in paperback. According to the blurb, it all seemed very simple. You wrote the book and uploaded it to the CreateSpace website. Incredible new technology then took over and transformed your text into a draft book which the writer could then proof-read on screen. When the author was satisfied with the way it was laid out and that they'd corrected any mistakes, they could then arrange for bona-fide copies of their new book to be printed and sent to them. One at a time, or in bulk. It seemed amazing!

McKenzie had heard about this before but never personally experienced it. It seemed like every Sunday there was some article in a paper or magazine revealing how an author who'd been rejected by traditional publishing houses, had then become an independent author – or 'Indie' as they liked to be known - and self-published their own book and then become a great success. Some had allegedly even made themselves millions of pounds!

McKenzie knew that there was no chance that the book he'd been reading would ever be so successful, but he could see how the Createspace vehicle had given Maggie, presuming it was her, the opportunity to create the book, print it and then distribute it. According to the website, this 'digital printing revolution' made all of this possible in just a matter of days!

But who should he contact to establish answers to the questions he needed?

More googling and reading quickly revealed that Amazon had purchased Createspace in 2005, and now offered the service to its growing tribe of indie authors.

Finding no simple way to find a telephone number on the Amazon site, he called Fettes Row and spoke to one of the police officers down there. She was a guru at getting unlisted numbers and it only took her ten minutes before she called him back with the telephone number of Amazon's 'KDP' Digital Publishing service in Europe, which was, she assured him, the organisation that dealt with the service Amazon had set up for Indie authors. The service helped Indie authors to publish their novels electronically on the Amazon Kindle, or have them printed physically using the Createspace service. The headquarters were in London, and within minutes McKenzie was speaking with the secretary to the KDP digital publishing service's director. She immediately transferred him to her boss.

"Hello, thank you for taking the call so early in the morning. I am Detective Chief Inspector McKenzie from Police Scotland in Edinburgh. I need to speak to you urgently regarding a matter of life and death."

"Hello, Chief Inspector. I am Gavin Booth, Director of Digital Publishing here at Amazon. How can I help you?"

"I'd appreciate if you would treat what I'm about to tell you with the utmost confidentiality, as no announcements have been made to the public yet while we try to track down next of kin to the deceased. However, I have a book sitting before me on my desk which we believe has been written by a serial killer who has killed three people in the past few days. The book quite clearly outlines the deaths of the victims. What's more, we have reason to believe that the one or two more people may die in the next few days, or hours, and we urgently need to determine the answers to several questions concerning the book."

"Which are?" Gavin Booth asked, his tone now very serious.

"I need to determine who wrote the book, when it was published, how many copies were published, where they were sent to, if possible, and any personal details relating to the author of the book or the person responsible for publishing it, such as a credit card number, or home address. If we can determine this information, it may help us to arrest the serial killer before any other people are murdered."

There was a heavy silence at the other end of the phone.

"Chief Inspector, I understand the urgency of what you are requesting. I really do. However, what you are asking for are personal details of a customer, and I'm afraid that without the permission of the author, I cannot divulge those details. It would not only be against company policy but would be against the Data Protection Act. It would be illegal."

"Three people have died, in the most gruesome, horrific ways imaginable. Within five minutes you could give me the name of the killer - the person who wrote the book. If you don't, one or maybe two people will die in the next day. You will be complicit in their deaths, and personally responsible for that happening, by virtue of not helping us. Are you prepared to accept that responsibility? And the media publicity around that, when I hold a press conference after their deaths and explain what happened?"

There was silence on the other end of the phone.

"I don't know what to say… I think I will have to talk to our lawyers… do you have a warrant to access this information?"

"Mr Booth, this investigation is happening in real time. In the past three days THREE people have died. Someone else may be dead in the next few hours. Please don't go down the lawyer route."

"I'm sorry, there's nothing I can do without talking to them."

"Okay, Mr Booth, let me promise you this. And I want you to listen very carefully. If you don't help me, voluntarily, in the next sixty minutes, I will immediately commence the process of obtaining a warrant. This warrant will entitle me to enter your premises and seize ALL your data storage systems so that our experts can commence investigations and a digital search of your servers and data banks in order to determine the answers we're searching for. We will seize all your servers. Your laptops. Your mobile devices. Anything digital. And then, because we only have a small number of people working on this case due to cutbacks, we will take months, possibly years to obtain the information we need before releasing the computers and servers back to you. During this time, all your digital services will be offline. We will also, I repeat, tell the media what we have done, why we have done it, and why you did not help. If anyone else dies, we will seek to hold you partially responsible for withholding information and therefore being party to the crime of murder. Do you understand?"

There was a stunned silence.

"Alternatively, you can give me the information we need, and I promise you we will never mention your name, or the source of that information publicly. You have my word. The choice is yours. Save a human life and do the right thing, or be a complete and utter prat."

McKenzie then spelled out the name of the book and provided the Amazon identification number of the book that was printed on the back cover.

He gave the Director his number, and told him he had one hour. After that they would obtain the warrant, and within hours police would be accessing the Amazon premises and starting quarantining all their equipment, even if that meant taking a complete data centre offline.

"One hour. It's your choice. Please, lives are at stake here, man. Just do the right thing. And don't forget, you will have to live with the consequences of your decision for the rest of your life."

When McKenzie hung up, his heart was pounding in his chest.

Fiona was standing in the doorway of his office.

She nodded, clapped her hands and smiled.

"Wow. I wouldn't like to be him!"

It took fifteen minutes for the Director to call back.

He didn't have the information yet, but he promised to have it all by lunchtime. All the information he needed, and more.

Tuesday
The Grange
The McKenzie Household
09.00

"I'm sorry, but I'm going to have to leave soon," McKenzie apologised to Fiona, pouring her another cup of coffee and sitting down at the breakfast table. He'd just whistled up some scrambled eggs, fried tomatoes and toast.

"I'll pack after breakfast, and then drive over to Jane's. I've already spoken to her, and she's made up the guest room in the caravan. Don't worry, I'll be fine."

"I'm not happy about it, but I think it's best. Once we get this case solved, I'll apply for some leave, and I'll look after you myself."

"I'd rather you saved the time until Little Bump is born. Then we can all spend some precious time together bonding."

McKenzie nodded, but Fiona could see that his mind had already begun to wander back to the case.

His face had just begun to turn white.

Then he stood up, thumped the table with his hand and swore.

"What's the matter? What's have you just thought of?" Fiona asked.

"I've messed up. I think I know who the killer is! And I can't believe I haven't realised it before!"

Chapter 38

En route to Portobello High School
Tuesday
09.10

McKenzie waited impatiently for Brown to pick up. He was driving en route to the school, calling Brown on handsfree, and probably driving a little too fast.

He was kicking himself.

McKenzie was usually on the ball, but for some reason, he'd missed something obvious.

Brown picked up.

"Where are you?" he asked, no preliminaries.

"I just parked my car. I'm outside the school."

"I think I know who the killer might be. I *think*. It's the old school headmaster."

"Interesting. But why?"

"I was up most of last night trying to read the book. It details all the murders and tells the story of Maggie Sutherland. In great detail. At first I thought it must be Maggie who wrote it, but then, after I'd called and spoken to Amazon – I'll tell everyone about that in the briefing – I suddenly remembered that Daniel Gray told me that he was a self-published writer! I even saw his laptop sitting beside the window on his desk, where he writes from!"

"Wow, I see where you're going with this."

"That's nothing... consider this... the guy has gone off the grid. Imagine that he's spent the past twenty years hating himself for what happened. He realises that the teachers were guilty. And he decides to take revenge on behalf of Maggie!"

"When was the book published? Before or after Maggie died?"

"I don't know. The guy from Amazon promised me that he'd give me all the details by lunchtime."

"If he published it after she died, then maybe he thought it was a way of telling the truth, finally. Letting the world know exactly what happened after all. I mean, Maggie didn't want the truth told when she was alive. Did she?" A moment's pause, then he continued. "According to Wishart's report, there're no surviving relatives or partners, so who would care today about her suffering and what she went through? Perhaps only Daniel Gray?"

"Good point." Brown mused. "How about this... do you think that there's any possibility that Gray killed Sutherland? I mean, we know she fell in front of a train, but could Gray have pushed her? I think someone else already suggested the possibility of a push instead of a jump."

"Possibly."

Another moment passed. Both of them were thinking fast.

"Ahh!" Brown suddenly exclaimed. "We're missing something else, really obvious!"

"What?"

"He was the headmaster. Apart from the caretaker, he probably knew more than anyone else about the school..."

"The tunnels!" It suddenly dawned upon McKenzie. "He'd have known about the tunnels!"

Tuesday
Outside Portobello High School
09.30

"Hop in," McKenzie directed, winding the window down as he pulled up beside Brown on the street outside the old school.

After the Eureka moment on the phone twenty minutes ago, McKenzie had suggested they both take a moment to mull over what they discussed. What was wrong with their ideas?

"I've thought of a problem with the hypothesis," McKenzie broke the news as Brown climbed in and sat in the passenger seat.

"His age. He's not powerful enough to overcome three younger men and carry a cross into the school. And the fact that he's on Coll."

"Exactly."

"I thought the same. As soon as you hung up. But, just because he's too old and probably too infirm and weak, it doesn't mean he didn't mastermind or oversee their killings. What's it cost now to put a contract out on someone? What's the going rate amongst the low-life in Edinburgh, for each person killed?"

"About one or two thousand pounds?"

It was a startling figure, that a human life could be worth so little, but unfortunately both knew that it was true.

"Okay, so we both still think that there's a possibility that Gray could be the killer, or at least be the person directing and resourcing the people behind the killings?" McKenzie asked his partner.

Brown nodded.

"Not only that Guv, but it all fits. Not only is there a possible motive, but he has the knowledge to possibly help make it happen. By writing the book, distributing it to everyone, and then killing the perpetrators of the rape, he absolves himself, and then manages to find peace, all these years later." Brown concluded.

"Okay. I think there's enough in the idea to bring him in. If he's behind this, we need to get him to tell us who else is going to die, who's doing the killings, and either get him to call off any more killings, or we warn the others, take them into protective custody and go after those who are carrying out the killings." McKenzie summarised the situation and the threat.

"Exactly."

"Okay, can you please go in and get everyone assembled, and I'm going to call PC Grant in Tiree and see if we can get her to cross over to Coll again, and bring Daniel Gray in for questioning."

"Grant? DCI McKenzie again. How are you?" McKenzie asked, having taken ten minutes to get her to answer her phone. Presumably the reception was limited or troublesome on the island of Tiree.

"Exhausted. I got back late from Coll last night. The ferry was delayed in Coll with engine failure. I had to hang around for most of the day. But the weather was good, so at least I spent some time on my favourite beach. It was all good."

"How do you fancy going back?"

McKenzie could hear her exhale.

"When?"

"Now. I want you to bring Daniel Gray in for questioning. It turns out, he could be the person responsible for coordinating the murders of Weir, Blake, McRae and possibly also even Maggie Sutherland. And it's urgent. We're expecting more fatalities any time soon, so we have to get to him and determine his involvement and, if he is responsible, somehow get him to stop all of this before the next deaths occur."

"Agreed, if he's guilty. But there's a problem, Guv. The next ferry isn't until tomorrow. At 17.40 p.m., I think. I won't get there until the evening, Guv."

"Are you serious?"

"This isn't the mainland, Guv. Things operate here at a different pace. And the ferry will only run if the engine's still working and the conditions are okay."

McKenzie closed his eyes.

"Can you hire a boat? Or are there any other ways you can get there?"

"Not at the moment. It's the ferry or not at all."

A feeling of dread began to overcome McKenzie. He was anticipating the PC's next question. He only had to wait a couple of seconds.

"Could you fly up again?" Grant asked.

An image of a sick bag and the colour green filled McKenzie's mind.

"I don't know. Possibly. I'll have to find out. Stay tuned. I'll call you back later."

McKenzie hung up.

Things were just about to go from very bad to much worse.

Tuesday
Operation Blue Building
Incident Room
10.10

McKenzie clapped his hands at the front of the room and everyone settled down.

He started off the session by conveying apologies from DCS Wilkinson who had called him earlier that morning to say that the promised criminal psychologist wouldn't be joining them for another couple of days. No explanation. Just lump it.

"With all due respect, Guv. This is all a bit of a joke… "

"Normally I would not really be too pleased to hear those sort of comments in my operation's meetings. I run quite a relaxed, but tight ship, and respect for behaviour and process is important. However, in this case, as usual, Lynch, you are entirely correct. This is, as you might say, complete bollocks. Three deaths from a depraved-killer don't yet seem to be enough to warrant more attention or resources."

He paused.

"Anyway, does anyone have anything urgent since last night? I have a few things to say, and I want us all to get back to work as soon as possible. Time is of the essence, and we've got to nail the killer before he strikes again."

McLeish went first.

"I've booked your car in for a security surveillance check at Fettes for 2pm this afternoon. We'll find out if your car's bugged."

"Do I get a replacement car?" he asked.

"Sorry, Guv. I was told to tell you to get the taxi."

"Are you kidding me?"

"Sorry, Guv. I'm not. They'll give your car back to you tomorrow morning."

McKenzie nodded. Maybe he wouldn't be needing a replacement car, if he was on Coll.

"Okay, thanks. Anyone else?" McKenzie invited.

There were no takers. Nobody had really had a chance to achieve anything since last night.

McKenzie then spent the next twenty minutes updating them on the book, his conversation with Amazon, and the realisation that Daniel Gray could be behind all of this, followed by an explanation of their reasoning. He'd then told them about his conversation with Grant, and warned them that he might be making another trip to Coll by helicopter, if DCS Wilkinson would agree.

"What about the remainder of the book… the bit you haven't read yet? Maybe it could tell us who the other victim or victims are going to be?" McLeish suggested.

"True. Right after I've spoken to DCS Wilkinson, I'm going to find somewhere quiet and read the rest of the book. If I find out anything, I'll get Brown to update you. She'll be in charge whilst I am away."

"Okay, we'll finish up now. Just let me encourage you all to act on any initiatives you come up with. What we all do in the next few hours could literally be the difference between life and death for those next in the crosshairs of this serial killer. Let's work hard, but work smart. Okay?"

Nodding heads. A few smiles. But a lot of tension in the room. Everyone knew what was at stake.

McKenzie clapped his hands, and everyone went back to work.

Tuesday
Stuart Nisbet's Private Jet.
10.30 G.M.T.

Stuart Nisbet's private jet bounced a few times as the tyres found traction with the runway and he wrestled with a strong headwind.

The plane taxied along the short runway before almost coming to a rest, and then turned back towards the hangars and the main building.

It had been a smooth and uneventful flight, with a very early start.
The good news was that they had now arrived.
Safely.
But now there was a lot to do.
Stuart had to be back in Edinburgh by the early evening. He didn't want anyone to know that he'd left the city or that he was really here.

However, over the next few hours Stuart had a lot to achieve. He'd planned his time down to the last minute.

He was here on important business.
In his line of work, every second counted.

After making arrangements with the copilot to refuel and have the plane ready at a moment's notice, he hurried to the taxi rank outside the main building and read out the address from the piece of paper in his hand.

Settling back in the comfort of the car, he closed his eyes and thought about the next few hours ahead.

For those he was about to meet, it could mean the difference between life or death.

Perhaps it was wrong, but knowing that their lives were in his hands, made Stuart Nesbitt feel strangely good.

McKenzie's Car
En route to McKenzie's home
11.00

"Another helicopter ride?" DCS Wilkinson screeched back down the phone. "Do you know how much these things cost our department? And you just got back! Could you not have planned this better?"

"Ma'am, I'm working with the resources I have. Which *you* have given me. Given I have the smallest team in history, I have to do what is necessary, when it is necessary. This case is unfolding hour-to-hour. It could be that the ex-headmaster living on Coll is the mastermind behind our killings. I have to bring him in and question him as soon as possible. The local PC can't get to him until tomorrow. I need to speak with him in the next few hours."

There was a silence at the other end.

"I'll do my best, McKenzie."

"Thank you, Ma'am. Also, can I ask, how did your conversation go with the Queen? You said you were going to call her and tell her to go home?"

Another silence.

"You're a cheeky bastard, McKenzie. But don't push it. Let me know how your trip goes. I'll get the pilot to call you directly and arrange when he can take you, if at all."

"Thanks Ma'am."

The conversation ended.

Chapter 39

The Grange
McKenzie's Home
Tuesday
12.45

McKenzie was just about to settle down at his desk at home to try and make some progress on reading the book, when his mobile phone rang.

It was the pilot from the police helicopter.

"Can you make it to the airport for 3pm?" was the main question.

McKenzie hurriedly agreed and laughed politely when the pilot joked about remembering to bring a proper sick bag this time.

Ha ha, very funny.

The pilot then reassured him that the flight should actually be much smoother than before, so hopefully a sick bag wouldn't be necessary.

But bring it along just in case.

The timing couldn't have been better.

It meant that McKenzie would have time to pack, take his car to Fettes and drop it off for its scan, then catch a cab out to the airport.

Hopefully he'd get his car back this evening, or early tomorrow, at least as soon as he could upon returning from Coll.

Dropping the book on the table, he stood up and was about to go and pack an overnight bag just in case, when his phone rang again.

It was the Director of Amazon KDP calling from its London headquarters.

"DCI McKenzie, I've been trying to gather as much information as I can for you. I understand the importance of your request, and we wish to help as much as we possibly can. At this moment in time I cannot yet give you the name of the author, however I hope to be able to provide you with this information by about 6pm this evening, or by close of play here. I'm sorry, I'm dependent upon someone delving into the records and the information we've archived from the old Createspace servers… and the technicians who will do this aren't yet available. Please bear with me on this. Rest assured, I will get that information for you, however, before I do, I'll need to ask you to provide me with a formal written request from yourself or your superior officer, for our records. You'll understand I can't just give you personal details without some proof of who you are. So far, we have only talked by phone. I'll need to verify this is an authentic police request. Can you arrange that please? I'm not asking for a formal warrant, I just wish to have proof of whom you claim to be."

The request was reasonable. McKenzie couldn't be too angry or annoyed. In response, he promised to send an email from his police account containing a letter on headed paper.

Then McKenzie explained that he would be heading north and there may not be reception where he was going. He requested that the Director keep trying him until they managed to talk, or to pass all the information across by email, as soon as it became available.

It was an amicable call. The delay wasn't helpful, but as long as the information was forthcoming later that day, it would still be significant progress.

In the meantime, after sending the email, McKenzie knew that he had to finish 'Remember Me?'

Settling himself back down again, and reaching out for his copy of the book, he looked at his watch to see how much time he had, and was shocked to see that it was almost half-past one.

He only had thirty minutes to pack a bag, get to Fettes Row, and then hurry out from there to the airport.

Now under time-pressure, he hurried up the stairs to his bedroom and packed a bag.

Ten minutes later, he was in his car, heading down to police headquarters.

En route he called his wife.

"Hi, are you at your sister's yet?" he asked.

"I'm with her just now. But there's a slight change of plan. We're in Callander. We're going to be staying in her caravan here for a few days before heading back to Stirling."

"Aha… that's good. Try to get some relaxation. Chill out. Take it easy. Please."

"I will. By the way, the caravan's not in the same position as before. Karen moved it to a better position that became available. It's now right at the back of the park on the left, overlooking the river. It's very secluded, not really overlooked and very pretty. We're very lucky."

"I'm jealous. I'm heading back up to Coll just now to talk to a suspect. We might not have reception there, but I'll call you as soon as I can, okay?"

Before they said goodbye, McKenzie made Fiona put the phone to her tummy, and he said 'hello' to Little Bump.

He missed them already.

McKenzie's Car
The Police Helicopter
En route to Coll
15.10

Stepping aboard the police helicopter and settling down into his seat, the pilot had warned him that the weather conditions had changed slightly, and that they were expecting some turbulence after all which may last about thirty minutes during the latter part of the flight.

The pilot had advised that if McKenzie had any work to do, he should do it as soon as possible. He might not feel up to it later, going on recent experiences.

It was good advice and immediately taken.

McKenzie was really now getting increasingly impatient and concerned about what the rest of the book might contain.

He needed to know as soon as possible if it mentioned anyone else that could be considered a target, and ideally he should finish it before they brought Daniel Gray in for questioning, and a possible arrest.

McKenzie had also warned the pilot that they may be returning with an extra guest, en route to a police station on the mainland.

He was still waiting for permission from DCS Wilkinson to take Mr Gray back to Edinburgh for questioning. Given their lack of resources the last thing McKenzie needed would be to have to take him to a local station in Oban or Glasgow, and then to commute back and forward to question him.

DCS Wilkinson had also promised to supply the documentation, if needed.

Accepting a hot drink from the crew, McKenzie opened the book and started to read.

He was soon engrossed.

Not that the writing style had improved at all, but he was now driven to digest as much of it as possible in the next few hours.

Fighting the text, McKenzie began to slowly plough through the pages.

He was about twenty minutes into his reading, when he began to realise that he had possibly made a terrible mistake.

Flicking back a few pages and rereading them, his hand began to shake a little, and he was forced to put the book down.

He felt nauseous.

Not from the turbulence, which had not yet started, but from the contents which he'd just read.

It was a new chapter.

It talked about the next victim.

It gave the victim's name.

Described their method of execution.

And outlined why they had to die.

McKenzie had got it all wrong.

McKenzie tried to stand up.

He needed to use the helicopter's radio immediately.

Just then the helicopter lurched forward violently and dropped a few metres through the air.

"DCI McKenzie, please return to your seat and strap yourself in, immediately!" The copilot shouted at him, his voice booming in McKenzie's headset. "The turbulence is just about to start, and it's going to be rougher than we expected. I'm sorry."

"I need to call someone on the ground. Immediately." McKenzie shouted back, grabbing hold of a strap hanging down from the ceiling.

"No-can-do. Not yet. Not until this bit of turbulence passes…"

The helicopter lurched again and McKenzie stumbled backwards, banging awkwardly against the wall.

He immediately sat down, and realised that he was quickly beginning to feel very queasy.

Reaching into his jacket pocket he pulled out a plastic shopping bag from ASDA and got it ready.

The pulsating drone of the helicopter outside had suddenly increased in volume and the static electricity in the air had quickly ramped up.

McKenzie shook his head.

He glanced back at the book, which he'd dropped on the seat next to his, and tried to focus.

He needed to carry on reading.

It was really important that he did.

But the wind had just increased, and the helicopter was beginning to become a very uncomfortable place to be. McKenzie could feel himself turning green.

Again.

The pilot looked back at McKenzie.

"Don't worry, it'll only last about twenty minutes. And there's no danger, let me assure you. It's just rather uncomfortable for some people."

McKenzie heard his words of reassurance, but did not feel assured at all.

On the contrary, he felt very bad indeed.

A few minutes later, he vomited for the first time that trip.

Which, it would turn out, would be the first of many such times that night.

Slowly, as the storm around them began to intensify, McKenzie began to think less and less about the case, and more about the contents of his stomach.

At one point, he even questioned his desire to live.

Then he thought of Little Bump and remembered the morning sickness that Fiona had gone through for months.

In theory, he knew, that should put things in perspective.

However, knowing that the pilot has assured him that in another fifteen minutes it would all be good again, it didn't stop those fifteen minutes becoming the most uncomfortable of his life.

Never, NEVER, did he want to go through that again, he thought to himself.

Unfortunately, he knew that it would very probably only be a matter of hours before he would have to.

Twenty minutes later, the copilot came back to McKenzie and offered some apologies.

"I'm sorry, that didn't go as well as predicted, but the good news is that it should all be good from here on in. And, you should be able to use your own phone for the next ten minutes. We're passing over a few villages where we know from experience that there is good coverage."

McKenzie opened his eyes. They'd been glued tightly shut for the past ten minutes in fervent prayer: '*Oh, please, make it stop.*'

Which it now had.

So perhaps his prayers had worked.

Or was it just the begging?

"If we need to, would it be possible to make a stop-over somewhere else to pick up another passenger after you drop me off? Then bring them back as soon as possible?" McKenzie enquired, before continuing and offering a more comprehensive explanation.

The copilot agreed that it could happen, if required, but McKenzie informed him he first had to get hold of the mystery guest to check their availability.

Pulling out his phone, he tried continuously for five minutes before he got a connection and the phone rang.

"Grant?" he shouted into his handset. "It's DCI McKenzie. I'm en route in the helicopter to Coll, as discussed. But there's been a change of plan. Can the helicopter pick you up on Tiree in thirty minutes and bring you to Coll after they drop me off? I think I'm going to need your help!"

"If you need me, yes." Grant agreed.

"Good." McKenzie replied, hesitating for a second before continuing. "I'm afraid I have some bad news. I've made a terrible mistake. Daniel Gray is not the serial killer. He isn't to blame for any of this. I've read the situation all wrong!"

"Then why the urgency? And why are you still coming up to arrest him or bring him in for questioning? Why do you need me?"

"I'm not. But I'm going to need you to persuade him to come into protective custody with us. Daniel Gray isn't the serial killer. He's the next victim!"

Chapter 40

Tuesday
Island of Coll
Above Port na Luing Cottage
17.15

Under McKenzie's instructions, the helicopter flew low over Daniel Gray's cottage.

"I need you to land as close as possible. Time is of the essence. As close as you can get."

They surveyed the ground around the cottage and then agreed a place where they could land, but just temporarily.

"We'll drop you off, but we'll have to leave you. We can touch down over there, on the road, but only for a matter of minutes. We'll open the doors and you jump down. Then we'll head over to Tiree and pick up Grant where you agreed and bring her back."

"Excellent." McKenzie shouted back.

"Don't forget, duck down and keep low as you move away from the helicopter. You're a tall man. Don't stand up, or you won't be a head and shoulders above anyone else anymore."

McKenzie nodded but wasn't really paying attention. He was surveying the cottage, expecting Daniel Gray to come out at any second to see what all the commotion was about. Then McKenzie remembered that if he wasn't there, there was a strong likelihood that he might be in the pub.

If McKenzie hadn't been so tense with worry, he might have enjoyed jumping out of a helicopter: it was all very Boy's Own stuff. Instead, he couldn't stop thinking about Daniel.

As the helicopter slowly dropped to the point above the road, McKenzie did exactly as he was told. When instructed and the copilot opened the door at the side, McKenzie jumped down, bent low, and hurried quickly away from the rotating blades into the grass beside the road.

He waved back at the pilot, then hurried further away. Behind him the blades starting rotating faster, and as soon as enough lift was generated, the helicopter took off, turned and headed off towards the Island of Tiree.

It only took McKenzie a few minutes to cover the ground to Port na Luing Cottage. Arriving at the door, he banged loudly. There was no reply.

He banged again, then after waiting a little longer, he walked around the property to the back. Looking inside through the window, he couldn't see any sign of Mr Gray, so he tried the backdoor handle, and as hoped, found the door was open.

He'd once heard that people didn't really bother locking their doors on the Islands. There was no real crime, and very few tourists on some of them. With only one ferry each day, if anything went missing, you just had to call the ferry and have it stopped, and you'd have the culprit then and there.

However, perhaps another reason why crime wasn't very high was because people lived very simple lives. Maybe, apart from the odd bottle of good whisky, most people didn't own very much worth stealing.

Once inside the cottage, McKenzie had called Mr Gray's name several times. No answer.

Moving through the house, everything seemed fine.

The laptop was open on the desk beside the window, and McKenzie was tempted to see what Mr Gray was writing, but decided against it. That was perhaps being a little too nosey. If Mr Gray wasn't willing to tell himself, then McKenzie knew he shouldn't look.

Moving through to the bedrooms, he also found them empty. No one was in the kitchen, or the bathroom.

The house was empty.

There was no sign of Mr Gray.

It was an hour's walk to the hotel where Grant had last found him. McKenzie called her midway. She'd just been picked up by the helicopter, and she agreed to meet him at the hotel.

"If he's not there, is there anywhere else I should look?" McKenzie asked.

"Not really. It's the only hotel in town. And to tell you the truth, apart from going out on a boat, or walking on a beach, there's not much else to do. Don't worry, I think you will find him in the bar."

Unfortunately, she was wrong.

He wasn't in the bar.

And no one had seen or heard from him since Sunday.

McKenzie was still making enquiries with the locals at the bar when Grant walked in.

Everyone looked up and shouted a mixture of greetings. Grant was obviously well liked by everyone.

"Any luck?" she asked, coming straight across to him.

"None. Are there any taxis on the island? I want to go straight back to his cottage."

"There's not really a taxi service here. Not like on the mainland. But if you're in a hurry, we just do this... " she turned to everyone in the bar and shouted quite loudly. "There's two glasses of whisky on the bar later for anyone who gives us a quick lift down to Daniel Gray's cottage at Arinagour."

Three people stood up.

"Take your pick, Guv. Just remember they've all been drinking. My best advice is pick the one who's drunk the least and remember to forget about Scotland's zero tolerance laws. It's their way ... or the highway. Literally."

McKenzie nodded and chose the one with the fewest glasses on the table in front of them. Luckily he was only on his third beer.

"Dina worry, Detective," Old Jimmie Meekle assured him. "I'm nae completely pissed. And there'll be no other traffic on the roads at this time. Anyone not in the bar will be watching Eastenders on the box."

Not exactly immensely reassured, McKenzie offered to drive, and Old Jimmie accepted.

They took fifteen minutes to get to the cottage. Thankfully it was still light, and whilst Old Jimmie decided to take a wee nap in the back of his car, McKenzie and Grant wandered down to the cottage from the road, and once again found no one at home.

"Have you checked the beach?" Grant asked. "He might be down there, or sitting reading or painting on his favourite rock on the headland?"

McKenzie kicked himself. Why hadn't he thought of that before?

Striding out the back door and across the moor towards the sea, McKenzie told Grant to take the beach, and he would check out Gray's favourite rock, where they had sat together and talked during his last visit.

Grant nodded and turned away from him down through the small dunes towards the curving beach below.

McKenzie walked forward about ten metres, rose up over a small dune, and then came to an abrupt stop.

Headmaster Daniel Gray was sitting on his favourite rock not far away from McKenzie. A bottle of whisky had fallen over on the rock beside him, its contents mostly now spilled.

Grant's body was sitting up straight, facing the setting sun.

From where McKenzie was standing he could see that it was resting on a piece of wood which had been positioned to prop up the body to stop it falling over.

To anyone else, the body would have seemed slightly slumped forward, because McKenzie could not see Daniel Gray's head.

McKenzie saw Daniel, however, and shuddered.

He knew exactly what to expect.

He'd read the book.

They were too late.

The killer had got there before them.

McKenzie took several deep breaths and steeled himself for what he knew he would find. Walking slowly forward, and looking around just in case the killer could perhaps be hiding somewhere, even though McKenzie instinctively knew he wouldn't, McKenzie came up to Daniel and walked around to his front to face him.

Even though he'd known what to expect, the brutality of it shocked him.

Daniel Gray's body was headless.

But it was not without the head.

The head was easily found resting in Daniel Gray's lap, his two arms and hands gently placed around it to stop it rolling away, but positioned so that McKenzie could easily read the two words which were written across his forehead, branding him forever in the afterlife.

Daniel Gray's eyes were open.

It seemed as if they were looking out over the sea watching the setting sun.

One. Last. Time.

Tuesday
Headquarters Ben Venue Capital Assets
St. Andrew Square
Edinburgh
18.00

Marie McDonald sat alone in the waiting room outside the board room of Ben Venue Capital Assets.

She'd been sitting there alone, for over an hour.

Having arrived ten minutes early for the appointment, she been given coffee and cake, then shown into the waiting room.

Periodically, a pretty receptionist had come through and apologised.

"We're extremely sorry. We're running a little late. Could you wait a little longer please?"

Marie had smiled, and said, "No problem."

At first she'd meant it, but after a while she began to wonder if this was going to be a meeting like so many others that she had attended: lots of nice words, but not really being taken seriously.

She was used to it. Finding funding for her children was an uphill struggle at the best of times.

However, at 5.50 p.m., when the pretty young lady had apologised one more time, Marie had not replied, "No problem." It was actually becoming a problem.

If they weren't going to give her any money, they should just say so. Not play these games and go through the motions. She would rather they were upfront and honest. Marie had other things on her mind too. She didn't want to be late for meeting Stuart at 7.30 p.m. outside the entrance to the North British Hotel in Princes Street.

At 6.00 p.m. the lady came through one more time, and apologised again.

"Could you wait ten minutes more?" she asked.

Marie smiled, then expressed her apologies and said that she did have a personal appointment that she needed to make at 7.30 p.m. She would have to leave at 7.15 p.m., but she was free up till that time.

The young lady smiled, thanked her, then left the room, returning to the board room where she and two others were waiting, and beginning to slightly panic.

Stuart Nisbet had arranged this meeting and instructed them in no uncertain terms that the meeting should go ahead. He also made it clear that he would talk to them further before the meeting and provide guidance for their discussion.

However, no one had been able to reach him all day. They knew that he'd taken his jet somewhere, but no one was able to contact him. They'd been sitting there, waiting to talk to him, as instructed, but not able to take the meeting until they'd received his final instructions.

Now they were worried that their guest might leave, before they had a chance to talk together.

"Ladies! Why are you looking so worried?" Stuart said, bursting into the boardroom from his office.

The Vice-President stood up, and rebuked him.

"Where on earth have you been, Stuart? We've been sitting here like idiots waiting for you for hours, and you've not been returning our calls!"

"Don't worry. I'm here now. But I can't stay. I've got a date later tonight and I can't be late." He saw the look of confusion on their faces. "But don't worry, you don't need me here. I'll tell you what to do just now, and then I'll leave."

Five minutes later he slipped out through the back door, grinning like a Cheshire cat, and hurried down to the gym to shower, swim and spend some time in the steam-room, before getting ready for his date.

"Could you come in now please?" a tall, very smartly dressed lady with beautiful blue eyes asked. Strikingly beautiful eyes.

Marie stood up and smoothed herself down. Her nice, 'fund-raising' skirt was all wrinkled from sitting for so long.

She was ushered into the board-room and greeted by two other women who introduced themselves as the Head of HR – now obviously not just a receptionist as first thought! - and the Head of Finance.

The lady who had fetched her, shook her hand and introduced herself as the Vice-President of the company. "Please, call me Valerie."

They offered her more tea. Or coffee. Or a glass of wine if she preferred?

And then they invited her to introduce herself, tell them about her 'children' and the orphanages she ran, but stressed that she should relax. She was, apparently, amongst 'friends.'

"I've brought my laptop. Would it be possible to connect to your projector and show you a presentation that details who I am, and what I am hoping to raise funds for?"

"Certainly," the HR director agreed, and jumped up and helped Marie connect everything up.

A few minutes later Marie was in full flow.

Impressing them. Depressing them with the sad plight of her children. But inspiring them with the dream she had for not only improving the lives of her children, but extending the network of her orphanages and building one or two more in other European countries.

She introduced some of the children she cared for. Told them about their lives. Made it personal.

She even succeeded in making two of them cry.

As she neared the end of her presentation, she told them of her ultimate dream, which was to help provide a better education to her brightest children by finding a way to fund some of her children to go to the best universities.

"Education is the best way out of poverty. It creates opportunity, inspires, and helps children to dream. Children who grow up with a dream, have something to live for. Before I met these children, most of them had neither. No dreams. And no futures. Please, help me change all of that, not for just one or two children, but for hundreds."

By the time she had finished her presentation, it was almost 6.45 p.m.

Things weren't looking good.

She knew that they would have lots of questions, and she didn't have much time to answer them.

"Thank you," Valerie said, nodding. "Thank you very much. That was... and I think I speak on behalf of all of us... very moving. You've obviously done this before. You know how to work your audience."

Marie winced. It seemed to be a pointed comment.

"That's true. Sadly, I have to do this a lot, because funding nowadays is very scarce. I have to work hard to obtain the resources I need, to keep our orphanages going," she defended herself.

"You missed out one small detail, Ms McDonald. The simple matter of what level of funding you are looking for?"

"I'm sorry." Marie replied. She could tell from her tone of voice what the outcome of the meeting was now going to be. Things were not going well at all.

"Okay, I know it's a lot, but I was hoping to ask to for a minimum of one hundred thousand pounds. More if possible."

"Surely that would not be enough to fund the dreams you have outlined to us. Do you already have other, significant funding?" the Finance Director asked.

"To be honest, no. However, I'm worried that if I tell you how much I really need, then it will be too much, and it will simply turn you off and I - my foundation - will get nothing."

"And how much would that be, Ms McDonald?"

"Five million. Pounds."

The three executives of Ben Venue Capital Assets exchanged several rapid glances.

"Before you say no, would you like to ask me any questions? I know I may not have provided you with enough information to... "

"Don't worry about that, Ms McDonald. We've had someone investigate your foundation today. We've done a significant amount of due diligence. And we've spoken to the British Ambassador in Poland, and had a quick ten minute conversation with the President."

"Of Ben Venue?" Marie asked.

"No. Of Poland." The Vice-President replied. "So, you see we have no further questions for you just now, but I'm sorry to say that we do have a problem with the figure you have just asked us for." The Vice-President continued.

"The five-million pounds? Yes, sorry, I know it's too much... but," Marie tried to interject and steer the conversation away from disaster. She knew what was coming next. It happened almost every time. It was going to be a 'no'. Polite. Regretful. But a 'no' all the same.

"Yes, the five million pounds. Unfortunately," the Finance Director interrupted and continued, "five-million pounds is too little. That figure is no use to us. You see, we need to arrange for a significant tax write-off this year. We need to invest in international aid and be seen to be doing it by the UK Government. We were hoping that you were going to ask us for at least thirty million. But since you are not... "

"Please may I have thirty million?" Marie immediately interrupted her. "I'm very flexible. Thirty million is perfect."

"But since you're not going to ask for thirty million," the Finance Director continued, "*per* year, for the next five years, it causes us a significant problem. We were really hoping that... "

"Thirty million per year is perfect for the next five years." Marie replied, quickly and surprisingly forcibly.

"Are you sure? That's not too much? You would definitely be able to cope with such a large number?"

Marie was just about to reply and give them assurances that she could spend as much money as they could spare, when she realised that they were winding her up.

Making fun of her.

Suddenly she felt the anger within her rise.

She stood up.

"I'm sorry. I can see now that I'm making a fool of myself, and you are having a good laugh at my expense. No, at the expense of my orphans. Children who have nothing but their own abilities. Abilities which I only want to support and help nurture. I was introduced to your company by someone who thought you might actually be able to help me. However, I see now that my trip was wasted. I think I'd better leave… "

"There would however be conditions… " Valerie announced, seeming to ignore Marie's little outburst. "We would contractually, initially, only give you full control of the first thirty million. That money would be for you to spend as you see fit. However, the remaining one hundred and twenty million would be conditional upon us receiving full status reports, every three months, along with approved accountancy records of how you are spending the money. To do this, we would insist upon someone from Ben Venue Assets being seconded to your organisation to oversee your spending and how the money was being used. We would also only release the funds to you a week in advance of the next financial year upon agreement of how you would spend the money. We would not seek to influence or dictate how the money was spent… that is your area of expertise and not ours… we would only seek to ensure that the money *would* be *spent*. And our employee would need to spend a minimum of three months a year working with you. Very closely. With full access to you personally."

Marie sat down. She was beginning to feel quite strange. A little dizzy. Quite faint.

The conversation had gone from being just words, a hypothetical request for a string of numbers which she could personally never really comprehend, to what seemed like the board of a major company seriously offering her a fortune in funding beyond her wildest dreams.

"May I have a glass of water?" she asked.

Valerie stood up, fetched a fresh glass from the side-board and poured some new water.

"You're looking a little faint, Ms McDonald. Are you okay?"

She took a sip, then looked up and tried to focus on first Valerie and then the other two women in the room. She took several deep breaths.

"Is this a joke, or are you serious?" Marie heard herself asking, and was shocked by her own unprofessional but direct question.

"I can assure you, Ms McDonald, that we are totally serious if you are. If you agree to take a charitable donation from us each year for five years of thirty million pounds per year, totalling one hundred and fifty million pound sterling over the five-year period, then yes, we are very serious indeed. We can have the paperwork drawn up in the next few days, and you may visit us here tomorrow night to arrange a bank transfer to your Charity, or we can issue you a cheque. As you wish. However, there is one other condition. We must agree tomorrow who it is that we may second to you for the coming years. Of course, if you know anyone in our company who you may prefer, or can recommend, and if we think they are suitably qualified, then we could look favourably on that recommendation."

Marie smiled. Could this all *really* be happening?

She looked at the clock on the wall. It was nearly ten minutes past seven.

She thought of Stuart, hopefully soon to be waiting for her on the steps of the hotel.

"Actually," she replied, trying not to laugh or cry, but now visibly very excited, "I can think of one person. But I would have to discuss this with them first. They may not wish to, but I believe they would be an ideal candidate for the job!"

"Good. Would it be possible for you to return tomorrow morning? To make a few further arrangements? We will require a copy of your passport, your charity's bank details. Names of your trustees, etc. We may also have a few extra questions for you. Would that be convenient?"

Marie couldn't help but reply, "Are you seriously asking me if I have the time to come back tomorrow morning to arrange to accept one hundred and fifty million pounds?"

"Yes, Ms McDonald. And if you would not object, we would like to arrange to have a photograph taken with you receiving a symbolic cheque tomorrow night. And last of all for now, do you think you may have time to attend a formal dinner tomorrow night? We would like to introduce you to the First Minister of Scotland, if you are able to attend. I'm sure she would be very interested to hear of your work, and our donation to your cause. We may even arrange for her to present you with your first cheque?"

It was a simple answer.

"Yes!"

Five minutes later, Marie McDonald left the building of Ben Venue Capital Assets. She managed to walk only ten metres before she had to reach out for a seat and sit down.

She was crying her eyes out.

Could all this really be true?

Amazingly, it seemed it was.

Chapter 41

Tuesday
Island of Coll
Port na Luing Cottage
19.30

McKenzie had spent the past hour on the phone, making arrangements. He'd had to drive back to the hotel to get good reception, with Old Jimmie Meekle still nodding off in the back, oblivious to what was happening.

McKenzie had left Grant with the body of Daniel Gray, promising to be back soon.

The first person he'd tried to call was Brown. He couldn't reach her so he'd left a message. It was the same story with Anderson.

He had however, managed to get through first to DCS Wilkinson, and then to PC Jordon, who he quickly updated.

DCS Wilkinson was audibly upset. She'd even used McKenzie's first name several times. McKenzie had over exaggerated the problem with lack of phone connectivity on the island, and DCS Wilkinson had promised to arrange everything for him with respect to contacting the local forensics department in Oban and having a team make their way to Coll as soon as possible. McKenzie had promised to send the helicopter back to collect them.

She'd then quickly moved on.

"Campbell, I have some bad news for you, I'm afraid."

McKenzie took a deep breath. Was it something to do with his wife? Was she in hospital again?

"As you requested, I looked into the threat level and the use of a code-word. It turns out that the code-word was quite old, but still valid. It was strange though, because no sooner had I made the enquiry, than I received an update on the terror level. It turns out that a bomb threat was made earlier today. We were able to get everyone to safety and even managed to find and diffuse the bomb."

"Blast." McKenzie had said, managing not to swear in front of his boss. That meant that he wouldn't be getting his missing team member's back anytime soon.

"No. There was no blast. We managed to find the explosive just in time. Actually, we had plenty of time."

McKenzie was momentarily confused, then realised what had happened. Rather than explain it, he moved swiftly on. "What type of bomb was it? Home-made? Crude or sophisticated? Are there any indications who could have made it?"

"Actually, it turns out it was made quite crudely from commercial TNT."

A small alarm bell went off at the back of McKenzie's mind.

"Commercial TNT as in the type that's used to blow up buildings? Like Portobello High School?"

"I don't know. Perhaps."

"I hope we don't have a problem here, Ma'am. I can't help but wonder if the TNT was taken from the school, by the killer, and used to make a point. Perhaps there was no intention to hurt anyone. Only to prove that the threat to the Queen was real, so that you wouldn't give me my staff back."

"Oh, come on McKenzie. You can't really be serious."

"I'm afraid I might be. I'll need to get the demolition company to check all their explosives in the building and make sure they're all still there!"

"Even if some are missing, it still won't affect the terror rating or get your staff back any sooner." DCS Wilkinson insisted.

"You're missing the point, Ma'am. If our serial killer has now managed to arm himself with TNT which he stole from the school, who knows how much more dangerous that makes him! This is just going from bad-to-worse!"

"Okay, check on it, and let me know. By the way, I heard from PC Jordon this afternoon that the bodies have all been formally identified now and the autopsies are complete. That means we can't really hold this back from the press much longer. It's going to get out. Perhaps we need to control the release ourselves and make a press announcement."

"Not until we've blown the school up. Otherwise we'll have thousands of people turning up to ogle at it and cause even more problems."

"When will that happen?"

"In a couple of days time, if you give me permission? The ball's in your court for this one. I asked one of my team to contact you to discuss that already."

"Sorry, I was busy most of the day."

"Well, I've asked you now. As soon as you give us permission and we can get forensics out of the building, then we can blow it up. And then you can have your press conference."

"Not me, Campbell. You. It'll be your press conference. You can hold it."

"Thanks Ma'am. But does that mean I can blow it up tomorrow then?"

"Campbell, use your judgement. If forensics agree, you have my blessing. But let me know when you do it. I want to come and watch. Oops... got to go... Sorry. Bye."

And she hung up.

A few minutes later McKenzie managed to call and reach Gary Bruce.

He sounded disturbed, but cheered up when McKenzie gave him the good news.

"We just need to find out from Forensics when they will release the rooms back to me. I suggest you start to prepare anything you can just now. Once we know when we can do it, we'll need to coordinate with the council to close the roads again. But, parking that one for now, I've got a bigger issue to discuss... "

McKenzie went on to explain the potential problem with the TNT.

Gary was livid.

"I told you this might happen! Who knows how much the bastard has stolen... I hope he blows himself up with it... "

"Calm down. Maybe he hasn't taken any. I just want you to check and get back to me as soon as you know."

McKenzie could hear Gary swear a few more times, but after a few minutes he calmed down and agreed to organise a check of all the explosives that had been set.

"I'll ask DI Brown to assign someone to go around with you first thing tomorrow. I want someone to agree your tally. Okay?"

Next, McKenzie tried calling Brown again. No luck. He left her a voice message, and then sent her a text message with some instructions.

Just as he was finishing that, his phone buzzed. It was a text message from Grant.

"Please call me on Gray's home number, Guv."

McKenzie got the number from his notes and called it straight back.

"What's up?" he asked.

"You need to come back here immediately. I've got something for you."

"What?"

"It's a note. Daniel Gray's torso fell to the side from it's upright position, and his head rolled off his lap. There's a note under his head. It's addressed to you."

Tuesday
20.00

Once more back at the cottage, McKenzie ran from the car down to the house. Before leaving the hotel, Old Jimmie Meekle had woken up, and was hungry. He'd agreed to let McKenzie have the use of the car and he'd stayed at the pub to have something to eat and get another drink. McKenzie had promised to drop the car off at the pub later.

Grant was standing at the back of the cottage, halfway between the body and the house.

"What have you got?" he asked.

"A note. But I haven't touched it. I don't have any gloves, and I'm worried about moving it until Forensics are here."

"They won't be here for another couple of hours. The helicopter's flying to Oban to fetch them as we speak."

Taking the lead, McKenzie hurried down to where Gray's body was. It had rolled over to the right, probably because of the wind buffeting the body. Gray's head had rolled forward, and was resting at an angle in the purple heather surrounding the stone on which the body lay, the word's 'Remember Me?' still visible across his forehead.

Grant pointed to just beneath Gray's crotch.

"Look, there's a note fallen between his legs. You can just make out your name on it."

McKenzie knelt down and bent forward.

For a few seconds he struggled to control his breathing. His heart was racing in his chest, and he couldn't stop himself from standing up and looking around the moor and the beach.

Was the killer watching him now?

Laughing at him?

McKenzie felt as if the world was closing in on him.

It was if the killer knew McKenzie's every move. He was taunting him. Goading him. Making fun of him.

This was the fifth time that the killer had targeted him with a message. Personally.

Why?

What was his motive?

Counting to ten, and waiting for his hand to stop shaking so much, McKenzie knelt down again beside Daniel Gray's body.

At first he was reluctant to touch the note, but he felt an urgency to pick it up. The killer had left the note here for him to read.

Every second counted.

McKenzie needed to read what it said.

Taking out his phone he took several photographs of the body and the note in situ, then pulling on the plastic gloves he'd borrowed from the hotel kitchen, he gently pushed his fingers in between Daniel Gray's thighs and retrieved the note.

It was an A4 piece of computer paper folded in two.

Two words were written on one side in red: 'DCI McKenzie'.

Opening the note up so both he and Grant could read it, he revealed five lines of large computer printed text.

McKenzie shuddered as he read it.

> **"With thanks to you,**
> **No longer Master of his Head,**
> **Number Four is dead.**
>
> **Although for now still alive,**
> **GasBag will soon be number Five!"**

Tuesday
20.30

Inside the cottage, Grant and McKenzie sat on Daniel Gray's sofas and drank tea.

For a while they had sat in silence, each person mulling over their own thoughts in private. Grant was the first to speak.

"Who is GasBag?"

"I don't know. That's one of the questions I was going to ask Mr Gray. I haven't finished the book yet, but I'm guessing she'll be the next person to die. Were you present when he mentioned GasBag before? She was someone whom Maggie Sutherland was very jealous of. Apparently Ronald Blake seemed to fancy her, or at least Maggie thought she did."

"It's almost as if the killer knew you were coming." Grant commented.

"Maybe he did." McKenzie replied, admitting that it may be true.

"It's rather spooky that he left the note for you. Do you think this is personal? Is there any chance you know the killer?"

"I don't think so. But possibly. More likely, he knows I'm in charge and he's messing with our minds."

"Why did it say, '*With thanks to you.*'" She asked.

"I don't know. But that part scares me." He replied. Quietly. He'd been thinking about that.

McKenzie got up. He didn't want to leave Grant alone, but he felt naked without coverage from his phone provider. He needed to make a million calls, and standing around here was getting him nowhere.

Almost as if Grant was reading his mind, she said, "I know you want to get back to the mainland or to the hotel, but don't forget you can use the landline to call someone if you need to."

McKenzie stared at her. He'd forgotten about that. Of course he could.

He wasn't thinking clearly.

"Can you make me a strong coffee please?" he asked Grant.

Looking round the room, the laptop on the table caught his eye, and McKenzie moved over to it. Sitting down he woke it up, and found that it wasn't locked. He was straight in.

McKenzie was wondering if the laptop could tell them anything.

What had Gray been writing about? What were the last sites he had visited on the internet?

It didn't surprise McKenzie however when he found that the browser history had been deleted, along with all the files. Even the recycle bin was empty.

Someone had literally wiped the computer clean.

"Unless they've been overwritten, the files will still be there. In the memory." Grant said, standing beside him and looking over his shoulder. She handed him his coffee.

"True. When the forensics team get here, please ask them to bag it up, and send it to the Fettes Row cyber team. I would prefer if they looked at the PC, just because they're closer and I can visit them more easily if they come up with anything or if they can restore it all."

McKenzie stood up, and moved across to the book case.

An idea had just occurred to him.

Did Daniel have a copy of the book?

It only took five seconds to find it.

It was on the third shelf, first book from the right.

Pulling it out, McKenzie found that it had been well used.

Flicking through the dog-eared pages, he came to the page in which Daniel Gray's murder had been described.

A blue pen had been used to underline the paragraphs which had described his death, and several notes had been written in pencil in the margins.

One of them said, '*Must get off the grid. Leave Scotland now and hide!*'

In that moment McKenzie understood why Daniel Gray was living on Coll, miles away from civilisation. Somewhere where no one could find him.

Then, a shudder ran down his spine, as out of the blue, McKenzie recalled the last words that Daniel had said to him as they were leaving the cottage the last time they were here: "*How did you find me here, by the way?*" Mr Gray had asked.

McKenzie swore aloud and suddenly felt dizzy.

"Shit! Shit! Shit!" he swore again in quick succession.

"What's the matter, Guv. What's happened!"

"Daniel Gray is dead because of me. It's my fault. The killer followed me here. Gray was in hiding. He was worried that one day someone might come after him, so he'd got off the grid and gone into hiding." McKenzie swore again and hit the wall with his fist. "The killer used *me* to find Daniel. It only took us a few minutes to track him down on our computers, but the killer could never get access to that information. We led him right to Daniel!"

"But how?" Grant asked, not understanding.

For a moment McKenzie just stared at Grant, his face blank. Then he moved quickly across to the landline phone and picked it up.

Reading it from his mobile, he dialled the number belonging to McLeish.

McLeish picked up almost immediately and went into overdrive, speaking far too fast and too loudly.

"Calm down, and start again." McKenzie instructed him. "I never understood a word."

"I've been trying to call you. We've all been trying to call you! You're not answering… "

"I'm off the grid. There's no mobile phone coverage here. I'm on Daniel Gray's landline just now."

"How is he? Did you arrest him?" McLeish asked.

"No. He's dead. He was number four."

"How? *How* did he die?"

"The headmaster lost his head. He was decapitated."

"Fuck… "

"Exactly." McKenzie agreed. "And I think I led the killer straight to him."

McLeish paused.

"Guv, the reason why I was trying to reach you,… you got my messages right?… Well, the reason I was trying to contact you was to let you know that you were right. The guys in Fettes scanned your car and found two bugs. A tracker and a microphone."

"What?" Another chill coursed its way down McKenzie's spine. "Where?"

"The guys in Fettes were impressed. The microphone had an inbuilt recorder and a memory chip. It can record hours of conversation and stores it until the person who controls the recording device drives by within a hundred metres and sends a signal to the recorder. The microphone then downloads all the recorded conversations via Bluetooth to the person managing the device. Then the person drives off, or walks away, completely undetected. Apparently it's a really professional device. And was really well installed. And the tracker tells you where your car is, as well as where to go to download the voice recordings. It's brilliant!"

"What do you mean brilliant? Thanks to that, the killer was probably listening when I told DCS Wilkinson exactly where I was going on Coll, and when I briefed the helicopter crew where I wanted them to take me!"

"Sorry, Guv, I didn't mean… "

"Where was it hidden?"

"It was part of your flip-down visor on the passenger side. You know, when the sun's too bright, you use it to shield your eyes. Or when your wife wants to put on make-up. The electronics and the battery were behind the mirror, but apparently when you install them you just replace the whole visor unit. It comes as a unit. All ready to go."

"That means we're dealing with a real professional here then. Someone with communications experience."

"Maybe Guv, or maybe not. Apparently you can buy these things easily off the internet. You just name the type of car you've got and its year, and it tells you which one to buy. The guy in Fettes row told me lots of stories about the types of people who use them or what they use them for. I couldn't believe it!"

"And the tracker?"

"Inside your wheel arch, above the wheel, front passenger side. It can last up to three months. Pinpoints your location exactly to anyone using the software that comes with it. It bounces its signal off a satellite. They're illegal in the UK."

"The guys a serial killer. I don't think he's bothered about that." McKenzie quipped.

"They've taken them out. And they're doing what they can to find out what they can tell us about… "

"Tell them to put the things back as soon as they're finished learning everything they can from them. I don't want the killer to know we're on to him yet. Maybe we can use this to our advantage. Somehow." McKenzie interrupted him.

"Good thinking, Guv. Maybe we can spring some sort of trap for him."

"Possibly. But it would be good to have that in our back-pocket. Just in case. Good work, McLeish. Don't forget, update PC Jordon on this. Who else did you say wanted to talk with me?"

"Probably everyone. When are you coming back?"

"Hopefully tonight, but I don't know yet. Can you get hold of DI Brown and tell her to call me on this number urgently?" McKenzie instructed.

Then he hung up and told Grant what he'd just learned.

"The killer's being listening in to everything I've said in the car, and has been following me wherever I go. That confirms that it was me who gave away Daniel's location. I told the helicopter where you were to meet me, and why. The killer was listening. In spite of everything Gray did to protect himself, I led the killer right up his garden path and handed him over to be slaughtered without even knowing it. Daniel Gray died because of me. It's my fault!"

Chapter 42

Tuesday
Island of Coll
Port na Luing Cottage
21.15

"I'm sorry to call you so late, Mr Booth. But it's absolutely imperative that you tell me everything that you've learned about the book and its author. I just checked and read your email telling me to call you on this number. Please call me back immediately." McKenzie said, leaving a voice message for the Director of Amazon KDP in the UK along with Daniel Gray's telephone number.

Frustrated that he hadn't been able to get his messages on his phone, and realising that he'd heard nothing from Amazon, he used Gray's laptop to connect to the internet and log on to his email.

Thankfully, there was an email from the Director at Amazon but when he opened it up, it had just said to call him. No details. Nothing.

McKenzie was furious.

He was just planning how he could personally destroy Amazon in revenge, when the phone rang.

"DCI McKenzie? Gavin Booth here. My sincere apologies, Sir, but I have been trying to reach you and couldn't."

"I told you I was going to be offline and asked you to send me everything by email."

"I haven't received your email yet, confirming who you are. I've got the information you want, but until… "

"I sent it. Have you checked your junk folder?"

There was a moment's hesitation. McKenzie could hear the man tapping away on his keyboard at the other end.

"Ouch… sorry. Yes, here it is… sorry. Just one second please while I read it."

McKenzie could hear the director at the other end mouthing the words aloud as he quickly read and digested the small email he'd sent.

"Okay, thanks. That's good enough for me. If you give me a moment, I'll send you the report I've put together for you. I've also got the original files and copies the author uploaded to CreateSpace. They may help in some way. The author made quite a few changes before the book was finally published."

"Good. Please send me that immediately, but while I've got you on the phone, please give me the basics now. For example, who published the book, and how many copies were printed?"

"The name of the original author was a Maggie Sutherland." The Director started reading from the report on his screen. "She printed only six copies."

The number startled McKenzie. It was totally unexpected.

"Only six copies?"

"Yes. After they were printed, the book was withdrawn from the website. No one else was ever able to access it."

"Did six people buy it from the website?"

"No, only she did. She ordered six copies and had them sent to her home. The delivery address is in the report I'm just sending you as we speak. There... it's gone. You should have it in the next few seconds."

"Have you got her credit card number?"

"Yes. It's in the report. Including the date the books were first printed, shipped and delivered."

"And when was that?"

The Director then told McKenzie the date of publication of the book. The date was immediately significant. According to the other information they now had, Maggie Sutherland was still alive then. It was two years before she committed suicide.

McKenzie thanked the Director.

"I'm going to read your file as soon as I get it. I may need to call you back. Please can you keep an eye out for any calls from me over the next few days? If I need to contact you, it may be urgent."

"I'm sorry it's taken so long. I hope it helps to save someone's life."

McKenzie thought about telling the Director about Daniel Gray's death, but it occurred to him that the news could traumatise the Director who may worry for the rest of his life that by not responding soon enough or quicker, he'd been partly responsible for Gray's death.

That wouldn't be true.

McKenzie knew that Gray's death was entirely down to him.

It was McKenzie's fault.

Putting the phone down he turned to Grant and excused himself. He needed to go for a walk and take a moment to think.

Stepping out the back door, he walked across the moor, and then turned left and head down to the beach.

Taking his shoes and socks off, he left them on a rock, and wandered over to the water's edge.

The water was cold. But not freezing.

It was refreshing.

Rolling his trousers up, he wandered into the water, until it was up to his calves. He then closed his eyes, stood still and listened to the sound of the water gently lapping the sea shore around him.

Only six copies of the book were printed.

What did that tell him?

Who else had been sent one?

If McKenzie could only tell who else had been sent the book, he might be able to warn them about a possible threat, or that they might be in danger.

Or he could call them in for questioning and see if they knew of any obvious reason they could be connected to the sequence of events which were currently unfolding.

Just working through the maths, and knowing now that Daniel Gray was a victim and that he had also received a copy of the book, that meant only two books were left over.

So, *who* had been sent the other copies?

If Gasbag, whoever she was, was going to be the next victim, then given that all the other victims had been sent a book, it was highly likely that she'd been sent a copy too.

And then a copy which Maggie Sutherland might herself have kept?

Or was one of the six books, a copy that the killer was using?

But, if Maggie Sutherland had kept a copy, and another one had gone to Gasbag, was it at all possible that the killer had never seen the book? After all, Maggie published the book and had seemingly sent the book to the victims before she'd committed suicide.

So, what did that tell them?

Had Maggie Sutherland commissioned someone to kill the others after her death?

Or was the killer someone else entirely that came along afterwards, that knew about the role these people had played in Maggie's life, but who did not know anything about the book?

Did McKenzie's awareness of the book give him any possible advantage in tracking down the killer or predicting the next death, anticipating it and preventing it?

If only he could identify who 'GasBag' was!

Then it occurred to McKenzie that perhaps Daniel Gray may have left a note on his computer about who GasBag may have been, and that's why the killer had deleted all the files? If so, then why not simply steal the computer too and throw it away somewhere far away, or into the sea?

Had they disturbed him at the scene?

Another question hit him like a brick: why had the killer not removed the book from Daniel's house? Had they disturbed him before he had the chance to do that, or did this also point to the fact that perhaps the killer did not know about the book?

Either way, perhaps, just maybe, could one of the many notes that Daniel seemed to have made in his copy possibly reveal the identity of who GasBag was?

"Shit!" McKenzie swore, just as he was beginning to feel a little bite more relaxed.

"SO MANY QUESTIONS!" he shouted aloud across the sea where his anguish was quickly swallowed up and drowned.

McKenzie turned and started to wade his way back through the shallow water to the beach.

As he sat down on a rock and brushed away the sand from his feet so he could put on his socks, yet another, and perhaps the most pressing of many remaining questions popped into his mind.

"What was the connection between the tunnels, Maggie Sutherland and what happened to her, and the murders that were now taking place?"

As he headed back to the cottage across the moor, McKenzie knew that he had to get back to Edinburgh as soon as possible

En route he needed to read the rest of the book and find out who GasBag was and how she was due to die.

And he needed to turn the focus of his team onto finding out who knew about the tunnels. His instinct was now screaming at him 'find the man in the tunnel, and you find the killer!'

At the top of the hill in the fork of the path, he turned and looked out to where the body of Daniel Gray lay on his favourite rock.

He suddenly felt very emotional.

He'd let the man down, and he'd died because of him.

"I promise you, Daniel, I swear to you. I'll find who did this to you. And I'll make sure that he gets his due deserves. I promise."

It was a solemn promise, and McKenzie meant every word.

He'd find the killer, even if it was the last thing he did.

Tuesday
Portobello Beach
22.00

Stuart and Marie sat on the sand, looking out to sea. After a wonderful walk up and around Carlton Hill, looking over the city centre, Marie had suggested that instead of going to a restaurant, they could head down to Portobello, buy a 'Fish & Chips' and eat it on the beach.

Stuart readily agreed. He loved the spontaneity.

So far the evening had gone amazingly.

When they met, Stuart had greeted her with a kiss and immediately asked her how the meeting had gone.

Marie had planned to tell him very slowly, building up to the final figure that she'd been offered, but in the end she couldn't control herself and she'd just blurted it out.

"One hundred-and-fifty million pounds!" she'd revealed, jumping for joy, and wrapping her arms around him and covering him with kisses. "And it's all because of you!"

"What do you mean?"

"It was your idea! You set up the meeting! I can't believe it. It's almost... no, *it is* unreal!"

"You're not seriously telling me that my company offered you one hundred-and-fifty million pounds? I can't believe it. If we've got that much money to give away, I'm going to ask for a pay rise!"

They walked to the top of the hill, sat down on the steps of the Grecian style ruins that dominated that part of Edinburgh, and Stuart made Marie tell her absolutely every detail of the meeting.

He expressed interest when she told him how senior the people were that she'd met, and was a little angry when he heard that she'd been delayed and kept waiting.

"Maybe that was just part of the game they were playing with you?" he suggested. "Testing you somehow?"

"I don't care. Not now. I honestly thought at the time that they were going to say no and give me nothing, but then they gave me one-hundred-and-fifty million pounds!"

"They haven't given it to you yet. I would hold back in the celebrating until you get the first thirty million in your bank account."

"Will you come with me tomorrow to meet the First Minister of Scotland?"

Stuart realised he was on tricky ground. He was on first name terms with the First Minister. She'd give the game away immediately.

"No. Sorry, I can't. Not tomorrow."

Marie seemed disappointed.

"There's something else I need to ask you, Stuart. It was one of the conditions of the money being given to me. But can I ask you after we've eaten? Later? I think we need to talk. A little. About us?"

"That sounds very serious."

"It doesn't need to be. But… "

"Okay. After our fish and chips. A serious conversation. A very serious conversation, if that's what you want."

Marie punched him in the arm.

"Stop it. I'm serious!"

"I know you are!" he laughed.

So, soon they were sitting on the sand. The sky had darkened, and dinner had been eaten. Marie knew the time had come to talk.

"Okay, so, Stuart Nisbet, I was meant to be going home tomorrow, but now it looks like I'll be staying a few days later. But I have to go home on Friday. Saturday at the latest. Now, obviously, with the money, there are a few things I have to do before I go. But, the truth is… I'm confused. I miss my children and I have responsibilities in Poland, now more than ever, but I'm going to miss you Stuart Nisbet. A lot. In some ways I don't want to leave."

She leaned her head against him and snuggled into him.

"This is really bizarre. I really like you. I'm going to be torn when I have to go."

Stuart wrapped his arm around her, and gently squeezed her.

"I feel the same. I wish you didn't have to go. But I can't ask you to stay. Not now, especially since… you know… "

"I know." She replied. "Stuart, remember I said that there was a condition to me receiving the money? At least, a condition for the remaining one-hundred-and-twenty million pounds after I receive the first tranche?"

"Yes. What was it?"

"The Directors of your company are insisting that they are able to assign someone to come and work with me in Poland to oversee and ensure that the money is spent. They claim that they won't dictate how the money should be spent, but just so that they can check and account for the money as it's used up. And to ensure that it is all spent each year."

"Okay. That sounds interesting."

"They also said, that if I knew anyone in the company, I mean, your company, then I could suggest them, if I thought they might be interested in the job."

"They did? And do you?"

"Do I what?"

"Know anyone? In my company?"

Marie looked up at his face, her eyes searching his, her expression one of slight confusion.

"Yes," she replied. "I know you."

There was a momentary pause, then Stuart laughed. "What? You want to suggest *me*?"

"Yes. It's just an idea. And I forgot to say that it's only for a minimum of three months each year, in total. Whoever takes the role, can do whatever they want the rest of the year, if they wish. But for three months a year, at least, they have to work with me and follow me around, everywhere."

Stuart laughed again, then stopped and looked at her very seriously.

"What? Are you seriously suggesting that I should give up my job and come to Poland with you?"

"No. Yes… I mean, no… it's only three months per year."

"But we hardly know each other? I haven't even kissed you properly yet. We haven't even spent the night together or made love to each other, and you're asking me to run away with you?"

"Then make love to me Stuart."

Stuart was about to speak, but although his mouth opened to formulate the words, no sounds came out.

Marie put a finger up to his lips, to silence him, and then kneeled up in front of him. She moved closer, removed her finger from his lips, and then kissed him, pushing him gently backwards until he was lying on the sand beneath her.

She kissed him again, and moaned slightly when after one of Stuart's arms went up and around her back, he lifted the other towards her face, but accidentally stroked her breasts en route.

She leant forward and whispered into his ear.

"Make love me to Stuart Nisbet. And perhaps, in the morning, you might be able to think about my idea a little bit more seriously."

Stuart laughed.

He was about to say something very clever in reply, but Marie never gave him the chance.

Her lips met his, and Stuart soon discovered how persuasive Marie McDonald could be.

Not once. But later that night, several times.

Chapter 43

Tuesday
Island of Coll
Port na Luing Cottage
22.20

The phone was ringing in Daniel Gray's house. For a moment Grant and McKenzie both stared at it. Should they answer? What would they tell someone at the other end if they wanted to speak to Daniel?

The truth?

Then McKenzie remembered he'd asked McLeish to get hold of Brown and get her to call him on Daniel's number.

McKenzie picked up.

"Hello, this is Daniel Gray's phone."

"Guv, is that you?"

"Elaine, thank goodness it's you. I've been trying you all night."

"Sorry, I was on the phone a lot. Then I went for a swim, and dinner. And then I got the messages and one from McLeish as well. I've got news for you, Guv, but first, did you arrest Daniel Gray?"

McKenzie explained the situation. Brown was shocked.

He also updated her on everything else that had happened, and shared the news he'd got from Amazon.

"Only six books? *Six*? And four of those who received them are already dead?"

"Yes. I'm on a mission to finish the rest of the book and find out who GasBag is, and establish if there's only one, or possibly two more victims still to be targeted. I'm hoping Daniel Gray's copy of the book might be able to provide some insight. I'll probably be up all night if I get the chance. The Forensic team arrived a while ago, and we'd literally just left them to get on with their work when you called."

"When are you coming back?"

"Hopefully this evening. I'm just waiting to hear from the helicopter pilot if he can still give me a lift back tonight, or if we have to wait till tomorrow morning."

"I'd better give you my news then, just in case you don't make it back in time for the morning meeting. The long and the short of it though, is that I've got good news. Remember we discovered that Mr Banner, the janitor at the old school, and his wife had fostered a couple of children? We knew they'd fostered at least two. A boy for six years and a girl for a couple of months. Then his wife had got ill and died. Poor guy. And the boy had died in Iraq."

"Yes, I remember all that."

"I looked into the girl. It may only have been a couple of months but you never know if she learned all about the tunnel or not. Anyway, it turns out the girl now lives in Canada. She's married, two children. I spoke to her. She's got a job. I spoke to her employer who vouches for her being in Canada for the past six months. I think we can rule her out."

"Okay. Agreed. For now. But let's remember her if we need to consider her again later. Anything else?"

"You also asked me to see if there were any other kids?"

"Yes... And?"

"Well, I've been speaking to several of the old members of staff at the school... Sally gave me their numbers... and two of them seemed to remember that there was another boy. Sally couldn't remember him, but the others could. This afternoon I went to one of their houses... she was a maths teacher at the school for a while, a Miss McIver. She showed me a photograph taken during one of the sports days and there was a group photo of Mr and Mrs Banner, with the boy who they had for six years, and there was another boy. Miss McIver thinks he was there for about a year, before Mrs Banner died. He was a year younger than the other boy."

"Did he go to Portobello High School?"

"No. The Banners were all Catholic. They went to Holy Rood High School, just up the road in Duddingston. It's another brilliant school just like Portobello High."

"Can you check it out?"

"I did already. I went to the see the Council and visited the department that looked after the foster parents and the children assigned to their care. They confirmed that there were three children. Brian, the boy who died later in Iraq, Alice, the girl, and Hamish Hamilton."

"Hamish?"

"Yes, Guv."

"So what happened to Hamish when the Banners stopped fostering? Where did he go?"

"Apparently he was only seventeen. He really loved the Banners, and didn't want to go into another care home or to any other foster parents, but he had to. He lived with with a few other families, each for a couple of months but he was really difficult to deal with, or so they claimed. He ran away once and went back to Mr Banner, but he was too heart-broken to really look after him, and the council wouldn't agree to it, as a lone parent who had a full-time job. So Hamish went into a home until he was eighteen, when he dropped out of school with only a few Highers and joined the army like Brian had done. He was sent to Afghanistan, about five years after Brian was killed in Iraq."

"And where is he now?"

"That's the interesting thing, Guv. He just doesn't seem to exist anymore. It's almost like he disappeared off the face of the earth."

"What you do you mean?"

"Well, after the army, he got a visa and left Britain and went to live in Australia... Before I go on, I just want to say that I called his regiment and I got some very good digital photographs sent over, and they are sending me his file tomorrow. I've also asked for copies of the passport photographs. I haven't got them yet, but I've been promised them first thing tomorrow."

"Good. Please try to print off copies for tomorrow's meeting and circulate the electronic copies to everyone too. So, what happened when he went to Australia?"

"That's where it get really interesting, Guv. After that, we don't seem to have any records. There's no recent records of him existing in Australia or here. I've been on the phone most of the day to various people, and also to the British Embassy in Australia about twenty minutes ago, but no one knows where he is now. It may be that he's dead, but there's no record of that. If he is still alive, then it's been suggested that one possible explanation is that he changed his name by deed-poll whilst he was in Australia. And possibly, as soon as he did that he came back to the UK. Or possibly, he assumed someone else's identity in Australia and is living there under a false name. Or he left the country to travel the world and is now living somewhere else abroad?"

"Or he came back to the UK and is living under a false name here?"

"Why would he, Guv?"

"I don't know. If he did change his name, why would he do that? Maybe something happened in his past that made him ashamed?"

"Maybe he just had a bad childhood and wanted a fresh start, and nothing to do with his original parents? Apparently they were both alcoholics and used to beat him up pretty badly, Guv. The council took him away from them and wouldn't let him go back."

"Did he have any natural siblings?"

"No. I asked that. Were you thinking about Maggie Sutherland, Guv?"

"Possibly. Surely if he changed his name by deed-poll the British Government would have a record of it?"

"I've asked for that. The Embassy is chasing it up, but I'm going to call the offices in London tomorrow and find out what the process is, and what records may exist, and how long it will take to find out his new name. If he travelled abroad on a new British passport, we must have his new name somewhere."

"Is it possible that he became an Australian citizen and then changed his name, and the Aussies have got all the paperwork? Maybe he's travelling on an Australian passport?"

"I don't know, Guv. But it's all early days. I just started my enquiries into this today, and Australia is twelve hours ahead. I'll get to the bottom of it, but it may take a while. A few days, or maybe even weeks. Anyway, Guv, I'm not saying that this guy is our man, but I'm just thinking that this is all quite suspicious. The guy has gone missing, perhaps deliberately, although maybe not. But the thing is that he would have known about the tunnels. If you put the two together, I think we have to consider him a suspect."

"I agree." McKenzie replied. "Great work, Elaine. Brilliant. But we don't have weeks. We may only have days before the next victim is killed."

He was silent for a moment.

"Right, if I can I'll get back to Edinburgh tonight. If not, tomorrow morning. In the meantime I want you to spend all your time chasing after Hamish. Get everything you can on him. But do your best to find out where he is now, and what his name is, if he's changed it."

"Will do, Guv."

McKenzie said goodbye, and hung up.

Tuesday
22.20

McKenzie heard it before he could see it. Although it was almost the middle of the night, at this time of the year, it never got completely dark. There was enough light for the helicopter to navigate its way across the island and land in front of the cottage on the road.

McKenzie was waiting for it as it arrived, and ducking low, he ran forward and jumped aboard when invited to do so by the copilot.

As they rose into the air, Grant waved at them, but McKenzie's attention was on the hive of activity that was visible just beyond the house.

A tent had now been erected around Daniel Gray's body, glowing yellow against the darkness of the grass as the forensics team went to work inside.

As McKenzie settled down into his seat, reassured by the copilot that it would be a smooth ride, he thought briefly about his last sight of Daniel Gray's head.

Just as the words written across his forehead had so clearly instructed him, McKenzie would never forget Daniel, or the horrific scene McKenzie had found at the site of his death.

For a moment, McKenzie thought about the words of the poem often read out at Remembrance Services for the Fallen Heroes of the Great World Wars. What was it they said? Something like, 'At the going down of the sun and in the morning, We will remember them.'

From now on, whenever he heard those words, or he heard the bugle being played in the future, he would remember Daniel Gray, his head resting in the bracken and heather, his eyes watching the setting sun.

McKenzie would also remember that it was he himself who had led the killer to Daniel Gray's door.

The helicopter gained altitude and Daniel's cottage receded into the distance. McKenzie then opened up Daniel's copy of 'Remember Me?' and started reading from where he'd left off in his own copy.

Accepting that the writing would never win the Booker Prize, but now also knowing who wrote it, he was quickly immersed in the sequence of events that the book portrayed.

Maggie had done her best to build a story around the true events that happened, and then use her imagination to spin a series of fictitious reprisals against everyone involved.

Knowing now he was reading Maggie's words, it was almost as if he was seeing the world through her eyes.

He began to feel some of her emotions. Feel some of her anger. Her frustration. To that extent the writing was successful. McKenzie became involved in her plight.

As the pages turned, he could see how the main character, quite clearly now Maggie, had carefully planned and carried out the executions of those who had somehow slipped through the criminal justice system.

McKenzie could also see that in some way, perhaps, the writing of the book had potentially been cathartic for Maggie.

In her imagination she had been able to mete out the justice she thought her aggressors had deserved, although perhaps the extent of it had been exaggerated by the anger she felt when they had walked away without blame or reprisal.

McKenzie had been involved in many rape cases in his career. The one thing he had learned from them was that they were often complicated. He was not an expert in these matters. The apportionment of blame, if there was any, was often very difficult to determine. Sometimes it was clear a rape had taken place. Other times it was not. When it was not just a matter of brute physicality but also of human emotion, then McKenzie always relied on those who were specialists and trained in all aspects relating to such cases.

Reading the words of Maggie Sutherland he had to keep reminding himself that this was one representation of the facts, written from the perspective of Maggie who was according to the testimony of Daniel Gray, already an emotionally troubled individual even before the sequence of events which she experienced. Unfortunately, McKenzie could not read the same story from the standpoint of Weir, Blake or McRae.

As he read the pages, he could feel himself beginning to side with Maggie, and felt a growing sense that Maggie had originally started out innocently, as probably many young women might do, but then she got in rapidly over her head, and was not able to cope with or control what happened next. And then she was raped. She reported it, but was scared to expose herself even more to the establishment and become even more of a victim. And so, with no parents she could turn to, she had innocently requested help from the one person she thought might be able to help her: the headmaster.

He was an adult, had seen things from another perspective. He'd wanted Maggie to report it to the police and let others pass judgement, not him. She'd been scared. She'd left it to the headmaster to take action.

He'd struggled with what to do. Had not been able to determine the truth of what had happened. And had then effectively sided with her aggressors.

In Maggie's eyes, the headmaster had then become one of them.

He had failed her. Blamed her. Looked down on her.

Not supported her.

Abandoned her.

She had begun to hate him.

Blame *him*.

And soon her writing had included him as a victim.

In her imagination she had found him as guilty and culpable as the others, and as an outlet for the whirlpool of emotions that ripped her apart every, single, day, she'd carefully plotted out how justice should be served on him too.

In her story, Daniel Gray's head had been cut off, and then stuck on the flag pole at the front of the school.

His body had been fed to the Koi Carp in the large pond in the centre of the campus.

Obviously, she had not been able to predict that in real life, Daniel Gray would go into hiding, or that the school would close.

Perhaps however, Maggie would have taken some comfort from knowing that Daniel Gray had been sentenced to years of torment, spending the rest of his life berating himself for the decision he'd made, questioning as he did every day whether or not he had done the right thing in response to her plea for help.

McKenzie could not judge what had happened - given the absence of facts and not able to question witnesses, the accused or Maggie - but he couldn't stop thinking that Daniel had also become a victim of the events that night. He lost his peace of mind, his home – he'd been forced to go into hiding, and ultimately, he'd lost his life.

Was he actually guilty of anything?

McKenzie would never know.

As he read the pages, McKenzie became aware that his thoughts were wandering.

For now, his focus had to be on what would happen next and the most urgent question that remained.

Who was GasBag?

Was she also destined to die, and if so, how?

As he progressed through the book, now trying to discipline himself not to skip pages or scan ahead, he discovered that GasBag was destined to meet as gruesome a death as the others.

Frustratingly, the pages didn't explicitly reveal who GasBag was. Neither did the notes which Daniel had periodically scribbled on the sides of the pages alongside the paragraphs.

Maybe Daniel had not known?

As he began to read about her death, it occurred to McKenzie, that surely, had Daniel known who she was, then he would have volunteered that information to McKenzie. Perhaps by doing so, Daniel could have sought some form of absolution for his past, and helped to save a life.

From the fact that he hadn't, it indicated he didn't know her identity.

McKenzie read on, desperate to find out what happened next.

He didn't have to wait long, and the pages soon told him most of what he needed to know.

Maggie had been furiously jealous of GasBag. As her emotions had become increasingly troubled, GasBag morphed into the one person on the planet who was preventing Maggie from attaining happiness.

Maggie seemingly became convinced that if GasBag had not existed, had not been so pretty, and had never attracted or flirted with Ronald Blake, then surely Ronald would only have had eyes for Maggie?

GasBag was the one person in the world who was preventing Ronald from falling in love with Maggie.

It was GasBag's fault that she had been raped.

If it were not for her, Ronald would have made love to Maggie. Passionately, Caringly. Affectionately.

Ronald would have been in love with Maggie.

Together they would have been happy.

When Ronald had blurted out GasBag's name during sex, it was the last straw.

In that moment Maggie had begun to plan revenge against GasBag.

She would die, just like the rest of them.

It would be Maggie that had the last laugh, exacting revenge on GasBag which was 'oh so sweet', and fitting.

GasBag would be put in a big bag, filled with gas, and then blown up.

Blown to smithereens.

From here to Timbuktu.

Chapter 44

Wednesday
Somewhere above the River Forth
02.15

McKenzie spent the entire helicopter flight immersed in the book. After he finished the story, he had scoured back through Daniel Gray's copy for any notes which he may have missed that could add some insight as to GasBag's identity.

He found none.

The book itself had ended - as far as McKenzie was concerned - rather disturbingly. It perhaps also revealed something about the state of Maggie's mind, which caused McKenzie to feel quite uncomfortable.

In the end, it turned out that following the rape, Maggie had been pregnant.

In her version of the story, she'd had the child.

It was a boy.

She'd called him Ronnie.

In her story she'd always assumed that the father was Ronald Blake, and not either of the other two men she mostly referred to as 'the rapists'. She'd brought Little Ronnie up as Blakes's son.

Little Ronnie would have been about two years old when Maggie had killed his father, in the book.

In real life, McKenzie couldn't help but wonder if Maggie actually had that child.

If she did, that boy would now be a man.

Capable of murder.

Had he found the sixth copy of the book, and realised his mother's dreams for vengeance?

Had Little Ronnie acted as an executioner appointed by his mother's court?

"Found guilty for the sentence of rape, or aiding, abetting, or flirting with the accused, I sentence you all to death."

If so, that would mean that Little Ronnie had murdered his own father in cold blood for raping his mother!

McKenzie shook his head.

This was a very sick world.

Certainly, if Little Ronnie existed, he would top the list of suspects.

Unfortunately, it was a very short list, with only two people on it.

Hamish, who didn't seem to exist anymore, and of whom no one could find any mention. And Little Ronnie of whom there was mention in Remember Me?, but who probably didn't exist in real life.

Certainly, if Maggie had a child, there was no record of it. McKenzie had already had his team look into it, and the answer was that Maggie had no surviving relatives.

Most likely, Little Ronnie was just a figment of Maggie's fertile imagination, and an indication of just how desperate she was for love, and for being loved by Ronald Blake.

When she couldn't have him, she'd fantasised about having his son.

It had been a short flight. With no winds to fight, and no turbulence en route, it had passed quickly. During the trip, McKenzie had learned a lot.

There would be only one more victim. And she would be blown up in a cloud of gas.

With only about ten minutes to go before landing at Edinburgh Airport, McKenzie's mind turned back again to the six copies of the books that had been printed.

Four had been given to the victims. That left two.

It seemed a logical conclusion that Gasbag would have one copy, and most likely Maggie Sutherland or the killer had the other one.

Therefore, finding out who had the other book, could be the way to finding GasBag and then saving her.

Right from the beginning, the killer had been taunting McKenzie. Rubbing his nose in it. Making him and his team acknowledge that the killer was always one step ahead of them.

McKenzie knew that he was tired. Exhausted. And not up to his normal self. He was beginning to make mistakes. Potentially miss leads. Get things wrong.

He desperately needed DCS Wilkinson to give him more staff.

What if the obvious was again staring him and his team in their faces, and they were missing it, just like they had missed the tunnel?

'What if... ' McKenzie began to scold himself. Berate himself.

Something was beginning to niggle away at him. He recognised the feeling. He always had it when he didn't feel comfortable with the facts.

When he'd got something wrong.

Missed something important.

But what?

It was just as the helicopter flew over the new road bridge across the River Forth, and his mind relaxed for a few moments as he looked out of the window and marvelled at what the engineers had first imagined, then created - and the sheer scale of it! - that another piece of the jigsaw puzzle fell into place.

It was almost as if up until that moment he was trying too hard to think.

His mind was trying to say something to him, but couldn't be heard.

Only when something else - the bridge - distracted him, was his subconscious able to yell at him and finally be heard.

But once the jigsaw piece had fallen into place, McKenzie knew exactly where he would find the next clue, and perhaps even be able to reveal the identity of GasBag.

McKenzie had been so busy searching for clues, that he'd missed the only one he had, practically given to him on a plate, and which he'd just ignored. Ever since then, McKenzie had been so keen to meet with Daniel a second time and then get him to reveal who GasBag was, that he hadn't realised that perhaps Daniel had already done it!

What was it that Daniel Gray had said to him during their visit when he'd first talked about GasBag and Maggie, who he'd called Amelia at the time?
"Apparently, she turned up at the ball looking exactly like Gasbag. Same dress. Same hair."

Maggie had known that Ronald was attracted to GasBag, so she'd started to copy her. And she'd gone to the final ball looking like her!

Trying to calm his breathing he pulled out his phone and started to dial, then stuck it under his helmet by his left ear.

He knew it was late, but it didn't matter.

"Pick up, pick up." He willed the phone aloud, his voice being drowned out by the throbbing engine of the helicopter.

McKenzie had begun to sweat, and his heart was pounding in his chest.

Why wasn't she answering?

Where was she?

At last, a very grumpy voice.

"Campbell… are you okay? Where are you?"

"Fiona, are *you* okay?"

"Yes, we're both fine. A few more Braxton Hicks but everything's okay. You just woke me, up. Sorry. I'm really tired. But happy to hear your voice. I'm a bit lonely. My sister had to go home back to Stirling to check her house and turn off the house alarm. It's been going off and she might have been burgled. She'll be back soon, I hope. We're not very far from Stirling. Only about thirty-minutes or so."

"You're alone?"

"Yes, but only for a few hours. I'll be fine."

"Good. I'm just about to land at Edinburgh airport. I need to ask you something. Can you remember the photograph we were looking at, at the Ball? The one of all the pupils taken at your school Prom, just after you'd left? I wasn't really paying attention, but I think you said you had a copy of it somewhere?"

Just then the line died.

He dialled her back and waited.

She picked up briefly, but then it cut out again before they were able to exchange any words.

McKenzie quickly redialled, this time with more success.

"The school photo of the ball? Is that what you want?"

"Yes. DO YOU HAVE A COPY?" he shouted.

"Yes," she replied. "I think I do. If so, it'll be in one of my many tins in the attic somewhere. You know, the ones with all my childhood stuff in them… ?"

The line went dead again.

He redialled, willing her to pick up.

"Where?" he asked, as soon as she did.

"The OLD BISCUIT TINS! IN THE ATTIC!"

McKenzie was really struggling to hear her now. The reception had become terrible, and the sound of the helicopter was drowning her out. It was becoming too much of a struggle.

He tried to say goodnight, and to blow her a kiss, but then she was gone again.

This time he gave up.

Instead he sent her a text message.

"*Almost home. I'll call you in the morning!*"
A few seconds later, she replied.
"Ok. NN. Kisses from me and Little Bump."
McKenzie smiled.
For a few seconds he closed his eyes, to picture Fiona and Little Bump.
He yawned, and then shook his head and shoulders, struggling to stay awake.
He'd been running on auto-pilot for days.
It was amazing just how debilitating stress could be.
He was tempted to let himself fall asleep, but they'd be landing in a few moments.
And there was something else.
Something more.
Another thought gestating at the back of his tired, tired brain.
Trying to get his attention. Trying to tell him something…
Something, important…

McKenzie awoke with a start, the copilot shaking his shoulder roughly.
"Sorry to wake you Guv, but you're here, and we all want to get home to bed! Although we've still got to fly back to Glasgow yet!"
McKenzie couldn't believe that he'd fallen asleep so intensely for such a short period of time. What was it? Five minutes?
That wasn't to say he wasn't grateful for it. He knew now how tired he was and how much he needed to sleep. For everyone's sake. The last thing he could afford was to miss things, to not see clues that were staring him in the face.
Like the one he may just have missed!
Thanking the pilots profusely, he hurried from the helicopter through the airport and managed to catch the only taxi on the rank.
It only took him about forty minutes to make it back across the city on the deserted roads, struggling the whole time to keep awake.
Once home, he passed the taxi-driver a fifty-pound note and impatiently waited for the receipt.
Hurrying up the steps to his house, he fumbled with the key in his door, then hurried into his hallway.
Dumping his overnight bag on the floor at the bottom of his stairs, he flicked on all the lights, then bounded up the stairs two at a time.
Fetching a chair from the spare bedroom he positioned it under the trapdoor to the attic, stepped up onto it and then fought with the latch above him.
Pulling the trapdoor and the ladder down, he climbed the steps and reached out into the darkness to switch on the light.
Once up in the attic he took a moment to orient himself and decide where Fiona would have kept her stuff amongst all the piles of boxes and debris they had accumulated during their lives but refused to throw out, just in case it became useful at some point in their future.
McKenzie realised this was not going to be a simple task.
By now his heart was pounding, and the heat in the attic was already making him sweat.
McKenzie peeled off the layers down to his shirt and trousers, dropping his other clothes through the hatch to the floor beneath, then got to work.

Kneeling down he started to go through the boxes, pile by pile.
It was like mining for gold.
With so little free space around, half the struggle was finding somewhere else to put the piles which he moved from one place to another.
He was almost thirty minutes into the search when he found the pile of tins which Fiona had been referring to.
Her school-day memories.
School books. Jotters. Pictures she painted. Her poems, essays and homework.
School reports, medals and exam certificates
And a tin full of photographs.
Bingo!

The photograph McKenzie was looking for was halfway down the pile inside the tin, but easily visible from the top: it was so long and wide.
McKenzie was looking for two people. From what Daniel Gray had said, *'she turned up at the ball looking exactly like Gasbag. Same dress. Same hair.'*
If he could spot two girls looking very similar, both wearing similar dresses, then hopefully he'd be able to identify one of them as Maggie. The other one would be Gasbag. McKenzie would then get Fiona, or someone else from her year, to tell him the identity of the other person.
There was something else too. Had Daniel not also said that she was wearing a red dress that night? That both of them were wearing the *same, red* dress?
How many people would be wearing red dresses in the photograph?
Hopefully not too many.
As he pulled the photograph out from amongst the pile, he remembered more clearly how he and Fiona had looked at it together in the school hall during the Reunion ball.
When they initially stood before the pinboard in the hall covered with all the school photographs, Fiona had pointed to the old photograph taken at their Prom and challenged him to find her amongst all the other pupils. Embarrassingly, he'd initially gone for another girl.
McKenzie's eyes immediately started to search for that girl, and quickly found her in the second row.
He could see now why he'd mistaken the other girl for Fiona. They were both tall and thin, and did both look quite similar, although Fiona had changed a lot since then.
The other girl looked similar in the face, but her hair was tied back, and she was wearing a green dress.
Fiona on the other hand, was standing in the front row, had her hair down on one side, and was wearing… a bright red ball gown.
McKenzie blinked and looked closer. His heart skipped a beat.
His eyes immediately started to scan the photograph for other girls wearing red dresses. Surely there would be more. Several. A lot?
It took only a second to realise that this was not the case.
At first it seemed as if only Fiona had been wearing a red dress.
No one else in the front row was, or the second.
But in the third row it was not so easy to see.
Then he saw her.

In the third row. Fourth person along.
Maggie Sutherland.
He'd recognised her from the photograph Wishart had shown the team: her face hadn't changed much over the years, and her eyes were still the same, bright blue piercing jewels that made her stand out from the crowd.
She was a very attractive young woman.
Her hair curled down beautifully on side of her head, just like Fiona's.
The people in front of her were blocking most of the view of her body, but McKenzie could still see the dress covering her right shoulder, and the side of her waist.
It was red. Bright red.
She was the only other woman in the picture wearing a red dress.
For a second he heard Daniel's voice echo in his head.
"Same hair. Same dress."
McKenzie felt suddenly light-headed. The photograph seemed to go in and out of focus, and his hands started to shake.
With a sickening feeling of dread, McKenzie realised the truth.
In spite of all the clues, he'd only now just discovered the identify of GasBag.

It was his wife.
Fiona.

Chapter 45

Wednesday
The Grange
McKenzie's House
03.40

McKenzie felt sick.

The world around him was spinning, and he had to bend forward and lower his head, taking deep breaths, until he managed to bring his breathing under control.

His heart was racing.

His mind numb with shock.

He found it strangely difficult to think.

Thoughts came to him in short, abrupt sentences.

Fiona, his wife, was GasBag.

The killer was going to kill GasBag.

She was the next target.

His wife WAS GasBag.

The killer was going to kill his wife.

And Little Bump.

A deep breath.

Another deep breath.

Turning onto his back, he lay on the floor, staring up at the ceiling of the attic.

He had to think.

He had to protect his wife. And his unborn child.

Think.

Think.

Okay, good, Fiona and Little Bump were not at home. They should be safe.

They were far away in Callander. In a caravan in the middle of nowhere.

He'd spoken to her only an hour or so ago.

She was safe.

Safe.

Calm down.

Good.

She was safe.

What next?

Bring her into protective custody.

Now.

Immediately!

But he had to call her first. Don't alarm her. Just check she was okay.

McKenzie reached into his pocket for his mobile, pulled it out and dialled her number.

Shit. There was no reception in the attic.

Get up. Go downstairs...

He struggled to sit up, taking deep breaths.

He edged towards the rim of the hatch in the attic, gripped the ladder and lowered himself slowly down.

Holding onto the bannister he walked slowly down the stairs to the kitchen.

The mobile reception was good there. He knew that.

Sitting down at the kitchen bar and taking more deep breaths to calm himself down, he called her.

The phone rang.

There was no reply.

He hung up and called her again.

He let it ring… and ring…

"Hello?"

Incredible, unbelievable relief.

MASSIVE relief.

"Fiona, H… Hi!", McKenzie stuttered and coughed. "Just calling to s… say I'm back home. How are you?"

"You woke me up."

"Is your sister there yet?"

"No. She's coming. She should be here soon."

"Good. Will you call me when she arrives?"

"Yes. But don't worry. The Braxton Hicks seem to have gone away for now, and I'm feeling fine. Honestly."

"Good….that's brilliant news." McKenzie hesitated… "Slight change of subject, but I was looking for a book earlier in the house. I was just wondering if we had a copy… Someone I was talking to earlier today said that everyone in your year at Portobello High School had been given a copy a few years ago, and she'd recommended I read it. Apparently it's very funny and worth a read."

"What's it called?"

"Remember Me?" McKenzie swallowed. "I don't suppose you ever remember getting a copy?"

There was a moment's hesitation at the other end of the phone. A few seconds silence that seemed to last an eternity. Then came the answer.

"No, sorry."

"What do you mean…you can't remember getting it, or you know you didn't get a copy?"

"I just can't remember getting it. But that doesn't mean I didn't."

McKenzie's heart sank.

"But, you know me, I never through anything out, especially books. When we moved from the flat to the house I packed everything up in boxes, and most of my book collection is still in the attic. If I got sent a copy of it, the chances are that it's still there, in one of the boxes. I know I never read it, but you could try looking there. The boxes of books should be easy to find…I labelled most of them with their contents when we moved."

McKenzie's eyes were shut tightly, his mind racing. This couldn't be happening.

"Campbell?"

"Yes, sorry, … Change of subject again…when did you say you think your sister should be there?"

"I didn't. But soon. Very soon." Fiona replied.

"Good. Listen, I don't want you going anywhere until your sister arrives. Don't leave the caravan at all until you speak to me or I give you permission. Do you understand?"

"Yes, Fine. But it's the middle of the night, and I'm not going anywhere...Campbell. What's this about? You're making me nervous now..."

"Remember I told you about the increased terror threat? To the Queen. Well, it's very serious," McKenzie lied. "I don't want you going anywhere just now. Just stay where you are? I'll tell you when the threat's passed. Okay?"

"Yes."

"Good, now go back to sleep. Lock your door, and call me in the morning. Okay?"

"Yes, fine."

"I love you Fiona. A lot. Please look after Little Bump for me. Say goodnight to him from Daddy."

"You need to get some sleep, Campbell, You're exhausted."

"I know," he replied. Exhausted was an understatement. "I will. As soon as I can."

McKenzie blew her a kiss, and then hung up.

Seconds later, McKenzie was scrambling back up the ladder to the attic.

He felt nauseous. Light-headed.

It only took him a few minutes to locate the boxes.

Fiona was as good as her word.

The word "BOOKS" had been scrawled in large black letters across the top of three cardboard boxes.

Pushing a few other boxes roughly aside to make space, he grabbed the first of the boxes and pulled it towards him.

He ripped open the top of the box and started ploughing through the contents, pulling them out and dumping them on the floor.

McKenzie's heart was pounding.

Reaching the bottom of the first box, he grabbed the second, and ripped the lid off in one go.

This time, he tipped the box on its side, scattering the contents across the floor, before wading through them with his hands.

Nothing.

He took a deep breath, wiped the sweat from his forehead and his eyes, and then bent forward and reached for the third and last box.

The top of this box was covered in duct tape, and McKenzie fumbled with his fingers to find enough purchase to rip it off.

Grabbing his keys from his pocket he forced one of them into the middle of the strip of tape, and pulled sharply backwards, forcing the lid open.

Standing up, he lifted the box up and dumped its contents onto the floor where the box had just been.

With the empty box still held in his hands in front of his chest, McKenzie looked down, and time seemed to grind to a halt.

On the edge of the pile, its cover facing up, and mocking him with its title, 'Remember Me?' glared up at him from the floor.

McKenzie fell to his knees and thumped his hands against the floor.

"FUCK!"

In that moment, all last vestiges of hope evaporated, and left in its place was only certainty.

Gasbag and Fiona were one and the same.

McKenzie collapsed forward, steadying himself with an outstretched hand, his head bowed, his thoughts racing.

An image of Fiona, heavily pregnant with Little Bump, flashed into his mind.

McKenzie took a long deep breath of air.

From now on every second counted.

A matter of life and death.

His wife's life. And his child's.

Standing up, he retreated from the attic, and hurried down the metal ladder. He took the stairs two at a time and dialled the number of Fettes Row as soon as he got reception on his phone in the kitchen.

McKenzie demanded to speak to the senior officer in charge.

It turned out he knew the officer. They were friends.

"Brodie, Campbell McKenzie here. I need you to do something urgently for me. I need you to call Stirling and send some cars and armed officers to a caravan park in Callander. We have a serial killer in Edinburgh, four dead so far in five days, and my wife is next on the list. I expect the killer to try to kill her in the next twenty-four hours. We need to pick my wife up, bring her into protective custody, and keep her alive."

"Fiona?"

"Yes, and she's pregnant."

"Campbell, I have to honest with you. I don't know if Stirling will have any men to spare just now. They've just found a bomb in Stirling and all officers have been assigned special duties. We also found a bomb in Edinburgh, and one was found in Glasgow. The threat level has now increased to its highest ever in Scotland since the system began. Someone is out to kill the Queen."

McKenzie was speechless.

"What type of explosives? TNT used in commercial demolitions? And warnings were given so that the bombs were *found* not *exploded*?"

"What are you getting at, Campbell?"

"It's my serial killer. He's deploying decoys, sucking up all possible police resources. Freeing up the streets to get everyone off my case, and give him a free rein to commit his string of murders."

"Are you serious?"

"Never more so, Brodie. Listen, if you need special authority, call DCS Helen Wilkinson. She's the Guv on this one. But I need you to help me, Brodie. Do the right thing now. I need a Tactical Team in an ARV to go fetch my wife now! Please! Help me!"

There was a moment's silence. Brodie was thinking.

Not whether he should help McKenzie or not, but *how*.

"Okay, I'll do my best. You need to text me the address and directions. And any special instructions."

"Good. I'm going to try and get there myself, but I'm in no fit state to drive just now, and I need to wake one of my team up and get them to drive me." McKenzie explained. "Brodie, once the Tactical Team is on the way, please get the team lead to call me on this number. Okay?"

Brodie agreed and promised to help as best he could.
As soon as they hung up, McKenzie texted the instructions over.
He then called DCS Wilkinson.
She didn't pick up.
He tried her again.
This time she did.
"McKenzie, it's four in the morning. This better be good."

McKenzie hesitated.
It was anything but good.
Where should he start?

Wednesday
04.20

Hanging up the phone on DCS Wilkinson, McKenzie flicked the switch on the kettle and went through the motions of making the strongest cup of coffee ever.

Whilst he waited for the kettle to boil, he rang Brown.

"Elaine, it's Campbell."

"Guv? What… "

"It's Fiona. My wife. She's next on the list to die."

"What? Are you sure?"

"Are you fit to drive?"

"I… yes… sure. Why?" she replied, trying to understand the reason for asking the question.

"My wife's in Callander. In a caravan. I've requested a Tactical Team to go fetch her and protect her. But it's dubious that they may have the spare capacity just now… " McKenzie explained to her about the increased threat level, and the bombs which McKenzie was almost certain came from TNT taken from Portobello High School.

"Can you come fetch me and take me to her? I'm in no fit state to drive, but I need to get to her. I can update you on what I've learned as we drive."

"I'll be there in twenty minutes, Guv."

True to her word, Brown arrived exactly on time.

McKenzie was waiting outside by the road.

He handed her a fresh coffee and climbed into the passenger seat.

She immediately drove off and headed through town towards the road to Stirling. At this time of the morning there was no need to use the bypass. The streets were still deserted.

McKenzie called Brodie.

"Good news Campbell. I've got an ARV with four officers en route to Callander."

"Thanks. When are they expected to get there?"

"They left ten minutes ago. I'm guessing in fifteen minutes."

"Tell them to put the blue lights on."

"I've already told them."

"And tell the lead officer to call me the moment they get there."

"He already knows."

"Our SatNav says we'll be there in an hour. We'll meet them there."

"McKenzie, what's going on? You didn't tell me much… "

It took McKenzie ten minutes to give him the lo-down on what had happened so far. Brodie was audibly shocked.

"And all of this has happened since last Friday?"

"Yes."

"How many are in your team?"

McKenzie named them all.

"Are you kidding me? Is that all?"

"Please, Brodie. Don't go there… It's a running argument with DCS Wilkinson. The Queen comes first. We mere mortals are dispensable. Listen, I've got to go. DI Brown and I need to talk."

McKenzie hung up.

Brown yawned.

"Sorry about this, Elaine. I appreciate it."

"You're lucky. When I got home I was so stressed that I almost got the red wine out, but I just went straight to bed. I was asleep within seconds."

McKenzie didn't hear her.

He'd put his head against the window and was staring out into the darkness.

Outside he probably appeared calm to Brown, but inside, he was shaking like a leaf.

He closed his eyes to picture Fiona. He imagined her stroking her tummy.

McKenzie yawned.

And within seconds, he was asleep.

Wednesday
Stirling
04.35

McKenzie awoke with a start. At first he didn't know where he was but quickly realised that Brown was shaking him awake.

"Your phone," she urged, "It's been ringing."

"How long have I been asleep?" he stretched, and then fumbled with the phone in his pocket.

"About ten minutes. Deeply. You were snoring your head off, Guv!"

"I don't snore." McKenzie protested.

McKenzie didn't recognise the number on the screen but called it straight back.

"Hello, this is DCI McKenzie. You just called me?"

"Yes, sir. I'm Sergeant Stewart. I'm leading the team sent to collect your wife and bring her into protective custody."

McKenzie was immediately alert.

"Are you there? Can I speak to her?"

There was a momentary pause.

"DCI McKenzie, I'm sorry. We're here at the caravan. But it's empty. Your wife is not here."

"What?" McKenzie sat bolt upright in his seat, shouting the reply, causing Brown to turn and stare at him whilst she continued to drive. "What do you mean?"

"Sir, there seems to be signs of a disturbance within the caravan. The door was open when we arrived. The nearest neighbours, about ten metres away, reported hearing a car arriving about half an hour ago. There were some loud voices, and then the car left. One of the neighbours came to investigate, and found the door of the caravan open. He looked inside, and found it empty."

McKenzie was beginning to panic.

"Are you sure she's not hiding somewhere? Have you searched around the caravan?"

"Yes sir. Your wife is not here."

"Keep searching. I'll try calling her. And her sister. I'll call you back in a moment."

McKenzie hung up. His hands were shaking.

Brown offered to pull over.

"No, keep driving. Fiona's not there." His voice was shaking. "I'm calling her now..."

Good. The phone was ringing.

Then it was answered.

"Hello?"

It was not Fiona's voice.

"Who is this?" McKenzie demanded.

"PC Williams. To whom am I speaking?"

"DCI McKenzie. Why are you answering my wife's phone?"

"Hang on sir, I'm passing the phone over..." A moment of silence, then the voice of Sergeant Stewart again. "DCI McKenzie, your wife has left her phone in the caravan. It was lying on the floor..."

"Fuck!" McKenzie swore loudly. "Hang on, I'm going to call my wife's sister."

He hung up and dialled the number.

It rang three times, then was picked up.

"Campbell, hi, are you okay?" she asked.

"Where are you? Is Fiona with you?"

"I'm driving back to Callander. Fiona's in the caravan still. Someone burgled my house, so I had to go back and switch the alarm off..."

The world began to spin. McKenzie felt very, very sick. He quickly pressed the button to let the window down and took several deep breaths of fresh air.

"Campbell? Are you okay? What's the matter?" Fiona's sister asked.

"How far away are you from the caravan?"

"I've just left the house. I'll be there in about thirty minutes."

"Maryln, I'll meet you there. Sorry, I've got to go." McKenzie hung up.

"What's the matter? What's happened?" Brown urged. "Tell me."

"Shit. Shit. **SHIT!**" McKenzie screamed, hitting the roof of Brown's car, and ripping the fabric.

"We're too late. We're too bloody late. The killer has got Fiona!"

Chapter 46

Wednesday
Callander
05.00

McKenzie stood in the centre of the caravan hugging Fiona's sister.
She was almost inconsolable, blaming herself for leaving Fiona alone.
McKenzie himself was barely holding on, and felt close to losing it.
It all seemed so unreal.
None of this could surely be happening.
After speaking with Marilyn by phone he'd spent the next ten minutes talking with the senior officer in Stirling, trying to persuade him to take further action.
Road blocks? A helicopter search?
Something! Anything!
The senior officer in Stirling had however, done all the right things. He'd agreed to set up several road blocks, and stop and search passing cars and vans, but had warned that realistically it may achieve nothing.
Circumstances were pointing towards the fact that she had been abducted. However, almost an hour had passed since her abduction and when the police arrived, and Callander lay in the middle of the countryside. Although there were only one or two routes north and south from Callander, the roads very soon came to junctions that presented multiple options north, south, east or west.
Worse still, Callander was a small town. CCTV coverage was limited and only covered the centre of the town. There was nothing on the caravan site or near its entrance.
Without any knowledge of a number plate to feed into the ANPR system, there was realistically no real hope of catching anyone trying to escape from the town.
By the time they'd been alerted to her abduction, the abductor and Fiona could realistically be anywhere within an eighty mile radius. By the time a roadwork was set up, they could be anywhere in Glasgow, Edinburgh, or quite far North.
McKenzie knew this to be true, but insisted they try, at least for an hour. If nothing by then, they could call them off.
By the time he arrived at the caravan, he was trying his best to regain control of his emotions.
As part of police training, they learned to cope with stress, and had studied techniques on how to focus under pressure.
McKenzie was grateful for all the training he'd received and now found it all invaluable. Breath, focus, breath. Repeat.
Arriving at the caravan and seeing the obvious signs of a disturbance, and being handed Fiona's mobile, was too much though. McKenzie had been forced to step outside the caravan, and walk round to the rear.
He knelt down, covered his heads with his arms and cried.

After a few minutes, he'd stood up. Walked back to the front of the caravan, swallowed hard, and stepped back inside.

"There are tyre marks outside on the edge of the grass and the gravel. Please make sure they're investigated and identified by forensics." He instructed Brown, who he'd already asked to liaise with the police department in Stirling.

Moments later, Marilyn had arrived.

McKenzie had sat her down, and calmly told her what had happened.

She'd cried. They'd hugged. Then McKenzie had mustered all his inner strength and regained control.

"Elaine, we're going back to Edinburgh. The team here know what they're doing. I'll speak to DCS Wilkinson on the way back and get her to arrange for some more officers to come here from Stirling and do what they have to do. We're needed back in Edinburgh."

McKenzie spoke to the officers on the scene, and told them that they also needed to investigate the break in at Marilyn's house. Get forensics all over the building. Check CCTV. Look for any cars in the neighbourhood driving on nearby roads at the estimated time of the burglary that could belong to the burglar. McKenzie explained that it was highly likely that the same person who abducted Fiona had either broken into the house in Stirling hoping to find them there, or had done it deliberately to set off the alarm and hope that Marilyn would return to the house and leave Fiona alone in the caravan. He also instructed to check CCTV for traffic in the Callander area in the minutes before and after the estimated time of Fiona's abduction.

Ten minutes later he, Brown and Marilyn were en route to Edinburgh via Stirling. After dropping Marilyn off at her home, McKenzie pulled out his notebook and started making notes.

He then called round his team, woke them up and summoned everyone into the office for a 7 a.m. meeting.

Lastly he called DCS Wilkinson.

"Ma'am, I have some bad news for you… " And he spent the next few minutes briefing her, waiting for the inevitable interruption, and worrying how the conversation would go.

"Campbell," she began, and he could tell from the use of his first name that this was the precursor to the 'serious conversation' which had to be had.

"Campbell, you know I have to take you off the case now. You know… "

"That I can't investigate the disappearance of my own wife? That there's a conflict of interest?" McKenzie interrupted.

"Exactly."

"With all due respect, Ma'am. What are you proposing? You've made it repeatedly very clear that there are NO officers available to help assist my investigation, the death toll of which is now four. Probably averaging roughly one a day. You've made it abundantly clear that until the Queen goes home to have tea in Buckingham palace, that not a single soul can be freed up to help save a Scottish commoner's life. But now, because my wife has been kidnapped, magically you are going to make a whole team available from the Kidnap Unit to investigate? Or are you really, realistically saying that you have to take me off the case, and then my case is on hold until the Queen goes home, and until normal Police service resumes? During which, by the way, my wife will be killed?"

"Campbell..." DCS Helen Wilkinson was about to reply, before McKenzie cut her short.

"Or, Ma'am, were you just about to say that until I formally file a missing person's report on my wife, that you do not have to do anything because no missing person has been reported? Or were you about to suggest that given the circumstances that I have a day to find the killer, and save my wife, before you would hand my case over to the Kidnap Squad?"

"Both of those. You have until lunchtime on Thursday. Then you're off the case."

"Thank you, Ma'am."

"Good luck, Campbell."

She hung up.

Wednesday
Edinburgh
Incident Room
Operation Blue Building
07.00

McKenzie stood before a sea of worried faces.

Everyone was there. Including DCS Wilkinson.

McKenzie was just about to clap, but he looked down at his hands and changed his mind at the last moment.

"Good morning everyone." He started.

All eyes were on him.

You could hear a pin drop.

"As you know we've had another murder. Daniel Gray. The ex-headmaster of the school. Decapitated, his head left on this lap. It also turns out that I led the killer to Mr Gray who had taken to living off the grid, presumably to avoid being tracked down and killed by the killer. Everyone who is now dead has had a copy of this book in their house." McKenzie held up Daniel's copy of the book. "The book details the plight of Maggie Sutherland, her experience of rape at the hands of the victims, now dead, and the alleged mishandling of her plight by the then headmaster, now also dead. The book details the deaths of the victims quite vividly, and as we have seen, where possible, the true-life murders of the victims have mimicked those described in the book."

"The book describes five deaths. Five victims. Four of whom are now dead. The last person to be named as a victim, and whose death is described in the book, is a girl at Portobello High School, who in the book is nicknamed 'GasBag' ". McKenzie's voice faltered. He reached for a glass of water and took a sip.

"Early this morning," he continued. "I remembered that Daniel Gray had told me that at the last school prom which Maggie Sutherland attended, the same evening that she claimed she was raped, GasBag and Maggie had come dressed to the ball in identical red dresses and hairstyles. Maggie had sought to look like GasBag, because she believed that Ronald Blake was attracted to GasBag and her looks. Maggie wanted to be just like her." McKenzie's voice cracked again, and he took another sip.

"After I returned to my house from my trip to Coll, I found a photograph taken at the ball, and discovered that the only two people at the ball wearing a red dress, and with similar hairstyles to boot, were Maggie Sutherland and my wife, Fiona…"

McKenzie took a minute, closed his eyes, and then continued.

"At about four-thirty this morning, police officers despatched from Stirling to my sister's caravan in Callander, where my wife Fiona had gone to rest and be safe, discovered that my wife had been abducted… "

There was a sharp intake of breath from everyone in the room apart from DCS Wilkinson and Brown. But no one talked. All eyes were on their Guv.

"Please forgive me… this is all quite stressful," McKenzie apologised. "I have discussed this with DCS Wilkinson and she has agreed to let me carry on leading the case, for now. Until tomorrow lunchtime, so we can maintain our momentum." McKenzie looked briefly at DCS Wilkinson, and she nodded.

"Okay. From now on EVERYTHING we do must count. We must not waste a second. In the next few days, possibly hours, it is very likely that the individual or individuals behind these deaths will try to kill my wife. I will not let that happen. And I am asking you to work with me to prevent it. To save my wife. And to capture the bastard behind all of this and bring him, or her, to justice."

He paused.

"I can tell you that I am exhausted. We all are. But imagine how the killer must feel. So far, he, or she, or they, are continually one step ahead of us. And we are running at full pelt. It's likely that they planned a lot of this in advance, but now they're executing their plans at such a rapid pace, I can promise you, they will make a mistake. Everyone makes mistakes. Especially when they're tired. And the killer must be even more exhausted than I am."

McKenzie paused.

"I have already made mistakes. Daniel gave me the clue about the similarity of Gasbag and Maggie on Sunday. I never picked up on it. A huge mistake. The time for mistakes is past. We won't make any more. From now on, I want everyone to question everything, double-check everything. Focus. Discuss. Share. And then re-check. *Everything*. Agreed?"

They all nodded.

McKenzie took a deep breath.

"Okay, moving swiftly on, early last night I received information back from the Director of Amazon KDP in the UK telling me the identity of the person who wrote Remember Me? and how many copies were printed. He confirmed it was Maggie Sutherland. The book was published two years before she committed suicide. Last night I was informed by the Director of Amazon that only six copies of Remember Me? were ever published. Just after my last conversation with my wife before she was abducted, I discovered that she too had been sent a copy of 'Remember Me?' quite a few years ago. That means that we can now account for five of the six copies of Remember Me? that were published. So, who has the last copy? It could be Maggie Sutherland, or probably the killer. At first, I thought the latter would be the obvious choice, but later I realised that there's a possibility the killer may actually be unaware that these books even exist. We don't know for certain that he is following instructions in the book, or from somewhere else."

"I don't necessarily agree," McLeish interjected. "On each of his victim's heads he's scrawled the words 'Remember Me?'. The title of the book! And the victims are being killed in ways which are pretty much described in the book. I think the killer has got the book. He's read it, and he's enacting the book in real life."

"I agree," Wishart said.

"But I can see the Guv's point. We don't know for sure. It's not sure." Lynch argued. "What I think we really need to know, is *why* the killer is doing it?"

"You're all right. And they're all good points. Which could mean that either the killer knew Maggie Sutherland intimately and knew all about the problems she'd had, and she told him about the book. Or, perhaps, somehow he was either given the last copy of the book from Maggie, or he got it from her once she'd died. To be frank, it could be we'll never know. For now though, let's proceed accepting that both options are possibilities: one he knew about the book, the other he didn't." McKenzie summed up. "Okay, let's park that one for now and recap what we know overall and decide what we need to do."

McKenzie turned to the whiteboard behind him.

"For now, we can put on hold all the actions we have pending. Unless you have new information that is immediately pertinent to the case, such as the identity of the killer, new suspects, or a possible number-plate of a van or car used to abduct Weir, Blake or McRae, then we start with a clean slate. There's no point in calling round any more staff or pupils. We know who the next victim is going to be. It's my wife."

McKenzie picked up a photograph of Fiona from the table behind him and stuck it with blue tack to the whiteboard for everyone to see. "You'll all get copies afterwards."

"First things first. Who are the suspects?"

McKenzie then told them about the last chapter of the book, and the possible existence of a child, Blake's child.

"If he exists, he's the number one suspect. But I don't think he does."

"I checked all that already. She had no relatives!" Wishart spoke out.

"Please check again. We have to rule this option out. Did she give him up for adoption? Daniel Gray said he saw her later that year, probably about five months later, but he never commented about her appearing to be pregnant. At least, she wasn't obviously showing. Check with her doctor and also her university. It's very important."

In the corner of the room, PC Jordon noted down the action.

"Apart from a possible son, the next and only other real suspect we have is a young man who we now believe was also fostered by the Banner's. I'll let DI Brown explain," and McKenzie handed over to Brown. She went through her findings and told the team everything she had told McKenzie the night before.

McKenzie wrote his name on the board, with a big number two beside it.

"Hamish Hamilton."

He stood back for a second, then took a step closer and ringed it with a red pen.

"We have two suspects. For now we have to pursue both. The moment we confirm that she wasn't pregnant and there's only one suspect on the list, we focus on Hamish." He tapped the board.

"Okay, I made a decision this morning, when thinking about what we all need to do. And next steps. I've read my way through 'Remember Me?', looking at the copy I got from Mark McRae's house, and then the one from Daniel Gray's cottage. There's nothing of significance on the first few pages, no author name, no dates, nothing. Just the title. The book's tough going. I read the whole book, but I worry that there are maybe clues in there that I missed. Perhaps notes written on the pages by McRae, Blake or Weir that could maybe give us some clues about who the killer is? Where to look? Something. Anything. So I'm going to hand out copies of the book, and ask volunteers who can read fast, to read the book cover to cover and see if I've missed anything. Hands up if you can read fast?"

There were four volunteers. McLeish, Wishart, Dean, and Anderson.

McKenzie tossed the books over to them, one at a time.

"Okay, and Lynch, I'm going to send you an email just now… " McKenzie pulled out his phone, tapped away on his keyboard for a moment, and then looked back up… "Done. I've just sent you the information that the Director sent me from Amazon. Can you read it all, go through it, check it? Anything you can find, let me know."

Lynch nodded, then started to play with his mobile. He opened up the email and started scanning the contents.

"Next up, it's official. My car's been bugged. The boys down at Fettes found a microphone and a tracker device on my car. I told them to put them back. I'll be picking up my car later on today, with the bugs and microphone still working. The killer doesn't know we found them. At least, hopefully not. Which means that we at last have something, a tool, that we can perhaps leverage to our advantage later on. I don't know how. But you never know. Let's just keep that in our back pocket for now. But we shouldn't underestimate it. We know he's listening. At first I was puzzled as to how the killer knew where my wife was. I'd agreed with her that it might be best if she went to stay with her sister. Which she did. In a caravan in the middle of nowhere in Callander in the Trossachs. Then I realised that the killer would have been listening when I was in the car and I was talking to Fiona and she told me exactly where she was. And also, I told Grant where to meet me on Coll and why I was going there. That's how the killer knew where Daniel Gray was on Coll, and where Fiona was… " his voice cracked a bit again, and he took another sip of water. "It's also how he knew where I was at all times, and how he was able to follow me… "

"GUV!" Lynch shouted excitedly. "I think I've got something. Something important… " He was already on his feet, moving towards the front, pointing to his phone.

"What?" McKenzie asked.

"You just sent me this from the Amazon guy. He mentioned in his email that he'd sent the original word document of 'Remember Me?' uploaded by Maggie Sutherland to the Createspace system, before she'd begun to edit it. I just clicked it open, and started to scan the first few pages… and look, on the very first page… there's a dedication in the book. You just said that on the printed copies there's nothing. But here, look in the original draft of the book sent to the Createspace system. It says, 'To Hammy.'" Lynch offered the phone to McKenzie, and pointed to the screen.

"To Hammy." McKenzie said again, aloud.

"Hamilton. To Hamish HAMILTON. *Hammie*. It's probably his nickname!" Brown stood up, and almost shouted.

McKenzie's face lit up.

"Bingo!"

Everyone in the room smiled. Several laughed.

In that instant the mood in the room changed.

"Okay, everyone, settle down. This changes everything. *Everything*. I want you to continue and recheck the possible existence of a son, but I'm almost certain you'll find he doesn't exist. This is it folks. This is our man. Hamish Hamilton. Maggie Sutherland dedicated her book to him. He's the only person we know that knew all about the tunnels. We know he was in the army. He'll be very capable and mission focussed. According to what we learned earlier, he's tall and powerful."

McKenzie took a deep breath.

"Okay, for me the four big questions are now, what's the connection between Maggie Sutherland and Hamish Hamilton? They must know each other. How? Were they lovers? Friends? Acquaintances?"

"And secondly, where is Hamish now? If he's the killer he has to be in Scotland. Thirdly, what's his name now? Is Brown right and he's changed his name?"

"Then last, but not least, why would Hamish be prepared to kill for Maggie, especially since Maggie's dead? This motive is important, but maybe it's something that we can figure out later. For now we have to find out where he is."

"Everyone. We find Hamish Hamilton, and we find Fiona."

Chapter 47

Wednesday
Incident Room
Operation Blue Building
08.45

There was a tangible air of excitement in the room. Everyone sensed that a corner had been turned.

Thanks to the original book file sent to Amazon and forwarded to them, they now had a tangible connection that linked the prime suspect to Maggie Sutherland.

"Okay, I'm just about to ask Brown to get up and brief us on Hamish Hamilton. But before she does, I just want us to all say to ourselves continuously, '*One mistake. He only has to make one mistake!*' That's going to be our mantra from now on. I promise, he'll make one. And you and I will find it!"

McKenzie paused.

"Also," he continued, "this case is dynamic. We have to be prepared to swivel on a dime, if you'll forgive a terrible American expression. It means we change course as soon as we know we should. Which means now we have a lead suspect, it's more important that we find *him* than have four of you spending the next couple of hours reading copies of the book. I'm cancelling that pervious instruction. For now, I only want Wishart reading a copy of Remember Me?, then scanning the other copies for notes made on the pages. The rest of you are focussing on tracking down any leads you can think of to help find Hamish Hamilton. Agreed?"

Nodding heads.

"Good. Now, over to you Brown."

Brown took the floor.

"About forty minutes ago, I received Hamish Hamilton's file from the army. I've emailed you all a copy of it. It makes interesting reading. First and foremost, though I've included digital copies of his photographs. We're going to make great use of them in the coming hours... "

"A quick summary. He served two tours. Was decorated twice for courage and showing great leadership under fire. He's calm and collected under pressure. Tall. Physically very strong. And good looking. I say that because apparently he used his charm to succeed. It was an attribute he knew he had, and he used it well. However, he was treated several times for depression, and his mental health was not perfect. The file says he suffered in his childhood, and was running away from his past. He found it difficult to form relationships, but when he did, he was fiercely loyal. After only serving a few months on his first tour of duty, one of his colleagues was wounded in Afghanistan and left behind. When Hamish found out, he went back to get him. He was wounded in the process, but rescued his friend, and apparently killed eight people in the process. He was then invalided out of the service. He's described as being clever. He has a knowledge of explosives, weapons and he worked in communications. Which explains the electronic bugs he placed in the car and his ability to track and listen to us. Lastly, he's very tenacious. He doesn't give up."

She then went on to explain in more detail about him going to Australia, possibly changing his identify and then going off the grid.

"No one knows where he is now. He just went off the grid. Why, we don't know. However, thanks to Lynch we now know there was some sort of relationship with Maggie Sutherland, and that can probably only really have happened because he met her during his time living at the school and when she was a pupil, or afterwards, when he left the army before he went to Australia, or since he may have returned to the UK after Australia. Or any combination of the three, I suppose."

She then outlined she was expecting to receive more information from the Home Office about a possible change of name, but that they didn't know if he had formally done this, or how, or even if the UK Government was aware of it.

"For now, we therefore have to try to find out via independent means, what his new name is. Or at least, what identify he may have assumed. If we can find his name, maybe we can find out where he is." She concluded.

"Or vice-versa," Dean spoke out.

"Explain?" McKenzie passed the floor to him.

"We have the photographs of him. Several. From different angles. We know his age at the time when they were taken and how old he would be now, so we can get experts in the cyber unit in Fettes to artificially age him and give us the equivalent photographs of how he would be expected to look now. We can then feed those photographs into Zeus, which is what the cyber team have nicknamed the Facial Recognition system in Scotland. If we tell Zeus to look at all the images we can get from live CCTV feeds, or even historical stored records, then we may be able to locate someplace where he was, or is. And if we can do that, the cyber team can do their stuff and possibly find a mobile number for him. And if we get his mobile number we can maybe get his identity, and an address. It's not that simple, - actually it's very complex - but I've seen it done lots of times before. And there's a new cyber unit called ACT – the Advanced Cyber Team been set up in London. They have connections to the National Security Agencies, as well as having other tricks up their sleeves. If we need to, we can ask them to help us. They can work magic. Trust me."

McKenzie smiled.

"They certainly can. They helped me on my last case. They basically saved my life. In fact," he said, flicking through the contacts list in his phone, "I have the telephone number right here of the top man in ACT. And an open invitation to call him anytime I need his help. But before I do, let's take a moment to brainstorm any places where we think Hamish Hamilton might have been. Can anyone suggest a location where we know the killer was at a certain time, so that we can kick-start Zeus and the CCTV analysis? Let's list them on the whiteboard!"

The first suggestion caught McKenzie by surprise.

"The Ferry to Coll." McLeish shouted out excitedly.

To McKenzie it was like a little light bulb had gone on inside his head.

"Genius! Thanks." McKenzie looked at his phone. "Brown? Can you takeover just now, I want to make a quick call. Also, Anderson, I know Brown assigned you to walk round the building with Gary Bruce to check the explosives. Could you do that now, if possible? Go and chase Bruce and find out where he's at. And please let us know as soon as you have the answer about any missing TNT."

The Sergeant nodded and immediately left the room. McKenzie followed him out, and stood just outside the door at the top of the stairs connecting the portacabins. He dialled PC Grant.

"DCI McKenzie? How is everything?" she asked as soon as she picked up.

McKenzie told her about Fiona. Grant couldn't believe it. She was shocked.

McKenzie then immediately explained to her the news about Hamish Hamilton, his career in the army and that they were now looking for him. He was the number one focus of their activities just now. They had to find him. Immediately.

"How can I help?" she asked.

"You're still on Coll, right?"

"Yes. I won't leave until tomorrow at this rate. I think I have to stay and liaise with the locals, and work with the Forensics team, as you requested."

"Exactly. Although there's been a slight change of plan. I need you to get down to the port as soon as possible and find out which ferry, I mean exactly which boat, would have visited Coll on Monday. We're all pretty sure that Hamish Hamilton is the killer. At least he's one of the killers. As soon as I finish this call, I'll send you a couple of digital photos of him. I need to you to get on the boat which Hamilton would have used to first visit the island and then leave it. Talk to Forensics about when they think the time of death was, but I'm pretty sure he died on Monday, sometime. Then get on the boat that would have visited the island on Monday, and check everywhere on the boat for CCTV. Get copies of everything. And if you're stuck on the boat between ports, please start going through it all. Hamilton must have been on one of the boats, and with any luck he'll have been captured on CCTV. Did he buy anything on board? Use a credit card? What car was he driving? What's the number plate? What name was he travelling under? At the moment we only have his photo and the fact that he must have been on Coll to kill Daniel Gray. He could have got someone else to do it, but I don't think that's the case. I'm beginning to think we have one guy, operating alone. Can you do that, please?"

"Yes, Guv." She replied. "Hang on a minute please... just let me check the time of the next ferry." A moment's pause. "Okay, Guv. The ferry should still be in port. It leaves at ten past ten. If I hurry, I should make it."

"Go for it. And let us know anything you find. Every second counts. There's a possibility that the killer will kill my... "

"Guv, that's not going to happen. We're going to get him first." Grant interrupted. Reassuring him.

"Call me. The moment you have anything. *ANYTHING.*"

McKenzie hung up.

Next, he called the number he had for the leader of ACT – the Advanced Cyber Team operating out of London. The man in charge was a guy called Ray Luck. On one of McKenzie's last cases, when the Scottish crimelord, Tommy McNunn, had killed one of McKenzie's officers, and then framed McKenzie for her murder, it was Ray Luck who had called McKenzie out of the blue and offered him the evidence needed to prove McKenzie's innocence. The ACT team had been monitoring the telephone conversations of the Scottish crimelord from abroad, and had telephone recordings capturing him making plans and issuing instructions to have McKenzie's assistant killed and the murder blamed on McKenzie. Thanks to Ray's team, McKenzie had been able to prove his innocence and Tommy McNunn was found guilty of the murder.

Ray ran a team of cyber experts. They were based in the UK, but also partly based in India.

McKenzie knew that it was the type of operation where you didn't ask too many questions. It wasn't above the law, but it used the latest technology to help support the rule of law. In cases where UK National Law may have frowned upon what they did, they conducted covert cyber operations out of an office in India.

From his conversations with Ray Luck, McKenzie knew that Ray had recruited the best of the best. If the boys in Fettes were brilliant, which they were, then ACT was out of this world.

And at this point in time, Ray needed all the help he could get.

"Hello, is that Ray? Ray Luck?" McKenzie asked as soon as the call was answered. "This is DCI Campbell McKenzie from Police Scotland… "

"Redirecting. One moment please… " A man's voice interrupted him. There were a few electronic beeps then two seconds later, a familiar voice.

"DCI McKenzie. how good to hear from you! How are you?"

"My wife's been kidnapped and has only hours to live. I need your help."

"Not good. What do we have?"

"Nothing but a photograph of the suspect, and his old name."

McKenzie quickly shared all the salient information.

"… and if you give me a few moments I can text you or email you a list of locations where we think the killer may have been, along with some approximate times."

"That's all you've got?"

"It's more than we had an hour ago."

"Send me the information to the email address that will appear on your phone in a few seconds. We'll take it from there. We'll call you as soon as we have something. And DCI Campbell, don't worry. We're going to do our best to help you find your wife."

"Thanks Ray."

"One question, are you also getting the boys in Fettes Row to help on this?"

"Yes… They're our first operational port of call, but you're the one we're counting on."

"No pressure then. But don't worry, the cyber team in Fettes indirectly report to me. I'll coordinate with them directly. We'll have everyone working on this. From now on, you can talk to me. But in a few minutes, I'll also give you the name of someone in Fettes you can send someone from your team to sit with, if you want. That person will be able to answer any questions and ask any questions of your team that we need to know." Ray paused. "DCI McKenzie, it's 9.20 a.m. now. Most of my team are just finishing another project of national importance. I promise you that as soon as they're finished, I'll make this a priority for them. Is there anything else?"

"No. Just find my wife please." McKenzie's voice quivered.

The line went dead.

McKenzie stepped back into the Incident Room. The room was humming with activity and excitement.

He looked at the whiteboard and found that Brown had made a list of places they knew that Hamish Hamilton may have been, tallied alongside possible times.

First one: the ferry. Monday and possibly Tuesday morning. Along with the times of the ferries landing on the islands and leaving it. Tuesday morning was ringed in red. Everyone knew that the killer would want on and off the island in the shortest possible time, so it was highly unlikely he would have been there and waited for the Tuesday ferry. He'd have left by then.

Next location: McRae's House, when someone attached McRae's phone to the underside of McKenzie's car, and the approximate time.

Likewise the time and location of when the second note had appeared on McKenzie's car at the bottom of Bath Street after Willy Thomson had been killed.

Then Daniel Gray's house at the time of Daniel's death.

David Weir's death from falling from the top of the school.

And Mark McRae's death when he was murdered in the Chemistry department.

Lastly, the caravan site in Callander earlier that morning when Fiona had been kidnapped.

McKenzie took a photograph of the board and sent it to the email address that Ray Luck had magically sent him during their phone call.

For a moment he stood and watched his team getting to work. They were all already busy on the terminals which yesterday they'd brought into the room and had assembled and connected up on tables which now ringed the room along the walls.

McKenzie clapped his hands and they all immediately turned to him.

"I'm going to leave you all to it. Feel empowered to do what you have to. If you've got a lead that you think you need to chase, do so. Just keep PC Jordon aware at all times of where you are. And make sure you don't go anywhere you think you might be in any danger. If you find him, no one goes anywhere near Hamilton without discussing it with me first. And, ... one thing more. I just want to say thank you to you all. Okay, let's get to it."

His team nodded. McKenzie was about to clap his hands, then realised it would be a waste of time. His team had already forgotten about him and were focussed on their computers, their phones or their files.

"A word?" DCS Wilkinson said over his shoulder.

"Two seconds... sorry... " McKenzie put his finger in the air, and then quickly moved across the portacabin to Dean.

"Tell PC Jordon I've assigned you to go and sit with the Cyber Team in Fettes. In a few minutes I'll text you the name of your contact. You're acting liaison between them and us. You can help them in any way you think you should. Finish what you're doing then head over there as soon as you can, or I can take you there in a few minutes if you want. I'm heading over there to pick up my car."

He patted him on the shoulder and turned and went back to DCS Wilkinson.

"I'm not needed here, Campbell. There's nothing I can add to your team."

"How about people?" McKenzie asked.

"Prove to me that the explosives come from here, and I'll give you some people back. Until then, Operation Crown takes precedence, sorry. But for now, I don't think more people will help. What you need is luck."

"I've already got it, Ma'am." McKenzie replied. "I've got Ray Luck."

"From ACT?"

"Yes."

"Then it's only a matter of hours, Campbell."

"I hope you're right, Ma'am. But I'm worried that even hours may be too long. Ma'am, can you keep some of the armed squad on standby for me? And can you move the helicopter to Edinburgh and keep it on standby too? The moment we find where Hamish Hamilton is, we might need to move fast."

DCS Wilkinson smiled and nodded.

She briefly thought about saying something clever or smart to make McKenzie feel better about the situation, but then thought better of it.

What could she say that would make a difference?

The killer had already killed four people in five days.

Fiona McKenzie was next.

Both she and McKenzie knew that realistically speaking, the odds were not in Fiona's favour.

Chapter 48

Wednesday
Corstorphine
10.20

Lynch parked his car on the high street on a double-yellow, stuck on the flashing lights, and hurried into the funeral parlour which the caretaker of Corstorphine Hill Cemetery had sent him to.

He had his fingers crossed.

Forty minutes ago, he'd been sitting in the portacabin staring at the files on his computer. One of the actions that Wishart had was to recheck that Maggie Sutherland had no surviving relatives, but for now she was busy reading the book which all the victims had been sent. Wishart's head was stuck down in the book, when suddenly an idea had come to her.

It was a long-shot, Wishart was interested in seeing if she could find out who went to the funeral. Maggie Sutherland had no relatives. So, if anyone had gone, they might be worthwhile interviewing.

Wishart already knew where Maggie had been buried. Someone should go to the graveyard, talk to the caretaker and see Maggie Sutherland's grave.

And the big question: had Hamish Hamilton gone to the funeral?

Unfortunately, Wishart was tied up with the book, so she'd delegated the idea to Lynch.

With the blue flashing lights on, it had only taken Lynch twenty minutes across the city.

Luck had been on his side. Lynch had quickly found the caretaker, and after five minutes in his office he'd located Maggie Sutherland's grave.

The caretaker had been working there for many years. He knew a lot about the guests he looked after. And he'd attended many of the funerals, standing on the side lines.

They weren't long into the conversation about Maggie Sutherland before the caretaker had volunteered that he could clearly remember Maggie's funeral for one simple reason.

No one apart from the minister had turned up.

She'd had no relatives or friends attend that day.

Jeff, the caretaker had found it very sad. It didn't happen often, but when it did, Jeff remembered them.

So, Jeff had stood beside the minister and spent a moment with him before the grave had been filled in afterwards.

"Have you ever seen anyone visit her at all?" Lynch had asked.

"Yes." He replied. "One man. He comes every year on her birthday. Lays a big bunch of beautiful Irises. Has a cry. Then leaves. I spoke to him once. He'd missed the funeral. Hadn't known about it. He was devastated."

"What does he look like?" Lynch had asked, reaching inside his jacket for the photograph of Hamish Hamilton. "Was this the man?"

Jeff had stared at the photograph, and very quickly replied.

"That's him. He was here just a few months ago too. Every year. Every birthday. Same flowers."

"Are you sure?"

"Do you know what his name is by any chance?" Lynch had asked.

"No. I never asked him. But I think he's the one that paid for the headstone. He came several times in the first few months, then it became every year. After the first year she still didn't have a headstone. He asked me about that. I think he talked to the minister, and then he came back and asked if I could recommend a good headstone that would last forever. Not like the other ones that faded or fell apart. I told him black granite. I gave him the name of the undertaker. I think he went there and ordered the headstone. It appeared about a month later. It's one of the best, actually. Beautiful."

Ten minutes later Lynch opened the doors to the funeral directors and walked in.

Fifteen minutes later he was staring at the copy of the invoice which had been paid for by the man who had chosen the stone.

Unfortunately, there was no name.

The man had paid in cash.

The signature on the receipt was just an indecipherable scrawl.

Lynch showed them the photograph of Hamish Hamilton but no-one recognised him.

Just before he left the shop, he took a photograph with his phone and sent it to PC Jordon and the rest of the team.

Aboard the Ferry from Coll to Tiree
10.57

Grant was lucky. Not only had she made the ferry, but it was the same ferry that had visited Coll on Monday morning and night and would have carried Hamish Hamilton if he were abroad.

It was a large ferry, capable of carrying many cars and lorries, and keeping all the islands supplied with all the necessities of life, including the vital tourists that kept their economies afloat.

Grant was quickly shown up to the Captain, to whom she explained the situation without giving too many details away, but just enough to be offered his crew's full support.

"We have digital CCTV throughout the ship. It's all stored on a server somewhere. I don't know how long for, but I'll ask Angus here to take you down to the Comms Room, and he'll introduce you to Chris, our IT technician, who'll see what he can do to help you. He manages all that sort of stuff."

The comms room, so-called, was several decks down, tucked away in a room with no view, and very hot.

Chris was busy with a soldering iron as Angus led Grant in, introduced her, and then left.

"CCTV? From Monday? That won't be a problem. It's all digital nowadays, and we keep about a month's worth on the servers before we wipe it."

"Where are the camera's located? Where do you think the most likely place would be that I might capture images of someone on board?"

"The bar, or the restaurant. Or just outside the toilets on the first deck when people first leave their vehicles, or before they head back." Chris explained.

"Excuse me for asking, but do you have any spare hard drives on the ship that you could download all of Monday's video onto and then give me? I didn't really come prepared… "

"Aye. No problem. Happy to help. But you'll no be getting back to Oban until nine-thirty tonight. We're heading to Tiree now… You can stay onboard between sailings if you like."

"I live on Tiree. I could either take it all home with me and watch it from there, or I could stay here and go through it all until we get to Oban later, and then hand it over to the local police there. I may even have someone waiting for it from Edinburgh. Since it's digital once they get it on a server, they could probably scan everything for our suspect much faster than I could ever do manually."

"Aye, well, it's up to you lass. But it'll be mighty boring going through it all hour by hour. We've got about thirty cameras on the ship. Maybe it's best if I set you up with a computer somewhere a little nicer than this. If you give me a few minutes, I'll get some kit and a few cables, and then I'll take up to the Captain's office. He'll no mind."

It took thirty minutes to set everything up. When he was ready, he selected a screen view which showed Grant all the cameras on the ship. All she had to do was select the camera she wanted and move a cursor along the bottom of the frame to go from one time to another. There was a fast forward, a super-fast-forward, a pause, and options to go backwards if she overshot something.

"If you want to take a snap shot, you do this… ," Chris showed her. "The pictures are stored here… and you can print them by doing this… ," he explained, then repeated the instructions a few times. "And you can watch three or four CCTV feeds at the same time by arranging the videos tiles on the screen like this and changing their size like this… The only problem is you might get a bit overwhelmed with all the data and you probably don't want to miss out any detail. And… last of all… I think… is that you can adjust the speed you watch things at by doing *this*… Don't worry, you'll get the hang of it very quickly." He reassured her.

Grant admitted that she was quite surprised that there seemed to be so many camera feeds to choose from. There was a lot of choice, with cameras covering all aspects of the ship.

"We have to be careful. People getting drunk, falling overboard, smugglers, people having sex where they shouldn't… you wouldn't believe it. It all goes on here!" he laughed. "Any questions, just call me on the phone on Extension 9."

"One question before you go… where should I start? Where do you recommend?"

"Who's the suspect? A man or woman?"

"A man."

"From where? How long's he been travelling for?"

"We think since Edinburgh."

"Okay, there're toilets on the shore before he got on the boat, but no café late at night. I'd guess he would go to the restaurant or the bar and get a coffee, if he was alone and driving. That's where most people go. It's too early to drink, but the bar's the most comfortable place, I think."

"Okay, the restaurant first, then the bar next, then the corridors outside the toilets."

"Aye, call me when you're done with them. By the way, you might want to get yourself a coffee before you start."

It was good advice.

She fetched a coffee, sat down and got to work, several photographs of Hamish Hamilton lying on the desk in front of her. She didn't yet have any of the aged-photographs of Hamilton, and she was just using the mugshots provided by the army.

She felt under a lot of pressure. She knew how important it was that she find Hamish Hamilton on board the ship. Fiona's life might depend upon it.

She started with the restaurant, flicking through the images, looking for someone - anyone tall and powerful - who might look like Hamilton. For now she decided to only view one video feed at a time. She didn't want to miss anything.

The journey from Oban to Coll was about two hours forty minutes, but people had started flooding into the restaurant even before the ferry had left the harbour in Oban.

It took Grant about forty minutes to go through the images of the restaurant. By that time the ferry she was on was about to arrive in Tiree. She had a choice. Get off the ferry now, and take the hard drive with the images home with her and work on it from home. Or stay on the boat.

It only took a moment to decide. She would stay on the boat and carry on working. If she got off now, she would lose an hour before she got home and got set up again, and right now, every second counted.

Having bitten the bullet and decided to stay on board, she loaded up the video-feed from the bar and started to process that.

She was twenty minutes into the video when she struck gold.

11.00

In the end McKenzie and Dean were both lucky, and were able move fast enough to get a lift to Fettes with DCS Wilkinson.

"Keep me updated every few hours," DCS Wilkinson told McKenzie, then headed off to her office. McKenzie wished Dean luck and went to collect his car.

After a brief discussion with the team who told him they weren't really able to learn any valuable intelligence from investigating the electronic bugs hidden in his car, other than that they were fairly sophisticated and quite expensive, McKenzie decided to get back to the Incident Room.

Before climbing back into the car, McKenzie called PC Jordon and arranged with her that she would alert the team that for now, any conversations acknowledging Fiona's capture should be avoided. He didn't want anyone listening to their conversations to know that they were aware that Fiona was missing. From an abductor's perspective, it would be perfectly reasonable to assume that McKenzie might not discover she was missing till later that day. So, for now, if it gave them any sort of advantage whatsoever, everyone should carry on as normal, just as if no one yet knew that Fiona had been kidnapped.

McKenzie then headed back to the school to be close to the team.

En route, Anderson called him. McKenzie had already talked to him by phone outside his car and knew what it was about, but he now wanted to repeat the conversation in the car, and give the illusion to anyone listening that they did not know about the eavesdropping bug in the visor.

"Sergeant, what have you got?"

"Guv, I've finished the rounds of the building with Gary Bruce. We found that four TNT charges had been taken. Each one in itself is very powerful and is probably enough to blow up a house."

"FOUR!" McKenzie shouted loudly to himself, and anyone listening.

"Yes, Guv. Whoever did this is extremely clever, and very dangerous. I'm worried that he always seems to be one step ahead of us. How did he manage to take the explosives from underneath our eyes without being spotted? Bruce is mad. He says that whoever did this has to have had specific training. He could easily have killed himself trying to steal the TNT. According to Bruce, whoever stole the TNT definitely knows what he's doing. He must be very clever, and we shouldn't underestimate him."

"I hear you. Okay, I'll be back at the school in a minute. I just picked my car up from the car park at Fettes. I'll meet you in the incident room."

McKenzie hung up.

The plan was to big up the killer whenever possible. Play to his ego. Make him think he was brilliant, and that they were stupid. It was one of several tactics that McKenzie was familiar with when playing a suspect, and one of several behaviour patterns that might help in encouraging the suspect to make a mistake.

Next, he called Brown. As before, he had already spoken to her before he got in the car. He'd already established that the forensics team would be finished with the school murder scenes later that day. Which left Gary Bruce open to demolish the school the next day, if all the other permissions were to be granted, and the council could put the required street closures and diversions in place at short notice.

"Elaine, I was just wondering if you'd managed to talk with the Forensics team yet about when they'll be finished with the school? When do we get it back, and when can we finally get the chance to demolish it?"

"Guv, they've agreed that they will be out of there in a few days time." She bluffed. "I think we're probably looking towards the end of the week. Maybe we could be looking at Friday for the final demolition. A week later than originally planned, but better late than never."

Ten minutes later, McKenzie was at the school, standing face-to-face with Bruce.

"If it's safe, can you take a sample of the TNT to Fettes Row and make sure it's left for the attention of DCS Wilkinson at the front desk?" He smiled, the first time that day, but it didn't last for more than half a second. "Tell the people it's the TNT. They'll know what to do. I'm going to call them just now..."

Gary Bruce agreed.

"And then come back and start making plans for blowing up Portobello High School up. *Tomorrow*. The sooner the better. I'll leave that to you. It's your area of expertise not mine. Just tell me when you're doing it, because when you do, I'm going to have to get my team out of here and into St Leonards."

11.20

After calling Fettes and alerting them to the fact that a bundle of TNT was on the way to them, McKenzie then made his way around his team, finding out what progress had been made.

Wishart was just about to finish the book. She was a fast reader, as promised. Once done, she'd start checking the other books for any informative notes and scribbles.

Apart from one point, so far the book hadn't revealed anything new. What had caught her attention however, was the question of how GasBag was projected to die. Where, and how?

In the book it was done in the Physics Lab. An unlit Bunsen burner had been left on and a big bag, containing GasBag's unconscious body inside, had slowly filled up with gas. When the whole bag was filled with gas, an electric spark had been passed between two cables fed into the bag, and the gas had been ignited and blown up.

"I don't want to dwell on it for now, but I think it's important to understand how it might be planned. We need to anticipate it and stop it from happening."

"Another reason for blowing this bastard up as soon as possible, so there's no chance it can happen here!" McKenzie swore, waving at the old school outside the window and revealing some of the tension he was feeling. In general, with the exception of this case, McKenzie never swore in front of his team.

"Heard anything from the Embassy on any possible name change?" McKenzie quizzed Brown.

"Nope. Not yet, Guv."

Lynch was back now. He showed him the signature he'd found and told McKenzie the news about Hamish Hamilton being identified within the graveyard.

"Great work. Now we know for sure that he's back in the country. He must definitely be operating under a pseudonym. We just have to find it!"

McKenzie had just finished suggesting that Lynch pass the signature on to the writing experts in Fettes Row when his phone buzzed.

It was PC Grant.

She was very excited.

Chapter 49

Wednesday
On board the Ferry en route to Barra
11.30

PC Grant was speaking too fast.

"Slow down, and tell me what you've found!" McKenzie instructed her, putting the phone on loudspeaker so everyone in the room could hear her.

"I was searching through the CCTV footage from the different feeds on the boat - there's about thirty cameras on the ship - and I'd already been through the feed from the restaurant. I was about twenty minutes into the crossing on Monday's trip and looking at the CCTV from the bar when a man with a hoodie came down and sat at the far edge of the bar. He ordered a coffee. He sat there for about ten minutes, and started to nod off. His head jerked forward, and he sat up. His hood was still up, but then he automatically pulled it back when he woke up, and looked around, then carried on drinking his coffee. After a few sips he pulled the hood up and covered his head again. I recognised him immediately. Exactly the same face as his army photograph. A bit bald on top, receding hairline, but the same face."

"Brilliant. Well done."

"I've printed off photographs and emailed screen-captures to PC Jordon for the team. Anyway," she continued. "He ordered another coffee, this time take-away, and then got up and walked away. I've got pictures of him standing up. Walking. I then moved to the feed from another camera and tracked him going along the corridor and into the gents. When he came out, he went to the restaurant and ate some food, but by now he'd put his hood back up. I've images of him in almost high res from quite a few angles. He was wearing a blue Super-Dry top, and blue jeans, and training shoes with red stripes on the heels. Easy to spot really. Noting the times he appeared, I managed to find him on several others feeds and track him going down to the deck. I was hoping to see him get into a car. Unfortunately, that didn't happen. He was on a bicycle."

"A bike?" McKenzie queried.

"Yes, Guv. When the ferry docked, he cycled off. It was the same ferry that would have taken him back later that night to Oban after he'd killed Daniel Gray, and I'm just about to start to look at those too. But the point is, when he got back to Oban, he would have been on a bike. Maybe he got the train up? Or most likely, he came by car, parked the car somewhere, unloaded a bike, and walked or cycled onto the ferry. I understand what he's doing Guv. He's trying to lie low, sneak across under the radar, and not draw any attention to his main mode of transport. It would have worked too, but he made a mistake. He took his hood down at the bar. And we got him straight away."

McKenzie thumped the table.

"Did you hear that everyone? He just made his first mistake, and we were all over it!" He turned his attention back to the phone. "Okay, it's obvious he must be really tired. If he got the morning ferry on the Monday morning at seven fifteen from Oban, he must have driven overnight from Edinburgh once he heard me give the details to the helicopter crew. He obviously jumped on the news he got about where Daniel Gray was living and took action straight away and went for the very next ferry. But it cost him a night's sleep. And he just made his first mistake. Grant, can you please check out the rest of the CCTV feeds on the return trip? We can't wait for you to get to Oban this evening. We need to act fast on the information you've given us now. We'll pass these images and information to DI Dean and the Fettes Cyber Team and Ray Luck at ACT, and see what they can make of it. Great work, Grant. Call us if you have anything new, okay?"

McKenzie hung up and walked across the room to the whiteboard.

He ringed Hamish Hamilton in red again.

"Team, we're making great progress. We now know that Hamish Hamilton is back in Scotland and it was almost definitely him that had some form of friendship or relationship with Maggie Sutherland and then killed Daniel and the others. He was at the graveyard and on Coll in the last few hours that Daniel was alive. Lynch? Do what you can to find out how Maggie Sutherland and Hamish Hamilton knew each other. What job did Maggie do? Where did she study? Did she have a Facebook presence? Anything. Wishart? Put pressure on the Home Office and try to get more help on finding out whatever name he's using now. We need a name folks. An address. And a telephone number so we can track him. Good, now everyone get back to work!"

11.45

Seconds later McKenzie was on the phone to Ray Luck.

He briefed him on what they now knew and had discovered.

In return Ray sent McKenzie an aged computer-generated high-resolution photo of what Hamish Hamilton would look like now. Incredibly, it was almost identical to the images McKenzie then sent to Ray from the CCTV capture on the boat.

"Okay. We're working on a few things, DCI McKenzie, but now you've given me this it will help. I've got to go. We'll speak soon."

There was no messing around. Ray was on the case.

McKenzie respected that. And it also reassured him.

For the first time since early that morning McKenzie allowed himself to feel the tiniest bit of hope.

He then closed his eyes and said a small prayer.

He thought about Little Bump. About Fiona.

But that was too much. He opened his eyes and went back to work.

11.50 a.m.

After hanging up on DCI McKenzie, Ray Luck issued new instructions to his team. They had recently finished their other project and had just been briefed by Ray when McKenzie had called, offering them fresh intelligence.

"Okay, pay attention everyone. We've got some new intel on board. So let's recap what we know. Okay, so we now we have five anchors to work from and some extras."

"The five anchors are, firstly, the number plate of the white van used by the suspect for at least the week before last Saturday. Second, the photograph of the suspect which we can put into the BloodHound system. Third, the army record of the suspect. Fourth, a physical location: we know he got off the Ferry in Coll and committed a murder and we can therefore guess that he got the first ferry back and got off at Oban on the mainland as soon as possible. On the Monday, the ferry arrives at Oban at 9.55 a.m. and leaves at 12.45 a.m., getting back to Oban at 15.25 p.m. Fifth, we also believe we know how the suspect was dressed when he left the ferry and that he was riding a bike. Additionals include the fact we think he may have changed his name in Australia, but don't know what it is. He's probably Catholic. He knew the deceased Maggie Sutherland who we discussed at the first briefing. We also have rough times and defined locations for where we think the suspect may have been, but which are not confirmed." He checked his watch. "It's now almost midday. You know what to do. Go for it."

The team immediately dispersed and hurried back to their terminals dotted around the walls of ACT Room 5. The walls were covered in large LED displays, showing an ever-changing dynamic tapestry consisting of video conferencing feeds, computer screen displays, statistics, CCTV feeds, and a big clock, which showed the recorded time since the disappearance of Fiona McKenzie.

On one of the screens was a picture of the cyber team in Edinburgh, where DI Dean could be seen sitting beside a terminal and assisting one of the seconded ACT team members in Police Scotland Fettes Row.

The ACT team knew what they were doing. They did this every day and knew every trick in the book.

They'd been split into several teams, each progressing a different lead. A jar full of £5 notes sat on the desk beside Ray Luck's terminal, the result of the traditional sweepstake to see which team would provide the vital clue that would locate the suspect and empower the local team on the ground to capture him, or her. The winning team got the contents of the jar and enjoyed a night down the local pub at the cost of everyone else.

Although Ray had not mentioned anything to DCI McKenzie, Ray was extremely hopeful.

Once they had a photograph of a suspect, and a confirmed location where they had once been, it was normally just a matter of hours before ACT could track them down.

In today's modern world, once the digital hounds had been unleashed, only an expert or the dead could remain hidden for long enough to evade detection and capture.

It was twelve o'clock now.

Ray's money was on the Green Team, so called because they normally made the other's green with envy. Going on past experience, with all the modern cyber technology at their disposal, Ray guessed that it would probably only take them several hours to complete the job.

12.05

McKenzie was worried.

Although DCS Wilkinson had agreed to letting McKenzie continue to lead the investigation, McKenzie knew that there was a serious conflict of interests here.

Under normal circumstances, he would be taken off the case immediately and it would have been handed over to the National Crime Agency. For the first time since last Friday, McKenzie was almost grateful to whoever was behind the terrorist threat because it was that threat which was allowing him to continue to manage the search for his wife.

Handing over the search now would be disastrous. The momentum they were building up would be lost just at the moment their reduced team was really gelling and being to function together, seamlessly.

If Wilkinson kept true to her word, he would have command until tomorrow at midday.

Two things could threaten that however, and McKenzie was concerned.

Firstly, at this moment in time, Fiona had technically been abducted, and she was the victim under threat. If, however, Hamilton made any contact with the team and made any demands regarding Fiona, technically, in the processes that Police Scotland followed, Fiona would cease to be the victim, and become the hostage, and the classification of victim would pass to McKenzie, and a Kidnap Team from the National Crime Agency would formally take over Fiona's case. At that point, McKenzie knew that the full processes and mechanisms for protecting a kidnapped person would kick into play, and he would be surrounded by processes, technology and people designed to help find the hostage. In most circumstances this would be brilliant news, however, in this case, it would be disastrous. McKenzie knew the killer had no intention of returning Fiona. His soul mission was to carry out the murder so vividly depicted in the final chapters of 'Remember Me?'. So long as he himself was in control, he believed he had a better chance of finding the killer and his wife.

So, what would happen if the killer contacted him?

Would he declare it, or bury it, potentially threatening his career?

McKenzie already knew the answer to that.

He would rather bury his career than his wife and child.

The second problem he faced was the question about the TNT which they had sent over to be analysed and compared with the explosives already found as part of Operation Crown.

If Fettes determined that they were the same explosives, from the same sources, then Operation Crown may take over command of his case. Although this may throw the full weight of Police Scotland behind the search for the terrorist, who was now obviously one-and-the-same person as the killer McKenzie was investigating, it would also result in an initial delay and result in the investigation losing precious hours. Even worse, if not handled properly, it could tip the killer off, resulting in him expediting the murder of Fiona and Little Bump and the killer then running for cover.

On the other hand, things were looking good.

For now, for the first time, McKenzie's team had several cards in their favour.

How long that would last, and how long McKenzie would remain in control, McKenzie did not know.

All he knew was that the clock was ticking, and with every second that passed, the threat to Fiona and Little Bump increased.

Some place, somewhere, McKenzie knew that the killer - almost certainly now identified as Hamish Hamilton - was making preparations to kill his family.

Tick. Tick.

Tock.

Chapter 50

Wednesday
Henderson's Vegetarian Restaurant
Edinburgh City Centre
12.15

Marie McDonald was crying.
She was sitting at a table at the back of the restaurant, feeling very strange and for the first time in years, not fully in control of her emotions.
She was scared. Excited.
And worried.
In the past few days, so many incredible things had happened.
Last night she had hardly slept a wink. For many reasons.
All of which had been truly, truly amazing.
Wonderful.
Fantastic.
First of all there had been Stuart.
They had made love.
In a hotel which they had spontaneously booked near Portobello Beach.
With an incredible view of the sweeping bay that led out to the North Sea.
Then there had been Stuart again.
As they had made love one more time.
She had drunk champagne, just two glasses, but it was enough to celebrate the occasion.
Then, slightly mysteriously, Stuart had been forced to leave. He'd received a phone call, and he'd seemed concerned.
He'd left, but promised that he would meet her today for lunch, and he'd assured her that he would give her his decision about Poland then.
After he'd left, Stuart had texted her several times.
Each time the mobile had pinged, she'd felt a surge of excitement.
She felt like a teenager again. Carefree. Reckless. In love.
After Stuart had gone, she started to get ready to go home.
She was in the process of dressing when she changed her mind.
She needed some time and space to herself to think about the money she'd been promised. She needed to process the fact she'd just been promised one hundred and fifty million pounds.
One hundred and fifty million pounds!
It was an astronomic sum.
With so much funding, all her hopes and dreams for her children could come true.
At the back of her mind, however, she couldn't stop herself from doubting that all of this could be happening.
She'd spent most of the night looking out of the hotel window across the bay, mesmerised by the lights dancing on the water, reflecting from the houses dotted along the shore or the boats at anchor.

At one point, she'd seen a shooting star, and she closed her eyes and started to make a wish, but then realised that perhaps, just maybe, all her wishes were already coming true.

Eventually she had fallen asleep, showered and then tried to check out, only to discover that the room had already been paid for by Stuart.
As she had climbed into a taxi, Stuart had texted her, apologising for having to leave the night before, but wishing her luck with the meeting that morning. He'd also suggested the restaurant where they could meet for lunch.
She'd tried calling him back, but it had gone to voice-mail. He must already have been at work.
After texting him back, she'd stopped by her house to pick up the information she'd needed, taken a quick shower and then dressed.

This time around, her visit to Ben Venue Capital Assets had been short and sweet.
The Finance Director had met her in reception, asked her a few questions, taken copies of the information requested, and then given her a letter with directions to the event in the evening where it had now been confirmed that she would meet the First Minister of Scotland, who would formally present a symbolic cheque for thirty million pounds made out to her charity.
"Would you like to bring a guest? Perhaps a significant other?" the Finance Director had asked. "Please feel free to do so. And may I ask, did you manage to speak with your friend at Ben Venue last night, about their possible nomination as someone who we could second to work with your charity in Poland?"
"Yes, and no." she had replied. "We discussed the idea. But he hasn't given me his answer quite yet. I'm meeting him for lunch. And he'll let me know then."

Marie had arrived early at the restaurant.
She'd been sitting there already for almost thirty minutes when Stuart had texted her saying that he might be late.
Something had come up.
She'd replied, 'no problem.'
Until that moment, she had not once worried about Stuart, but it was then that it occurred to her for the first time that perhaps she was coming on too heavy.
Why had he really left her last night, after they had made love so beautifully?
Was she scaring him off?
Was he having second thoughts?
Was this, after all, going to prove too good to be true?

12.35

Lynch sat back at his desk and considered what he'd just learned.
Almost immediately a possible link between Maggie Sutherland and Hamish Hamilton popped into her mind. It was certainly feasible.

According to what they already knew, from what Daniel Gray had told Grant and McKenzie, and which he had since checked and corroborated, Maggie Sutherland had studied Psychology and Philosophy at St. Andrews University.

Maggie's first job had been at St. Andrews, working in one of the Union Bars. From that Lynch had learned Maggie's National Insurance Number.

With that number, and her personal details, the HMRC were then quickly able to provide the details for a series of employers for Maggie after she left university.

It turned out that she had become a Psychiatrist.

What Lynch had just now discovered, having called the Hospital which had been recorded by the HMRC as paying her first wage, was that while studying for further qualifications, her first job straight out of university was working in a hospital with soldiers suffering from Post-Traumatic Stress Disorder.

Bingo!

The time-frame was excellent and coincided with exactly the time Hamish Hamilton would have returned from serving in Afghanistan in early 1997.

Hamilton had been wounded whilst rescuing a friend. According to the Army file they'd been sent, he was sent back to the UK for further hospital treatment.

What happened if Maggie had helped treat him for PTSD, and they'd formed a relationship of some kind?

PC Lynch sat and stared at his notes.

Then he nodded to himself and walked across to speak with DCI McKenzie.

12.45

Ray Luck stood by the desks of the Blue Team, appraising their progress. They were doing well.

They had started with the number plate of the white van and gone back the full two weeks to when it had first been reported stolen. Ray's organisation, ACT, had significant resources at its disposal. Some in the UK and answerable to UK legislation. Some not so answerable, and not in the UK.

Technically, nothing his team did in the UK was against UK law or illegal. Anything which was, was not done in the UK.

What the Blue Team was doing now was above board, although the resources at their disposal were greater even than those available to the National Crime Agency.

On an ongoing basis, the systems available to ACT were able to hoover up all the data gathered by the Automatic Number Plate Recognition systems throughout the UK, and store it for at least six months in vast server arrays buried deep under the ground in air-conditioned bunkers.

The cameras of the ANPR system were able to examine the number plate of any car that passed by underneath one of its cameras, and then identify the car, its owners, and process any details recorded against that number plate. For example, was it stolen, had the owner paid its car tax, or did it belong to a Subject of Interest being investigated or followed by any of the UK law enforcement agencies?

In this case, the Blue Team had simply typed in the number plate and waited for the system to do its work and tell them what it found.

In the old days, the system would spew out a vast list of undecipherable data, which would take a police officer days or weeks to go through and understand.

Nowadays, complex data analytics were able to interrogate the data, find patterns amongst that data, and then draw pretty pictures, maps, or charts and project them up onto the overhead screens.

In this case, when the data first started populating the screens above their desks, the Blue Team were immediately able to see that there were several distinct clusters showing where White Van had been spotted in the past few weeks. Two of those clusters were of particular interest.

One was close to the old Portobello High School in Edinburgh in Scotland. This was not a great surprise, since it was suspected that the van had been used to deliver the murder victims to the school where they were imprisoned and then killed.

The second cluster of sightings appeared as white lines going back and forward on a map of the roads south east of Edinburgh along the roads between Edinburgh and North Berwick.

What was of particular interest to the team was the fact that the lines which connected where White Van had been spotted seemed to come to an abrupt end on the same spot on a long stretch of road south east of Gullane.

At first this puzzled the team.

It could indicate that White Van was being parked on the road somewhere, and could indicate a possible location for where the subject, or driver of White Van, was living.

However, when one of the Blue Team suggested that they should look at Google Maps to see what was there, they found only a clump of trees and a small patch of gravel.

At that point another member of the Blue Team suggested using CCTV feeds from a nearby garage a mile further down the road and to look for any similar white vans seen passing through that stretch of road at similar times to those when White Van had disappeared from the ANPR feeds.

The result was interesting.

In almost every case they checked they found that about twenty minutes after White Van had disappeared from the ANPR system going south-east or twenty minutes before it first appears heading towards Edinburgh, a similar white van had passed the garage, but with a different number plate.

"Clever bastard," one of the analysts had announced, as he realised what was happening. "The driver is passing the garage en route to or heading back from Edinburgh, then pulling into the clump of trees, and changing the number plates on the van before carrying on down the road."

"Yep, he's protecting his den." Another member of the Green team had agreed.

Even more interesting was when they ran a check on the other new number plate, they found that it belonged to a car that had reported its number plates stolen, although the owner still had the car. "Clever," the analyst mused. "Everyone would assume it was just kids that had stolen the number plates, and no one would be taking any real action to track them. The police have got better things to do."

When they ran the new number plate through the ANPR system, they found that they had records of the White Van driving further up and down the road towards North Berwick, but somewhere along that road it disappeared off the screen.

This time however, when they repeated the same trick, they found it brought no new answers. The nearest CCTV camera on the road was on the other side of North Berwick, miles away, and White Van never showed up again.

The van also never showed up on the cameras on the roads into North Berwick.

The team then concluded that White Van had taken a turn down a side road either into the countryside inland or in the other direction towards the coast roads.

A quick scan of the ANPR showed that there was practically no CCTV or ANPR coverage for that part of the world once you left the main road.

Which meant that the van had effectively disappeared into an area covering hundreds of square miles.

They'd learned something, but not enough to win the cookie-jar full of £5 notes.

The Green Team however was also doing quite well.

They had started with ANPR and upon finding the two clusters of sightings, as the Blue Team had done too, they had immediately chosen the tactic of instructing Bloodhound to sniff out their Subject of Interest.

Although the ACT team were now getting used to its capability, every time they used the Bloodhound system, they still couldn't help but be impressed by how much better their capability was than the Zeus system which the NCA and national cyber teams were stuck with using. The Bloodhound system could best be described as Zeus on steroids. Like Zeus, its tiny little sister, Bloodhound was a facial recognition system, but it used a digital array of quantum processors about twenty times more powerful than Zeus, and was powered by a self-learning AI algorithm. Whereas Zeus could take hours to go through its databases and pull up all the matches to the digital map created from a human facial image, and often got it wrong to boot, Boodhound seldom made mistakes and could trawl through the databases in about a fifth of the time.

What's more, the ACT databases went back further than the NCA databases. Because ACT was not based entirely in the UK, it was able to store more data, for longer.

Which meant that instead of trying to find out where a person was last week, they could dig down historically through all their image databases and establish almost exactly where the person had been seen not just last month, but up to two years ago, when the system first started collecting and storing data.

The only caveat they applied to working with Bloodhound was that when they were in a hurry, the longer they asked Bloodhound to search backwards in time, the longer it took to find anything.

The best practice was always to first see what you could find as close to the original time of an incident, and then to work backwards from there.

Not everyone was able to use the system. Yet. One day it would turn the world of fighting crime upside down, but for now, only ACT had access to it.

Starting with the cluster of ANPR recordings for the first number plate of White Van, the Green Team had told BloodHound to show them wherever the aged facial images of Hamish Hamilton could be found in a period going back three weeks.

Five minutes later, they had a list of thirty sightings.

It wasn't much, but as they started to look through what BloodHound had found, they realised that a lot of the time, the Subject of Interest, or the SoI, as they normally called their suspects, was routinely walking around or wearing a hoodie or baseball cap to cover or shade his face.

Scanning through the sightings they found them to be fairly random, not belonging to any particular pattern and not revealing anything in particular.

Knowing that a prerogative for them was to find an identity for the SoI, they decided to filter down the sightings to places where the SoI might choose to make a purchase using a credit card.

The normal practice for this was to look at BloodHound sightings recorded on CCTV cameras within petrol stations, or in supermarkets, or betting shops.

Frustratingly, Bloodhound came back with six sightings of Hamilton being picked up in petrol stations, but in the first five they looked at, in each case, Hamish Hamilton was seen to pay for the petrol in cash.

The sixth image they looked at however, was different.

Bloodhound had identified a man with a face similar to Hamish Hamilton walking into a petrol station, recorded on CCTV video footage from a petrol station on the route heading south east out of Edinburgh towards North Berwick.

The man was seen to look at the papers on the shelves before approaching the kiosk to pay for his petrol.

His hoodie was up, but the CCTV camera still had a good enough view of the front of his face for Bloodhound to identify him.

As the man – Hamilton – turned towards the desk, the analyst watching the video feed saw him reach into his pocket and pull out a phone. The SoI looked at the screen of the phone and then touched the front of it to accept the call. He spoke to someone for a moment, then hung up, before placing the phone back inside his pocket.

"BINGO! SHOW ME THE MONEY! Show me the money!" the analyst jumped up from his seat and started to dance.

The others in the Green Team got up from their positions and walked across to Kyle, the analyst of the moment, and patted him on the back.

"Do it!" the team-lead laughed and watched as Kyle went to work.

First, after shaking his fingers and hands in the air, Kyle sat back down at his station and clicked on the icon on his desktop that opened up the program called Audirex.

Audirex was another of the wonder apps that those at ACT now found indispensable. As with CCTV and facial recognition images, the massive server farms under the auspices of ACT were also able to collect and store almost a year's worth of data downloaded to them from all the national Communications Service Providers, which they mostly nicknamed the CSPs. The data from the CSPs provided them with everything they needed to know about phone calls made across their networks, both from mobile or fixed landlines.

If an analyst provided Audirex with a telephone number, the system would tell him who the phone belonged to, who that person had called in the past year, and who had called that person, all with a whole host of metadata describing those calls. In combination with another system, it could also tell you what IP activity took place on that phone, for example, it could tell you what websites the phone's user had visited, or which social media sites they were active on and what they had said on any forums. It could also provide an analyst with insight into any messages that had been passed back and forward via that phone.

If the analyst didn't know the phone number, but knew a location, Audirex would listen to all the calls that had been made in that area at that time, and by triangulating the signals from all the different phone masts, it could provide the analysts with a list of all the phone numbers of phones active in that area at that time.

If you didn't know their identity, it couldn't tell you exactly which one belonged to the SoI, but you would know that at least one of them did.

In the case of the petrol station, Kyle soon discovered that there were one hundred and twenty-six phones active within an area of eighty-six square metres around the petrol station.

Kyle was disappointed, but not surprised. His mood sobered slightly, and the others in his team returned to their stations.

Sometimes they got lucky and only found one or two phones, but the location and time that Kyle had given Audirex was in the middle of the afternoon, and on a busy main road with lots of passing cars.

Nevertheless, Kyle was not despondent.

One of those phones on the list belonged to the SoI.

He just had to find out which one.

Looking over at the clock on the wall, he noted the time.

Only fifteen minutes had passed since the challenge had been kicked off.

He saved the list of phone numbers on his system and logged the details of what they represented and then went back to work.

He knew exactly what to do next.

Chapter 51

Wednesday
Fettes Row Cyber & Comms Unit
12.50

Dean sat beside the cyber team in Fettes Row, totally impressed by the capability and expertise which they possessed. These guys were sharp. They knew their stuff.

As soon as they had been given their brief, they had started to search for and find CCTV feeds for the area around the port in Oban where the ferry had come in.

Within minutes the map on the computer screen had located all possible CCTV feeds which they had access to – an increasing number of CCTV feeds were now digital, and online, and often the NCA had direct taps into the systems, or were able to access the servers where the video from the cameras had been stored.

Not all CCTV feeds were yet connected to the system, which meant that as Dean had done in Leith, you still often had to trudge around the streets looking for shops and private cameras which might pick up images of SoIs passing by. However, the official ones run by the councils, police or military were increasingly all included.

The team in the cyber centre in Fettes soon had a number of screens showing CCTV footage of people coming off the boat and streaming into the streets nearby, most of them in cars that rolled off the ferry and soon headed out of Oban to other destinations.

Several bicycles came off the ferry in quick succession when the doors came down.

One of them was Hamish Hamilton, easily recognised by the clothes and training shoes he was wearing.

The team followed the bicycle as it headed through the gates of the ferry terminal and tracked the cyclist as he went from one street to another.

They followed him for what would have been fifteen minutes in real-time, but only minutes when fast-forwarded on the screen, from one camera to another.

Eventually, on the outskirts of Oban they struck pay dirt.

The cyclist drew up to a parking area on the left of the street heading out of town, behind a large red Ford estate hatchback.

They watched him open the back of the car, put the bicycle into the back of the car, and then get into the car and drive off.

A red box automatically appeared around the number plate at the back of the car, and a drop-down box appeared on the right of the screen, which soon populated with details of the car from the DVLA.

It was a rental car from one of the top rental firms.

Within seconds, one of the analysts working the data feeds had opened up a direct link to the database of the rental firm and was formally requesting information on the car which had been identified from the rental company. The analyst also provided details of the warrant which had been organised by DCS Wilkinson and signed by the Home Secretary in the past thirty minutes. The warrant gave UK law enforcement agencies the requisite permission to access numerous databases and request information from partners with respect to their named Subjects of Interest.

Once the warrant details had been entered into the system, cooperation from the rental agency was swift.

In took only a few minutes for the digital interface to the rental agency to provide details of where the car had been hired from, the name of the driver, the address of the driver, a mobile number for the driver, his age, date of birth, a copy of his driving licence, and his credit card.

Dean's heart began to thump faster and faster.

This was it.

They'd done it!

Eureka!

"Hang on a second," the analyst cautioned him. "Before you get too excited, we need to verify the details."

"What do you mean?" Dean asked.

"Watch the green box on that screen. Keep an eye on it... " the analyst directed, pointing to one of the large monitors on the desk. "If it stays empty, you can celebrate."

Dean didn't understand, but his eyes stayed glued to the green box.

Fifteen seconds passed, then text began to stream into the box.

"Sorry,... but it's a stolen identity. Very professionally done, but as you can see the credit card was cloned about two months ago. The driver's licence and everything else is fake. We see this a lot now." The analyst pushed back in his chair and swore.

"Shit... and worst of all, if you look at that, it tells us that the phone is a burner. No details. A SIM card bought in Tesco. For cash."

"So, what, we get nothing from this? No intelligence at all?"

"A little. We have the number. And even though it's a burner, we may be able to do something with it. Keith, can your pals in ACT do anything with that?"

The analyst pushed back in his chair and looked over at his colleague Keith. Keith was nodding, but already passing the details from what they'd learned from the hire car over to his colleagues in London.

"What now then?" Dean asked.

"Now we try to track the rental car back to where he drops it off. Then see if we can follow him on CCTV and find out where his real car is, and try to get the plate number of that. This guy's a pro. He's not going to drive the rental car home and park it outside his house. He may even dump it somewhere without returning it, but I doubt that. Even though he's got a false identify, I don't think he'll want to draw any undue attention to himself, by having the rental company report a theft. Personally I wouldn't get my hopes up on this, but you never know. We should still do the plod work."

Dean nodded.

"He only has to make one mistake, and we might have him."

The analyst laughed.

"Too bloody right!" he agreed. "It doesn't matter how clever these bastards think they are. It only takes one mistake and we'll nail them hard!"

12.55

McKenzie finished the Greggs sausage roll and wiped the corners of his mouth with the white paper napkin provided.

He felt guilty, and in his imagination he could hear Fiona's voice telling him off for eating such rubbish. *"That stuff just clogs up your arteries and Little One will need a Dad all his life, not just until you drop dead with a heart-attack."*

She was right, he knew, and he just wished she was here now to tell him off in person.

He promised himself then and there, that when he brought her home with Little One later that day, he would give up Greggs sausage rolls on the spot.

He felt a message arrive on his phone and he pulled it out of his pocket.

A voice message. Dial 121.

Licking the rest of the grease from his finger, he tapped in '121' and prepared to listen.

"You have one voice message, left today at 00.56 a.m. The caller withheld their ID."

McKenzie instantly recognised the voice after the first syllable and a cold shiver shot down his spine. He immediately tensed in anticipation of what was to come.

An evil, computerised, deep voice.

"With No.4 out the way, I wonder what will happen today?
Hint: it's not long to go until we reach five,
At which point GasBag will no longer be alive."

McKenzie's hands began to shake. The room began to spin, and he found himself struggling to breathe. His heart was beating wildly.

Breath. Take long. DEEP. Breathes.
Focus. Breath. Focus.
Find. The BASTARD. The **BASTARD!**
Focus.
Breath.
Another deep breath.

Gradually the room slowed down, and the world began to stop moving.

His heart started to beat slower. More steadily.

A few minutes later he was able to think clearly again.

He listened to the message once more, and then forwarded it to Ray Luck at ACT.

McKenzie knew that theoretically he should now inform DCS Wilkinson, but he had no intention of doing so.

He'd spoken to Luck at twelve o'clock. Luck was confident that they were making great progress and that it was a matter of hours, not days, before they would track Hamish Hamilton down.

McKenzie dialled Ray's number.

"I just finished listening to it," Ray said, without any formalities. "So, you reckon we only have until five o'clock?"

"That's what it looks like," McKenzie admitted.

"Okay, I'll tell the team to pull out all the stops. We need a name and address in the next hour if we're going to be able to arrange a rescue."

"He may not be holding her at his home. That would be unlikely."

"True, but let's cross that bridge when we come to it, DCI McKenzie."

Then Ray hung up.

Henderson's Restaurant.
Edinburgh
13.00

Marie was smiling again.

Stuart had just walked into the restaurant carrying the biggest bouquet of flowers she'd ever seen, and she couldn't help but notice that everyone was turning their heads as he walked past them.

"For me?" she asked, hopefully.

"For you." He offered them to her with both hands. "And I'm sorry. For leaving you last night, when I had to go. And for being late just now."

It was just then that Marie saw the big scratch on Stuart's face.

"How did that happen?" she asked, reaching out to stroke it as he sat down beside her and kissed her. Rather passionately. Full on the lips.

"The scratch? Oh, it's nothing. I went to the gym first thing this morning, and I did some sparring with my coach."

"I didn't know you could box?" she asked.

"There's a lot you don't know about me, Marie. Not all of it good. But with you beside me I hope to put my bad boy days behind me and turn over a new leaf."

"Does that mean you've decided to come with me to Poland and work for your company there with our charity?"

"If you'll let me?"

"Stuart, yes. Definitely! Can I tell your company the good news?"

"Yes. By the way, did you get that cheque they promised you?"

"No. Not yet. But they promised that they'd give it to me this evening. By the way, are you free this evening? Ben Venue Capital Assets is going to introduce me to the First Minister of Scotland, and she's going to present me with a cheque tonight. They asked me to invite my other half."

"You want me to be your other half?"

"*Please*?"

"I don't know. Meeting the First Minister. I don't know if that's my scene..."

"Don't be shy, I'll hold your hand!"

He laughed.

"I'm sorry, I'll be tied up with meetings until after six. I've got something happening then. I don't know if I can get out of it."

"It's not till six-thirty." She said, and paused. "Please come. But I'll understand if it's short notice, and you've other things to do."

Stuart looked deeply into her eyes.

"I'll tell you what. I'll try to be there. If I can, I promise I will, but if I can't, then please don't be upset with me. What would I have to wear, anyway?"

"You'd be meeting the top person in Scotland. Smart! Dess smart!"

"I've already met the top person in Scotland," he said, truthfully, and kissed Marie. "And I made love to her last night. Twice." He whispered in her ear.

Marie blushed. Then after sniffing the flowers and putting them down on the bench seat beside her, she looked at Stuart, quite seriously.

"I've been wanting to ask you. Is this too fast for you? I'm not scaring you away, am I?"

"First of all, Marie, it would take a lot to scare me. And second, my only regret so far, is that this didn't happen twenty years ago. This... ," he said, "is just amazing."

He kissed her then. Long and passionately.

When he pulled back, it took a moment for Marie to be able to open her eyes.

Almost as if she'd been hypnotised.

For a moment, she was speechless.

Then she said one word.

"Wow!"

Chapter 52

Wednesday
ACT
London Bunker
Room 2
13.05

Ray looked at the clock.
Several hours had already passed.
Things had not been progressing as fast as he'd hoped for.
The SoI, Hamish Hamilton, was obviously very clever at what he was doing, and seemed to have covered many of his bases.
Ray knew that if he had twenty-four hours, Hamish Hamilton would have no chance.
With the technology now at his disposal, no human being could hide any more. It was always just a matter of time. Normally minutes. Seldom hours.
Time was not on their side, however. It seemed that from the warning just received it would all be over by five o'clock this afternoon.
There were three teams in the room today. The Green Team, The Blue Team, and The Red Team.
He summoned them all together.
"Okay, things have changed. We have less than four hours before we're rescuing a corpse. Forget the competition between you. From now on, you're talking to each other. One person from each team is keeping the other teams aware of what you've each got or have found. I want cooperation. If we find Mrs McKenzie and bring her home alive, I'll treble what's in the pot, and we'll all get drunk tonight. Okay? Good. Make it happen!"

Hannah from the Red Team considered the latest news. The number of anchors had just increased. Their team-member in Edinburgh had passed down the information they'd found from the rental company.
She knew, as did other members of ACT, that there were two ways of going about this now.
The SoI had started committing a series of murders in the past week. He'd probably been planning it for a while. As a result, it was likely that most of the subterfuge he was using to cover his identity and tracks was probably recent, intended for the time during which he was committing the murders.
Hannah knew that if she went back in time far enough, she would be able to find a period when the SoI would most likely have been acting normally, just being himself. At that point he would probably have had nothing to hide. He'd be driving his own car. Making calls on his own mobile. Living in his own flat or house. If so, they would be able to track him down. However, going back in time would take longer. And there was no guarantee how far they would have to go back.

They would be able to do it, no doubt, but could they do it in the next few hours? She didn't know.

On the other hand, if Hannah and the others started 'pairing', then they may come up with the answer they needed sooner by analysing more recent data.

Pairing was basic training for those in ACT. It was based upon the basic principle that when people started committing crimes, criminals in the digital age mostly now started to use burners - pre-paid mobile phones which they could use during a crime and then throw away afterwards. However, almost all criminals still kept their own private phone. The cleverest ones didn't carry their private phones with them when they used a burner. But most criminals didn't know that modern technology enabled the law enforcement agencies to find and track a mobile phone even if the phone was switched off and the battery was taken out. Most just switched it off and didn't use it. Sometimes they didn't even switch it off.

This meant that when the law enforcement agencies were able to detect a burner on an SoI, they mostly also found a second mobile number, sometimes even a third, belonging to a second phone or third phone which the criminal was carrying.

If you knew the locations where criminals were operating, and you could get the CSPs to identify all the numbers for all the phones in that area, then simply by comparing the lists of phones detected in each area, and then finding which phones were also appearing in the other areas, would the analysts be able to determine which phones were owned by the criminal.

When Hannah had first been trained on it, she'd found it a little confusing, but as soon as she started to work it in practice, she'd understood it completely.

And now, looking for Hamish Hamilton, the principle should, *in principle*, help them find what they needed.

In principle.

The only way to find out if it would work here, was to try.

Glancing across at Kyle, she saw that he was already hard at work. Although Ray had said the competition was over, if anyone was going to beat her to the answer, it would be him.

First of all, she took note of the physical location that Hamish Hamilton had rented the car from which he had then subsequently driven to Oban and then parked, before offloading a bicycle. From the information that the rental firm had made available to DI Dean in Edinburgh, Hannah then noted the time that he had signed the document in the office. She then put the time and location into Audirex and waited for it to give her a list of all the mobile phones active in the area at that time.

There were about ninety numbers on the list.

Hannah then took the location of the caravan from where Fiona McKenzie had been abducted, as well as the time the neighbour had told the police that they had heard a commotion coming from the caravan. She put both into Audirex.

A few minutes later, she was sent a list of twenty mobile numbers.

Hannah then took both lists, copied them and dropped them into another app which compared the lists and pulled out any numbers which appeared in both of the lists.

There were two numbers on the list. She called them 'A' and 'B'.

One of them was the number DI Dean had learned about from the official application form for the rental car. The other one was a new number.

Maintaining her momentum, she ran the location of the original petrol station where the SoI had been seen receiving a phone call, and she generated the list of phone numbers again.

She then copied that list of numbers and compared it with the list of numbers from the car rental firm. This comparison generated two numbers as well. One of the numbers was the one found originally in the rental firm application by DI Dean, but the other was a new one. She called them 'A' and 'C'.

Lastly Hannah then took the list of all the numbers found at both the Caravan and the Petrol station and dropped them into the computer app which compared them and she found that two numbers popped up. She already knew both of these numbers. They were 'B' and 'C'.

From this work, Hannah had found that Hamish Hamilton had at least three phones. She knew that he was the person carrying those phones and that he had two of them at each of the places he visited. What she didn't yet know was the name he had used on the records as the owner of those phones, or the address he had used on the mobile phone service application forms.

DI Dean had already got the details of the owner of phone 'A', but as of yet she knew nothing about the identity recorded against the ownership or mobile phone service subscriptions for phones 'B' and 'C'.

She didn't have long to wait.

Entering both numbers 'B' and 'C' into Audirex, she pushed back in her chair and crossed her fingers.

She only had a minute to wait, then Audirex answered her question.

Unfortunately, it turned out the 'C' belonged to a burner phone. There was no subscription associated with it with any telephone company. The number belonged to a pre-paid SIM Card which Hamish had bought over the counter in a supermarket.

'C' however, was a different kettle of fish altogether.

According to Audirex the phone belonged to a Neil Macbeth. He lived on a farm on the outside of a village about ten miles from North Berwick. The good news was, that unlike number 'A' which had turned out to belong to a stolen identity, Neil McBeth's name was not triggering any alerts. It could be the real deal!

Hannah was excited.

The news seemed really promising, but she was trained to remain calm in these circumstances and to also check the facts as much as she could.

Still smiling, she cast a glance across at Kyle.

He was smiling too, and already looking across at her.

"You look like the cat who's got the cream!" she teased him.

"So do you!"

She hesitated, then stood up and walked across to him.

"I've got something, and I'm just about to extend the search and see if I can ratify my findings with extra data. But given that the clock's ticking and someone's life is on the line… "

"You want to compare notes?" Kyle offered.

"Yep."

Kyle didn't hesitate.

"Pull up your chair and show me what you've got. I'll show you mine, if you show me yours!" he added, flirtatiously.

Hannah reached across and picked up her notebook and then grabbed the back of her chair and pulled it over.

"What basis did you use for your Audirex searches?" she asked.

"The first petrol station. Then I took the location of the clump of trees where he kept changing the number plates and I also took the bottom of Bath Road in Edinburgh and the time when the detective said the suspect put a note on his car."

Hannah nodded.

They were good choices.

"And what did you come up with? What numbers, and which identities?"

"I got one burner and another which I think is the SoI's main phone, which he was carrying at the bottom of Bath Road."

He pointed to his screen showing Hannah the name of the man who, according to a subscription to T-Mobile, owned the second phone which had come up at several of the locations Kyle had investigated.

Hannah took one look and did a fist-pump in the air.

"YESSSSS!" she exclaimed loudly. "Same guy! I've got him too. Neil McBeth. From just outside of North Berwick!"

Kyle took a quick look at her notes, and she explained her logic, and he confirmed it was all good.

He stood and hi-fived her, and they turned to go find Ray Luck.

There was no need.

He was standing right behind them, and they hadn't even noticed.

"Good work." Ray nodded, smiling. "But before we go absolutely crazy, I want you to do two more things. Kyle, take the number you've got for McBeth's phone, and see if it's the same one that we saw being called at the petrol station on the CCTV. Check the phone records from T-Mobile. If it's the same phone that we saw being used at the same time we logged it on the CCTV, then see if you can get the telephone number of the person who called him. Then do a search on Audirex and see what we can learn about the person who called him. Perhaps we cold-call them and see if we can learn anything about McBeth without alerting or alarming him. Second, take the number for McBeth, go back a week in time on Audirex, and see what it can tell us about all the locations the phone was in that week. Try to build up a pattern of life for Neil McBeth. Can it tell us where he works? Where he hangs out in his spare time? And can it confirm that during the night, the phone is stationary at the same address that is recorded on his subscription contract?"

"Hannah? Take another three locations… Say, the flat in Leith where the first note was put on DCI McKenzie's car, and Mark McRae's house, and then perhaps also the place where the burnt-out white van was found. Run the number for Mcbeth through Audirex and see if the phone was ever recorded as being present at those addresses. Let's just do a little more homework to try to confirm this is really the guy, and that we do know where he lives, before we send the cavalry in and try to find Mrs McKenzie. Agreed?"

They both nodded.

And jumped to it.

Incident Room
Operation Blue Building
13.10

The atmosphere in the Incident Room was buzzing.

After days of continuously being on the back-foot, now at last, progress was being made. And rapidly.

After Lynch had told McKenzie about a possible connection finally being made between Maggie Sutherland and Hamish Hamilton, McKenzie had immediately requested him to try to get hold of Hamish's medical notes.

It was surprisingly easy: now they had his national insurance number from the HMRC for the pay he'd received at the army, Dean had managed to get a colleague in ACT in Indian to hack into the NHS medical database and access Hamilton's online medical records. They confirmed that he had been treated for PTSD at the same hospital that Maggie Sutherland had worked. It didn't connect them directly, but it was the next best thing.

Whilst this was happening, McKenzie had asked Anderson to find out what they could about Maggie Sutherland's career.

It seemed that everyone was now turning to Dean, and that he had quickly become the most popular person in the team.

Anderson had simply asked Dean to talk to his new best friends in ACT, and see what they could find out about Maggie.

It only took them about ten minutes to pull records from the HMRC, her insurance company, the Home Office, and the Passport Office, to find out that after about five years working, she had applied for a working visa to Australia, got insurance and gone to work in Perth.

She'd been there for about two years, before coming home.

Anderson was impressed.

The guys in ACT knew exactly what they were doing. Without even asking for it, they had produced what could only be described as a mini-dossier on Maggie Sutherland.

There was one single fact that interested the Sergeant, however.

On the passport form to apply for the working visa, she'd had to state the name of a sponsor in Australia, and the address of where she would stay.

It was a very easy name to remember.

It was a good Scottish name.

Neil McBeth.

One third and very relevant fact had come back from the forensics team.

It was the analysis of the dirt that was found entombed within the melted rubber of the tyre on the burnt-out White Van.

According to the report, an exact location of where the dirt came from could not be determined in such a short period of time. However, this much was possible at this stage: it was soil from a farm from the east Coast of Scotland, near the sea. It contained traces of fertilisers, minerals and tiny pieces of volcanic rock commonly found near areas of volcanic activity, as well as sea-salt and sand possibly blown in on the air.

If the forensics team were to hazard a guess at a more exact location, they would suggest somewhere near North Berwick.

Chapter 53

Wednesday
A Secure Conference Call
between
Incident Room Operation Blue Building, Fettes Row & ACT London
13.30

"Thank you all for joining me. And thank you all for the amazing work you're all doing. This is actually probably a first for us all. The first time we've got ACT and the Fettes Cyber Team hooked up to a video conference call with a Police Scotland incident room briefing." McKenzie greeted everyone who had joined the video conference call.

There were two large monitor screens on the desk in front of him: one projecting a view of DI Dean and two others in the Fettes Row cyber room, and another with Ray Luck. Both of the screens had video-conferencing cameras attached to the top of them. The incident room itself was full of the rest of McKenzie's team. Including Mather who had come in early to help.

"Things have been moving so fast that I think we first need to get everyone up to speed. So, shall I recap the situation, and what we know, and then we can move on to deciding a course of action?"

McKenzie nodded at the cameras on the large monitors. He was not very comfortable with the technology, and hadn't really used it much.

"First of all, let's note the time. It's one thirty GMT. We've reason to believe that by five o'clock the killer, who we believe to be Hamish Hamilton, will have killed his latest abductee. That abductee, is my wife, Fiona McKenzie." McKenzie paused, and swallowed hard. "To avoid confusion, the killer refers to her as GasBag, and he seems to be following the plot of a book – Remember Me? – which details how all his victims to date have died. Or near enough."

"Moving on, we suspect that Hamilton has changed his name, or is at least operating under a pseudonym since he returned from living in Australia. For the past few hours our new-found friends in ACT and Fettes Row have been helping us to track down that pseudonym and also to establish where Hamilton may currently be living or hiding. They've done an outstanding job."

"To cut a long story short, we've established that Hamish Hamilton is now using the name Neil McBeth. We don't know if that's the name he's living with, or just using as a cover. We've got an address for him several miles north-west of North Berwick. It's a farm. CCTV and ANPR footage show that he's been driving back and forward from Edinburgh down the A1 to somewhere very close to the farm, where he disappears off down a side-road. We also have confirmation that the soil found in the tyre that partially survived the fire of Hamilton's old van, came from an area that would meet that description. We also know that it's very likely that Maggie treated Hamish Hamilton for PTSD, and that she subsequently went to live in Australia for a while and that she listed Neil McBeth as being her sponsor at that time, and that she named his house in Australia as her residence."

Some of the team in the incident room hadn't heard all of this yet, and were furiously copying down notes and smiling: this was fantastic progress!

"Before we can move on though I have two questions, which I've been told our guests on the screens may already have answers for. I'll ask the questions for the benefit of everyone, and then hand over first to Fettes and then to ACT to explain what they've found."

McKenzie looked at the screen which showed the Fettes team.

"My question is this: what do we know about Neil McBeth? Is it a made-up name? Why Neil McBeth?"

The man on the screen to the left of Dean answered.

"We ran a check on Neil McBeth. He's a real person. Active credit cards, active NI number, active council tax payer. He's got an active driving licence and a job. And this is the photograph on his driver's licence... " The man held up a facsimile of a driver's licence and held it just in front of the camera lens on the screen so that everyone on the other side of the connection could see it. It was Hamish Hamilton.

"However," he continued, "and this is the interesting part. The identity also flagged up another person with that name. He was in the army, and apparently served in the same regiment as Hamish Hamilton in Afghanistan. According to the army records, however, Neil McBeth went missing in Afghanistan. He never came home. We also found out that Neil McBeth was an only child whose parents died in a car crash while Neil was in Afghanistan."

"We have one last piece of information which you may be interested in at this time... " the man teased them.

"Go for it," McKenzie rewarded him with the theatrics Fettes obviously craved.

"The parents of Neil McBeth were farmers. And their farm is not far from North Berwick. In fact, it's the same address that appears on Neil McBeth's current driver's license."

McKenzie clapped his hands together.

"Brilliant. Great job. So, that's basically it then. That's the answer. Hamish Hamilton goes to live in Australia to start a new life and to forget his old, unhappy childhood. He wants to start afresh. He assumes the name of someone who he served with in Afghanistan and who McBeth knows is so far only declared missing in action but not yet confirmed dead. Except McBeth knows he's dead. He may have been a close friend, we don't know, but certainly close enough to know that McBeth's parents were dead, and he was an only child. McBeth then somehow manages to convince everyone that he's the son, now living in Australia. Before he went to Australia, Hamilton was treated for PTSD. It's likely that's when he met Maggie Sutherland. After Hamilton goes to Australia, Maggie Sutherland comes to live with him. Then comes back to the UK. A while later Hamilton comes back to Scotland too, but now under the name of Neil McBeth. Assuming the role of the prodigal son now returned, he goes to live in Neil McBeth's house and takes on the rest of his identity. Somehow, he gets away with it."

McKenzie strolled the floor in front of the screens, thinking aloud.

"Okay, so we still don't know the extent of the relationship between Maggie Sutherland and Hamish-stroke-Neil McBeth, but we have to assume it was quite close. But we also know that he never went to her funeral, so possibly they fell out, maybe in Australia which explains why she came back before him. Although we don't know that for sure. Maybe they returned together? But from what Fettes says... , sorry, your name?"

"PC Menzies, Guv."

"But from what PC Menzies has just said, it sounds like she came home alone, and Hamilton aka McBeth followed her later. There could be a relationship between them that we don't know about, and my guess is there was. Otherwise, why the hell is he killing everyone just like Maggie described, and why was the book dedicated to him?"

He picked up a glass of water and took a drink.

"Okay, over to you Ray. My last question is, do we know where McBeth is *now*?"

"From what we can tell, he's at the farm near North Berwick. There're not many mobile masts in that part of the world, but the triangulation we have from the nearest ones shows us that his phone is somewhere in the area that the farm buildings occupy. Give or take a couple of hundred metres. It would also appear that he drove home around six a.m. this morning, and has been there ever since."

McKenzie smiled. Broadly.

"Thank you, Mr Luck. Thank you very much." McKenzie clapped his hands in front of the camera. "Oh... sorry, there's still one thing, Ray. Please can you ask someone to monitor his phones and let us know if any of his phone numbers move away from the farm?"

"Absolutely. It goes without saying, DCI McKenzie."

McKenzie turned to the team in his Incident Room.

"Okay, so it's now one-fifty. We've got roughly three hours left. Time is running out..."

McKenzie was just about to start discussing ideas with the team concerning what could happen next, and open the floor to ideas, when he felt his phone buzzing against his leg.

He quickly pulled it out of his pocket and checked the caller display. It was a voice message.

A cold feeling of dread swiftly permeated his senses.

Excusing himself from the meeting for a moment, he dialled 121.

As soon as the message began, he reached out to steady himself against the bannister on the stairs that linked the three different levels of the portacabins.

Fighting the urge to vomit, he closed his eyes and steeled himself.

> **"Isn't this fun! Now the count-down has begun!**
> **With two for the price of one!**
> **They're both going to die,**
> **Automatically blown sky-high,**
> **When the clock reaches five,**
> **Big and Little Gasbag will no longer be alive!"**

Leaning back against the wall, he felt very weak, and his legs were no longer able to support him. He slid slowly down the edge of the portacabin until he was sitting on the ground.

For a few minutes he rode out the wave of confusion and fear.
Then slowly he opened his eyes, and looked up at the sky.
It was blue. The sun was shining.
The world was still there.
Some birds flew overheard.
He pressed a few digits on his phone and listened to the message again.
Then again.
Getting angry.
Learning from the words, and exactly what was said.
Turning the threat into intelligence which he could use to save his wife's life.

He also knew that he was now on thin ground.
That was the second message he'd received from the 'kidnapper'. He should now really report them and hand over the case to the NCA.
His career would depend on it.

Or he could just pretend he hadn't heard them - 'yet'.

McKenzie stood up. He took several rapid deep breaths and swore several times in quick succession and then stepped back into the portacabin.

"Okay, team, sorry about that. But I also needed just a moment to myself. To think and to plan."
He took a few more breaths.
He could feel the adrenaline kicking in now.
His hands were shaking.
The anger was building.
The words of Hamish Hamilton echoed in his head,

"With two for the price of one!"

He closed his eyes again and blocked the sound of the metallic voice out of his head.
When he opened them, McKenzie looked around the room, briefly scanning the Video Screens.
Everyone was looking at him. Waiting.
They didn't have to wait long.

"Okay, things have just changed. We're no longer going to be on the back foot. It's now time to let the hunter become the hunted. And to get my wife and my child back... Safe, sound, alive, and in the next three hours! I have a plan. This is what we're going to do... "

Chapter 54

Wednesday
Two miles from Sea View Farm
North Berwick.
15.00

It had taken fifteen minutes to organise everything. It had then taken another forty-five minutes for everyone to drive down to the location close to Sea View Farm where they had selected to set up operations, and where they now believed that Hamish Hamilton was hiding at the old farm which once belonged to Neil McBeth.

They didn't yet know if Fiona was also there, but McKenzie knew time was running out. For both him and Hamish Hamilton.

But, if Hamilton had driven there first thing that morning after snatching Fiona from the caravan and had not left, the chances were that he also had Fiona there.

In some ways, it made sense.

It was a remote location, far from anywhere else.

The ideal place to hold a hostage.

McKenzie had left his car outside the portacabin in Portobello, hopefully giving the illusion to the tracker device that he and his team were still there.

He had also requested the use of the helicopter, but at the time it was on the west-coast near Arran.

It was now on its way, just in case it was needed to ferry Fiona straight to a hospital, and was due to arrive shortly.

The first part of McKenzie's plan was just about to come to fruition.

It was in fact, the only part of his plan. What they learned in the next fifteen minutes would determine what happened next. If anything.

"Is there a problem?" McKenzie asked, standing beside the two large drones which sat on the ground, with their handlers playing with their remote controls and occasionally bending over the drones and tweaking something or other.

"No, they're both ready to go. We're only going to send one up, though. The other's the backup."

When McKenzie had called Fettes to arrange everything he hadn't appreciated just how large the drone – or 'Remotely-Piloted Aircraft System' as he was politely informed by its handler – actually was.

The drone had two separate cameras, one optical and one fixed-mounted thermal imaging camera: one would give them high definition clear sight of what they could see normally, and the other would pick up any thermal images, potentially showing them anyone inside the farm buildings, depending on their construction.

They had already viewed images of the farm on Google Maps, but now they needed to see live detail. Was there a car there? If so, they could maybe get its number plate and then use ANPR or CCTV to track its movements earlier that morning and to see if they could identify any passengers. Although most likely, it would be a van, or a car with a large boot in which Fiona would have been hidden.

Was there activity on the ground they could see?

Would they be able to see Hamish Hamilton?

Or Fiona?

"We're ready," the drone's handler announced, stepping towards McKenzie.

"You can see everything the drone sees on the screen in the van. It's slightly larger, and everyone can watch that one together." The drone man continued.

"Will the people in the farm-house hear it?" McKenzie asked, having last minute nerves and wondering if the plan was going to work.

"I doubt it. We're initially going to be flying it really high until we get an idea of what we can see on the ground. If it's looking good, we can fly the RPAS down lower so we can get a better view with the thermal camera."

McKenzie nodded.

"Just be careful... we mustn't alert anyone we're watching."

The man nodded.

McKenzie felt a little guilty. A quick passing thought about grannies, eggs and sucking, came to mind. He hurried away to the van.

At the door, he turned and saw the drone steadily rise into the sky, tilt, and then head forward towards the farm.

The image on the screen was surprisingly detailed. And bright.

For now, it was zoomed out so they could see the geography passing by underneath as the drone headed towards its pre-programmed SatNav coordinates.

It only took a few minutes to get there, and suddenly it slowed, came to halt and hovered above the farmhouse.

The image on the screen then zoomed in slightly, now showing details of a large bungalow style farmhouse and several outbuildings surrounding a courtyard.

Everyone spent a moment checking for signs of life but found none.

"How do I tell the drone handler what to do next?" he asked one of the technicians sitting in front of the console in the van.

"Just close the door behind you, and speak aloud. The RPAS handler has headphones on now, and he can hear you."

McKenzie nodded.

"Okay, can you zoom in on the courtyard first please? What's that black stuff?"

As soon as they'd established there was no one visible on the ground, the next most obvious feature they were looking at was a large black mass in the courtyard, surrounded by several other black items around it.

The drone camera zoomed in.

As they were watching, the door to the cottage opened and a man stepped out, carrying some more black stuff. He dropped it on the ground and disappeared back out of sight.

"Shit... did he see us? Do you think he saw us?" McKenzie asked loudly.

The technician immediately reached up to one of several consoles in front of him on the wall of the van, and switched it on.

He then typed away on his keyboard and manipulated a command interface on the screen.

Suddenly the other screen jumped to life and they could see the recorded imagery of the man opening the door and stepping out.

They saw him drop the black material on the ground, and then turn around and walk straight back into the cottage without looking up.

"Nope. He didn't see us."

"Can you replay that and blow the image of his face up, and then print it or send it to me?"

"I can do both. No problem. What's your email address or phone number?"

"Never mind. Just print it off and give it to me. You can send it to me later."

As instructed, the technician enlarged the image of the man's face on the screen.

"Hamish Hamilton!" McKenzie shouted, alarming everyone else in the van.

Brown nodded.

"Yep. It looks like we've got him." She said. "But what's all this black stuff?"

"It looks like plastic sheeting," the operator said, zooming in as far as he could go. "Maybe the stuff you use to wrap haystacks in for the winter?"

McKenzie leaned forward, screwing his eyes up to get a better look.

The courtyard was littered with the stuff.

It only took a moment, but he suddenly realised what it was for.

His pulse started to race, and he forced himself to take several deep breaths.

"I know what he's doing." McKenzie said monotonically. "He's sealing off one of the rooms in the house. He's turning it into a big bag. And when he's finished, when he's sealed it all off, he's going to fill it up with gas!"

Brown exhaled loudly, and involuntarily raised her hands to her mouth. She looked across at McKenzie and shook her head.

McKenzie reached out and placed a hand on her shoulder.

"Elaine, don't worry. It's not going to happen." He reassured her.

He turned back to the technician and spoke loudly so the drone operator could hear him.

"Can you give me a thermal image of the inside of the house?"

"We'll try, but it depends on how well insulated the house is."

"Try."

The image on the screen changed, and now they could see a greyish ghost-like image of the structure of the building.

"THERE!" McKenzie shouted excitedly, pointing to a second image in the middle of one of the rooms. It was stationary, and from the angle the drone was looking down through the side of the cottage, they could see through the cold wall and discern a human form in a sitting position, with arms wrapped behind its back."

"She's probably tied to a chair. You just can't see the chair," the technician said.

The other image was standing on the side of the room, reaching up with outstretched arms.

"He may be carrying or trying to fix some more plastic sheeting to the wall. You just can't see the sheeting."

"And he can't see us either. The windows are probably covered over."

McKenzie looked at his watch.

It was three-twenty. One hour and forty minutes to go.

"Okay, resume a monitoring position higher up, and keep me informed of any sudden changes."

McKenzie opened the door and stepped out of the van.

He and Brown walked across to the head of the armed response unit who had travelled down from Edinburgh and joined them soon after McKenzie had arrived.

"How're the preparation's going?" McKenzie asked the lead officer, Sergeant Galbraith who had helped them out only a few days before in the tunnel at the school.

"Good. I've got ten officers in the team. Eight of the team are now almost in place at different places dotted around the farm. We're going to come in from all sides, making sure we've got all the exits covered, and ensuring maximum possibility to access the property undetected. We'll probably be set and ready to go in ten minutes?"

McKenzie looked nervously at his watch again. Only a few minutes had gone by since the last time he'd looked.

"Good, thanks." He said to Sergeant, almost absentmindedly. Something was beginning to bug him at the back of his mind.

A thought. Something. But McKenzie knew it could be important.

He thought back to what the last phone message had said.

> "**They're both going to die,**
> **Automatically blown sky-high,**
> **When the clock reaches five…**"

Then he realised what it was.

Hamilton was going to blow her up remotely. When the clock reached five.

"Elaine. Please. Over here a moment," he said, walking her away from the armed response unit.

"What is it, Guv. Are you okay?"

"Yes. Listen, and don't judge. Just listen. I got a message from Hamilton. About an hour ago."

Brown's face went blank.

"And what did it say, Guv?" she asked, excitedly.

McKenzie told her.

"The thing is. I think he's going to do this remotely."

"Which is good, because the moment he's leaves, we go in."

"Possibly." He said. "But it could also be bad. If he gets any wind of us being onto him, he'll blow her up immediately. And take us out too."

"Yes, but that's only if he does it remotely via a phone message or text, or phone signal. He may just do it the old-fashioned way with a clock or electronic timer… In which case we just rush in and disarm it quickly… "

"He could. But for some reason I don't think he will."

"Then if you think it's going to be a phone message, you've got no choice but to jam any mobile signals so that no message can get through to the detonator no matter how hard he tries."

"Or have the phone network switched off. That would work too!"

"Can you do that, Guv?"

"Yes. It's not easy. But it's been done before. My only worry is that it might take a while… and we haven't got much time."

"When is Hamilton going to leave?"

"How do I know? Maybe right at the last moment."

"Unless we can get him to leave earlier?"

"How?"

"I don't know. It was just a suggestion… "

McKenzie stared at her. Maybe it wasn't such a stupid idea after all.

"We've got another problem, too, though… " McKenzie carried on.

"Which is?"

"He's making a gas bag. When he sends the signal the bag of gas will blow up. If we go in too heavy-handed we might create a spark that ignites the gas."

"True, but I think we can get round that. But that's not what worries me most, Guv."

"So what does?"

"The gas. If we don't get in there quickly, Fiona won't be able to breathe. She'll be poisoned and die. And even if she doesn't, the baby might be harmed from breathing in the gas."

"Shit, I hadn't thought about that."

"And there can be no shooting. Maybe they can use rubber bullets, or tranquiliser darts, or something, I don't know. But no metal bullets. The heat of the bullets will ignite the gas and blow everything up."

McKenzie stared at Brown.

For a moment, he just carried on, staring at her, thinking furiously.

"You okay, Guv?"

"I've got an idea. It might work. It might not. But we're running out of time and we've got to do something."

"So what's the plan, Guv?"

"Like you just suggested, the way I see it, we've got to get Hamilton out of the building as soon as possible. That way maybe we can get in there and burst the bag and let the gas out before it reaches toxic or combustible levels."

"True, but I've got another idea Guv. Why don't we switch the gas off?"

"How?"

"Get the gas-board to switch off the whole area. Stop the supply."

"But Hamilton will notice it."

"Not if we time it right. We get him to leave the building. As soon as he does, we switch the gas off, block the cell network and go straight in as soon as he's clear. We have to do all three, just in case he's not using the gas from the taps. Maybe he's using canisters? Or maybe he's using some of the TNT he's stolen, and he's going to set that off with a signal from his mobile. Like I said, Guv, we have to do all three. The big question is how do we get him to leave the building and leave her alone? Do we just wait until he's ready, or do we force him out of there early? Maybe even *before* he's ready?"

"The latter, if possible." McKenzie decided. "And I think I may know how we can do it. Or do you think this sounds too crazy…? "

McKenzie told Brown his idea.

Chapter 55

Wednesday
Portobello High School
McKenzie's Car.
16.35

The helicopter had landed in the Figgate Park, and McKenzie and Brown had sprinted across the grass, up into the street and round to the front of the school.

McKenzie was scared.

Was it too late?

The helicopter had taken longer than McKenzie had expected to arrive, but he'd used the time while he'd waited to make all the necessary arrangements and ensure everything was in place.

McKenzie had been torn.

Every sinew in his body had cried out to him to stay and be there when the Tactical Team went in to the cottage, but McKenzie knew that his plan would only stand a chance of working if he was here now, back at the school, and in the car.

So, he'd left everyone else behind, hidden close to the farm and with strict instructions not to use weapons in the open, and not in the direction of the cottage.

However, McKenzie had made sure that Sergeant Galbraith and the rest of the Tactical Team were fully briefed as to the risks that Hamish Hamilton posed. They knew his sole intention at this time was to kill Fiona McKenzie and that he had already killed four others. Given that a major concern was that Hamilton would be intending to remotely detonate the gas explosion within the cottage, and that he would almost certainly trigger this immediately he suspected that he was being watched or had been discovered, it was decided that should he emerge from the cottage and obviously react in a way which suggested he knew he had been detected, then a Critical Shot was required. This would immediately destroy his brain stem and induce instant flaccid incapacitation, with the result his fingers would relax on any remote controls being held, and remove the danger of him sending any signals remotely to a detonator.

If, on the other hand, they did not believe that Hamish Hamilton had suspected anything, then they were to allow him to get into his car and drive away from the farm, thus allowing the Tactical Team to go in and rescue Fiona.

The rest of the plan was so far, touch wood, all going to plan – if you could call it a plan. McKenzie knew he was flying by the seat of his pants. Winging it. Making it up as he went along. But every time he closed his eyes and thought of Fiona and Little Bump, he knew he had no choice. This was the only plan.

If it worked, they all had a chance.

If it didn't...

The telephone companies had not been happy. McKenzie and his team didn't know how many phones Hammy Hamilton had. He could have one for each network, as far as they knew... so they'd had to switch them all off.

All of them.

He'd promised it would only be for thirty minutes. No more.

McKenzie had had to lie. He'd said it was part of Operation Crown. He'd sworn blindly that the drastic action was needed to stop the terrorist who was threatening to kill the Queen. He'd been careful with his words. But it was essentially true: whilst he'd been waiting, an important call had come through from the forensics team in Fettes. It had been confirmed that the TNT which McKenzie had sent over for analysis, was from the same type and batch which had been recovered from locations targeted by the terrorist threatening the Queen. So, McKenzie was telling the truth. What's more, McKenzie knew that this knowledge was explosive in its own right. As soon as he told DCS Wilkinson, the case would be taken off his hands and all the police and army in Scotland would descend on North Berwick and almost certainly, Hamish Hamilton would kill Fiona. For now, that news could wait.

He'd spun the same story to the gas company, instructing them to shut off all the gas supply in the area. They'd complained. Kicked back. But McKenzie didn't need a warrant to ask them to do it, and existing protocols and his authority were enough to make them comply.

The telephone company also had little choice but to agree.

They both agreed to switch off the local phone network and the gas supply instantly, as soon as McKenzie called them and gave them the command to do it.

"Stay by the phone. Wait for my call!" he commanded.

"Any movement with Hamilton?" McKenzie checked with the technician in the van in North Berwick, who now also had Wishart and Anderson in the van with him.

"Nothing significant yet. We think we know where his car is now. It's in the outbuilding across the square from the house. He came out of the cottage about five minutes ago and was carrying a suitcase and a rucksack which he took into it. I think it's the garage. A few minutes ago, he came back across the square, picked up some more black plastic and disappeared back into the cottage. From what we can see with the thermal imaging, he's still working on making the room airtight to keep the gas in."

"And Fiona?"

"She's still in the chair in the middle of the room."

That part of the news was good.

She would still be alive. The gas hadn't been switched on yet.

McKenzie and Brown had rehearsed McKenzie's plan over and over again on the helicopter trip back to Edinburgh.

By the time they'd landed, they both knew what to do.

The only thing was they didn't know if it would work.

It was a bit far-fetched, but the plan was designed to play upon the frail mental state that Hamish Hamilton was obviously in just now. Not to mention that he must now be so tired that he was probably no longer capable of rational thought. He was probably only either functioning due to some drugs he was taking, or because of some incredible, overpowering emotional tie to Maggie Sutherland.

Which this plan was designed to exploit.

Put another way, McKenzie was going to fuck with Hamilton's brain.

It was time for McKenzie to take back control.

The Pentland Hills
16.37

Stuart stood at the top of the Pentland Hills, looking out over Edinburgh.
He hadn't felt stressed like this for years.
He'd needed to get away. To walk. To breathe. To think.
He felt a strange mixture of emotions. Excitement. Amazement. Awe. He had fallen head over heels in love with Marie, and it was, honestly, an incredible feeling. He was also in awe of her and amazed by everything she did, and had done.
His trip to Poland to find out more about her, her work, and her children had been an eye-opener.
That people like her existed was unbelievable. Selfless. Incredibly caring. So loving.
Before he had decided to invest in her, he'd needed to understand more about her and her work. In business, they would call it 'due diligence'. It wasn't spying. Just a normal business process.
He felt guilty however that he had not told her. Almost as if he had been intruding on her life.
And now he was scared.
At first, he'd thought that he could get away with it. Just give her money, spend time with her, visit her and work with her in Poland. Get to know her better. All without telling her who he really was.
It had been his idea to make a condition of the deal that someone from his company would have to spend time working alongside her to oversee activity and ensure proper allocation and spending of the funding.
That too could be excused as 'due diligence' or 'standard business process'.
It was, after all, a lot of money that was being spent, and it was perhaps a legitimate concern that when spending such vast sums in Eastern Europe, he should be worried about corruption. The gift he would give her could attract a lot of unscrupulous attention, and good oversight may need to be established both to make sure the money was spent properly and not stolen, and also to protect Marie from any dangerous people who may now be attracted to her. In Eastern Europe, the money could be a flame that might attract a lot of dangerous moths.
However, Stuart felt uncomfortable about it all.
The thought of telling Marie who he really was, scared him. She was a wonderful person, a *pure* person. He'd never met anyone like her before. Money and wealth meant nothing to her, except for its power to save the lives of others and transform them in a positive way.
Yet, not to tell her was even more wrong. Stuart could see the white lie turning into a huge lie, and deception on a massive scale.
At some point she would find out.
Or, if their relationship deepened, it would be based upon a lie, and at its very core, distrust.
He needed to tell her.

But Stuart was scared. He knew from experience what money did to people. It corrupted everyone. And everything.

It wouldn't corrupt Marie, that much he was sure.

But it would corrupt their relationship.

Destroy it.

And Stuart could not bear to lose her.

Not now.

Not after he'd finally found her.

Yet, he had no choice.

A relationship based upon lies was no relationship at all.

McKenzie's Car
Outside the Old Portobello High School
16.39

McKenzie opened his car door and sat down inside. He switched on the engine and started driving his car towards the bypass that would take him to Stirling.

A minute later, as agreed, Brown called him on his mobile.

"Elaine. How are you? Any news?"

"No. I can't seem to reach my wife. I've called her several times but her phone is not answering. I'm just leaving to drive up to Callander to find out if she's okay. I'm just worried that there might be a problem with the baby. I'm leaving you in charge. Can you please just check with PC Jordon on the status of things and call me straight back? Can you get the team together for the 5 o'clock meeting as normal and can you lead it? Apologise to everyone but I've got to go and see Fiona. And can you please tell everyone not to leave me any voice messages at the moment? The fault with the voicemail that Fettes told everyone about this morning is affecting me too. I haven't been able to listen to my voicemail all day. Fiona may have left me a message but I can't listen to it yet. Tell everyone that if anyone needs to speak to me, they have to keep calling me until they get through to me, okay?"

"Yes, Guv."

She then hung up.

McKenzie then waited for the text message.

It was a gamble. For what they were going to do next to work, they needed Hamish Hamilton to be listening to them.

Incident Room
The Old Portobello High School
16.40

Brown immediately called the Drone operator in the field several miles from the cottage in North Berwick.

It was good news.

"We've been watching him constantly on the Infra-red. The moment you started talking to McKenzie, we saw him stop what he was doing and walk across to the other side of the room and bend down. As if he was listening to something. Then a couple of seconds ago he stopped and went back to work again."

"Good. He's listening to us."

Brown hung up, her heart beating faster.

Typing away as fast as she could, she typed a message to McKenzie and sent it: "North Berwick confirms he's listening."

Then she called McKenzie straight back and played out the rest of the scene.

McKenzie's Car
En route to the bypass
16.41

"Guv, I just spoke to PC Jordan and DI Wishart. They've both been calling you and trying to get hold of you urgently. They've left you voice messages... "

"I told you, I can't get the voice messages just now."

"I know, Guv. I told them. Anyway, it's not good news. It's very bad. And weird. You asked DI Wishart to supervise the exhumation of Maggie Sutherland's body to check if she was murdered, and to establish if she really did commit suicide or not?"

"Yes."

"It happened this afternoon. About 1 p.m. They had to wait for the minister to be there, but he had a wedding. Anyway Guv, the things is, they got the coffin up, and they opened it. But it was empty. There was nobody inside. Just several bags of sand to weigh it down ... "

"What do you mean? What are you talking about, Elaine?"

"Guv. Maggie Sutherland's body was not in the coffin."

"Are you serious? So where's the body then?"

"That's the other thing, Guv. DI Wishart immediately contacted the Advanced Cyber Team in England and they used Maggie Sutherland's photograph and ran a scan using the new facial recognition system that's been implemented. Maggie Sutherland's face immediately came up. Hundreds of times. She's alive and well!"

McKenzie paused, adding a dramatic silence to the scene they were playing out. It was all made up. A dramatic storyline cooked up to get Hamish Hamilton's attention, and get him out of the cottage.

McKenzie pulled the car over to the side of the street and stopped.

He knew his car was also being tracked via the tracking bug, and the whole story had to tie in if it was to be credible.

"Sorry, Elaine, I just pulled over. So, what are you telling me? That Maggie Sutherland is alive and well? She faked her own death? And that she could be behind all the killings all this time? She'd hoodwinked us all? Made fools of us? The whole time it was her?"

"Possibly Guv."

"Shit...! " He exclaimed, adding extra colourful language, and a surprised tone of voice.

"So, where is she now and what's her name?"

"The cyber team have been tracking her for the past hour. Using the facial recognition system they got her new name from a driving licence that came up on the system and has her photograph on it. She's living in Balloch just north of Glasgow. She's using the name of Margaret Nowak. It's a fake polish identity. It literally means 'new Maggie!" She's taking the piss, Guv."

"I can't believe this." He paused. "Okay. I want you to get the cyber team to continue to monitor her. I want you to plan to get a team over to Balloch this evening. If the cyber team can confirm where she is, and can then tell us when she gets home using her mobile phone signals or local CCTV, then we'll get a warrant issued and wait until she's ready for bed and we know she's definitely there in her new house. What's the address?"

"48 Parkside Road, Balloch."

"Hang on, I'm just writing that down... 48 Parkside Road?...Thanks... Okay... Get the team over there for 9.30 p.m. Hopefully I'll be able to join you as soon as I've spoken to Fiona at the caravan or found out where she is."

"Yes, Guv."

McKenzie hung up.

He left it a moment more, and then called Fiona's mobile and left a voice message. Again, just for effect.

"Darling, it's me again. Where are you? Call me please. I'm worried. I'm coming up to the caravan. I'm on the way. I'll see you soon."

He then stepped out of the car and walked a few metres away before calling DI Wishart in North Berwick.

"Are you in the van with the drone technician?"

"Yes Guv."

"What's happening?"

"It looks like Hamilton has gone berserk... "

"Is Fiona okay?"

"Seems so Guv. He hasn't gone near her. He crossed the room again and bent down and was stationary for a few minutes. Then it looked like he was hitting the wall, or punching the air or something. Then he just stood there for a moment. Just staring. Then suddenly he started moving around the cottage really fast. He walked over to Fiona for a moment, then turned and walked to another room... and then came back and has been doing something to the door to the room Fiona is in... " She paused, "Hang on, Guv, he's just left the cottage. We're pulling the drone back up and away. Switching to visual. Zooming in. Okay, we've got him. He's looking really flustered, Guv. He's walking over to one of the outbuildings... he's gone inside. We've lost visual... "

McKenzie was pacing the road beside his car. He could tell from Wishart's voice that she was as nervous and excited as him.

"He's back, Guv. A car's reversing. It's in the courtyard... Guv, we've got a number plate."

"Track it. Get it straight over to ACT. Get them on it now!" McKenzie almost shouted.

"Will do, Guv... I'm passing my phone to Anderson."

Another moment of silence.

"Guv, Anderson here. He's out of the cottage. The car's started to drive down the driveway."

McKenzie glanced at his watch.

4. 51 p.m.

"He's clear?" Campbell asked.

"Two hundred metres away now! He's on a small dirt track, heading towards the main road."

"Murray, give the signal for DS McLeish to contact the telephone company and issue the agreed codeword, *now*. And tell Lynch to issue the codeword to the gas company too. Get them to switch off the phone network and the gas *immediately*!"

"Yes, Guv. Doing it now… "

McKenzie could hear Sergeant giving the instructions to the others in the van, who were both on open hotlines to the utility companies.

"I'm back, Guv. Hang on… McLeish is telling me they're saying it's done. And the gas is off too. Both done. I confirm they're both off, Guv!"

"Excellent. Now, give Galbraith the signal to go in with the Tactical Team now. *GO!*"

"Roger that, Guv."

McKenzie immediately hung up. He was so nervous, his hands were shaking. The plan had worked.

Hamish Hamilton had heard the news that Maggie Sutherland was still alive.

In his tired, sleep-deprived, exhausted state, the news must have come as a bombshell to him.

Whatever his relationship was with Maggie, it must have been significant.

Significant enough for him to kill four people, possibly five.

And discovering that she was alive, but that police were going to arrest her tonight, for the murders that *HE* was committing, for *her*, in *her* name, must have driven him to the point of insanity. If he was not already there.

He'd dropped everything. Hopefully even abandoned his plan to kill GasBag, the fifth person he was planning to kill for the memory of his beloved 'dead' Maggie Sutherland.

Who was not dead after all.

Who had faked her own death.

Who had LIED to him. Had HIDDEN from him.

Who had made a fool of him.

Possibly even spurned his love.

Alternatively, there was another course of possible thought.

Maggie Sutherland would know nothing about the work Hamilton had done to glorify her memory. The revenge he had taken in her name.

When she found out the justice that he had exacted on all her aggressors, by him, for her, against all those who were guilty, she would be overjoyed!

Surely.

There was one problem. Either way, Hamish Hamilton had to get to Balloch before the police.

To warn her.

To save her.

Or to kill her.

Chapter 56

North Berwick
16.52

Galbraith was the first to make it to the cottage across the fields. All the time he had been kept aware of the infra-red feed from the second drone which had been sent up to give them eyes on the cottage. The first drone was now following the car with Hamish Hamilton in it as far it could: its operator had jumped in the white van and was now pursuing Hamilton's car at a distance.

The news was neither good nor bad. Fiona, assuming it was her, was still sitting centrally in the middle of the room. She had been seen over the infra-red moving her legs. It meant she was still alive. Hopefully there had not been much gas in the room - in the 'bag' - before Hamilton had left, and hopefully he had not harmed her at all.

And there was one more thought.

Hopefully, hopefully, the last amount of TNT that they suspected Hamilton had, was not also now waiting for them on a local timer.

As they approached the cottage, they had less than seven minutes left.

His team approached the cottage from four sides. At least one man on each side of the building. Galbraith got to the front door and found it closed.

Normal options would include forcing it open, but they didn't know how much gas may have been released or built up in the room. The worry was that if there was already enough, a small spark could ignite it.

Hurrying around the cottage to another side, he found a window leading to a lounge.

One of his team was standing in front of it. He was busy covering the glass with sheets of very wide duct tape.

Galbraith immediately dipped into his own rucksack and quickly added two more broad strips to the window.

Then nodding at his colleague, the man smashed the window with a Halligan bar.

The glass collapsed, but did not fall into shards on the floor. Instead his colleague simply pulled the sheets of tape backwards and let it fall outwards onto the ground. He immediately formed his hand into a loop, and the Sergeant placed a foot on it and his colleague gave him a leg-up through the window into the lounge beyond.

Galbraith hurried through the room to the kitchen on the other side of the cottage.

He could smell gas.

He came to the kitchen door.

A large plastic sheet covered it from the outside. It had strips of duct-tape sealing it around the door, but it looked as if it had been applied very quickly.

"Are you okay, Mrs McKenzie?" he shouted loudly. "We're here to rescue you. Is there any booby-trap we need to know about?"

He heard a muffled response. But nothing intelligible.
He looked at his watch. Four minutes left.
There was no time for thinking.
Only instinct.
Galbraith immediately pulled the long knife from its sheath on his calf, and started to slice the inside of the plastic away from the door.
He ripped it open and pulled the centre section away.
On the other side of the sheet, the door had been closed.
The sergeant reached out to the door handle.
He was just about to turn it and push the door open when he thought twice about it.
Perhaps the door was booby-trapped.
He glanced at his watch.
No time.
Instinct.
INSTINCT.
Hamilton had been tired. Upset. Panicked. He'd rushed out, and probably forgotten to set any booby-trap even if there was one.
Galbraith closed his eyes and prepared to turn the handle. He knew that if there was a booby trap and there was enough gas, he could also potentially be killed by the blast.
If he was going to die, he wanted to die with his eyes open.
His eyelids opened.
He stepped to the side of the door so he was shielded by the wall and turned the handle and pushed...
"SHIT..." he shouted. The door was locked!
His eyes glanced down at the door. What now?
Something caught his eyes on the floor, just beneath the handle.
A key.
The key?
Perhaps it had fallen out as Hamilton had turned it rapidly, in haste, or dropped it deliberately, before the door was sealed with the plastic.
He grabbed it off the floor, and thrust it into the keyhole, applying pressure.
It turned.
He twisted the door-handle and pushed.
The door opened.
"I'm entering the room," he said into his comms microphone. "It's sealed everywhere on the inside with the black plastic sheeting. I can smell gas. Confirm I smell gas. But not at toxic levels. Mrs McKenzie is in the middle of the room sitting on a chair beside the kitchen island. Her eyes are open. She's gagged. But I confirm her eyes are open and moving. There are two words written on her forehead in red... Remember Me?... I'm now locating and turning off the gas taps on the cooker, although it seems like there's no longer any gas coming out... I confirm, I have now switched off the gas."

Galbraith rushed back to the chair on which Fiona was sitting and quickly scanned her and it with his trained eyes.

Immediately underneath the chair, but sitting independently and not connected to anything else, was a small bundle. A clock. Small cables. And two sticks of TNT.

"Shit... there's a manual detonator on two sticks of TNT. There's no mobile. Could be sensitive to movement... "

"Shit... " he said again, noting the time on the clock on the detonator. Two minutes to go.

Slipping his rucksack from his shoulder to the floor, he stepped to the front of the chair, bent down and picked her and the chair up.

Little Bump pushed against him. He couldn't lift them in that position. He couldn't get the balance.

He put her down again and then swiftly stepped around and behind the chair. He breathed in deeply, bent forward and lifted.

Summoning all his strength, he picked them both up and with the same effort and momentum launched himself and his passenger through the kitchen door.

Two other Tactical Team members were now in the corridor.

The front door was now open, having been checked for wires and any booby trap by the others and then opened from inside to create a draft and vent the gas.

As the Sergeant and Mrs McKenzie emerged through the kitchen door, the others pushed and redirected them down the hall and through the open front door into the courtyard beyond.

They'd made three metres into the courtyard when the blast caught them from behind.

It pushed them over, propelling them onto the ground, Fiona's chair landing on its back and then turning onto its side, the wooden struts of the chair splintering and absorbing most of the shock, and acting as a buffer from the impact of the fall.

Behind them, the windows of the cottage blew out, and some masonry shot across the courtyard, a few bricks and small pieces of stone peppering the cobblestones.

Immediately following the blast there was a moment of strange quiet and calm.

"Man down!" a voice echoed across the comm's unit linking them all together. "Medic required, immediately!"

Galbraith opened his eyes, feeling two sets of powerful hands pulling him up onto his feet.

Galbraith quickly surveyed the scene. One of the men behind him was lying on the ground writhing in agony, a large piece of shattered glass protruding from one side of his thigh. His left arm appeared to be broken. The single quick glance from Galbraith told him that it was a non-fatal wound. It had missed the artery. It needed taking out carefully under supervision, but the man would live, and the leg would recover.

Fiona McKenzie was lying on her side, one arm trapped beneath her on one side, both arms still tied behind the remnants of the chair. Her eyes were moving wildly, darting from side to side.

The other man from inside the building was kneeling up, and reaching towards Mrs McKenzie. His hands touched her face and then pulled the gag from her mouth.

"Are you ok?" he shouted, the blast still ringing in his ears.

She coughed several times, then vomited onto the cobblestones in the courtyard.

Galbraith had lost his knife in the explosion, but reached across and pulled one from the leg of his colleague lying on the ground.

He quickly cut through the ropes tying Mrs McKenzie to the back of the chair, and set her free.

Together he and his colleague helped Mrs McKenzie up onto her feet.

"How are you?" they asked. "How much gas did you breathe in? How's the baby?"

She coughed, then smiled.

"I'm okay, and I think Little... the baby, is okay too. Not much gas. It was okay. The man turned the taps on, then hurried out... I heard the gas coming... then it just stopped..."

Galbraith spoke quickly into the comms microphone on his lapel.

"Mrs McKenzie is fine. Baby seems fine. Mrs McKenzie reports all well. We need a medic to check her over and fix a flesh wound on PC Davies and a broken arm. But all looks well. And I now have a visual on all members of my team. Mission successful. I repeat, Mission successful. Victim secured alive and well, and there is a baby kicking, apparently!"

Thirty miles away DCI Campbell McKenzie collapsed onto his knees.
And wept.

McKenzie had just spoken to Fiona. It had been a short conversation, but a reassuring one.

The ambulance which had been waiting in the field near the cottage with the rest of his team had quickly made its way to the cottage, and the medics had given Fiona a once over. So far, everything seemed fine, but they were just about to take her into the hospital in North Berwick for a full investigation and ultra-sound scan of the baby. The paramedic had reassured McKenzie that it was only a precaution and that everything seemed good. Apparently one of the Tactical Team had been injured though, but he would be well too, once his arm and leg had been given time to heal.

Before the ambulance left for the hospital McKenzie had insisted on talking to Fiona.

There had been a few tears and McKenzie had apologised for sending her away and putting her and Little Bump in danger.

Deep down, McKenzie knew it was not his fault, but he would never have forgiven himself if anything had happened to them.

He was proud of Fiona though. She seemed to have been strong, and even after the explosion and coming close to have being blown up, she seemed to be coping with the stress of it all, even to the point of insisting she give him a quick de-brief before she was taken away.

"Campbell, before you go, I have some information I think you need to know," she had insisted. "I got to see his face. At first he wore a mask, like the face of an Indian Chief you see kids wearing at Halloween, but he took it off just before he started to write something on my forehead. I asked what he was doing, and why, and he just said that it was '*so I would remember in Hell what I had done, and who I'd done it to.*' I told him I didn't understand, and he shouted at me and said '*Shut up, you Gasbag. She's dead because of you. You killed her.*' I asked him what he was talking about, and he got even more upset and shouted that '*you killed the only person I ever loved, and the only person who ever loved me."* He said that he was doing this for her, '*making her wishes come true, just like in her book.*' Campbell, does that make any sense to you?"

"Yes. It does. A little. I think that he and Maggie Sutherland had a relationship once. They split up. I'm guessing that she killed herself because she couldn't cope with life and what had happened to her, and when that happened, he decided to exact revenge on everyone in her book. Obviously, he must have been given the last outstanding copy of the book that was printed. We know she dedicated the draft copy to him. She must have wanted him to have a copy, and given him one at some point."

"Campbell, I've got to go… the ambulance driver needs to get one of the Tactical Team to hospital. He's broken his arm and has got a flesh wound."

McKenzie promised to come straight to the hospital as soon as he could, then Galbraith had come on the phone and had requested a conversation with McKenzie.

The news had not been good.

"I saw two sticks of TNT under the chair. Not more. According to what you told me, there are four pieces still not accounted for. Hamilton may have them with him in his car."

McKenzie thanked Galbraith profusely for saving his wife and child. He'd then hung up and called Wishart.

She was still in the van with the technician and the drone operator.

"Status" he asked.

"About ten miles from Edinburgh, on the dual carriageway."

"Okay, keep him under observation. I'm going to call in the reinforcements."

The next call he made was to DCS Wilkinson.

"Ma'am, what time does the Queen leave today?"

"Tomorrow morning now. She's staying one more night in Holyrood."

"I got the news back on the analysis of the TNT from the school and the comparison with the TNT taken from your supposed terrorist attacks. It's the same TNT Ma'am. The same."

McKenzie could hear her take a breath, quickly processing the implications of what he'd just said.

"Okay, something tells me you're not finished." She carried on. "What else have you got, McKenzie?"

"The terrorist you're looking for under Operation Crown is Hamish Hamilton, also known as Neil McBeth. He's currently heading towards Edinburgh in a blue Nissan. We have him under observation and we're following him. That's the good news. The bad news is that we think he has three sticks of dynamite left and he's possibly got them with him in the car… We also know that he is very upset, and thinks he has just killed my wife, who by the way, thanks to Sergeant Galbraith and his Tactical Team, is alive and well. As is, we hope, our baby."

"Fiona and the baby are okay?"

"Yes. They're going to hospital as we speak for an examination, but the paramedics are happy."

"Great news. Congratulations Campbell. I couldn't be happier for you!" She exclaimed, some real emotion sneaking through in her voice. Then her tone changed, and she became more serious. "So, you're handing the case over to me or the National Crime Unit?"

"Ma'am, there's a terrorist heading to Edinburgh with three sticks of TNT. He's killed four people already and placed numerous bombs targeting the Queen. What are you going to do about it?" McKenzie replied.

She replied with only two words.

"Stop him."

It took twenty minutes for DCS Wilkinson to pass over all the relevant information that McKenzie had provided to the appropriate authorities responsible for preventing and terminating a live and ongoing terrorist threat to the Queen.

By the time all the relevant parties were informed and resources had been deployed, Hamish Hamilton was on the three-lane bypass heading around the outskirts of Edinburgh en route to Glasgow or Stirling.

McKenzie had been waiting and watching for him to pass by, sitting patiently in an elevated but hidden police viewing point, at all times full informed by Wishart exactly where Hamilton was.

As soon as the car passed by, McKenzie dropped back down onto the road, and followed from behind about twenty metres away.

The traffic on the road was light today, and there were only a few cars ahead of McKenzie's between him and Hamilton's Nissan.

A large and expensive white Land Rover, and a green Audi.

McKenzie was no longer in charge.

The Combined Response Firearms Team working on Operation Crown had taken over.

The plan was simple. Already several Tactical Teams and armed response units with Counter Terrorist Specialist Firearms Officers were waiting to enter the motorway at the next junction behind Hamilton. They would then close the motorway behind him.

Likewise, the traffic in front was already being diverted off the motorway ahead of Hamilton's Nissan, and all traffic in the opposite direction on the opposing carriageway had been terminated.

The C.R.F.T. had done this many times before. If everything went well, only a few cars in front of the Nissan, and those immediately behind it would be left travelling down the next stretch of the motorway, with armed response units immediately filling the road in front and behind, and setting up barricades on either side of the road.

Helicopters would then descend from the heavens, bristling with hardware and megaphones blasting threats and instructions, with armed officers rappelling down ropes onto the motorway.

Within minutes the remaining traffic would be stopped and encircled at a suitable distance on the motorway by very scary armour-plated CRFT vehicles.

Heavily armed CTSFOs would immediately move in and secure the safety of passengers in any of the other vehicles, leaving only Hamish Hamilton alone in his vehicle in the middle of three lanes of empty traffic.

The plan sounded simple. And it was executed well.

Unfortunately, however, one vehicle – the expensive Land Rover - was travelling too close to Hamish Hamilton's Nissan and was eventually stopped and became stationary, only metres away. It had entered at the last junction beneath the Pentland Hills and had been in a hurry.

"Remain in your vehicles. Do not attempt to leave."

The helicopter's megaphones blasted out the instructions as it hovered above the two vehicles.

McKenzie had come up slowly behind the CRFT vehicles in front of him, and he was now safe on the other side of the barricade as the CRFT took control.

From where he was, it was obvious Hamish Hamilton was going nowhere fast.

The Edinburgh City Bypass
17.48

"Marie, I'm really sorry, I genuinely want to be there with you at six-thirty for the meeting with the First Minister and the photograph. I was heading over there now ..." Stuart was explaining to Marie on the phone. "There's a lot I need to talk to you about. There're some things I want to explain to you. It's important I get the chance to tell you something before we meet the First Minister and have the photograph."

"So where are you now? How far away are you?" Marie had asked.

"Actually, there's a problem. I may be a little late…"

"Why? What's happened?" she asked, sensing an excuse coming.

"Well, I seem to be trapped on the Edinburgh Bypass. I'm completely stationary and can't move. There's one car just in front of me. Two police helicopters directly above my head, and a fleet of armed vehicles in front and behind me… As far as excuses go, I think this is a pretty good one."

"Are you serious? What's going on?" Marie asked, now a little concerned.

"Actually, I don't know… but I think I have to go now. There's about six armed men surrounding my vehicle and ordering me to get out… I think I have to go…"

The Edinburgh City Bypass
17.55

Hamish Hamilton sat in the front seat of his car. He was still gripping both sides of the steering wheel, the white of his hands showing through his knuckles.

There was a helicopter above his head.

A fucking helicopter.

And armed vehicles and heavily armed police officers everywhere.

"Where the fuck did they come from?" he swore aloud.

Still gripping the steering wheel, he swivelled his head around, taking in the scene around him.

The crazy, chaotic, madness that was unfolding around him.

"Where the fuck did they come from?" he repeated.

He was tired.
So tired.
And so confused.
He needed to get to Maggie before the police arrested her.
To see her.
She was still alive!
Hamish knew that it would all be alright when she saw him again. She would love him again. They would be together again.
They would have what they had before.
She was alive.
That was all that was important.

"Hamish Hamilton. Open the door slowly and step outside your vehicle. Put your arms in the air and keep them there. Leave everything else in the vehicle."

The helicopter had now lifted up higher into the air, and to the side, backing off.

The voice that was almost blasting his eardrums to pieces was now coming from a wall of loudspeakers mounted on a nearby police vehicle.

Glancing in his rear-view mirror he saw another man step out of a white Land-Rover. His hands were in the air. He was immediately surrounded by armed officers in uniforms that made them look like something from Star Wars, and the man was swiftly ushered away.

Within seconds it was just Hamish. Alone.

Against what seemed like the whole fucking Scottish armed police force. There were armed cars and police in strange uniforms and weird helmets everywhere, all carrying weapons, all of which were pointing straight at him.

He was tired.

What was happening... He had to get to Maggie...

"Step out of the vehicle, put your hands above your head..."

Hamish glanced down at the passenger seat. Three sticks of dynamite.

And a detonator.

He picked it up in his hands and held it close to his chest.

He was tired... so very, *very* tired...

Closing his eyes for the last time he started to dream about Maggie.

It was a nice dream.

And Hamish didn't want it to end.

Maggie smiled at him. Hamish saw her wave.

"Come..." she said.

Hamish pressed the red button gently with his thumb.

Chapter 57

Wednesday Evening
The Scottish Parliament
Dining Hall
Edinburgh 19.00

By the time Stuart arrived, the reception was already underway.
As soon as the CRFT had released him he'd been bundled into a police car and driven down to the Scottish Parliament buildings beside Holyrood Palace.
His own car had been destroyed in the explosion which he too had almost been killed in.
Apparently, just a minute later, and he would have been toast. Or at least, little pieces of toast. Charred and black.
A terrorist had blown himself up, only metres in front of his car.
Wrong time, wrong place.
The universe was obviously punishing him for telling lies.
He'd tried several times to reach Marie, but she wasn't picking up.
Stuart was going to tell her the truth.
She was either fed up of him and his excuses, or was already busy chin-wagging with the First Minister of Scotland.
He managed to make it through to his personal assistant and told her he was on his way, and she in turn had informed him, that the situation was now even worse than before.
The Queen had decided to stay another night. She would now be in the Dining Hall with the First Minister.
Both of whom knew him by his first name.

He'd arrived at the Parliament building at 7.15 p.m. Fashionably late and slightly char-grilled.
As he'd walked into the Dining Hall, all eyes had turned to him.
"I'm so sorry." He'd announced, hurrying across to the table at which six places were set. The Queen. The Duke of Edinburgh. The First Minister of Scotland and her husband. Marie McDonald, and an empty space for himself.
The look of relief on Marie's face as she glanced over her shoulder and saw him arrive, was incredible.
Her face lit up. Her eyes sparkled. She smiled.
And then it happened.
The Queen coughed. Marie looked back at her. The Queen smiled and sort of waved and said, "Hello Stuart, did you forget your watch tonight, you naughty boy? You're late!"
Followed quickly by a laughing First Minister.
"Stuart, we've been hearing all about you. Apparently you're going to live in Poland for a while?"

Stuart Nisbet stopped in his tracks, bowed slightly to the Queen and turned red in the face.

Almost ignoring the First Minister he turned back towards Marie McDonald, whose face was now as white as a sheet.

"I guess, I've got a lot of explaining to do." He said, sheepishly.

"Don't you worry," the Queen said. "The Minister and I shall just talk amongst ourselves for a moment. We'll give you the opportunity to explain to this beautiful young lady, just who you really are! But make it quick, the soup's going cold!"

Thursday
The Old Portobello High School
17.00

DCI Campbell McKenzie, his wife and her large Little Bump stood outside the portacabin, looking over and up at the towering blue hulk of the Old Portobello High School.

All the roads had been closed off and all the necessary diversions were in place.

The crowds of onlookers were smaller this time around, since very little notice had been given about the impending demolition of the school.

McKenzie was determined that it should happen today.

Hamish Hamilton was dead. He'd committed suicide and evaded capture and they would probably never know the true nature of the relationship between Hamilton and Maggie Sutherland.

But did it matter?

Perhaps it did, but that could wait until another day.

For now, McKenzie wanted to fulfil a promise he'd given to Gary Bruce. That they'd let him finish the job he'd started the week before, and help him to do it before he too became a permanent victim of a case that had already claimed five lives, including the murderer himself.

In a few hours, press releases would be given out to announce the deaths of David Weir, Ronald Blake, Mark McRae, Daniel Gray and Hamish Hamilton. No mention would be made of Maggie Sutherland. Or the book 'Remember Me?', the reason they had all been killed, or the injustice that may or may not have been done to Maggie Sutherland. That part was DCI Wilkinson's decision.

Everyone involved in the case was now dead. There could be no benefit in dragging up a past that could only remain in the past if there was no way to shed any further light on it.

Everyone had agreed that before the announcements went out, the Old School should also be allowed to die a dignified death, without becoming a mecca for tourism for sick individuals who thrived on the suffering of others.

Portobello High School was, for the majority of pupils who attended it, a wonderful, much-loved home for over six years of school life.

It had shaped lives, created lives, and fostered and nurtured dreams that had lasted whole-lifetimes.

The building was loved by tens of thousands, and would be remembered warmly by all those who had once walked and been educated within its beloved walls.

Portobello High School had been the centre of a warm community. And now it was time to lay it to rest.

Gary Bruce stepped forward, his final checks now complete.

He nodded to Fiona McKenzie, and held out his hand, gesturing at the big red button on the desk in front of her.

"It was your school. It's time to say goodbye."

Fiona turned, and looked around at the team of people present that had saved her life, and the life of Little Bump.

Sergeant Anderson, DI Dean, DS McLeish, DS Wishart, PC Lynch, DI Brown, Sergeant Galbraith, DI Mather, and her husband.

Smiling at them all, she looked back for one last time at the towering eight floors of the school that had once been such an important part of her life, and then she pressed the button in front of her.

Just then she felt Little Bump kick. Fiona laughed and grabbed her husband's hand, pulling it towards her and letting him stroke their 'Bump'.

DCI Campbell McKenzie smiled, and kissed his wife on her forehead.
There were tears in his eyes.

A moment later, when they both glanced upwards, the school was gone.

THE END

A Personal Note from the Author

"*Hi,*

Thanks for reading this novel. I am really flattered that you chose one of my books to read, from all of the millions of books on Amazon. I hope you enjoyed it. I would love to hear from you if you did! You can contact me on iancpirvine@hotmail.co.uk .

Although I am not a new author, most of you may not have heard of me before you purchased this book. If you did enjoy it, may I ask you personally if you would consider writing a review on Amazon, telling others what you thought? Positive reviews can really help new books and new authors succeed and could really help others to decide whether or not to purchase a book. Writing a review is easy. All you have to do is go to the Amazon book page you bought the book from and scroll down to where it says, "**Customer Reviews: Write a Customer Review**".

If possible, I would like to stay in touch with you by asking you to sign up to my email list. If you do sign up, I promise I will not spam you. However, if I write another book, I would like to be to email you to tell you about it in the hope you might want to read it too! To entice and encourage you to sign up to my email list I would like to offer you a copy of one of my ebooks - for free!

You can choose from a children's ebook to read to your grandchildren!
OR
A tense, page turning thriller with over 1500 Five Stars on Amazon!
To get this free offer please type the below URL into your browser:

http://eepurl.com/dE-3pf

Details of my other books already available on Amazon can be found at www.iancpirvine.com.

Good luck with your next choice of book!

Kind regards,
Ian C.P. Irvine."

Ian C.P. Irvine is fast becoming one of the UK's leading independent authors, with over 2,010,000 books downloaded from Amazon.

For a full list and to download all of his **FREE EBOOKS**, now available for a limited time, visit **www.free-ebook.co.uk** . Download them all now! And read them soon.

To visit his website please go to www.iancpirvine.com .

Printed in Great Britain
by Amazon